Forgotten

Don & Stephanie Prichard

Other books by
Don & Stephanie Prichard

Stranded: A Novel

Review by Dr. Betty Ray—

Stranded is a spellbinding adventure story. I sped through it to discover what would happen next and was thoroughly captivated by it. I marveled at the resourcefulness of Jake, a Marine trained and tested in Vietnam. Co-author Don Prichard's firsthand knowledge gained as a member of the United States Marine Corps in Vietnam brings authenticity to the life and death struggles on the island.

Then I slowly re-read *Stranded,* savoring each word. What a depth I had missed on my first read. Embedded in the adventure was the sovereign God using adversity to mold the lives of His people. The symbolism, most of which I missed my first-time through, was a rich blessing. The truth of the book's epigraph, Isaiah 40:21-22, comes alive in this great adventure.

Review by Danielle Hanna, author—

The first thing I look for in a story - before plot, before prose, before any of the millions of writing "rules" an author is supposed to follow - is HEART. Don and Stephanie Prichard nailed it. Don't expect an easy read - and by "easy," I mean read-and-forget. I came dangerously close to flinging my new Kindle across the room on more than one occasion. The authors' pen was like a lancet at times, probing the tenderest parts of my heart.

One of the main themes in the book was the role of fathers, physical and spiritual, and how their presence, absence, or performance can either leave us well-equipped for life and a relationship with God, or leave us emotionally and spiritually starving. As a fatherless daughter, I can attest that the authors wrote on this subject with compete authenticity.

Beyond that, I was delighted with the writing style and imagery, and was impressed by the survival knowledge, which no doubt Don had from personal experience as a Vietnam veteran. The characters were authentic - even the villains. I'd be hard-pressed to pick a favorite. (Perhaps the Lone Soldier? Haha.) Debut authors frequently struggle with their sense of timing, but I think Don and Stephanie dwelt on all the best parts.

Dedicated to Brenda Anderson
Mentor par excellence
Who taught us the difference between a sow's ear and a silk purse

The Lord is in His holy temple,
The Lord's throne is in heaven;
His eyes behold,
His eyelids test the sons of men.
The Lord tests the righteous,
But the wicked and the one who loves violence His soul hates.
Upon the wicked He will rain coals;
Fire and brimstone and a burning wind
Shall be the portion of their cup.
For the Lord is righteous,
He loves justice;
Upright men will see His face.
—Psalm 11:4-7

PART 1

Chapter 1

June 1982

A voice reached down and nudged her into consciousness. Sweet words—crooned, stretched out into long, soft syllables. "Beau-ti-ful laaay-dee." Enticing words, drawing her through an ocean of darkness like a fish to a lure. Her nerves tingled, eager to respond.

She opened her eyes. White walls, white sheets, white lights overhead. Something stinging her nostrils. Disinfectant? She wrinkled her nose. None of it made sense. She closed her eyes and spiraled back into the darkness.

The voice prodded her again, poking light into the blackness, prying her eyes open. She frowned. *What?*

Rustling nearby. She turned her head, squinted at a smooth, cinnamon-colored face. Dark almond-shaped eyes, delicate nose, gleaming white teeth smiling at her. Attached to a white uniform. The significance hit home: a nurse.

"Beautiful lady, how are you feeling?" A slight foreign accent stretched out the nurse's words. "Please, I need to ask you questions before your surgery."

The word pierced her grogginess. Surgery? Alarm pinched her cheeks with heat and lifted the fog behind her eyes.

In a flash, fragments of memory snapped together like pieces of a jigsaw puzzle. The central piece: she'd been airlifted from a yacht to a hospital in the Philippines—today, only hours ago. Why? Adrenaline jolted her like a hot

3

wire and she remembered—the yacht, her captors, the gunshot to her head.

More pieces locked in—a jungle island, the man she loved bound to a tree and beaten. "Jake!" she cried, heartbeat escalating. "You've got to save Jake!" Two more pieces: people with him—Crystal and Betty, hiding. She struggled to sit up and say their names, to grab the nurse and tell her to hurry, to send help.

"Please, can you tell me your name?" Small hands against her shoulders pressed her head back onto a pillow.

The room swirled. The puzzle pieces vanished. Her name? "Eve." Or was it Eva? Eva Gray?

"Can you tell me what year it is?"

She gripped the bed rails, palms sweaty. Her answer came out thick, sluggish. "19 … 82."

"Good. And, please, your age and birthdate?"

"Thirty- … four."

The room tipped, and the black vortex swallowed her birthdate. She spun away with it.

***

Pain wrenched open her eyes. She groaned and put her hand up to touch the right side of her head. Stopped when she spied a wire clipped to her forefinger and tubing taped halfway up her arm. Dully, she followed the tubing's path to a bag of clear fluid suspended from a metal pole. Next to the pole a monitor traced a pattern of intermittent peaks and valleys.

She jerked fully awake and looked around. She was in a bed in a hospital room. Her heartbeat quickened, locking the air in her lungs.

She snatched in a breath, put her hand down, raised the other to her head. Bandages. She explored farther. The entire top of her head was swathed in them.

Her fingertips triggered a jackhammer inside her skull. She yelped and yanked her hand away. A young Filipina nurse, almond eyes full of concern, dashed into the room.

"Are you feeling pain?"

"My head." She clenched eyes, teeth, fists against the crushing implosion.

The nurse's footsteps pattered off and returned. She opened her eyes to see the nurse poke a syringe into the I.V. line. Within seconds the pain melted away like candle wax. She took a shuddering breath and sank gratefully into the bed sheets.

She started over again: bandages on her head. She touched them gingerly. What had happened? Before she could ask, the nurse spoke. "Your surgery went well, but you need to lie still. Please, can you tell me your name and birthdate?"

She blinked.

Inside the bandages, her mind raced back and forth, arms outstretched, searching, searching, until finally it halted, shattered. Nothing. No memories. Only emptiness.

Her breath heaved from her chest, shot back in, catapulted out again. "I …" Her vision spun in erratic circles. "I don't …" She gasped out the last word. "Know."

A sticky syrup, dark, menacing, melted over her brain. Crept to her face. Absorbed her eyes. The last thing she heard, as if from a deep subterranean well, was the echo of her nurse's voice: "Doctor!"

***

The door creaked on its hinges, admitting yet one more person into the crowded hospital waiting room. Jake knew immediately it was Detective Lee. Looking for him.

Jake stood—not that he was hard to spot, the only white male in a room of cocoa-skinned Filipinos. It was just that the contrast between the detective's coat and tie and Jake's tattered shorts and shirt—a tee with orange and blue flowers the size of elephant ears he'd been given to cover his bare chest—demanded defiance. Shaggy hair and beard tangled below his shoulders didn't help. There'd been no time to clean up.

In the chair beside his, Betty Parker stirred, her wrinkled face creasing into a frown as he rose. Crystal, her twelve-year-old grandniece, slept against Betty's left shoulder, leaning on her from the next chair. Both were as ragged as Jake. The year of bare-bones survival on a jungle island had stripped them of civilization's sheen. He flashed a twitch of a smile at Betty to assure her all was well.

"Colonel Jacob Chalmers?"

At the use of his military title, heat flushed Jake's cheeks. There'd be no *oo-rah* from the Marine Corps at the state of his appearance. He gave a curt nod.

"Detective Lee." Though he was a good half-foot shorter than Jake's six-two, the detective managed to peer down his nose at Jake. He didn't offer to shake hands. "You accompanied Eva Gray from the yacht?"

"She goes by her nickname, Eve. Yes, I flew in on the medivac with her."

"Could we step into the hallway? I'd like to ask you a few questions."

"No." The noise in the room hushed as ears locked onto the two men. "I'm waiting for the doctor to report on Eve's surgery."

Lee's nostrils flared. "I spoke to the doctor. Ms. Gray is in recovery."

The words landed a hard punch to Jake's belly. "Recovery? Why didn't anyone inform me?"

"When we're finished, you can check with the doctor."

"No!" Jake grabbed the detective's arms. "I want to see her. Now."

The biceps under Jake's grip tensed. Lee's eyes narrowed. "You won't be allowed to see her." The muscles in his cheeks tightened. "Eva Gray—Eve—is under arrest for suspicion of murder."

Chapter 2

Jake's arms dropped to his side, and he stepped back from Detective Lee. "Are you talking about those two thugs on the yacht with her?" His voice rose. "They kidnapped her!"

"Perhaps now you'd like to step into the hallway and answer my questions?" Detective Lee turned and stalked through the doorway. The averted eyes of everyone in the waiting room shifted from the floor to Jake with unabashed interest.

Betty touched his hand. "Go," she whispered. "Crystal and I will wait for you here."

He followed Detective Lee into the hallway. The man stood waiting for him, eyes studying Jake. No arms folded haughtily across his chest, no chin raised in disdain. The tightness in Jake's gut eased at the detective's thoughtful gaze.

"Colonel, I seek your cooperation."

Jake's lips tightened. "I want to see Eve."

"That may be possible after we visit the island you were stranded on. Show me evidence of Eve's innocence, and she is free for visits."

"Evidence? Those two goons on the yacht clearly killed each other—and almost took her life as well! What more evidence do you need?"

Lee's gaze bore into Jake. "That yacht was stolen, and the owners and first mate disappeared—probably murdered. Eva Gray may have been a participant."

7

Jake sputtered. "She was kidnapped! I'm a witness to that, and so are Betty Parker and Crystal Oakleigh, sitting right"—he jabbed his finger at the waiting room door—"there."

Detective Lee's eyes narrowed. "There's also the matter of three dead men on the island—reported by you when the Coast Guard rescued you and your companions."

Jake's shoulders slumped. Prison was a possibility after all. For both him and Eve. Their innocence needed every bit of support he could give. "All right, I'll go with you. But I want to see Eve first."

"Not an option, Colonel. A helicopter is waiting to transport us to the island. The Coast Guard is already there."

Jake's voice rose. "I want to see her." A nurse at the far end of the hallway turned her head toward them.

"We can't." The detective spoke softly, as if calming a wild-eyed horse bucking his lead. "She is in the ICU in an induced coma."

Jake's chest turned to lead. "Coma?"

"To protect her brain. There's been some swelling. The doctor said it needs to go down to help her brain heal. She will be fine until we get back."

Jake clenched his teeth so hard his jaw hurt. "I'm not leaving her."

"All right." Lee's chin jutted forward. "Then I will have to arrest you and your two friends in the waiting room on suspicion of murder."

The two men, rooted in place, stared at each other.

"Look," Lee finally said, the tone of his voice begging for reason. "In three days the doctors will reverse her coma. Plenty of time to fly to the island and return. I promise."

Jake's lip lifted in a snarl. "I'll go. But if anything happens to her ..."

Lee's eyebrows raised over steely eyes. "That sounds mighty close to a threat, Colonel." He nodded toward the waiting room door. "Tell your friends you'll be back in three days."

Three days. Jake's stomach twisted. Not only did he have to abandon Eve, but now Betty and Crystal too. He swallowed back the helplessness slithering up his throat, squared his heart to trust nothing bad would happen in his absence.

***

Bradley Henshaw punched the speaker button on his office phone. Not too often the State Department called the Department of Justice in Chicago. "District Attorney Bradley Henshaw."

"Mr. Henshaw, this is Linda Faris at the U.S. State Department. You issued a BOLO for an American woman under the name of Eva Gray or Evedene Eriksson."

Henshaw frowned. That *"Be-On-the-Look-Out"* was a year old. "Yes …" Tension prickled up his spine.

"The U.S. Ambassador's office in the Philippines called us. A red flag tripped your watch list item when four Americans were rescued from a remote island yesterday. They claim to be survivors of the cruise ship *Gateway*. One of them is a woman named Eva Gray."

The room emptied of oxygen, taking Henshaw's breath with it, creeping back in tiny pinches down his throat. "She's … alive?" His mind staggered at the possibility. Grabbing a pen, heart beating faster and faster, he scribbled the details Ms. Faris shared.

When the call ended, he punched in the number for the U.S. Marshals.

***

The whir of the police helicopter blades softened to a *wop, wop, wop* as the copter hovered over the landing deck of the Philippine Coast Guard cutter. The aircraft landed with a jolt and the blades whispered into silence, yielding to the slap of ocean waves against the ship's hull and the cries of alarmed seagulls at a distance. Jake stepped onto the deck and gazed at the island. Two days since he'd left, and memories squeezed his heart as if it had been two years.

A motorboat awaited him and Detective Lee, who had changed his coat and tie for jeans and a tee shirt, while Jake discarded his flowery tee for a bare chest. The captain shook hands with them, and the three of them and four guardsmen boarded the craft and shoved off for the coastline. Jake had never approached the island from a boat, and the swiftness of their advance jarred him with the reminder of their purpose: to collect three dead bodies and explain their deaths.

They entered the cove where he, Eve, Betty, and Crystal had lived for a year. A crescent of white sand bordered the water like a businessman's starched collar. Past the beach, a field of long, sun-bleached grass slanted uphill to a steep terrain of rocks. Towering in the distance like a giant anthill was the cone of the island's volcano.

"This is where the pirates kidnapped Eve?" Lee asked.

"Yes."

"Where were you while this was going on?"

Jake's teeth ground on the question. "There, on the other side of that stream. I was tied to one of those three trees."

"By your wrists?"

Jake glanced at the raw, meat-red bracelets burnt into the skin behind his hands. "Yes. Hanging by them."

"They beat you?"

Jake snorted. His cracked ribs would ache for months. "I didn't count any hugs."

Lee nodded as if he were done with questions for now.

Jake pointed to where grass and rocks merged. "Up there is our cave, dug out probably forty years ago by a platoon of stranded World War II Japanese soldiers. Nearby is their burial cave. Do you want to see them?"

"Everything," Lee said. The guardsmen murmured their assent. An undercurrent of excitement rippled their breaths and lit their eyes. This was something schoolboys dreamed of, and the story world was about to become theirs.

They pulled the motorboat onto the beach, and Jake led them across the sand to a rocky path on one side of the field of grass. "Careful where you step. That's a minefield to your left. A defensive barbed-wire fence is buried inside those long blades of grass." The men formed a straight line behind him and cautiously placed their feet where Jake stepped.

He beckoned them to his side when the ground leveled before a steep wall of rock. "Hear that crash of waves? Thataway,"—he pointed to the west— "the ground drops off about forty-five feet in a sharp cliff to the ocean. The other way"—he pointed to the east—"is the soldiers' defensive trench behind the minefield and barbed-wire fence. And here"—he descended a few feet into the trench and pulled aside long blades of grass with both hands—"is the last defender of the island, fondly dubbed by us as the Lone Soldier."

The men crowded around the fully clothed skeleton and gawked at its uniform, boots, and the nearby rusty machine gun he had manned. "Japanese uniform, all right," the Coast Guard captain said. "Looks like the rank of lieutenant. Where's his head?"

Jake winced. "A victim of my rage at the pirates, I'm afraid. A story for later? Right now, it'd be good to look at the residential cave while there's still daylight. And since you brought flashlights, I can take you through the burial cave."

Stepping close to the rock wall, Jake bent, pressed his hands against it, and pushed up. Lee grunted in surprise when a portion of the rock slid knee-high to reveal an opening.

"Works on a pulley." Jake couldn't help a grin. "Wait until you see what they did inside." The seven of them crawled through the aperture, the guardsmen murmuring in appreciation as they found themselves able to stand with plenty of headroom in a large chamber. Like the proud owner of a manor, Jake took them on a tour, pointing out the slitted window that let in light and allowed the soldiers to spy on the sea lane to the north; the large hearth with its tripod and cauldron; the long bamboo table with ten chairs; and the sleeping corridor with ten bunks carved into the stone. "All the comforts of home," he beamed. "And here are our hash marks on the wall to keep track of the days. Almost a full year."

Lee peered out the window. "All four of you were survivors of the *Gateway* shipwreck?"

"Not a shipwreck," Jake growled. "Captain Emilio herded all the passengers onto two small boats and deliberately killed them at sea with explosives." Heat swept through his body at the memory, and his stomach shredded as if stuffed into a meat grinder. "Including Ginny, my wife." His lungs locked, and with effort he pulled air back inside. "The *Gateway* sailed away unharmed."

"Yet four of you escaped?" Lee's voice fell just short of incredulity.

Jake bristled. "Everyone except me was at a staged event on deck. I was in my cabin, reading. When they found me, Emilio forced me overboard at gunpoint. Then he,"—Jake flared hot—"then he deliberately gave the signal to a crewman to set off the explosives so I'd see he was responsible."

His lower lip trembled. "I should have been with Ginny." The words choked out of his throat. "I would have seen the ruse. Could have saved Ginny, all the passengers."

"Colonel, I'm sorry." Lee's tone softened. "She and Betty and Crystal were in the boats?"

"Different boats. Betty and Crystal fell overboard and Eve swam out to rescue them. It saved them from the blasts."

"You rescued them?"

"No. The boats were made of a material that prevented major damage. I found Ginny's body and sailed the boat she'd been in to the island. Until I got there, I had no idea anyone else had survived."

"The other three sailed to the island in the second boat?"

"Yes. I'm guessing an ocean current took all four of us there."

"Why didn't you use the boats to leave the island?"

"Mine cracked apart; the other needed repair. The monsoon hit and we had to delay sailing."

The captain stood at the window. "Sun is setting. I suggest we start gathering the three bodies tomorrow."

They exited the cave, and Jake pointed to the far end of the trench. "Burial cave is down there. You want to wait until tomorrow?"

"We've got flashlights." Lee pulled his from his belt. "Let's go."

"How about a pistol?" Jake scanned the six men for weapons. "Just in case a python is at home."

"Part of our equipment. No worries," a guardsman said.

Ten to one they'd wet their pants at the size of the beast. Jake nodded and led the way.

Chapter 3

"No door on a pulley this time." Jake knelt in the trench and shoved aside vegetation concealing a hole barely larger than his head. "Their escape tunnel in case the enemy overran them. You'll have to squeeze in on your belly, but it will open up to where you can walk at a stoop. Who wants to go first?"

Detective Lee grinned. "Be our guest."

"Then I'll need a flashlight and pistol. Until we get to the burial chamber, there's no room to see around me to shoot any lurking critters."

The captain motioned one of the guardsmen to cede his flashlight and pistol to Jake. The edge of the hole scraped solid rock against Jake's shoulders as he scrunched them to his neck and wiggled inside. He grunted at the extent of the flashlight beam down the tunnel. Sure beat the scanty light from the twisted grass torches he's used his first time in. He rose to a stoop and counted twenty footsteps forward. Behind him, the excited murmurs of the guardsmen ricocheted off the walls. Halloween would be a tame holiday after this adventure.

"Turn right and you'll enter the burial chamber," he called over his shoulder. "You'll be able to stand, but don't go all the way in until we check for snakes." The voices behind him quieted.

One by one the men filed into the chamber. Their flashlight beams brightened the room with details that had escaped Jake's paltry torchlight. Goosebumps erected every hair on his body. As if choreographed, the men's breaths punched into the chamber in one horrified gasp, followed by gags as the foul odor of decayed flesh hit their nostrils.

Encircling the chamber were niches cut into the stone wall. Twenty Japanese soldiers, empty eye sockets gaping above grisly grins, lay with uniforms rotted by flesh in every niche but two. Tucked against the side of each soldier were items of battle gear and a few personal possessions. Jake focused his flashlight on each alcove, ending with a thorough search of the two empty ones. "All right, no snakes," he announced.

"Look, but do not touch, do not take," the captain bellowed. His voice boomed off the walls as if the twenty ghouls had joined in.

Hands over their mouths and noses, the men visited the niches and whispered comments. With the enhanced light of his flashlight, Jake discovered several photos on or near the soldiers. Photos of family. Sadness gripped his chest. Family who for forty years had wondered what had become of their loved one. Or who had died never finding out.

Lee approached and stood at his elbow. "Is there an escape tunnel out of here?"

"At least two. Difficult to maneuver, and both end in the jungle. The sun will be down."

"Let's save it for tomorrow then, if there's time," the captain said. "We should return to the ship now."

Jake led them back through the tunnel to the trench. Tomorrow they would trample through the jungle to two corpses only days old. Worse ghouls than the ones in the cave. The thrill of a storybook adventure would continue for the excited guardsmen.

But not for him.

Not if he ended up arrested for killing a man.

***

A storm roared in at night and shot cannonball waves at the Coast Guard cutter. "Because we violated a gravesite," the men whispered.

"You can moor in the cove, Captain." Jake was feeling white around the gills himself. "It's more than deep enough, and certainly calmer. A good night's rest will make a hard task easier tomorrow. Sounds like some of the men are on edge already."

The captain didn't protest. He put down anchor in the cove, and boat and men settled down at once. Didn't help Jake sleep much. Problems with solutions he couldn't control always set him into a wrestling match with God, the equivalent of Jacob's the night before he encountered his brother Esau. Tomorrow was Jake's Esau.

After an early breakfast, the same guardsmen accompanied Jake and Detective Lee to the beach. This time they carried two body bags. The third corpse was midway down the east coast of the island, where it was easier to sail the cutter than tromp through miles of jungle.

Their feet sank into the sodden beach, leaving footprints and disturbed sand in their wake. Slogging up the stream that emptied into the cove, they passed the three lone trees where Jake had hung by his wrists. Further inland, they slipped through an opening carved by the survivors into the dense vegetation bordering the stream. A narrow, trampled path snaked through thicker and taller vegetation toward the towering trees of the jungle proper. The pungent odor of rain-bathed wood and leaves savoring the morning sun welcomed them, as did a committee of tiny, winged insects determined to explore every orifice on their heads.

The first corpse was easy to locate. The nasty smell of decomposing flesh as good as pointed an arrow at it. The body, covered in a shroud of competing insects, lay several feet off the path. "I used the choke maneuver to subdue him," Jake explained, "then tied his hands and feet together with his shoelaces behind his back. If I'd killed him, I wouldn't have bothered to restrain him to prevent his escape."

"Clear the body for photos," the captain barked. Three of the guardsmen dispersed what bugs they could while the fourth guardsman snapped pictures.

Detective Lee leaned closer to the corpse. "I know that man. Miguel Galit." He stepped back and swatted at a battalion of blowflies attacking his face. "He's been in and out of jail more times than I have hairs on my head. I suspect the second corpse will be his sidekick, Philippe."

An electric current zapped from Jake's heart and sizzled across every nerve in his body. Suddenly, hope was a reality. Miguel's criminal record, the shoelaces obviously tied to avert escape—Jake's innocence was an easy conclusion.

"Why a choke maneuver?" Lee's voice was stiff.

Jake blinked. "He had a pistol, so I came at him from behind. The other pirate had captured Eve, and I had to hurry." What was Lee's problem? Jake huffed and turned back to the path. Best keep his mouth shut and take them to the next corpse. A confrontation with the detective would not help Jake's case.

"Bag him," the captain instructed his men. "We'll get Miguel here on our way back with the second corpse."

A ways down the path, Jake left it to follow another one not as obvious. Within moments, they entered the rain forest, a hothouse of tree trunks that soared like skyscrapers to a leafy canopy obscuring sun and sky. Hoots and screeches from the canopy's denizens slammed their eardrums. He hoped the detective was a city boy and would find the surroundings unnerving.

They rounded a twist in the trail, and sunlight spotlighted the jungle through a hole in the canopy. The tree that had occupied it lay toppled into a taller tree's branches, forming a steep but accessible bridge to the tree. Jake led them to a mound at its base. A second battalion of blowflies occupied it.

Jake tipped his head back and squinted against the sunlight. "He fell from up there."

Lee followed his gaze. "What was he doing in the tree?"

"Eve broke loose from him and fled to it. He climbed up after her."

"Handy that he fell."

Jake's jaw stiffened. "She said she didn't push him, if that's what you're inferring."

"Did you see it happen?"

"No. I found her after she descended. She scraped dirt and leaves over him to hide his death from the other man."

"Whew, that was quite a fall." The captain nodded his head at the corpse. "Evidently he landed feet-first." One of the man's femurs protruded from his abdomen, staking him in a crouch in the humus of the forest floor. "Is it Philippe, Detective?"

Lee nodded. "Bag him, and let's pick up Miguel. I want to get the third body before dusk."

Bearing the two body bags between two guardsmen apiece, the group returned to the cutter, Jake leading the way, then the detective, followed by the four guardsmen and the captain. It was a dour funeral procession that Jake couldn't shake off as being his own. Perhaps with the third corpse, Detective Lee would relent and come around to Jake's side.

Chapter 4

Again, memories pinched Jake's heart as the Coast Guard cutter anchored off the beach where the four castaways had arrived a year ago. He had dragged himself out of the ocean, broken-hearted at the death of Ginny, aching to join her in death if only God would take him home. Instead, God purposed him with the protection of three women's lives, created a family from the pieces of their shattered souls, and comforted Jake with a new love.

A love who now lay in an induced coma. Who might awake to an unjust incarceration for murders she hadn't committed. Or to a fiancé incarcerated for a murder he hadn't committed.

From the motorboat, Jake's view of the gravesite was lost in the expanse of white sand fronting a lineup of sentinel palm trees. The men landed and left behind a guardsman to putter alongside their onshore search. Evening shadows grayed the sand by the time Jake spotted the four sticks marking the grave.

The body the guardsmen dug up was badly deteriorated. "I found him a few days after we landed on the island," Jake said. "From his clothing, I guessed he was a sailor. His throat was slit."

The captain examined the corpse. "Might be the sailor lost at sea from a freighter last year. Rumor had it he was murdered." His eyes rounded, and he shot a glance at Detective Lee. "Murdered by that scum Jojo after an argument in a card game."

"Jojo!" Jake exclaimed. "That's the brute who tied me to the tree and kidnapped Eve!"

Detective Lee pursed his lips. "Looks like we have a pretty clear picture of what happened on the island. We'll talk to Eve tomorrow and see if she learned anything about the disappearance of the yacht's owners and first mate before she got shot."

It was all Jake could do not to shout, *Halleluiah!* "I can see her, talk to her tomorrow?"

"You and Betty and Crystal." Lee said. "We'll call them from the airport and tell them to meet us in the hospital waiting room."

Jake stuck his hand out, and Lee shook it.

***

"Eve's gone!"

Weary from his two days on the island, Jake braced himself as Crystal Oakleigh sprinted across the recovery waiting room and threw herself into his arms. Behind her, Betty Parker's distraught face and full-body sag in a waiting room chair confirmed the child's news.

He swallowed the spike of alarm that zapped from his stomach to his throat. "Whoa there, pumpkin! Let's check it out at the nurses' station. They probably took her to X-ray or—"

"No, Jake!" Crystal's chest heaved a sob. "They took her away after you left for the island."

He released Crystal and wheeled to confront Detective Lee, who had accompanied him to collect Betty and Crystal for the visit to Eve's room. Or at least that's what the detective had told him.

Lee back-stepped out of Jake's reach. "They're mistaken."

Supporting herself with the cane Jake had made on the island, Betty shuffled over to them, her fluff of white hair bobbing as she shook her head vehemently. "No sirree, young man, my niece is not mistaken." She stopped in front of Lee and glared at him from fatigue-darkened eyes. "U.S. Marshals took her. Eve's nurse told us so."

The surprise that flitted across Lee's face was genuine. It was the only thing that kept Jake from grabbing him and shoving him against the wall.

"I'm checking this out." Lee strode out of the waiting room, with Jake,

Betty, and Crystal close on his tail. At the nurses' station, Lee halted and drew himself into a stiff stance in front of the nurse on duty. He flashed a badge at her. "Room number for Eva Gray."

The nurse riffled through two files before answering him. "She's been dismissed."

"On whose orders?" Lee barked. "This patient is under arrest."

The nurse's eyes widened. Shoulders crunched forward, she huddled over the second file. "By order of the United States, sir." She pulled a piece of paper from the file and slid it across the counter to the detective.

Before Lee could pick it up, Jake flattened it under the palm of his right hand. "U.S. Marshals," he read out loud. "Eight o'clock p.m. yesterday via ambulance to Villamor Air Base." Heat, lava hot, suffused his face. "What's going on, detective? You sent her to the United States as a prisoner while you and I were on the island?"

"I know nothing about this." Lee grabbed the telephone next to the nurse. "But heads will roll when I find out who allowed this to happen. She was *my* prisoner!"

Jake's body quaked with anger. Lungs and diaphragm punched air in heaving volleys. *Eve, gone!*

"Jake." Betty's fingers touched his cheek, directed his eyes to hers. "Find out where she is." She let the words sink in. "We'll go after her."

Go after her. Yes. He grabbed Betty in a fierce hug.

Chapter 5

"Eve's alive."

The two words hit drug lord Danny Romero like a bullet between the eyes.

His head recoiled and he clutched the phone to his ear to keep from dropping it. The shadows of his office swooped in on him like awakened ghosts. "How ...?"

"Philippine Coast Guard found her on a stolen yacht four days ago. Shot in the head."

"Four days, and you're just now telling me?"

"I called as soon as I found out." The voice on the other end quavered. "U.S. Marshals brought her to the United States last night. That's the first anyone here in Chicago knew of it."

Romero's knees gave way. He dropped into his chair, heart pummeling his chest. He had to open his mouth to breathe without rasping. *She can't be the only one still alive.* He steadied his voice. "Who else was on the yacht?"

"Two Filipinos. A convict and a ship's officer, both dead."

Romero cursed. "What happened?"

"No one knows. She's had brain swelling and has been put in an induced coma. Doctors are reversing it today. She's under minimal security at Cook County Hospital. You could finish her off before—"

"No!" His hands shook. "Not until we know her story. If she's alive, my son could be alive."

A spasm of coughing choked off his words. Irritation that the informant knew about his emphysema and was waiting for him to catch his breath—maybe even hoping he'd drop dead right there on the spot—made it worse.

"Stay on top of it," he finally hissed. He slammed down the phone and leaned back in his chair, chest tight, eyes closed. Four days! Four days since Eve surfaced in the Philippines equalled four days of lost opportunity to get to her. But now she was in Chicago. On his turf. Within his reach.

Basta! Enough! He straightened his back and cautiously inhaled a deep breath. He needed a plan, but this time it had to be flawless.

***

The noise drew her upward—up and up, beckoning her through the darkness until at last she could reach the light to discover it. The sound deepened as she drew nearer—a muffled rumbling, far away and low like thunder. She opened her eyes and squinted. Bright light framed a dark figure next to her. It turned toward her and she saw the face of an aged man.

Dad?

She closed her eyes, and her heartbeat filled her ears with a thrum of joy as she sank back into darkness.

When she heard the noise again—his voice, she was sure—she opened her eyes immediately. Her heart swelled at the sight of him. He sat in a chair next to her, holding her hand. She was in a hospital bed. She peered around the room—what was she doing in a hospital?—and returned her scrutiny to him. His head was bowed and his eyes squeezed shut, yet he was talking. His voice was familiar somehow, deep and rumbling, like thunder rolling off a distant mountaintop.

She waited for him to look at her. His hair was white, combed straight back, his face somber. When he saw she was awake, he smiled, and the leathery skin around his eyes and mouth crinkled into a thousand tiny smiles.

"Hello there!"

"Dad?" She held her breath.

"I'm George Peterman, chaplain at Cook County Hospital."

"Oh." Disappointment swept through her like water swirling into a deep chasm.

"I've been praying for you."

She tried to remove her hand, but he brought his other hand over hers and started patting it. She gazed at him dully. "Why?"

His face sobered again. "I've been praying for your life."

He pointed to an area behind her, and she twisted far enough to glimpse an army of medical instruments standing guard over her. She traced wires and tubes to her right arm and her chest. Her eyes darted back to the chaplain.

"You've been out four days," he said. "You've had a lot of people worried."

Who? she wanted to ask. Then she remembered she couldn't remember. Not anything. Not anyone. She glanced at the chaplain. Not even her father.

***

Dusk squeezed the bright square of her hospital window into an empty shadow of gray. She stared at it, identifying with it—hollow tube of flesh and bandages to hollow square of glass and aluminum.

No one would tell her anything about herself. Not the chaplain, nor the doctor who hurried in to examine her, nor the nurse who brought a paltry meal of orange gelatin and ice water with a straw. She was a floating soap bubble in an empty universe, and no one seemed to care.

"You awake?"

She followed the trail of the deep voice to a tall, craggy man in a blue suit and striped yellow tie, standing in the doorway. He crossed to the side of her bed and nodded at her.

"Eve. How are you doing?"

Her heart thumped against her chest. *Eve.* Was that her name?

The man folded himself into the chair the chaplain had used and scooted back a few feet so he could extend his long legs in front of him.

"Eve?" she whispered.

He pursed his lips and tapped them with a long, slender forefinger. "Evedene Eriksson. You don't remember?"

"No."

His lips thinned into a grimace "Nor where you've been this past year."

Her breath left her. *Year?* She shook her head. *How about a lifetime?*

She waited for more questions, more information, but the man fixed his eyes on the floor and tapped his fingers on the edge of his chair. *He doesn't know what to say, and he's going to leave.* She clutched the bed sheets and blurted, "Who are you?"

His eyebrows shot up and he looked at her with eyes sparking. "Your boss—Bradley Henshaw, District Attorney at the Everett Dirksen Courthouse in Chicago. You flew to Guam last year as Eva Gray to get information on Danny Romero's drug trade, and when you vanished"—he slapped his hands together in a loud pop—"the case against Romero vanished."

She jutted her jaw out and flashed narrowed eyes at him. "Thanks for caring."

He laughed. "You may have lost your memory, Eve, but you haven't changed a bit." He stood and tugged his suit coat into place. "You're going to be okay. We just need to give this some time."

"Please!" She had so many questions. She grabbed at his coat sleeve. "I don't remember anything. I don't know what year it is, what my job is, nothing about myself. No one will tell me anything."

He put a hand on her shoulder and gave it a gentle squeeze. "The doctor says your memory will come back in bits and flashes. Your father is flying in tomorrow; let's wait and see if his visit prompts anything. Then we'll talk."

She inhaled sharply. Her father. She had forgotten him along with everything else in the tsunami that had swept away her memory. Yet left behind, uncovered by the waves like a buried treasure chest, lay an intense yearning to see him. Talk to him. Be with him.

Why? Why such a fierce longing?

She exhaled and drew a long, slow breath into the hollow space in her chest. Tomorrow she would find out.

Chapter 6

Eve's hospital window greeted her in pastel sunlight the morning after her boss's visit. It matched the tiny ember of hope warming the empty space inside her. She reviewed what she'd learned: her name, Evedene Eriksson, alias Eva Gray. Her location, Chicago. Her boss, District Attorney Bradley Henshaw. And today her father was coming.

She noticed with a silly sense of delight that the contents of her breakfast tray had been upped a notch from gelatin and ice water to oatmeal and orange juice. Why was it she could remember the identity of food and other items but not her own name?

A new nurse introduced herself as Susan. She removed Eve's breakfast tray and turned to leave. Eve arched her left eyebrow. Why wait for her father's visit for a memory prompt?

"Susan, do you think I could have a cup of coffee and a newspaper?"

Dear Susan complied, and Eve glanced at the date before shoving the newspaper out of sight between her bed sheets. Her hands shook with the deliciousness of her audacity. Today was Saturday, June 19, 1982. And just like that, she knew her date of birth and that she was thirty-four years old. Tears sprang to her eyes.

Susan dashed back into the room. "Where's that newspaper?"

For a second, Eve considered fighting to the death for it. But of course that was foolish. She meekly handed the paper over. *The Chicago Tribune* stood out in bold letters across the top. "Is there a problem?"

"Orders." The previously friendly voice was now cold and clipped.

Eve stiffened. Was she a prisoner? Anger burned her face like a flame hitting gasoline, but just as quickly it dissipated and she sank listlessly into her pillow. A hammer thudded dully inside her head. She closed her eyes, just for a minute …

She awoke to the sound of a distant rumble. She knew even as she opened her eyes that it was the chaplain. He had pulled the chair closer to her bed, and she could see his eyebrows were thick and white and that tiny tufts of white hair poked out of his nose and ears.

Inanely she said, "I'm thirty-four years old."

He threw back his head and laughed. "Top priority information for a woman to know."

She grinned, giddy with her knowledge and a friend with whom to share it. "My name is Eve, Evedene Eriksson; today is June 19, 1982; and I'm in Chicago."

"You remembered all that?"

"Just my birthday." She told him about her boss's visit last night, the newspaper this morning, and her father's impending visit today. "Why is no one telling me anything?" she grumbled.

"Orders. We've been told not to help you."

"Why? Whose orders?"

Peterman lifted his shoulders in an exaggerated shrug. "To tell you would be helping you. But you said your father is coming." He winked at her. "I suspect he doesn't share those marching orders."

"He'd better not." She glared at him. "Fathers look out for daughters, unlike bosses and chaplains who won't say anything."

"Everyone here wants to help you, Eve. You can't take big leaps when your legs don't work. Focus on getting well. That's what you need first."

"There's no reason I can't do both." She folded her arms over her chest.

Peterman stood. "I'm not involved with these orders except to cooperate with them." He reached over and patted her hand. "Invest some trust in them, Eve. Everyone is on your side."

He excused himself to continue on his hospital rounds, and she mulled over his advice. Invest trust in whom? And in what? If there was a plan, why wasn't she privy to it?

Fatigue grabbed her thoughts and melted them into sticky syrup. She dozed off, waking with a start to find herself still alone. Where was her father? Had her boss told her the wrong day?

Unbidden, a memory of her mother materialized, young but faded like an old sepia photograph, and she knew without a doubt that her mother was dead. *Dad held me and we cried together.* She tried, but she couldn't remember her father's face. A sob shook her chest. That was what she wanted—his arms around her, telling her everything would be okay.

***

She jumped every time someone entered her room, but it was always hospital staff. Chaplain Peterman brought her a crossword puzzle book and she distracted herself with it, filling in page after page of little boxes with letters. Why could she answer the downs and acrosses of these puzzles but not remember the details of her own life? They'd come in "bits and flashes," the doctor had said. She threw the puzzle book across the room. Where was her father?

Lunch and dinner were a series of soups and crackers, juice and more gelatin, this time red. She barely touched them.

Evening brought a new nurse on duty, Roxanne. She greeted Eve, left the room, then poked her head back in a minute later. "Your father is here."

Eve froze.

A man stepped into the doorway. Nordic, wearing a white dress shirt and pleated black trousers, no tie or jacket. Huge hands reached for her as he rushed across the room. He grabbed her and held her tightly. A whiff of cologne tugged at her memory.

"Eve! I thought I'd never see you again." His voice caught on the words, and his chest jerked against hers as he caught his breath.

She had wanted this, longed for it, but she stiffened into cardboard at his embrace. She didn't know these arms. Didn't know this man. She drew her head back and pushed him away.

He let go of her with a sigh and sat in the chair next to her bed. "Do you remember me, Evie?"

She shook her head. Nothing about him was familiar, from his fading blond hair to the spit and polish of his shoes. His cologne lingered in the air, and she blinked. Yes—Ralph Lauren. The fragrance tingled on the outer edges of her mind.

"No memories of anything?"

She swallowed back tears and pressed her lips together. In spite of her efforts, a jagged moan escaped.

He reached over and caressed her cheek. "You never could talk when you were emotional, Evie. Do you remember that?"

He knows me, better than I do. She ached to grab his hand and press her face into his big, strong palm, but she couldn't move. She watched him put his hand back into his lap.

He started talking about their family. She took another breath and leaned back into her pillow, studying him, looking for a button to spring open her memory. Late fifties or early sixties, tall and a bit stoop-shouldered, a slight paunch rounding out his shirt above his belt.

Nothing.

He told her about her mother, and tears welled in her eyes. Her mom had died in a car accident when Eve was five. Was that when he'd held her on his lap and cried? She looked at his hands again. He wore a class ring on his right hand and a massive black jewel on his left. No wedding ring.

"You have an older brother, Dax. He lives in New York with me." He paused. "Do you remember Dax?"

"No, I don't." The hammer started tapping inside her skull and she winced. Her eyelids fell to half-mast. "I'm sorry, I need to rest. Can you stay, or come back tomorrow …?"

"Eve, come home with me."

He grabbed her hand, but her eyelids were too heavy to keep open. She sank into darkness …

She awoke to a night-blackened window. Light from the hallway seeped in between the door and wall to reveal her father asleep in the chair. *He stayed!*

Her heart percolated. She wanted to jump out of bed and fling her arms around him.

Was she crazy? He was a stranger. She didn't know him.

His head was tilted back against the chair, his nose pointed at the ceiling, his mouth wide open. She laughed when a horrific noise of half-gasping, half-snarling emitted from his throat.

"Hey, wake up, you're snoring."

His eyes popped open and he sat up and looked at his watch. "Eve?"

"I'm awake. I'm sorry I—"

He rubbed his eyes. "Listen, honey, I have an overseas flight to catch, but I want you to come home with me when I get back. Please, let Dax and me take care of you until you're back on your feet."

Leaving already? She choked back her disappointment. "I ... I don't know."

He moved to sit on the edge of her bed and hold her hand. "I have something difficult to tell you first."

A thousand possibilities swept into her brain like autumn leaves caught in a whirlwind. But there was no landscape in an empty mind on which to land, and just as quickly they blew away. She stared at him, her heart pounding in her ears.

"I was a bad father, Eve. I didn't stand up for you when I should have." His voice broke, and he cleared his throat. "You haven't spoken to me in years. That would be important to you—to know that before you say yes and come."

She darted her eyes in bewilderment over his face. "What happened?"

"You and Dax and his friend ... there was trouble." He shook his head and tried several times to speak. He avoided her eyes. "I didn't look out for you when you needed me. I failed you, Eve. You never forgave me, and when I heard that you'd died ..." His voice trailed off and his chest heaved in gasps, shaking the bed.

"I don't remember. I don't know what you're talking about."

"Please, give me another chance. Give *us* another chance."

No! She didn't know this man. Didn't know what bad thing had happened. Didn't want to take chances.

But she couldn't make herself yank away her hand. She *needed* to know. An ache strangling her heart told her his apology was a treasure chest buried long ago, long before her memory loss. Maybe it was time to uncover it, to open it up.

She squeezed his hand and forced herself to say the words. "I will, Dad. I want that chance too."

Chapter 7

Jake exited the Indianapolis Express taxi and stood immobile as the cab disappeared into the dark. Across the street, his house was the only one in the neighborhood with no lights on. Exactly the homecoming he had dreaded. Empty house, kids unable to meet him, memories of Ginny everywhere.

And no idea where Eve was. Detective Lee's office had run into a dead end.

A dog barked inside a fenced yard nearby, and within minutes every dog on the block was yapping. A door opened three houses down, and light and the evening news spilled into the dark. Jake crossed the street. Last thing he needed was a neighbor sending the police to check on things before Jake got the word out that he was alive and well. And home.

He started across the lawn but stopped when his overnight bag caught on something. A lawnmower. He looked closer. The grass between the curb and the mower was cut; the grass between the mower and the house stood at eight inches. His left cheek twitched. Young Toby Miller, hired to mow their lawn, would be getting a phone call tomorrow.

He retrieved the spare key from the crack in the bottom of the fence post and entered through the back door to the kitchen. The odor of mice and mildew hit him like a two by four. Wasn't someone supposed to be cleaning the place while his kids were gone? The house had only been vacant since Brett and Dana returned to West Point two months ago.

He checked the refrigerator—empty, but the light was on. Good, electricity was working. Water on at the kitchen faucet too. He wouldn't use the lights because of the neighbors, but a shower would be a welcome relief. He might even work on his beard.

He ran his fingers through the eight-inch tangle of hair on his cheeks and head. *A disgrace.* Why had he let Crystal talk him out of a haircut and shave? He'd asked himself that every time someone had looked at him with wary eyes. A Marine was a Marine from the inside out, but wild and crazy hair did not communicate "Marine within."

Of course, no one had known on the trip back to the United States that he was a Marine. But the real answer, the one that came from his heart, was always the same: Crystal didn't need any more stress than what she already faced going home—no parents, only grandparents whom Crystal didn't think loved her. And so the razor had stayed at bay.

He missed her.

And Betty.

And most of all, Eve.

Today was June 20, 1982, and for the first time in over a year he was utterly and completely alone. His shoulders slumped.

He was home.

Within minutes his eyes adjusted to the dark, and he walked through the kitchen to the living room. Everything was tidy and in order, exactly as he remembered it a year ago. Almost as if the kids had preserved it as a memorial to their parents. No, he corrected himself, not a memorial but an expression of hope.

"Dana and I never gave up, Dad." Brett, who even as a child had seldom cried, had wept on the phone yesterday.

Jake walked down the hall toward the four bedrooms. The guest bedroom and Brett's room were spotless. Dana's was a wreck. Bed unmade, clothes tossed everywhere, cola bottle on the dresser. Jake smiled. Evidently a year at West Point Military Academy hadn't spoiled her nesting skills.

He stopped at the door to the master bedroom and took a deep breath. He'd had to tell Brett only half their hope had been realized. "I survived, son. Your mother didn't."

He gasped in fresh grief and walked into the bedroom.

Ginny was everywhere. Annual photos of the family on the wall, a stack of favorite cassettes next to a boom box, her mother's worn Bible on the nightstand. He opened the closet door. Her clothes were still there. He grabbed an armful and buried his face in them. *Ginny.* Her fragrance clung faintly to them.

She had died a year ago. He needed to say goodbye.

But not tonight.

Tonight he would see her strawberry blond hair pulled back in a ponytail on their first day at Sherman High. He would be bold and steal a kiss from her at the county fair and not get another for six years. He'd watch, heart pounding, as she walked down the aisle in her mother's satin-and-lace wedding gown, never to stop kissing him again.

Until a year ago.

But tonight … tonight Ginny was alive. Tonight he was not alone.

***

He awoke the next morning flattened by a steamroller. He dragged himself to the shower and stood in the hot water far longer than was decent for a man of economy. He made a mental list to get himself going. *Find the source of the mildew odor—best bet, a leak beneath the kitchen sink. Set mousetraps. Call Toby Miller about the lawn.*

He'd be flying out to see the kids while Betty contacted a private eye she trusted to search for Eve. *Check credit card account, buy a ticket to West Point. By all means, get a haircut and shave.*

He toweled off and stood naked in front of the mirror. Arm and chest muscles lookin' good, man; ribs sticking out, not so good. He ran his fingers over the two jagged scars on his right cheek that continued down the right side of his chest. Pit bull. Bullet holes on the left side formed contrasting circular scars. Nam. He turned to examine the reflection of four sets of claw marks on his backside. Clouded leopard.

Pit bull, Nam sniper, clouded leopard. There was no room on his body for additions to the list.

He put on clean briefs and plaid shorts from his dresser. The shorts were way too loose. He got out a belt and cinched it at the tightest notch.

The mirror reflected a wild man. He just couldn't walk into a barbershop looking like this. He found a pair of scissors and attacked his beard over the bathroom sink.

He stopped halfway through. The scissors were dull and he looked like road kill.

A sharp knife would do. He headed for the kitchen.

Ginny's perfume bottle on the vanity stopped him. His throat tightened. She'd worn it for as long as he'd known her. He didn't even know the name of the fragrance—it was just … her. The essence of Ginny distilled. He removed the stopper and brought the bottle to his nose. Tears flooded his eyes.

He took the bottle with him to the kitchen. He'd give it to Dana. She'd want her mother's perfume.

No. The fragrance would haunt him. He'd toss it, bring closure. It was time to move on. Time to focus on finding Eve, bring her home. On finding Captain Emilio, bring him to justice.

He held the bottle over the trashcan. Grimaced. Put the bottle on the kitchen counter.

He poked around in a kitchen drawer until he decided on a knife sharp enough to slice through his wiry hair. He also decided about the perfume. Dana should have it—she could decide what to do with it.

He picked up the bottle, grunted as it slipped from his grasp. He caught it in midair, but not before half the perfume splashed onto the floor. The sweet aroma fluffed into the air like a ballerina's tutu in *Swan Lake*. Disgusted at the waste, he slipped the kitchen knife into his belt and grabbed the shirt he'd been given in the Philippines. Orange and blue flowers the size of elephant ears weren't quite his style—no harm using it for the spill. He was going to get rid of the shirt, anyway. Maybe he'd give it to Toby Miller, make him wear it while he finished mowing the lawn. Jake snickered at the picture. He wadded the shirt into a ball, mopped up the spatters and hung the shirt on the back of a dining room chair.

A pile of mail strewn across the dining room table caught his eye. Brett had told him he'd picked up the mail from the post office before dashing back to West Point. Jake's mouth fell open. He had expected a few envelopes, not an avalanche. He added *sort mail* to his list, plus *visit post office to start up delivery*.

The post office. He halted. Perhaps there'd be a letter from the U.S. State Department. It had been only two days since he'd called them from the embassy in the Philippines, but they had been eager for his information, had asked him to FAX the details about Captain Emilio and the murders on the cruise ship. It wasn't unreasonable that he'd have an answer from them by now.

The doorbell rang, and he jumped.

Toby Miller? Jake put on his best scowl and stalked to the front door.

Chapter 8

Orville Marsh cast another glance across Chalmers' yard. Not at all what he had expected for this interview. He eyed the lawn mower. Dull blades, gauging from the path of torn grass, but still no excuse for abandoning the machine mid-lawn. His gaze shifted to the taller grass bearing tiny beads of seed next to the house, and from there to the weeds spiking above brown clumps of, well, what surely must have been flowers. Petunias, perhaps?

Orville huffed. No doubt the neighbors had hoped for more than this from a Marine Corps Reserve officer. A Viet Nam hero no less, decorated with a Purple Heart and the Navy Cross. Promoted to full colonel only a month ago. For a moment Orville wondered if he'd made a mistake and come to the wrong address. But no, the house number matched the address given him by the U.S. State Department and further documented in Chalmers' military file.

He ran the palm of his left hand over his bald spot and smoothed a thin film of sweat into his hair. Too hot for a suit. He should loosen his tie.

The front door burst open and Orville's heart leaped into his throat as a half-naked man with wild chestnut-red hair and a mangy beard glared out at him.

Orville swallowed and gripped his briefcase tighter. "I'm looking for a Mr. Jacob A. Chalmers."

"Are you a salesman?"

"I'm here on business. Orville Marsh from the U.S. State Department."

The man's eyebrows jumped and his mouth formed an *O*. "I'm Jacob Chalmers. Come in." He stepped back and beckoned with his hand. "Please, come in."

Orville squared his shoulders and stepped inside. The room was dark except for the outline of drapes drawn tightly over two windows. The odor of neglect and animal filth hit his nostrils, and his stomach lurched. It took a few seconds for his eyes to adjust and see that Chalmers had extended his hand to him to shake.

"Could we have some light?"

"Of course."

A light in the ceiling switched on, and Orville took in a quick glimpse of his surroundings before focusing on his host. At the sight of Chalmers he sat down hard on the nearest chair. The man's body was covered with scars, front and back. A knife—a kitchen knife with a long, serrated blade—was stuck in his belt. Orville could count every rib above the belt.

"I'm sorry, I wasn't expecting company," Chalmers said. He disappeared into the next room.

Orville craned his neck and saw it was a dining room. The table was piled high with unopened mail. He straightened when Chalmers came back into the room. He had put on a wrinkled T-shirt featuring large orange and blue flowers. It looked like it had been worn non-stop for weeks. Orville cringed at the thought of the stench he was in for if Chalmers got too close.

"Mr. Chalmers, if you could have a seat over there, we can take care of matters quickly enough. I'm sorry to have disturbed you—"

"I'm in no hurry. This is important to me." Chalmers sat down on the couch. He brushed something off the end table next to him and turned on a lamp with a red shade.

Orville's eyes widened at the sight of Chalmers' chopped-up beard. It looked like he had used the lawn mower on it. Orville averted his eyes and fumbled to turn on the lamp near him. Dotted across the dark cherry wood was what Chalmers must have swept off his end table. Mouse droppings. A long-legged, pale spider dropped out of the lampshade, and Orville saw his hand had broken the creature's web.

"Maid must be on vacation," Chalmers said.

Orville managed a weak smile. He opened his briefcase and took out Chalmers' FAX. "Before we begin, Mr. Chalmers, I need to see your I.D."

Chalmers withdrew a wallet from his back pocket and stepped forward to hand a piece of plastic to Orville. The sweet bouquet of a woman's perfume wrapped itself around Orville like a boa constrictor.

Orville sneezed. Several times. His skin itched and his shirt clung to him in wet blotches on his back and stomach. "Would it be possible to open a window?" He took off his suit coat and laid it next to him, decided to remove his tie as well.

"Sorry, I'm used to the heat." Chalmers drew back the drapes and opened both windows. The warm air wafted the perfume like a peacock tail behind Chalmers as he moved about the room.

Orville held his breath as long as he could and examined the piece of plastic Chalmers had handed him. Driver's license. The face was a match for the man now back on the couch, but with a military haircut, no beard, and two thin, jagged scars on his right cheek. Orville examined the data. His eyebrows twitched. "It's expired."

"Not much opportunity to renew it last year."

Orville compressed his lips into a straight line. He put the license on the table as if he might need to look at it again. Anything to avoid the cloying power of Chalmers'… scent.

"Your communication, Mr. Chalmers, claims the explosion of the cruise ship *Gateway* was—"

"Claims? Are you disputing my report?" Chalmers' face turned as red as the lampshade.

Orville could see the bulge of the kitchen knife under Chalmers' shirt. "*Informed* us," he said. "You informed us the *Gateway*'s explosion was not an accident but that the cruise ship passengers died—"

"Were murdered," Jake exclaimed. "It wasn't the cruise ship that exploded. The passengers were herded into two boats, set adrift, and intentionally killed by explosives. My wife was among them."

So that was it. Orville nodded his head in sympathy at the poor man. First

Nam, then the wife. "I'm not clear on how you survived, Mr. Chalmers."

"I was below deck. When Captain Emilio discovered this, he forced me to jump overboard. After the explosions, I secured one of the boats and sailed to the nearest island."

Orville jotted down notes. *Lifeboats can survive explosives? Equipment includes a sail?*

"And what became of the captain and crew, Mr. Chalmers? There's been no word of their survival—"

"Their escape. They fled with the *Gateway*. That's why I contacted you, to set the record straight and start the hunt. I want that murderer Captain Emilio found."

"Of course. And you say you ended up on an island for a year with three women …"

"Yes. The four of us survived the massacre."

"Can you give me information about them? Names, birth dates?"

Chalmers rattled off the information with ease. "Eve… rather, *Eva* Gray, May 3, 1948. Betty Parker, September 18, 1917. Crystal Oakleigh, spelled O-a-k-l-e-i-g-h, October 16, 1970."

Orville wrote the names down and read the information back to Chalmers for accuracy. "Thank you, Mr. Chalmers. This is all I need to get started." He stood, gathered his coat and tie in one hand, his briefcase in the other, and made a beeline for the front door.

He looked back when he reached his rental car. Chalmers had closed the front door, but Orville had no doubt the man was watching him through one of the windows. A bead of sweat dribbled down Orville's forehead. He mopped his face with his handkerchief, then got into his car and turned the air conditioner on full blast.

He'd heard stories from his colleagues about Viet Nam veterans falling apart. Now he had a story of his own to tell.

Chapter 9

At precisely five o'clock p.m., as agreed upon in their flight home yesterday, Crystal Oakleigh slipped into Aunt Betty's living room to call Jake. Her heart thumped in pace with the stuttering ring of the phone on the other end.

"Hello?" A deep voice, warm and way too far away, answered.

"Jake?"

"Crystal?"

They laughed. She pictured Jake's eyes twinkling with smiles the way they had the time she'd discovered him sitting on the beach, reading his pocket Bible, his bare feet in the water and tiny crabs crawling all around him.

"How was the homecoming, Pumpkin?"

She shrugged. "Fine. We arrived a couple hours after you got off. Grandpa met us at the airport but not Grandma because it was so late." Grandma used an oxygen tank now, hooked up to her nose. She said it was because Grandpa's smoking had ruined *her* lungs instead of his. Grandpa just snorted and said a cigar now and then didn't hurt anyone.

Crystal turned her back to the living room doorway and lowered her voice. From the kitchen came the clink of dishes as her grandmother set the table, and the grumble of her grandfather complaining about something. Probably about the burnt onions soaking everything in the house with their blackened odor.

"Aunt Betty's mad," she whispered as loudly as she dared. "Really mad, I can tell. Grandma is her sister, and she and Grandpa moved into Aunt Betty's house because they thought she was dead. They changed things all around and even took over her bedroom." Crystal looked at the four couches rearranged into a large square in the middle of the living room, and the antique highboy moved from the dining room to a recess behind the couches. Grandma had also replaced all the paintings and pictures on the walls with her own. "I'm glad, though, because this way I'm not living all by myself with them again."

"They love you, Crystal. They're happy to have you back and know you're alive. Both you and your Aunt Betty."

Crystal's lower lip trembled. "When are we going to look for Eve? And come live with you like we planned on the island?"

"We've been back two days, Pumpkin. Even the Marines can't act that fast."

A corner of Crystal's mouth tucked up. "Do you still have your beard?"

"Shaved it off this morning. But I got a picture before I did. It's being developed now. I'll mail it to you first thing after I get back from West Point."

The news popped tears into her eyes. She remembered the first time she'd seen Jake on the cruise ship. He'd been sitting on the other side of the dining room with his wife. He didn't have a beard then. But the Jake she'd come to love as a father did.

No, she reminded herself, what would make everything perfect was not Jake keeping his beard, but finding Eve. Then Eve and Jake could get married and be her mom and dad, and she and Aunt Betty could move in with them.

"How long till you come back from West Point?"

"I'll go this weekend. If the private investigator hasn't located Eve yet, then Brett and Dana and I will take a little vacation."

She bit her bottom lip to silence the sniffles attacking her nose. On the island, she was the one who went everywhere with Jake. Now it was his kids who got to go with him.

"Is Betty there, sweetheart?"

She forced a big swallow in order to answer him. She was no longer a crybaby, remember? The island had made her tough, not even afraid of snakes anymore. "Uh-uh. She's gone to get that private investigator. She said she'd be back—"

"Crystal, time to eat." Her grandfather's voice boomed across the room, and she whipped around, a second big swallow leaping into her throat.

"Jake, I have to go."

"Okay, I'll talk to you tomorrow."

"I miss you," she whispered. She wanted to say more but her grandfather had stepped into the room and was glaring at her. Already the palms of her hands were sweaty. She hung up without waiting for Jake's goodbye.

Her grandfather's eyelids lowered halfway as they shifted from her to the telephone. "Who was that?"

"Jake."

"That man from the island?"

She nodded.

"I don't want you calling him. He's busy with his own life now, and he doesn't need you bothering him."

All the air in the room slammed into her lungs and exploded out again in hot tears. "I'm not a bother!"

Her grandfather's mouth fell open, and her heart stopped. Before her year on the island, she would've never yelled at him. Her heart started up again like a scared jumping bean. She took a step backward. "I'm sorry," she mewed.

Her grandfather's eyebrows furrowed lower over his eyes, and he turned on his heels toward the kitchen. "We always eat at five o'clock, remember? No more being late."

She clenched her fists and choked back sobs until they were only little hiccups. *It's okay*, she told herself over and over. She wiped escaped tears with the back of her hands, then her hands on the back of her shorts.

All she had to do was wait. It wouldn't be long. Aunt Betty was getting the phone number of the private investigator right now. Just a few more days, that was all.

***

The taxicab pulled away from the curb, braked, and honked along with three other drivers at a car ahead of them. It had stopped at a yellow light instead of dashing through the intersection. Betty Parker stood on the sidewalk and heaved a sigh of relief. Thank goodness she had taken the cab rather than attempt to drive in downtown Detroit traffic at 5:00. She was nervous enough as it was, just thinking about what she was going to have her lawyer do.

Pigeons scooted away from the tap of her cane, but only far enough to avoid her reach had she wanted to swat them. She didn't, but she knew a few people she'd like to. Neal Oakleigh, her sister's husband, for one. Made the hair on the back of her neck bristle, the way he had insinuated himself into her life—and her house—since she'd returned home. He deserved a whop.

She craned her neck to look up at the office building her husband had built two decades earlier. Taller buildings rose above it now, but none as handsome. Leaning heavily on her cane, she mounted the steps to the entryway one at a time. Pink Rosato marble, her favorite, framed the doorway. She paused to run the flat of her hand over the stone. In spite of the summer heat the marble was cool under her palm, its glossy surface soft as a satin pillow.

The entry door outweighed her, and she struggled to balance herself on her cane and at the same time pull on the heavy wood. Finally a man exited, held the door open for her, and she hobbled inside. A year ago she wouldn't have needed help. Not that she regretted her life on the island with Jake and Eve and Crystal. God had given them to her as the family she'd always wanted. Her foot injury was worth it.

She took the elevator to the top floor. *Parker and Snyder, Attorneys at Law*, embellished the frosted glass door of the office suite. With satisfaction, she noted Oakleigh, her brother-in-law's name, hadn't been added even though he'd told her he was now a partner in the firm.

The receptionist announced Betty's arrival, and Leroy Snyder came out of his office to greet her. Tall and gaunt, if he'd had a beard he'd have looked like Abraham Lincoln. He opened his arms wide and enveloped her in a hug, stooping to align his head alongside hers and kiss her on the cheek. "Betty, Betty, Betty. How good to see you! What a wonder you're here!"

She glowed at his welcome. "Thank you for the late appointment, Leroy. It's good to be back."

She liked Leroy. He was practical and unpretentious. When her husband had taken Leroy on as a partner thirty years ago, brain and charm had melded together in a match between the two men that skyrocketed the law firm to success. How in the world had Leroy found Neal Oakleigh, of all people, suitable to replace Franklin Parker's charm?

"Coffee?"

"Please."

Leroy buzzed his secretary to bring in two coffees while Betty sat down on the red leather couch she and Franklin had bought eight years ago for his office. Two matching chairs completed the suite, but the Bottocino marble-topped coffee table next to them was a prize they had found later in Belgium. She leaned forward and sniffed fresh flowers arranged in a crystal vase on the table. No doubt the receptionist still changed them every three days.

Sighing, she straightened and looked around the office. Until a year and a half ago it had belonged to her husband. Leroy had changed everything in the room except the suite where she was sitting. Franklin's massive mahogany desk was gone, the matching credenza too. In their place were a smaller desk, four overflowing bookcases, and three filing cabinets. *Please, don't tell me Franklin's furniture is in Neal's office.* It would be just like her brother-in-law to request the furniture on the basis of bogus sentimentality, and just like Leroy to give him everything.

Leroy sat down across from her. He leaned forward, elbows on knees, and beamed at her. "I want to hear all about your adventures this past year, Betty. But first, let me assure you that your money from Franklin's portion of the law firm is secure and should be available soon."

Betty pinched her lips together. She needed that money for her plan. "Why the delay?"

"No problems. Simply the torture of everything taking more time than it should."

"I don't like being financially dependent on my sister and brother-in-law."

"Tell you what. I'll have my secretary write you a check for as much as you'd like. You can pay the company back when your money's released. How about that?"

Her sister had told her she'd come back from the island changed. Feistier, she'd said. Betty toned her voice down. "Thank you, Leroy. I'd also like the phone number of the private investigator your company uses. MacBride, is it? I want him to help me find a lost friend." She briefly told him about Eve's disappearance from the Manila hospital. "There's another matter too. I'd like to draw up a new will."

Leroy's eyebrows rose. "Replace the one with Crystal as your beneficiary and Neal as her trustee?"

"Yes, I'm adding a second beneficiary and changing trustees."

Leroy sat back. "I'm in court the next two weeks. Is this something Neal can take care of?"

"Absolutely not. It's none of his business."

For a second, Leroy looked at a loss. Finally he said, "Then I'll make it my priority."

"Not in two weeks, Leroy. If you're too busy I can find someone else."

The muscles in Leroy's jaws tightened. "You don't want to take Franklin's business to his competitors."

Betty blinked. She certainly wasn't disloyal to Franklin. "All right then, let's get that coffee and start in right now."

And tomorrow, with MacBride's number in hand, Jake would set up an appointment to start the search for Eve.

Chapter 10

Neal Oakleigh put on his suit coat and straightened his tie. He popped a mint into his mouth, chewed and swallowed it, popped in another. Nothing worse than cigar-breath in a private conversation with his senior partner. Hopefully, Snyder was summoning him to do something worthy of inclusion in the company name on the office door. *Parker, Snyder, and Oakleigh, Attorneys at Law.* Or better yet, *Snyder and Oakleigh, Attorneys at Law.*

Outside his window, Detroit's Monday morning traffic was already snarled at the intersection. He walked down the hall to Leroy Snyder's office and found Leroy waiting for him on the red couch. So, this was to be an off-the-record chat. Neal's chest puffed out. It was conversations like this that had led to his becoming a partner in the firm. He sat down in a chair and made himself comfortable. Leroy wasn't one to waste time with small talk.

"Betty Parker came by my office."

Neal's heartbeat quickened. He'd seen his sister-in-law in Leroy's office, but she had said nothing about the visit when she came home. He'd wondered about it all weekend. "Everything okay?"

"I have some concerns."

Neal's face stiffened. Had she complained about him taking over her house? He'd thought she was dead, for Pete's sake—not off on some island in the Philippines playing Robinson Crusoe with his granddaughter and two other nut cases. He cleared his throat. "Concerns?"

"Under normal circumstances, I wouldn't share Betty's business with you.

46

But I'm involving you in this matter, Neal, because you're a family member. I feel a deep obligation to Betty because she is Franklin's widow."

"Thank you. I appreciate that."

"Betty asked me to take several actions that alarm me. One of them entails finding a missing woman who has amnesia."

"Eva Gray—Betty told me about her." Neal bobbed his head to show he was in the loop.

"Yes. Betty wants MacBride Investigations to contact her to start the search. You've worked with Mack, right?"

"Numerous times. He's provided invaluable information for several of my cases."

"Betty wants Mack to meet with a man in Indianapolis named Jacob Chalmers. That's where you come in."

Neal's stomach tightened. *What is Betty up to?* Snyder wouldn't be talking to him like this if Betty simply fancied unearthing a friend.

"Get ahold of Mack and tell him we want to hire him for the same work. Two birds with one stone—although our bird will be confidential."

"You want him to keep us apprised of his search for Eva Gray?"

"More importantly, I want him to uncover any dirt on Jacob Chalmers. I suspect he's after Betty's money."

***

The next day, Neal Oakleigh met Ian "Mack" MacBride for an urgent appointment at Neal's favorite downtown Detroit restaurant. The private investigator had the face of a cherub and the mind of a rocket scientist. The combination of innocence and intelligence often cinched a case's win when Mack took the witness stand. Juries hung on Mack's every word, mouths gaping like nestlings for a worm. His reputation for uncovering hard facts made his evidence and testimony untouchable.

Neal waited for the waitress to bring their sandwiches and pour coffee before jumping past the small talk. "Mack, I'm bringing you a tough nut to crack."

"Good."

"This guy's so tough he makes a baby's dimpled behind look like a warthog's."

Mack laughed.

"Only it's the other way around. He's a warthog, but he's got my sister-in-law believing he's the baby's behind."

"Franklin Parker's widow—Betty?" Mack whistled and paused to add cream and sugar to his coffee. His spoon clinked against the ceramic mug. "I heard she'd risen from the dead. Shipwreck, something like that? She's worth a few million, isn't she?"

"At least. And this warthog will convince you he doesn't know a thing about the money."

"Wants to marry her?"

"No, she wants to adopt him."

Mack whistled again, this time an octave higher. "How'd he manage that?"

"Of all things, they were marooned on an island together." Neal tapped the manila folder on the table between them. "It's all in here. He was quite the hero and weaseled his way right into Betty's heart. Into my granddaughter Crystal's, too. She was with them, plus a woman named Eva Gray. It's quite a story."

Mack looked hungrier for the folder than he did for his sandwich. "Want me to expose him?"

"Find me anything, *anything* I can use to catapult him out of Betty's life. And Crystal's."

Mack reached for the folder, but Neal put his hand on it. "There's more."

"Okay, you talk, I'll eat." Mack bit into his Philly steak sandwich and used his napkin to blot juice off his mouth and chin.

"Betty wants to hire you to find this other castaway, Eva Gray. She has amnesia."

Mack took another bite. "This gets better and better."

The story or the Philly? Neal eyed his own sandwich, and saliva sprang to his tongue. "Betty wants to send you to Jake Chalmers—her prospective son."

Mack stopped chewing. "Jake Chalmers? I have an appointment with him tomorrow."

"I knew it was soon. Only you're not supposed to know about the adoption, mind you. When you meet with him, that's when you start working for me." He corrected himself. "For *Parker and Snyder.*" In his mind he added *and Oakleigh.*

He slid the manila folder to Mack. "Everything you need to know is in here."

Except for one thing—and Mack didn't need to know about that. Neal grabbed his Reuben and took a big bite. By including Jacob Chalmers in her will—by planning to *adopt* him, for Pete's sake!—and, worse, replacing Neal as Crystal's trustee, Betty had forced him to take Chalmers on as a personal foe.

***

Jake and Mack MacBride carried glasses of iced tea from Jake's kitchen to the patio and sat in two wooden chairs at a matching round table. Overhead, a tall cottonwood tree showered specks of sunlight on their faces and arms and across the pattern of weathered orange bricks and redwood furniture.

The pungent smell of mowed grass, freshly baked in the oven of the noonday sun, permeated the air. Mack set his glass on the table, and the ice cubes crackled in the heat. He pulled a black leather notepad from his shirt pocket. "Since Mrs. Parker referred you to me, I called her last night for a confirmation. I hope you don't mind. In our conversation, she shared the basic information you two are interested in."

"Go ahead and read it to me." Jake folded his arms across his chest. Really? This fresh-faced kid was competent to find Eve?

"Okay, you want me to locate Eva Gray—nickname, Eve—a single, childless, Caucasian female, age 34, born May 3, 1948, assumed to be a citizen of the United States, occupation unknown. She suffered an injury to the head and memory loss on June 14 of this year in the Philippines, and was flown comatose to the United States for further medical help on June 16."

"Yes."

"She was a passenger along with you, Betty Parker, and Crystal Oakleigh on the cruise ship *Gateway* sailing out of Apra Harbor, Guam, a year ago on

June 12, 1981. Destination: Manila, the Philippines."

"Yes."

Mack flitted a glance at Jake's folded arms and back to his notes. "Detective Lee of the Philippine National Police informed you U.S. Marshals escorted her back to the United States."

"That's correct."

"I understand Detective Lee gave you the Marshals' phone number. May I see it?"

"I've already called them. They refused to help. Said not to call again."

Mack nodded. "They won't help me either, but the phone number will."

Jake frowned at the smile teasing the corners of Mack's mouth. He fished the number out of his wallet and handed it to Mack.

"Area code three-one-two. Chicago." Mack gave the phone number back.

The air in Jake's lungs stilled. Chicago was only three hours north of Indy.

"That's the Seventh District," Mack continued. "It's based in Chicago but covers Indiana, Illinois, and Wisconsin."

Jake nodded encouragingly. Remembered to breathe.

"Any thoughts on why U.S. Marshals would be interested in Eva Gray?"

Jake tipped up a weak smile. "She's in law enforcement?"

Mack's eyelids flickered. "Possibly. Equally possible she's a criminal."

Heat ran up Jake's neck to his cheeks. "No. I lived with her on that island for a year. I know her. She's not a criminal."

"If you want to find her, we need to consider that possibility before we dismiss it."

Jake put his elbows on the table and rubbed his hands over his face. His skin was warm next to the two jagged scars on his right cheek. No doubt the scars were glowing like neon signs against his flushed skin. "All right, for the sake of argument."

"Mrs. Parker said 'hooligans'—to use her words—came to the island and captured Eve. Two of them died on the island before the others took Eve away on a yacht. Could the marshals have arrested her for the two deaths on the island?"

Jake's head shot up. "She didn't kill anyone. One of them chased her up a tree and fell to his death. She wasn't even around when the other died."

"What happened to him?"

"I told Detective Lee about it. I used a military take-down maneuver on the man, and evidently—accidentally—it killed him."

One of Mack's eyebrows rose. "The detective dismissed both deaths as accidental?"

"Yes, and he didn't hold Eve responsible for the deaths of the two men on the yacht either."

Beads of sweat flecked Mack's forehead like miniature Bubble Wrap. He chugged down his iced tea, looking for all the world like a fourteen-year-old fresh off the field from a close soccer game. He set his empty glass on the table and grinned. "Mr. Chalmers, I'd say we can put prisons at the bottom of our list and start with the U.S. Marshals' office in Chicago." He rose to his feet. "I'll drive up there tonight, get started tomorrow. You and Mrs. Parker can expect a report no later than the end of next week."

As Jake walked Mack to the front door, an uneasy feeling gnawed at his stomach. He watched the private eye drive off. Mack's departure seemed abrupt. Something had flip-flopped in the interview about Eve, and it wasn't the mere flip of prisons to the bottom of Mack's list.

He recalled the sudden cock of Mack's eyebrow when Jake told him Detective Lee had dismissed the two men's deaths on the island as accidental.

He stiffened. Mack's reaction, slight as it was, said the man had found the information significant. But why?

Chapter 11

How could he tell his children he was in love with Eve?

Jake stared out the plane's window at the cloudbank shrouding Stewart International Airport below. He sighed and rolled the airline magazine in his hand into a tube. Ginny had died over a year ago. He loved her, always would. Her death had sent dark storm clouds roiling over his soul. He had lived in the shadow of their gloom until Eve brought back the sun. Could they understand that?

Eve. He ached to see her, to know she was okay and hold her in his arms. The doctor said she'd shown symptoms of amnesia. Was it permanent? Where had the Marshals taken her, and why? Why as good as kidnap her and hide their destination?

The airline magazine crunched between his fingers. He relaxed his fists and flattened the magazine onto his lap. No matter how long it took, he would find her. He and Detective Lee had run into a dead end with the U.S. Marshals, but that wouldn't stop him. MacBride would make short work of locating her—get into places Jake couldn't, root out the details he and Betty didn't know.

He sighed. Meanwhile, he had to decide when to tell the kids about Eve. For them, the death of their mother would be as fresh as if it had happened yesterday. They would see him in the airport in a few minutes but not their mom. The reality of her never coming back would crash down on them then. How could he impose the topic of Eve on them?

He couldn't. He wouldn't. He'd wait until the time was right.

The plane landed and he filed out with the other passengers. People of different ages and heights and shapes milled around the gate, gawking, murmuring, here and there faces lighting up and bodies meeting in brief hugs. He searched the crowd for Brett and Dana.

Dana's eyes snagged his. Her face crumpled, her mouth sagged open, and her chest heaved in jagged sobs. Jake caught his own breath, and tears rushed to his eyes. Next to her stood Brett, eyes soaking up his father, his lower lip quivering, chin jerking. Jake cried out. Their year of separation smashed against him, and he rushed to crush his children against him and never let go.

***

The three of them sat in Jake's hotel room, stomachs stuffed with a celebratory steak dinner. Even more savory for Jake was the update on the twins' year at West Point Military Academy. He and Ginny had taken them to the college the day before leaving for the Philippines. He'd expected to hear on a regular basis about the kids' activities and studies and friends. Had looked forward to it. Instead, he had missed it all.

"Dad, tell us what happened to you and Mom."

The air in Jake's lungs stilled at Dana's request. He drew in a deep breath. His turn to update them.

"After leaving you we flew to Hawaii for a few days, then to Guam." The tension in the twins' faces told him to skip the details of that part of the trip and get to the hard part.

"We boarded a small cruise ship in Apra that carried about two dozen passengers from Guam to the Philippines. Third day out, I was in my cabin reading when a crew member came and told me the captain wanted to see me—said there was a problem. The captain pointed to two small boats on the water about a hundred yards apart. Said all the passengers, including your mother, were in them. Told me at gunpoint to jump overboard."

Dana and Brett were so still he suspected they were holding their breaths.

"I'd barely surfaced when he pointed at the two boats with one hand and gave a signal with his other. The boats ..." He stopped. A lump the size of a boulder rose in his chest and lodged in his throat. He squeezed the last three words past it. "The boats exploded."

Dana gasped. Brett's face paled.

"It was deliberate?" Brett's voice was barely audible.

"Yes."

"Why?" Dana cried out.

"I don't know, sweetie." How many times had he asked himself that question?

Silence hung heavy in the room. Then Dana choked out, "What about Mom?"

Jake took another deep breath. Reliving the events scraped his soul raw. "I swam to the first boat and found her. She was dead. All the passengers were. The explosion collapsed their lungs. They died immediately."

Dana wept, and Brett put his arm around her shoulders. "Go on, Dad," he rasped.

"The boats were 'lighters,' designed with sealed air pockets to float high on the water to explore beaches. The explosions damaged both ends of the lighter your mom was on, but it was still floating because of the air pockets. I retrieved it and sailed to an island, where I discovered three other passengers who had escaped the explosion."

"How?"

"They'd been in the second lighter. Two of them fell overboard and the third jumped in to rescue them. The rough waters carried them far enough away to avoid the blast."

Silence again, then questions about surviving on the island. The tension seeped out of Jake's muscles, and he began to relax. These answers were bearable—the adventure of events rather than the anguish of loss.

"Tell us about the three people you were stranded with," Dana said after a while.

Jake's heart lifted. Yes. The three people he loved; who had become his family on the island; whom he wanted his children to love. He started with Betty—a childless widow in her late sixties, on the cruise with her grandniece, Crystal. Then Crystal—eleven years old, an orphan who lived with her grandparents. And finally, Eve—courageous, caring, capable, the one who had rescued Betty and Crystal, had towed them back to their damaged lighter to sail to the island. She had gathered fruit each day on the island, had sewed him up after a leopard attack.

He stopped, suddenly conscious he had talked more about Eve than the other two.

"You didn't say how old she is." Dana sat erect in her chair, eyes focused on her father.

"Early thirties."

"Married?"

"No."

"What's she do for a living?"

Jake shrugged. "She never told us."

"All that time on the island and she never told you?"

Jake flinched at the sarcasm in Dana's voice. "She ... avoided it, and we didn't pry."

"So she could have been a criminal, for all you knew?"

Brett frowned at her. "Dana, what's the matter with you?"

"Can't you tell?" Her voice leaped at Brett like a wild tiger. "Dad's in love with her!"

"That's ridiculous." Brett let out a loud guffaw. "He's hardly said a thing about her—"

Dana thrust her chin at him. "Only twice as much as about the other two. A year on an island with someone that fantastic—what do you think, Brett?"

Jake's cheeks burned.

Brett stared at him. "Dad?"

Not the timing he'd wanted for this news. He cranked out a weak smile. "Dana's right. We fell in love just before we were rescued."

Dana turned her face to the wall. Brett studied the green and beige carpet.

Jake's mouth went dry. "I'll always love your mother. Her death tore me apart. I thought I'd never stop hurting."

"But you aren't hurting now. You've moved on," Dana sniped.

"C'mon, Dana," Brett said. "After you met Bentley, you didn't grieve as much."

Dana's face turned a bright pink shade, and she darted a glance at her father. "It's not the same thing. Bentley's not replacing someone I love."

"Bentley?" Jake said.

"My boyfriend. You'll meet him tomorrow. And when will we meet this, uh … *woman*, Dad?"

"Eve," Jake said. "Eva Gray." He hesitated. "Soon. When we're all ready."

Which, gauging from his daughter's response, might need to be longer than he'd expected.

Chapter 12

July

"Dad?" Eve's hand shook at the weight of the telephone receiver. She pressed it tighter to her ear as a nurse wheeled a clattering hospital bed into the room next door. All Eve wanted was to hear her father, to talk to him again.

"Eve, are you okay?" Her father's voice crackled across the line from Firenze, Italy.

"I am." She squeezed her eyes shut to forestall brimming tears.

For a week she hadn't been able to talk to him. Only Chaplain Peterman had been allowed to visit as she lay rigidly in bed, afraid to move lest she set the room spinning. She could peek at her dear friend, glimpse his closed eyes and his lips moving in prayer, feel the warmth of his hands enclosing hers, smell the faint musk in his aftershave. But hear him she could not. She was a prisoner, cut off by a whirling room and the dead quiet of a tomb between her ears.

She opened her eyes and relaxed her grip on the telephone receiver. "My hearing came back yesterday. I was able to sit up without getting dizzy, and this morning I stood. I'm sitting in a chair now."

"You can come home then?"

"The doctor says I can go after the Fourth of July weekend—on Monday—if I continue to do okay." She dropped her hand over the edge of her chair and ran her fingers across the silky leather of the suitcase he'd sent from Italy. "Thank you for the luggage. And for the money for clothes."

"So you got to go shopping?"

"Not before the vertigo hit. So I asked Stella and Marianne, my co-workers at the district attorney's office, to pick up some things for me yesterday. They're coming over this evening to help me try them on."

"Those are the two girls you remembered a week ago?"

"Yes." She smiled. Both women were well into their fifties, not quite *girls*.

She had recognized the office manager and the receptionist the second they stepped into her room four days after her father left. Stella—short and round, but with a mod haircut and expensive clothes to ward off frumpiness—and Marianne, with her pug nose and a smile perpetually stretched from ear to ear. Their mouths had dropped open when Eve called out their names. Only after she saw their expressions did she grasp the fact that she remembered them. *Remembered them—at first sight!*

The next day vertigo nailed her to her bed.

Her father's voice brought her back to their conversation. "You sure you'll be well enough to travel? Monday is only three days away."

"The doctor said no planes, but a car will be fine. The drive will give Dax and me time to get reacquainted."

"I … hope you'll like him." Anxiety cemented her father's words together like mortar between bricks.

"Dad, please tell me what happened with Dax and his friend and me. What kind of trouble did we get into?"

The line was silent.

"Why won't you tell me?" She began to tremble inside. This was the third time she'd asked him, the third time he'd refused to answer. "You know I'm going to ask Dax."

Her father sighed. "I'm sorry, I never should have said anything to you. Can we just move on—"

"No! I don't like people knowing something about me that I don't know."

When her father didn't say anything, she clamped her jaw shut. He had erected a brick wall between them. This time she wasn't going to be the first to speak.

At last he said, "All right, Evie. I promise we'll talk about it when we get together."

She exhaled raggedly. That was probably the best she was going to get out of him. "I'm still going to ask Dax about it."

"You can do that. But you'll wish you'd waited."

"I'm tired of waiting. Why should I?" Her voice reverberated in the room.

There was a long pause, and then words heavy with sadness. "Because it's bad, Evie."

Suddenly she remembered his telling her she had refused to speak to him for years. It was she, wasn't it, who had put up the barricade.

A shiver ran up her spine and spread goose bumps over her arms. Maybe, just maybe, it was best not to know what lay on the other side.

***

Eve's suitcase stood at the door. A straw summer purse, a gift from Marianne, lay at the end of the stripped hospital bed. Inside the purse were a federal employee identification card and a checkbook with a year's back pay. She sat in the chair, teeth brushed, hair combed, dressed in a new shirt, slacks, and sandals—and shook. Today was Monday. Today she would meet her brother and drive from Chicago to New York. Would she remember him?

She got up and paced the room, refusing to poke her head into the hallway to look down the corridor. The clatter of dishes on trays and the acrid odor of coffee and overcooked bacon drifted into her room. Her mouth watered at the thought of food. Her dismissal papers had been signed before breakfast, and she'd now have to wait to eat until she left the hospital.

She wished Chaplain Peterman would make an exception to his schedule and come by. He usually made his visits after lunch. He had stopped by Sunday night to watch the Fourth of July fireworks on TV with her, and to say goodbye.

It struck her for the first time that she didn't know his full name. She dug into her purse and pulled out the business card he had given her. His first name was George. George Peterman. Warmth softened the tight ball in her stomach. He had asked her to look him up when she got back from her father's in New York. Chaplain Peterman would help her find an apartment, help her find a church. She would have asked him, in any case. Without him she was alone in Chicago. No one else here counted. Not as friends she could share her heart with anyway.

She thought of his question from Sunday night. He had asked her about God—did she remember Him, know Him at all? Joy had burst in her like one of the exploding firecrackers on TV. "Yes," she'd said. She had found Him in the deep caverns of her soul when the hospital room whirling over her head and the silence echoing between her ears had sent her running for a refuge. A safe place where she could curl up and be still, call out and be heard.

"I was so alone," she told Peterman. "I didn't even have myself for company—what was there to share?" She hunched her shoulders to her neck. "No memories. No history. No mistakes to ponder. No joys to relive. Only questions."

She looked at him, her brows knit together, her eyes scanning back and forth between his. "Who am I? That's what I kept asking myself. What if I never remember?"

Her lips pinched together and her gaze dropped to the floor. Peterman's hand covered hers and the warmth lifted her eyes back to his. "That's when I remembered God. Not just that I knew of Him from your prayers, but that I *knew* Him."

Peterman's grin wrapped around her and lifted her like a soaring kite. Emboldened, she shared her fear with him—how, like a caged animal being released into the wilds, she was clinging to the open door of the cage, afraid to venture out into the unknown.

"I've remembered my birthday and my coworkers Stella and Marianne," she said. "That's all. I've met Bradley Henshaw, my boss, whom I can't remember, and ten coworkers I also can't remember. I've learned I'm a federal prosecuting attorney, but I have absolutely no recall of the law, nor of any cases I ever tried, and especially nothing of this ... this Romero case." She glanced at her suitcase, where she had stuffed the files Henshaw had thrust at her with the demand she get current on them.

"I have a father I can't remember. He tells me I've rejected him for a reason he refuses to tell me, and I have a brother I also can't recall, who was somehow involved in that reason."

She glowered at the chaplain as if he were to blame. "So here I am, entering life at age thirty-four, having lived all of three weeks that I can remember— one of them flat on my back with vertigo." She flicked her hand dismissively. "And tomorrow? Oh, well, hey, off I go on my own. Easy-peasy."

"Oh, you're not so badly off." The chaplain winked at her.

This time Eve's scowl was genuine.

"There's a precedent, you know." His eyebrows rose, and he locked eyes with hers. "God brought Adam and Eve into the world as fully-grown adults with no memories. They had knowledge, communication, personalities, and unknown skills and aptitudes they would discover over time. They weren't blank slates, Eve. Neither are you."

She smiled, recalling Peterman's parallel and the comfort it had brought her Sunday night.

As if knowing she was thinking of him, Peterman appeared next to her suitcase. By his side was a tall, skinny man with blond hair reaching past his shoulders, a yellow T-shirt, and blue jeans ragged against the heels of dirty tennis shoes.

"Hey, little sis."

Everything inside her went rigid. Dax.

She remembered him.

Remembered his hands imprisoning her arms.

Remembered his friend lowering his jeans.

Remembered every detail her father had refused to tell her.

She felt her eyes bulging. Ceiling and floor crackled with electricity, blazed white-hot across every nerve in her body. She flared her nostrils and sucked in air so blistering it exploded into red-orange flames inside her head.

"Get him out of here!" she screamed. "Get him *out!*

Chapter 13

Stella barged into the District Attorney's office, startling the spit out of Bradley Henshaw. His heart jumped again as she slammed the door. "Boss! Eve's bodyguard, Sam, on the phone. Trouble at the hospital."

Brad swept the receiver off its cradle. "Henshaw."

"Sam here. Eve's brother showed up, but she threw him out. Screamed bloody murder until he fled. The doctor had to sedate her."

"Where's the brother?"

"Down the hall, pacing."

"Talk to him and call me back. Eve okay?"

"The chaplain's with her."

"No matter what, don't let her leave the hospital."

He hung up and regarded Stella. "We've got a problem."

She dropped into the chair across from his desk, eyes glued to his.

He repeated Sam's information. "Do you know what this is all about?"

She shook her head. "The nine years I've known Eve, she's never talked about her family. Never spent a holiday with them either, as far as I know."

Brad drummed the fingers of his right hand on his desk. "I don't want her leaving our protection. Too risky."

Stella gave a knowing look. "That phone call from the U.S. embassy in the Philippines this morning—you got new information, didn't you."

Brad handed her a sheet of paper with his handwriting scrawled on it. "My notes. Type them up and attach them to the report. I asked the embassy if there was any update on Eve's appearance there—beyond the medivac transporting her from a yacht with two dead men on it. Turns out the Philippine Coast Guard rescued three additional people that day. Americans. They claim they were marooned on an island last year with Eve—or rather, Eva Gray."

Stella's eyes widened and she sat up straight. "If she used her alias 'Eva Gray' and stayed undercover, it means—"

"She knows something." Brad slapped his hand on the desk and stood up. "It stinks of Danny Romero. And until she remembers, she's getting a bodyguard around the clock, starting this minute."

"You know she won't put up with that."

Brad scowled. Stella was a mother hen to the women in the office, and she knew her chicks well. "Okay, an undercover agent, then."

The phone rang and he snatched it up. "Sam?" He punched the speakerphone button so Stella could hear.

"Yeah." Sam let loose a number of expletives connected to Dax's name. "No wonder she screamed. All he'd say at first was Eve must have remembered him and the fact that she hated him. Family history, none of my business, you know."

There was a pause, and Brad could all but see steam billowing from the phone.

Sam continued. "With the threat of a night behind bars with Chicago's best, he told me he and a buddy got drunk one night when Eve was twelve years old. Brad, he held Eve down while his buddy raped her."

The news jolted the air from Brad's lungs. Across from him, Stella's face turned ash white. He slammed his fist on the desk. "Where is he?"

"He left."

"All right, stay with Eve. I'll get back to you." He switched off the speakerphone.

Stella was bawling now. He thrust a box of tissues at her and stalked down the hall to the water cooler. Her wails trailed him, and he groaned when all the office staff stepped out of their cubicles to gape at him.

"Get back to work," he barked.

He got a cup of water and brought it to Stella, this time making sure he closed his office door. She wiped her eyes and blew her nose several times while he sat and waited.

"I'm okay," she said at last. "What do you want me to do? The hospital dismissed Eve early this morning."

"Book a hotel room. Sam can stay with her until I decide on someone."

Stella stared daggers at him. "That's ridiculous. You can't leave her to herself like that after what's happened." Her face fell. "I'd let her stay with me, but …"

"I know. You've got enough to handle with your son."

"What about Marianne? Eve is comfortable with her."

"And by tomorrow everyone in the office will know everything there is to know."

Stella huffed. "Marianne can keep a confidence."

Brad drummed his fingers. The drama of the past ten minutes guaranteed whispers in the office, no matter what restrictions he laid down. "All right, but she needs to know she's putting herself at risk with Eve there."

"Of course."

Five minutes later, Stella was back. "Marianne is up for it. I told her to go straight to the hospital and get Eve. I'll find someone to cover the reception desk for Marianne until tomorrow."

"Make sure Sam knows to stick with them."

Stella left, and Brad kicked Dax Eriksson as hard and far away from his mind as he could. He forced his thoughts back to the embassy's phone call. Their update included three others dead on the island. The carnage reeked of Danny Romero.

Brad pursed his lips. He needed more than an undercover agent to protect Eve. He needed some way to get Romero off her back once for all.

***

Danny Romero let the office phone ring five times. On the sixth ring he lifted the receiver to his ear. Never let the caller believe he was readily available. "What?" he grunted.

"New information. The *Gateway* didn't sink."

For a moment Romero couldn't move. Couldn't think. *Emilio is alive?* Joy erupted in him like a geyser. Then rage that his son hadn't contacted him. Then fear that Emilio's silence was because something had happened to him.

"Emilio shanghaied it," the informant said.

Shock ripped through Romero. Emilio had swindled his own father? Rage shook him again. "Eriksson remembered this?"

"No. Information Henshaw got about three Americans rescued by the Philippine Coast Guard."

"Henshaw." Romero spat the name out. "How reliable is this information?"

"Unknown."

"What does Eriksson say about it?"

"She hasn't been told."

Romero clenched his jaw. "I'm done coddling her amnesia," he snarled. "Bring her in, *now*."

Chapter 14

The dream impaled Eve against Marianne's couch cushions. She was lying on the decayed leaves of a jungle floor, a myriad multi-legged insects crawling over her skin and wriggling under her clothes. Overhead, the cacophony of animal life in the towering treetops suddenly fell silent. *Someone was coming.*

Footsteps pounded the path next to her. A short, cocoa-skinned man ran past. Sunlight glinted off his glasses and the metal of the gun he carried in his right hand. He was not the one to fear. She scrunched lower into the foliage.

The *thwack* of a hand methodically slapping aside leaves came closer. The musky odor of her terror filled her nostrils, then the acrid fetor of urine as hot liquid dribbled down the inside of her thighs. *He would smell her.* She should run.

Before she could jump up, huge hands reached down and clamped onto her arms. A face ravaged with scars peered down at her. She screamed as he lifted her off her feet.

"Eve, wake up."

She opened her eyes to find Marianne leaning over her.

"You're having a nightmare."

Eve bolted upright. "Two men. They found me."

"Your brother …?"

"No. In a jungle—" Eve stopped in confusion.

"Oh, I bet it was that island in the Philippines." Marianne gasped and clapped her hand over her mouth.

"What island?"

"I shouldn't have said that. Please, please don't tell Brad. I'll be in such trouble for gossiping."

"Tell me!"

Marianne twisted her fingers, blinked rapidly. "I don't know much. Just that three people said you were marooned on a jungle island with them this past year."

Eve's heart palpitated. "Who are they?"

"Brad's checking them out. He thinks they're Romero's men and they were holding you prisoner."

Eve rubbed her fingers in a circular pattern on the soft velour of the couch. "So … maybe my dream is actually a memory …?" She jabbed the velour with her fingernails. "Yes, I'm sure of it. Brad's right. I'd never stay voluntarily on an island with those two men."

"If you were a prisoner, you'd have no choice."

"Until the yacht," Eve said. "That's why I was on it. It was my escape."

"But why keep you a prisoner in the first place, when Romero wants you dead?"

Eve's head jerked back. "How do you know that?"

Marianne sucked in her lower lip and turned away. She picked up a brown paper sack at the front door and scurried down the hall to the kitchen. "I brought home Chinese carryout," she called over her shoulder. "From Chicago's best. Are you hungry?"

She wasn't, but she'd had enough with lying on the couch for four days while the memory of her rape played over and over in her mind. She plodded down the creaky hallway and took a seat at the kitchen table. Rain pattered on the windowpane next to her. Water spots blotched the paper sack and Marianne's skirt where the umbrella hadn't protected her.

Eve removed the cardboard cartons from the sack while Marianne set the table with plasticware and oatmeal-colored paper napkins.

"You didn't answer my question."

"I can't, Eve. I've already said too much."

"All right. I'll take some of that Moo Goo Gai Pan." Eve dabbed a few spoonfuls of rice and Moo Goo onto her plate.

They ate in silence.

Finally Marianne sighed. "You were always a threat to Danny Romero. You won three big court cases against him, but he's got them all on appeal. You and Brad believed all you needed to finally send him to prison was some last piece of evidence you went to Guam for. That's when the word came out Romero wanted you dead."

Eve nodded but kept her eyes on her food. "Thanks."

Marianne took two more bites. "What you hated was not his drug dealing so much as his human trafficking. But that was a dead end street, so you went after what you could nail him for—drugs."

The face of a young Asian girl popped into Eve's mind. *Mid-teens, maybe sixteen. Face, neck, chest, arms black-and-blue with bruises. Lying in a hospital bed. One eye swollen shut, the other eye—golden-brown—peering at Eve. Pleading for help.* The face blurred, came into focus again. *Eyes closed now, lids painted turquoise, lashes blackened with mascara. Lying in a coffin. Slender fingers made to clasp a small bouquet of petite, white flowers. Sampaguitas.*

Eve leaped to her feet. Chinese food and white cardboard cartons flew as she pushed past the table. She dashed into the bathroom and bent over the toilet, vomited until there was only brown bile.

"Eve, are you okay?" Marianne stood in the doorway.

"A girl." Eve rasped. She sank to her knees on the vinyl floor and clasped the rim of the toilet bowl. Between convulsive gasps, she described the teenager to Marianne.

"Marikit," Marianne said. "Marikit Santos Torres. About half a year before you disappeared on the *Gateway*, she asked for you at Cook County Hospital and told you she wanted to testify against Danny Romero. It was your first big break to nail him on human trafficking. His men beat her up and dumped her into the Chicago River. Police rescued her and took her to the hospital, but before you could move her to a safe house, she … she ended up in that coffin."

Marianne knelt beside her, and Eve collapsed into her arms. They held tight to each other and cried. Four days ago she had wept in Marianne's arms and told her everything about the rape. Once again, Marianne's sympathy enveloped her in a cocoon of tenderness.

Finally, Eve got to her feet, washed her hands, rinsed her mouth. She returned to the table and pushed away what was left of her food. "I don't remember anything about Danny Romero." She thrust her jaw forward and glared at the rain-streaked window. "I don't remember any of the cases against him. I don't want to. *I want nothing to do with him.*"

"Good." Marianne dumped the spilled cartons into the trash and sat down. "Because he tried again."

"What do you mean?"

"Romero. He sent someone here—here to my apartment—to get you."

Horror clawed the back of Eve's throat.

"You're not supposed to find out, but Brad is wrong to not tell you."

"Romero ... still wants to kill me?"

"To take you prisoner again. He wants answers from you."

"About what?"

"Something about his son. He didn't say specifically."

"You talked to him?" Eve's mind spun. She grabbed the edge of the table to steady herself.

"No, no—Brad got permission to wiretap Romero's phone. That's how we found out his plan. He sent someone disguised as a pizza delivery man, and we nabbed him just as he was about to knock on the door."

Blood rushed to Eve's face and pulsed against her skin. "How dare Brad not tell me! He used me as bait. And put you in danger."

"Omigosh, Eve, please don't get me in trouble. Brad would never put you in harm's way. He cares deeply about you and has had someone watching you every minute since you got here."

Brad cared deeply about her? She straightened. "Were, were Brad and I ... was there ever 'anything' between us?"

Marianne giggled. "He wasn't your type, honey. Rich and glitzy was what you went for, and what you got without a problem."

"Rich and glitzy?" Eve had to laugh at the description. It didn't match up with the poverty and starkness she felt inside. "How about a serious romance or two?"

"If a man took a step toward serious, you moved on to the next guy."

"C'mon, Marianne, that sounds pretty fickle. I hope I wasn't like that."

"Not fickle, just dedicated heart and soul to your job. When you worked, you gave your utmost, and when you played, you wanted nothing but fun and glamour. Your clothes, your shoes, your jewelry—you put every penny you had into them. You were the Cinderella whose life brought sparkle to us plain old office girls."

"Cinderella." Eve stood and slammed her chair under the table. "But with no Prince Charming, huh? I guess my father and brother took care of him, didn't they."

She shuffled back down the hallway to the couch, feeling every bit an ancient hag. "I won't say anything to Brad about what you told me," she called back to Marianne. But she *would* talk to him tomorrow.

She had a plan now, and it didn't include Federal District Attorney Bradley Henshaw. Nor drug lord and trafficker Danny Romero. Nor her father, and certainly not her brother.

Her memory was gone. Her past was gone. She didn't want her future to disappear too.

Chapter 15

The next morning, Eve dug out Chaplain Peterman's business card and invited him to Marianne's for a lunch of any carryout except Chinese. She needed someone to talk to. Someone she could trust.

He arrived with a large sack and a broad grin. "Since I didn't know your favorite, I brought mine."

She opened the sack and inhaled rich, spicy tomato sauce, garlic, and pasta. "Good thing I didn't invite you yesterday. You'd be in jail, wondering why lasagna and breadsticks were a crime." They sat at the table, and she divided the food onto two of Marianne's plates while she told him about the pizza delivery and Romero's thwarted attempt to abduct her.

"Sounds like the sooner you head for your father's, the better."

"My father's?" Eve stabbed a piece of noodle onto her fork. "I won't be going there. Ever." Peterman's brow creased into deep furrows. Confusion, or disapproval? She wanted desperately for him to understand, to be on her side.

"The night my brother ..." Eve's throat closed, and tears seeped into her eyes. Peterman nodded, signaling he knew which night she was talking about. She had sobbed out the whole story in his arms at the hospital after Dax left.

"That night"—she cleared the hoarseness from her throat—"when my father and his boss returned, Dax and the boss's son met them at the door. They ... confessed." Tears spilled onto her cheeks, and she brushed them away with her fingers. "My father decided—before he even came to check on me—to not prosecute his boss's son.

"I didn't know about the law. All I knew was that my father didn't want to touch me. He didn't take me into his arms to comfort me. He wouldn't even look at me. He just … stood there staring at the floor and mumbled he was sorry, that he was afraid he'd lose his job. At dinner, he had been promoted to vice president of the company."

She inhaled and released the air slowly until she could gaze steely-eyed at Peterman. "He chose his career over his daughter. He'll *never* get me back."

The sympathy in Peterman's eyes set her lower lip quivering.

"Are you sure that's what you want, Eve? When you came out of your coma, the first word out of you mouth was *Dad*."

"That's because I saw you and thought you were my father." She knew it was more than that. She remembered the delirium of her joy, remembered the longing. From the depths of her soul she had wanted to love and be loved. By her father.

"You also told me you could tell your father was sorry about whatever had happened between you. You wanted to deal with it. Shouldn't you at least talk to him before you cut him off?"

"No. All that was before I remembered. Now I have the facts, not emotions born of ignorance."

Peterman looked unbearably sad. His expression dragged her to the edge of the despondency she had just spent four days fighting.

She put her fork down and reached over to touch his hand. "I know what I want to do now."

"What?"

"Use my back pay to go to graduate school and start a different career."

"And not be an attorney?"

She shrugged. "I don't remember any of it. If I have to start from scratch, I may as well start with something I like. Something that doesn't send a drug lord stalking me." She could add to the list: An office where she could be a rising star, not a fallen one. Co-workers who didn't know more about her than she knew—and certainly not about her rape. She winced at the thought of their eyes following her, knowing her dark secret. Why had she ever confided in Marianne?

She scrunched her nose. "The hard part is—I don't know what I like."

Peterman's bushy eyebrows shot up. "How about another possibility—a business venture with my niece? She's looking for someone to invest in a new shop with her. A fashion boutique, I think. With your beauty to advertise it and her experience as a buyer for Macy's, you two couldn't help but succeed."

Eve blushed. She was wearing no makeup and had pulled her hair straight back into a frumpy ponytail. The scar from the bullet made a bright red bulge on her forehead, like the budding horn of a unicorn.

Still, hadn't Marianne told her she was the Cinderella who brought sparkle to plain old office girls' lives? "I'd like to talk to her." A spark of confidence burst inside her and raced along her nerves to buoy her heart. She had two options now: education or business. Neither was a magic wand, but for the first time since she'd lost her memory, she was holding the reins of her life in her own hands.

***

As soon as Chaplain Peterman left, Eve called Bradley Henshaw. Best to get her boss off her plate right away, wipe the District Attorney's office out of her life. Somehow she'd make sure Danny Romero was included in the crumbs scraped into the trash.

She sat on the couch, one leg folded under her, and dialed Brad's direct line included in the files he'd handed her. He answered immediately. Her nerves pulled drawstrings on her stomach. "Uh, hi, it's Eve."

"Eve, how are you doing?" The genuineness of his concern made her feel like a traitor. She was going to dump him and everyone in the department simply because, well, because they meant nothing to her. How could they when she had no memory of them?

She planted both feet on the floor and sat erect, stiffening her backbone and shoulders. "Better, thanks. I've been thinking, and—Brad, I'm sorry— I've decided not to come back."

"What? What will you *do*?" His voice rose in astonishment.

"I've thought about it for four days on Marianne's couch." She told him her two options.

"But why leave something you excel at for something you don't know?"

"Because I don't remember what I excel at," she snapped. "Not one tiny bit of the law."

"The doctor said your memory would come back. You've already remembered some things, haven't you?" Brad stopped abruptly. No doubt he was thinking about her brother.

The *whirr* of the window air conditioner broke into her consciousness, and she realized she was sweating. She stood and turned her face to catch the cool air. "The doctor said *maybe*. No guarantees. I'm not going to sit around waiting until I wake up one morning and remember how to be a lawyer. I need to find a way to be who I am *now* instead of chasing after who I *was*."

"Have you read the files I gave you at the hospital?"

"About Romero? No. And I don't intend to."

"I see. Is that what you're worried about—Romero?"

"Shouldn't I be?"

"Yes, you should."

She blinked in surprise.

"I was waiting to tell you …" He cleared his throat. "Romero sent someone to Marianne's apartment to abduct you."

He gave her more details than Marianne had. She started trembling, then shaking so hard she had to sit. Her lungs tightened into a fist and she couldn't get the air out, couldn't get more in.

Then the fist let go and she gasped in oxygen, breathed out fire. "That's it, right on the bull's eye! I don't want Romero coming after me. I don't want him thinking I'm a threat. I don't want him getting me killed." She slumped forward and closed her eyes. "There's no reason any more," she whimpered. "I want him to know that, to get the news I'm out of the picture."

Brad drew in a deep breath that snuffled through his nose. "You want Romero to believe you'll leave him alone, even if you get your memory back?"

"Yes."

"And would you believe him if he told you he'd leave you alone, no matter what?"

Her chin jerked in a spasm. No. She could never trust Romero.

"Eve," Brad said softly, "going into another career won't stop him. And I won't be able to protect you if you're in another job."

Her mind raced. She'd have to use her back pay to disappear. She didn't even have a life yet, and here she was needing to leave it.

"Help me get away. Please." She fought to keep her voice from mewling. "Someplace where Romero can't find me."

The faint, rhythmic tapping of fingers on wood echoed on the phone. She paced back and forth in the small living room. Each footstep set the floorboards creaking. The squeaks climbed vertebra by vertebra up her spine until the hair at the nape of her neck stood on end. She stopped and held her breath for Brad's answer.

"I'll make a deal with you," he said at last. "I'll send Marianne home with a box of your earliest cases. I'll keep you on payroll, and you take a couple of days, weeks if you want, to read them. If you decide to leave after that, I'll help you."

She wanted to laugh out loud. Did he think the cases would prod her memory? Ha! They'd only convince her to run faster. "I don't want to be cooped up here all that time. I want to get on with my life."

"Go anywhere you want while you're reading. I'll send a bodyguard to look out for you."

A bodyguard. She'd need a bodyguard the rest of her life, wouldn't she?

She touched the scar on her forehead and flinched at the stab of pain that shot through her. It was her or Romero, wasn't it? One of them had to go.

The only person she could control for sure was herself. That meant it was she who would have to go. Whatever it took, that had to be her plan. To disappear. For good.

Brad broke her silence. "You used to work out at Ace's Gym. Start there. It will be good for you, help you recuperate."

She gritted her teeth. "All right. One box of files."

One box, then she'd vanish.

Chapter 16

Light flickered over the surface of the indoor pool as if a hovering spaceship were about to land. Eve sat on the cement lip, feet dangling in the water while she gasped in gulps of air. She had swum one lap, *one lap*, and she was done. Shopping for her bathing suit had taken more time than the number of laps she'd spent wearing it for a whole week at Ace's Gym. She'd never get well at this rate.

"Take it easy," Ace had said. "Don't get yourself all wore out and discouraged. Stop while you got some gumption left so next time you can push further."

The old man had more gumption in his scrawny, seventy-year-old body than she had at half his age. He had set up a schedule for her of three days swimming alternating with three days jogging on the indoor track. Puny as her efforts were, she was at least sleeping better. No more jungle dreams jerking her awake shaking and sweaty.

The door to the men's locker room on the opposite side of the pool opened. Eve stiffened. Two young men emerged wearing skintight Speedos, caps and goggles in their hands, towels draped over their shoulders. They had been swimming laps the first time she returned to Ace's Gym. From then on, she made sure she arrived before them. Today they were early.

Her gulps of air jammed to a halt in her throat. Were they Romero's men? Next in line after the pizza deliveryman to abduct her?

Her stomach tensed as her bodyguard stepped forward to greet the men.

Lisa's voice was friendly, but Eve knew Lisa's eyes were like an X-ray machine examining them for weapons under their towels or any kind of threat. When the men slipped into the water and began plowing steady furrows down the pool, the grip on Eve's stomach relaxed. She got up and walked to the ladies' locker room.

Lisa joined her and checked out the room before she let Eve enter a shower stall to wash off and dress. Eve was grateful, but she couldn't help but picture Lisa as standing in front of the stall, feet spread, arms crossed, chin up, eyes piercing steel.

She liked the protection. But did life from now on mean enduring Wonder Woman or other bodyguards as her sidekick because of the danger posed by Romero?

***

The receptionist's voice, competing with a Detroit news broadcast in the background, crackled over the intercom into Neal Oakleigh's office. "Ian MacBride on the line."

"Thank you, Barbara."

About time. Neal squeezed his irritation into a tiny ball in his fist. He'd expected Mack to call immediately after the P.I.'s interview with Jake Chalmers, and here it was a week later. Mack's thoroughness was an asset in court, but an exasperation when you had to wait and wait and *wait* on him.

He relaxed his shoulders, tilted back his chair, and put his feet on the mahogany desk that had once been Franklin Parker's. He picked up the receiver. "Mack, how's it going?"

"Slower than I thought. I need to stay over an extra week."

"What's the problem?"

"Dead ends. I'm going to have to use contacts in the police department, and that's always touchy."

"About Chalmers?"

"No, my report on him is complete. I'm talking about finding Eva Gray."

Neal dropped his feet from the desk. How long had the report been ready? He couldn't care less about his sister-in-law's missing friend. "Snyder's been breathing down my neck for that information, and I don't like postponing him. What did you learn about Chalmers?"

"Perhaps I should report directly to Mr. Snyder then." Frost coated Mack's words.

"I'm paying for the Chalmers information. I'd like it now."

"I'm billing you directly for it?"

"Yes." Mack didn't need to know Neal would get reimbursed.

"Then I'll put the report and the bill in this afternoon's mail."

"I'd like it now, Mack. A verbal report over the phone will do."

"My reports are based on facts. Written facts that can be validated. A copy for you and a copy for my files."

"Fine. But today is Friday, and I won't get your report until Monday at best."

Mack didn't answer.

Neal huffed. He'd better take a different approach. "I'm concerned for Betty, Mack. The sooner I can act on your report, the sooner I can help her. I need to know what I'm facing with Chalmers."

"Okay." A pause. "I'll add a note that I gave you a preliminary verbal report, at your request."

"Fine, good. Send everything to me at my office."

Mack started in with Chalmers' full name, birth date, and place of birth. Neal grabbed a pen and notepad and started scribbling.

"Married Virginia—nicknamed Ginny—O'Donnell on June 10, 1961, presumed dead and lost at sea in the sinking of the *Gateway* in June of 1981. Two children, Brett and Dana Chalmers, twins, born January 22, 1963, currently attending their second year at West Point Military Academy."

Neal put down his pen. Not the information he was looking for.

"Served on active duty with the United States Marine Corps ..." Mack gave dates and locations. "Served as a reservist ..." More dates and places.

Neal leaned back in his chair and waited. Mack was going to make him pay, wasn't he?

Chalmers' military honors came next, culminating in the Purple Heart and the Navy Cross. At these, Neal grimaced. War hero wasn't helpful.

"On June 14, 1982, the Philippine Coast Guard picked up Chalmers from a tankard that found him floating in the ocean and took him to the yacht where they found two men dead, and Eva Gray barely alive. The same day, the Coast Guard rescued Betty Parker and Crystal Oakleigh—"

"My granddaughter."

"—from a nearby island in the remote eastern sector of the Philippines and escorted them, along with Jacob Chalmers and Eva Gray, to Manila. Detective Lee of the Philippine National Police interviewed them, as did Ambassador Armacost later at the U.S. Embassy.

"Also on June 14, Detective Lee traveled with Chalmers to the island that he, your granddaughter, Betty Parker, and Eva Gray had lived on. Chalmers and the detective stayed there two days and returned to Manila on June 16. The next day, on June 17, Chalmers, Parker, and your granddaughter flew to the United States, arriving at their destinations in Indiana and Michigan on June 19.

"Do you want a verbal on Eva Gray's part in this?"

"No. I'll catch it in your written report."

Mack continued. "I interviewed Detective Lee on the telephone. The Philippine Coast Guard retrieved three bodies from the island—a Filipino sailor reported missing a year earlier from a freighter, and two sailors who died two days before the Philippine Coast Guard returned to the island for them."

Neal picked up his pen and pulled the notepad closer. Mack's arrows were finally closing in on the bull's eye. He leaned forward, as if Mack sat whispering across the desk from him. "Were they sailors from the yacht?" He held his breath, the taste of his last cigar thick on his tongue.

"Yes. The two sailors attempted to abduct Eva Gray." Another pause. Long. Significant. Then the arrow, slicing the air with its shrill whistle, punching into the exact middle of the bull's eye. "Chalmers saved her by killing one of them."

Neal exhaled an exuberant typhoon. Interesting that Betty had failed to divulge that little detail in her litany of praises for Jacob A. Chalmers.

***

A half hour later, Neal tapped on Leroy Snyder's office door. The door stood ajar, revealing Leroy writing at his desk, a six-inch leather tome open beside him. He glanced up, motioned Neal to enter, and kept writing.

Neal stepped inside. "Mack called."

Leroy raised his face and looked squarely at Neal. He put down his pen. "Close the door."

Neal shut the door and took a seat across from Leroy. "Chalmers killed a man on the island. No charges were brought against him."

Leroy sat back and folded his hands, his face expressionless.

"He claimed self-defense in protecting Eva Gray," Neal said.

"Heroism is not what we're looking for."

"There were no witnesses. Betty and Crystal were hiding in a cave, and Eva Gray saw the body only after Chalmers killed him."

Leroy lowered his chin and gazed at his folded hands, a sure sign he was thinking. He straightened and shook his head. "Not what we need. It won't discredit him in Betty's eyes."

"No, but a charge of second-degree murder would remove him from the picture."

Leroy shook his head a second time. "A conviction won't change her mind. We'll have to let this go, drop the whole idea."

"Okay." Neal hid the snarl leaping with sharp claws from his stomach until he exited Leroy's office. No way he'd let this go. As Crystal's grandfather, he should have power over Crystal's inheritance, not this manipulating hero who had weaseled his way into Betty's affections. By adopting Chalmers, Betty had made it next to impossible to go a simple legal route to usurp the man.

But not impossible. He calmed himself with a fresh cigar in his own office. It'd take a bit of work, but he could still carry out the plan he'd suggested to Leroy.

Chapter 17

The clatter of footsteps in the hallways of the Harry S. Truman Building faded as most of the employees in the Washington D.C. State Department left for the day. Orville Marsh studied the last two letters his secretary had slipped onto his desk for final approval before he put them in the mail tomorrow.

The first was an answer to an inquiry by Bradley Henshaw, District Attorney at the Everett Dirksen Courthouse in Chicago. Orville checked to make sure his secretary had correctly copied the dates this time. The information Jake Chalmers had given him for Betty Parker and Crystal Oakleigh had proven false. Crystal Oakleigh didn't exist, and the closest birth date for a Betty Parker was different by several years. The only castaway whose identity could be validated was Jacob A. Chalmers.

Orville loosened his tie and reread the description of his interview with Chalmers. Still made his knees knock at the memory of that long, serrated knife in Chalmers' belt. Bottom line, the man's story wasn't to be trusted. But Orville had been fair—a psychological profile of Chalmers, he wrote, should be sought for confirmation.

The second letter was addressed to Jacob Chalmers. It was short and simple: The U.S. State Department's investigation into the *Gateway* was proceeding on schedule. Orville's conscience was clear. He had yet to check out the cruise ship's officer, Captain Emilio. No doubt it would be another dead end.

***

Betty Parker swung the door wide open when Private Investigator Ian MacBride rang the doorbell on her front porch Thursday afternoon. "Come in, come in." It was all she could do not to grab his hand and rush him to a seat in the living room. He had taken a week longer than expected. Did that mean he had found Eve? His expression gave no hint.

"Good afternoon, Mrs. Parker." Clad in tan shorts and a navy T-shirt, the detective looked for all the world like a newspaper boy collecting his fee and hoping for a generous tip. The day had proven to be one of Detroit's hottest, and sweat formed a glistening mustache on his upper lip. "I hope you don't mind I didn't change clothes. It's been a long drive."

"Not at all. Please, come in and sit down. Can I get you a drink?"

"Water would be good, thank you." Mack took a seat on one of the four couches Betty's sister, Clara, had arranged into a large square in the living room.

"I'll get the water," Clara announced from the hallway.

Betty suppressed a scowl. She should have guessed Clara would find a way to insert herself into the meeting. Clara had no business taking Mack's phone call about his visit instead of waking up Betty to talk to him.

Betty sat on the couch with Mack. "You found Eve?" At his nod, firecrackers lit the night sky that had been darkening her heart over her missing friend.

"Yes. I called Mr. Chalmers to tell him, but he didn't answer. I left a message on his answering machine, although I imagine you'll talk to him first."

"You can be sure of that." Betty beamed at Mack. "He's visiting his sisters out west, but I have his number."

Clara joined them and handed Mack a tall glass crammed to the brim with ice cubes and water. She settled herself into the corner of the nearest couch and parked her mobile oxygen tank at her feet. "I'm Clara Oakleigh, Betty's sister." She fixed her eyes on Mack and didn't look at Betty.

"Thank you for the water." Mack took a sip and lowered the glass to his knee. "I know your husband, Mrs. Oakleigh. We've worked together on numerous occasions."

Betty spoke before Clara could take over the conversation. "Tell me about Eve. Is she okay? Where did you find her?"

Mack's boyish face sobered. "Finding Eva Gray turned into more of a challenge than I'd anticipated. The reason, I discovered, is because her name is not Eva Gray. It's Evedene Eriksson. Eva Gray is her alias."

Betty felt the blood drain from her face. *Alias?* She clutched the edge of the couch cushion. Jake had told her Mack insisted on considering Eve a possible criminal. "You mean *alias* as in an illegal alien … or a criminal?"

"No, no, Mrs. Parker, as an undercover agent. Evedene Eriksson works for the United States government."

"As a spy?" Betty released the cushion and clasped her cheeks. Her mind spun, readjusting and shifting everything she knew and didn't know about the woman Eva Gray.

"Your friend is a federal prosecuting attorney. She boarded your cruise ship, the *Gateway*, incognito as Eva Gray to uncover information for a federal lawsuit."

Betty dropped her hands and sagged into the couch. "We lived together a whole year on that island. Why didn't she tell us?"

"Maybe that man Jake you're so fond of is a criminal and she knew it." Clara's lips pinched shut in satisfied smugness.

"Jake is *not* a criminal."

"Oh? You thought you knew Eva Gray. Maybe you don't know Jake Chalmers either."

Betty leaned as close to her sister as she could without getting out of her seat. The odor of Neal's cigars emanated from her sister's hair and clothes like a week-old ashtray. "Clara, why are you here in my meeting with my investigator?"

The ice in Mack's glass collapsed in a noisy *plop*, drawing their three pairs of eyes. He raised the glass to his lips and drank until the ice cubes batted his mouth. The sisters watched him in stiff silence.

He smiled weakly at their stares and set the glass on an end table. "Mrs. Parker, I didn't attempt to contact Evedene Eriksson. My understanding was that you and Mr. Chalmers want to do that."

"Yes, that's right." Betty, catching the hint that he wished to conclude the meeting, cast a final glare at her sister. "How do we get ahold of her?"

"She works in downtown Chicago at the Everett Dirksen Courthouse. That's where you could meet her, or find out where she is staying."

"Neal would never give out an attorney's address," Clara huffed.

Mack retrieved an envelope from his briefcase and handed it to Betty. "Do you want to go over this together?"

She peered inside at two typewritten sheets and a bill. "No, I'll read it and call Jake. He's been … eager for an update." She smiled at the understatement.

Mack's mouth twisted into a boyish grin. "Have him call me if he has questions."

She walked him to the front door, caught sight of Crystal walking up the driveway, and hurried to intercept her before Clara got ahold of the child's ear.

Crystal would be excited that Eve was an undercover agent—a federal prosecutor, for heaven's sake.

But Jake? How was he going to take it, that the woman he loved had deceived him?

***

Adrenaline spiked every cell in Jake's body, and he sprang to his feet at Betty's news. His heart hammered his ribcage, pummeled his lungs, crashed lightning bolts in his ears. "Wait a minute, Betty." He'd missed everything she'd said after those first three words, *Mack found Eve.*

In his excitement he jerked the phone off the cabin's tiny, rustic desk. The base dangled precariously between the wall plug and the spiraled cord of the receiver clasped to his ear. He grinned like a goofy younger brother at his two sisters, who stopped lunch preparations to stare at him.

He restored the phone to its rightful location. "Start over again, Betty. My heart was doing somersaults and I didn't hear a thing you said."

"Eve is in Chicago."

Chicago—only three hours from Indy! Except here he was in Estes Park, Colorado. Didn't matter, he'd take the next plane out. "Where in Chicago?"

"Mack didn't get an address. There was a problem, Jake. That's why Mack took so long. Eve isn't Eva Gray, she's Evedene Eriksson."

"Evedene," he mused. "That's why she preferred *Eve* over *Eva*."

"That's not all, Jake. She's a federal prosecuting attorney."

At this he threw back his head and laughed. "We knew she was hiding something. That takes the cake and turns it upside down, doesn't it?" He shook his head in amusement. How about that—he was in love with a prosecuting attorney!

"That doesn't surprise you?" Betty sounded put out.

"The way that woman could nail down an argument? Did you ever win one?"

Betty chuckled. "You're right, it makes perfect sense." She paused, then lowered her voice and spoke so softly Jake had to strain to hear. "But why didn't she tell us? A whole year on the island and she never told us."

"Stubborn—simple as that. She and I hit heads the minute our feet touched the island. How long was it, half a year before we could speak civilly to each other? By then our world consisted of surviving from one day until the next. Life before the island wasn't an issue anyone thought about."

His last night with Eve flashed through his mind. They were sitting close to the hearth fire in the cave, his arm around Eve. She was shivering, snuggling tight against his side, quelled by the memory of the python that only hours before had wrapped her in its coils. Her skin was faintly moist with perspiration. He sat with eyes half closed, conscious of his fingertips touching the satin of her skin, of his cheek pressed against her hair. Betty and Crystal sat nearby, Betty beaming like the harbor moon outside, Crystal chattering about their plans. When they got rescued, she declared, Jake and Eve would marry; they would adopt her; and Aunt Betty would move in with them.

"Jake?"

"Sorry, Betty. I just remembered, Eve told me our last night together that she would tell me everything she'd been holding back. I couldn't ask her that night. Not after the snake. We were going to talk the next morning."

Betty's sigh rasped through the telephone. No doubt she was thinking about that next morning on the island. The morning their rescuers arrived—pirates—to destroy them.

"What do we do now? Mack said we should go to the Everett Dirksen Courthouse to meet Eve, or see if they'd give us her address."

"I'll get a flight out tomorrow and meet you in Chicago."

A chorus of wails erupted behind him. "We've got plans for tomorrow, Jake. You can't leave. Marc and Samantha are driving up with the kids. You can wait until Sunday."

His sisters herded him against the wall, hands on ample hips, glaring eyes pinning his against the back of his skull. Pure intimidation. The trick had worked until he turned thirteen.

"Jake," Betty shouted. She must have heard the commotion. "I already checked with the airlines. Everything's full tomorrow, and government offices are closed on the weekend. There's a flight available Monday—I can meet you then."

"Monday is good." Jake glared at his sisters. They backed off, smiled prettily, and returned to making sandwiches. The United States could have won the war in Nam with monsters like them.

"Eve may still have amnesia," Betty said. "What if I send a special delivery letter and tell her we're coming?"

"Good idea. I think she'd jump at getting a piece of the puzzle to help her memory. Please, do it." They hung up, and he checked his ticket. His current flight to Indianapolis left Denver at three-thirty on Sunday, with a two-hour layover in Chicago. He'd get a hotel in Chicago instead of continuing to Indy. Monday morning would find him at the Everett Dirksen Courthouse, seven o'clock sharp.

Question was, how do you approach the woman you love when she has no idea who you are?

Chapter 18

Danny Romero had four sons, and one of them he loved.

The secret trembled in the left trouser pocket of his heart—a secret he'd sorrowfully laid to rest a year ago with the news of his son's death. His son, who might be alive after all! He couldn't help the hope clasped to his bosom. Couldn't help dropping everything to find his beloved Emilio.

He trudged down Roosevelt Road, snarling under his breath at the Friday night revelers who dared jostle Chicago's premiere drug lord. They were lucky his mission required avoiding attention. A phone booth, its glass smeared with bird droppings and the grime of city living, stood empty halfway down the block. Romero stopped outside it and checked his watch. Behind him, his bodyguard, first cousin to Darth Vader without a facemask, diverted pedestrians simply by glaring at them.

The phone rang, and Romero stepped inside and closed the door. Just him and the stench of urine and five kamikaze flies inside. Outside, his bodyguard stood alert, certainly not looking curious about why his boss who could barely breathe fresh air would shut himself inside a nasty phone booth without the door cracked.

On the phone's second jangle, Romero lifted the receiver to his ear. He looked at his watch again. Second-hand on thirteen. If the caller's phone were tapped, Romero would be finished with the call and strolling down Roosevelt before the call could be traced.

"One-Bee," a voice said.

Romero gripped the receiver and squeezed it as if it were One-Bee's neck. "I'm in this filthy box because of you."

The time span of a hard swallow passed. Then, in a monotone, "U.S. State Department reported two of the American castaways are duds; the third, a looney."

Romero slumped against the grungy wall of the booth. Why had he hoped to find anyone besides Eriksson to help locate his son? He should have known better. Hope relied on people; success relied on clout.

His bodyguard peered through the smudges on the door. Romero straightened and waved him away. "Looney how?"

"Nam veteran. Henshaw thinks he's one of your men."

Romero sniggered. The hotshot district attorney had duped himself this time. "What about Eriksson?"

"No changes."

"There's a slab waiting in the morgue if you can't bring me anything better than that."

"I told you she's going to Ace's Gym every morning."

"I can't touch Eriksson now, thanks to that wiretap. They'd finger me the minute anything happened to her."

Fifteen seconds left. He grabbed his pen and tore off a piece of the booth's soiled phone book cover. "Give me the Looney's name and telephone number."

He stuffed the information into his pocket, slammed the phone down, and yanked the glass door open. One-Bee lived only because a mole inside the Justice Department was allowed nine lives.

"Take me to Sylvia's," he barked. His bodyguard signaled Romero's chauffeur parked down the street, and the black Cadillac pulled up. Romero climbed inside and sank into the padded black leather of the back seat.

His wife would call him a fool for trusting a novice like One-Bee to keep him on top of something important like a phone tap. But Rosa didn't know about One-Bee's phone calls. Rosa of all people must never know. Three of his four sons were Rosa's. The three he didn't love.

Just like he'd never loved Rosa.

The Cadillac stopped, and Romero got out. The diners at Sylvia's Restaurant filled every table stuffed along the sidewalk behind the waist-high, wrought iron fence. A waiter spied him, and by the time Romero walked through the restaurant to the outdoor area, a potted plant had been swept aside and a table and chair set up for him, complete with tablecloth, silverware and glassware. The diners paused, forks in midair, to watch the big shot stroll to the table as if he were the owner of the restaurant.

The manager, a portly man with ruddy cheeks and a brown cowlick spilling onto his left temple, stepped up to the table. "Signore Romero. Welcome." His English accent butchered *signore*.

Romero grunted and placed his order. Archie didn't like him. Didn't like his coming to the restaurant. Didn't like having to wait on him. Romero's lips twitched a flicker of a smile. The Brit's dislike doubled Romero's pleasure.

But Martha—*la cara,* his dear one—was why he came, why he kept coming. Only here at Sylvia's was his heart free to talk to the woman he loved. He sat back and prepared for his rendezvous with her, letting his tension drain cell by cell, muscle by muscle, until all his concerns lay in a pool under his feet and evaporated away. All his concerns but one. Their son.

Most men remembered their first love the way she had looked on the day they met. Romero remembered Martha Bennett not only from when she was eighteen and he, twenty-five, but from when he found her again six years after she'd fled. A memory he refreshed every year after that when they met for one stolen week, sometimes two, in a Swiss chalet or a villa on the Riviera or a castle on a fiord.

He should have made her marry him. But at eighteen she'd shaken like a leaf in the wind when she discovered his parents topped the list of crime families in Chicago. She ran away, hid in England with family he didn't know existed—until they came seeking his help. That's when he'd found out he and *la cara* had a son.

Archie loomed into Romero's peripheral vision, carrying a tray. He set a plate of bangers and mash in front of him. His English *cara's* favorite. The rich smell of freshly ground sausage and fried onions simmered for hours in ale filled Romero's nostrils. He cut a slice off the sausage and scooped mashed potatoes and sauce onto his fork.

La cara had named their son Miles Bennett, with the middle name of Romero. Miles had changed his name to Emilio Romero after she died and he went to work for his father. She wouldn't have liked Emilio's slide into crime. But Romero had seen it coming, had simply waited. The boy was a natural. Outshone Romero's other three sons like a supernova.

"Coffee?" Archie asked. He brought an espresso at Romero's nod and didn't attempt to hide a cheeky smile when Romero dismissed him with the paid bill and an oversized tip.

Romero watched the manager's eager retreat. Their relationship was a two-way street, and Romero took care not to push Archie too far. Archie Bennett needed Romero to protect the restaurant, and Romero needed Archie, Martha's nephew, as the only tangible link to *la cara's* family.

La cara. She was dead, and he didn't believe in life after death or spirits conjured from the grave. He wasn't a tottering fool like Vito down the street, who muttered nonsense to his dead wife all day long. No, *la cara* lived only in Romero's memory, but he knew what she would want him to do. Everything possible to find their son.

He left the restaurant and returned to Roosevelt Road. At the first phone booth he encountered he got out of the car, dropped coins into the slot, and dialed the number of the Looney.

The phone rang five times before a man answered. "Jake Chalmers—"

"What do you know about the sinking of the *Gateway*?" Romero growled.

"Leave your name and number, a short message if you'd like, and I'll get back to you."

An answering machine. Romero hung up. He slammed the metal wall of the booth with his fist.

He exited, and in a flash the perfect plan came to him. *Sicuro!* Of course! Chortling, he re-entered the telephone booth. This time he left the door open while he fished for coins in his pocket. He dialed and waited through Chalmers' message, then counted as his watch's second-hand ticked off the length of the empty tape. Using the scrap of paper he'd scribbled Chalmers' phone number on, he recorded the number of seconds.

Bravo! He stepped outside, his footsteps light enough to dance on clouds.

Henshaw's wiretap had thwarted Eriksson's abduction; now Romero would flip the trap and foil Henshaw.

The Nam looney was the perfect bait. What he wouldn't give to be with Henshaw when the fool swallowed it.

Chapter 19

Brad Henshaw recognized the name on the return address. Betty Parker. He cussed a stream of invective—safe enough since Saturday insured no one else was in the District Attorney's office. Only after he ripped open the Special Delivery envelope did he realize the letter was intended for Eve. He read it anyway.

Friday, July 9, 1982
Dearest Eve,

I've been told you have amnesia as a result of your head injury, so it may be that you won't recognize my name, Betty Parker. You and I and Jake Chalmers and my grandniece Crystal Oakleigh were stranded for a year on a remote Philippine island until our rescue four weeks ago. You were there with us, dearest Eve, but you disappeared from the hospital in Manila, and we were at a loss to find you until Jake and I hired a private investigator.

Now that we know you work at the Everett Dirksen Courthouse (and as a federal prosecuting attorney—how impressive is that?), we would like to come to Chicago to visit you. Jake and I will be there on Monday, July 12. Our hope is that we can help you overcome some of your amnesia when we talk to you.

And most of all, we can hardly wait to see you again, dear friend!
Betty

Brad drummed his fingers on the desktop. Should he give the letter to Eve? Sit in on the visit? Marianne had told him about Eve's nightmare and Eve's agreement that Romero's men must have held her captive on the island.

He opened the dossier on Jacob Chalmers that Orville Marsh from the U.S. State Department had sent with his report. Inside was a headshot of Chalmers. Two jagged scars clearly marked his right cheek. Almost exactly as Marianne had described the monster of Eve's nightmare. A monster further matched to the scarred veteran Orville Marsh detailed in his interview of Chalmers.

Groaning, he cranked back his shoulders to loosen the knots creeping up his neck toward a full-blown headache. Eve was already set to desert the Justice Department because of Romero. Why traumatize her and give the rabbit further cause to flee the wolf? But Chalmers was a decorated hero, recently promoted to full colonel. He couldn't discredit Chalmers on the basis of an amnesiac's nightmare.

He punched in numbers on the telephone keypad. Perhaps an update on Romero's wiretap would tip the scales one way or another.

It did. Big time.

A direct communication from Danny Romero's office to Jacob Chalmer' tape recorder: *Kill her.*

***

Jake could easily imagine workhorse Eve starting her workday early. He couldn't sleep anyway, so why not arrive at the Dirksen Federal Building before the first government employees started crowding in? His heart was hammering so fast he'd skipped the morning caffeine. Breakfast too—no good with a stomach full of wasps. One minute his feet floated on clouds, the next minute they mired in quicksand.

Betty insisted he not meet her plane but wait for her at the Dirksen building. He stared up at the 30-story glass and steel high-rise shadowed in the parasol of the morning sun. One of Mies van der Rohe's contemporary beauties. "Skin and bones" architecture, the man had dubbed his creations; "less is more." Jake had done little design work as an architect, choosing instead to focus on construction. But gazing up at the building's simplicity and beauty reminded him of his longing to try his own creative powers someday.

Almost in the blink of an eye, as if arriving through a magic portal, traffic jammed the streets and pedestrians bumped shoulders on the sidewalks. Jake stationed himself outside the double glass doors of the building to spot Eve, trying not to look like he was ogling every blonde beauty who paraded into the building in a tight skirt and high heels. The self-conscious flush heating his face didn't help, nor the tremulous breaths his heart was shoving out his lungs.

He stuffed his hands into his pockets to hide their silly shaking and sweating, but he couldn't hide his smile. *He was going to see Eve!*

A rap on his leg diverted his attention. Betty stood in front of him, cane in hand, grinning. Gone was the gaunt, straggly-haired, little old woman he'd known on the island. In her place was an elegant, silver-haired matron leaning on an intricately carved ebony cane.

"Betty?" Then, "Betty!" He grabbed her into his embrace, lifting her off her feet, laughing in pure joy.

"Jake, put me down before you crush every bone in my body!" Laughter accompanied the admonishment. Settled onto her feet again, she reached up and grazed his face with her fingertips. "Look at you, all shaved and handsome. If Eve doesn't remember you, she'll certainly want to make your acquaintance."

Grinning, they entered the lobby and sat where they could observe everyone who passed. Jake thought of at least a dozen possible things to say to Eve if she didn't recognize him. And discarded them all. No, if Eve didn't remember him, it made more sense for Betty to take the lead. Less intimidating for Eve's sake to be approached by a woman, plus Betty had paved the way with her special delivery letter.

The crowd didn't thin for a good half hour, and even then Jake was reluctant to give up for another half hour. Finally Betty spoke, the corners of her mouth drawn down. "Jake, if Eve still has amnesia, would she have any reason to come to work?"

His cheek twitched. His shoulders sagged. His buzz of anticipation crashed. So, he'd ended up with his feet in quicksand. "Okay then, we'll go ask for her address."

He'd already looked up which floor the U.S. District Attorney's office was on. He helped Betty to her feet and trudged at a snail's pace alongside her tapping cane to the bank of elevators around the corner.

The lift hummed tunelessly during their ride. They were alone, and Betty slid her hand into his with a tight grip. Tenderness tweaked tears into his eyes. He remembered the time on the island when he'd been at his lowest and Betty had sandwiched his big hand between her two small ones. "God doesn't abandon His loved ones," she'd said. He curled his fingers around her tiny hand now and squeezed gently. His chest glowed with warmth.

The elevator doors opened with a soft hiss. They padded through the hallways, Betty suddenly chatty, cane thumping. "I thought about bringing Crystal. She'd love to see where Eve works. I didn't want Neal and Clara to know where I was going, though. Crystal and I are miserable living with them. We can't wait until we come live with you."

Cane and chatter came to a halt outside the glass doors to the U.S. District Attorney's office. Neither Jake nor Betty moved. Couldn't move. On this side of the door, hope held their hands. On the other side, a monster could be waiting, their dreams already in its stomach.

"Eve might be in there," Betty whispered. "She could have slipped by us. Or come in another way."

Only two people were visible in the office. A middle-aged woman with a pug nose, sitting at what must be the receptionist's desk, and a man in a suit and tie, standing idly across the room. A big dude. In a barroom he would have been the bouncer. The hair on the back of Jake's neck pricked to attention.

The man saw them, strode across the room, plucked open the door.

"Thank you." Betty, chin in a regal lift, swaggered in. Jake followed, gave the man a nod, received a blank stare.

"Evedene Eriksson, please," Betty said to the woman at the desk.

The woman looked at her with deer-caught-in-the-headlights wide eyes. She licked her lips, swallowed, punched a button on her telephone.

Jake's stomach crimped into a corkscrew. Something wasn't right. He put a hand on Betty's shoulder.

A short, broad woman with an ultra-mod haircut stepped into the room and crossed to the desk. "Can I help you?"

"I'm Betty Parker, here to see Evedene Eriksson. I sent a special delivery letter she should have received on Saturday. And this is Jake Chalmers."

The second woman's eyes swept across Betty to include Jake. "I'll need to see your IDs first."

Betty dug into her purse, but Jake wasn't about to comply. Since when did you have to show identification to talk to a federal employee? "Is Ms. Eriksson here?"

A tall, craggy man joined them from a hallway in back of the receptionist's desk. The way he held his shoulders and head, the half-frown on his face—all clamored *authority*. Best bet, Jake speculated, he and Betty were meeting Bradley Henshaw, U.S. District Attorney. The man's voice filled the room. "Ms. Eriksson is under the care of the U.S. Justice Department. Before we can proceed any further, we must see your IDs."

"Is there a problem?" Jake asked.

"Yes."

How do you counter that answer? Jake took out his wallet, removed his fortunately updated driver's license, and handed it to the presumed D.A. Betty also complied.

The man gave the licenses a cursory glance and returned them. "I am Bradley Henshaw, U.S. Attorney for the Northern District of Illinois." He nodded at the big man in the suit and tie, who then stepped forward and handed a document to Jake.

"Jacob Chalmers and Betty Parker," the man said, "the State of Illinois has issued a protective order against you for the safety of Evedene Eriksson. You may not contact her in any form, written or verbal, nor may you appear within the order's stated distance to her, her place of residence, nor her workplace."

Every drop of blood in Jake's face, arms, chest, on down to his toes, drained away. He was a cardboard prop, no heartbeat, no breath. Only barely enough brains to ask, "Why?"

The answer was something about conspiring with Danny Romero. Didn't matter that Jake claimed not to know him. That Jake swore he wasn't a threat to Evedene Eriksson. That, as a matter of fact, Jake was her fiancée.

The quicksand of justice swallowed him whole.

Chapter 20

Was there a telephone booth in Chicago that didn't stink? To circumvent detection by Bradley Henshaw's wiretap, Danny Romero made sure he didn't use a booth a second time or move among their locations in anything other than a random pattern. As long as his informant wasn't wiretapped, they should be good to go.

This booth smelled of vomit. With one hand he whipped a handkerchief out of his pocket and covered his mouth and nose; with the other hand he retrieved the ringing telephone's receiver and pulled the cord taut to stand outside the folding glass door. No way he was going to step onto the booth's floor.

"One-Bee."

He briefly pulled aside the handkerchief to identify himself with a grunted "What?"

"Your plan worked." The voice had a smile to it. He allowed one corner of his mouth to twitch up. Of course it had worked.

"Henshaw caught your message to Chalmers on Saturday afternoon and immediately got a judge to issue a restraining order."

"That's all?"

"Not enough evidence for anything else. But timely. Chalmers and Parker came to the courthouse on Monday to see Eve, and Henshaw sent them packing."

"I want him to do far worse."

The voice softened. "I ... saw Chalmers. He's no looney."

"Good. All the better to embarrass Henshaw when he discovers his blunder. What does Eriksson say?"

"She doesn't know about it. Henshaw is keeping her in the dark. He's determined to protect her … especially from you."

"He won't. I've got a better plan. It's fail-proof." In spite of the handkerchief wadded against Romero's nose and mouth, the stench from the booth penetrated his defense zone. The contents of his stomach lurched upward. He choked back a swallow, slammed the receiver onto its base, and stumbled backward two steps. Too late. He bent at the waist and retched a sizeable contribution to the dried lumps inside the booth.

Ah, bene—better, much better than a coughing fit. He wiped his mouth with the handkerchief, dropped it onto the pool of chunks, and walked away. For once, he was satisfied with the informant's phone call.

With the Viet Nam veteran and the old lady out of the way, he could proceed with step two of his plan.

***

"What recourse do I have?" Betty's voice was shrill even halfway across her huge living room.

Neal Oakleigh rubbed his left ear. Bad enough his wife's voice could hit that pitch when she was mad. Living in Betty's house, he had twice the challenge to dodge the two sisters' emotional outbursts. "I'd let it go, Betty. It appears the Justice Department has taken on Eve's care in light of her amnesia. It won't get you anywhere to tangle with them."

"They were right there waiting for us," Betty fumed. "Handed us the restraining order as soon as Jake and I walked through the door."

"Who was 'they'?"

"The sheriff—or whatever law officer he was—and Eve's boss, District Attorney Bradley Henshaw, and then everyone inside all those office cubicles. The janitor, if he was there."

"Your friend? What did she say?"

"Eve wasn't there. If she was, she would have come running after I screamed her name enough times."

"You screamed? In the law offices of the Everett Dirksen Courthouse?" He groaned. His wife wasn't kidding when she told him Betty had come back from that year on the island a totally different person. *Feisty* was an understatement. "Sounds like confirmation for the need of that restraining order."

Betty all but stuck her tongue out at him. "I'm going to write Eve another letter and get this all cleared up."

"*Another* letter? You've been writing to her?"

"I wrote one letter. I don't have her address, so I sent it to the courthouse since she works there."

"Which explains why they were prepared to serve you the restraining order." He approached Betty and put a ham-sized hand on her frail shoulder. Smiled. "Betty, why don't you tell me about these things? Let me help you?"

"Have you been smoking cigars in the master suite?" she snapped. "You reek of it."

He removed his hand. Kept the forced smile. "Tell you what. I'm flying to Chicago this weekend. How about if I go to … Bradley Henshaw, you said? … and he and I will have a little talk, attorney to attorney, get this all straightened out. The restraining order forbids you corresponding with her, so writing a letter would be a violation."

Betty cocked her head to one side, squinted at him with eyes worthy of Doubting Thomas. "All I want is to talk to Eve. Someone could even be there—her boss, if he wants."

"The restraining order included, uh, that man from the island … Jake Chalmers?"

"You know his name. Crystal has talked nonstop about him."

Enough that he and Clara were planning to send Crystal off to a boarding school. "Just wanted to make sure I got everyone covered, Betty, that's all."

Perfect. He'd take the information with him that Mack had dug up about Chalmers. Neal had a feeling District Attorney Bradley Henshaw would find a man dead at Chalmers' hands a mighty interesting bit of news.

And before the weekend arrived, Neal expected to hear from the attorneys he'd contacted in the Philippines. Attorneys eager to file a suit for a poor, destitute family grieving the loss of their son murdered by a U.S. citizen.

***

Eve sat at Marianne's kitchen table, unread case files stacked on her left, space for files as she finished them on her right, strong brew of coffee front and center. The only way to get Bradley Henshaw's cooperation was to plow through her early case files so she could take advantage of his promise to hide her from Romero. If she skimmed them, she'd get through all the files by the time Wonder Woman picked her up after lunch for her Wednesday workout at the gym.

Her first file was slim. Surprisingly, Brad had put her into the courtroom on her own after serving only a few months as an assistant attorney. Her first solo, while not a simple case, had been fairly straightforward—like tossing peanuts to monkeys—but she couldn't recall the law of the case.

Funny, what she totally remembered was what she'd worn. She'd put every cent she owned into that outfit. An apple green, double-knit wool suit by Kimberly with stitched tucks, skirt modestly just above the knees but showing off her legs in spite of the low, blocky heels fashionable back then. Clearly a confirmation that going into business with Chaplain Peterman's niece was to be seriously considered.

By the fourteenth file, her heartbeat was up and her passion for the law— for the underdog helped by it, anyway—glowed like neon lights on a dark city street. Six more files, and it was clear Brad had put his finger on what made her heart pound, her temperature rise.

Human trafficking.

Even now, her stomach quivered, radiated hard gasps to her lungs, shook her hands as she flipped pages. She went back over the files and reread every detail. Buried herself in the horror of unchecked human lust.

Her emotions swirled around her like a typhoon, dark, mighty, violent, then surged into a single silver mass and struck down on her like a two-edged sword. *This was her heritage from her father's rejection—the ugly seed taken into her heavenly Father's hand and planted to bear fruit. Fruit from Him, to her, to the helpless.*

The fruit of Justice. The law.

***

"You haven't said a word since I arrived at your apartment." Lisa the Wonder Woman followed Eve into Ace's Gym. "Are you okay?"

The sour odor of perspiration only slightly set off by air conditioning settled into Eve's nasal passages. "Marianne's apartment, Lisa, not mine." She set her bag down and changed her shoes. Today she ran on the indoor track. Ace had moved her up from jogging a half-mile to one mile, finishing with a half-mile walk. "I'm fine, thanks. A bit brain-dazed from reading case files, that's all."

And from being thrust through by a two-edged sword.

She warmed up with leg stretches, then set off at a comfortable jog. Four times around the track was a mile. She counted five other people—two women, three men—on the track with her. Whereas her nerves had pricked warily at the proximity of strangers before today, she felt empowered now. As if a two-edged sword was protecting her.

She smiled at the image that came to her mind: a handsome, ruddy-complected man with a beard, auburn hair to his shoulders, muscular arms and legs, a sword sheathed across his back. A warrior. An angel?

Definitely not Wonder Woman.

Confidence flowed into her heart. Her brain. Her bones. Sinews. Muscles. Guts. She stretched out her legs and ran. Ran on clouds. Ran with winged feet. She flew past the other joggers. Laughed. Joy welled up, streaked out her eyes in tears. Blew with her hair, her shorts, her tee.

Yes! She knew exactly what to do. Exactly where she was going. When she got back to Marianne's apartment, she would call Brad, tell him she would be finding her own apartment, buying a car, moving on with her life.

No more Wonder Woman. No need for her because Romero no longer had Eve cowering in a corner. From now on, she would go to the courthouse office every day. Sit at her desk. Read the rest of her case files. Study. Prompt her memory. Relearn what she'd forgotten.

She was returning to work. To the law. To putting Romero behind bars.

It was Romero who had better look out—for her, and for a sword-bearing warrior who had her back.

PART 2

Chapter 21

September

The Metropolitan Correctional Center in Chicago, only a few blocks southwest of where Eve worked, was an architectural marvel to Jake. Row upon row of five-inch by seven-foot windows perforated the twenty-seven stories of bare concrete like a giant IBM computer punch card. The design shouted an unmistakable message: *criminals will pay their dues*. Jake had driven past the building several times since its opening seven years ago in 1975. What he had never expected was to see it from the inside out. From a cell. As a prisoner.

Incarcerated. The reality of his situation alternated between the seething anger of an erupting volcano in his gut, and a bizarre nightmare filled with Picasso-like creatures in outsized Pierre Cardin shirts hunting him down. Justice lurked far out of reach. Without Eve's testimony that he'd been protecting her, was there any chance of release?

The restraining order left him helpless to contact her. But not hopeless. Betty's attorney brother-in-law, Neal Oakleigh, had promised to appeal the order. And of course there was always the hope Eve would recover her memory. Hope in God too.

But hopelessness found him anyway. Wended its way halfway around the world from the Philippines to his front door a month ago in August. Forced his hands into handcuffs behind his back. Carted him off to jail.

He looked up as footsteps slapped the floor of the jail corridor and stopped outside his cell. A guard peered in at him. "You have a visitor."

Jake's heart pounded in spite of his brain scoffing at the hope of anything good coming his way. It certainly wouldn't be Eve visiting him. Nor Betty, off in Virginia with Crystal. That left Neal Oakleigh. Jake scowled. The man had presented a weak-kneed, addlebrained defense in the courtroom half an hour ago.

He stood for the guard to perform the now-familiar procedure of securing Jake's hands and feet in chains before escorting him at a clinking shuffle down the hallway. Inmates growled, spat at the guard, rattled the bars of their cells. Harry Weese, the jail's humane architect, had aimed to appease the detainees' lot with "accommodating" lodgings, but had failed to consider that no palatable trade-off existed for loss of freedom.

At the visitor's room, the guard freed Jake to take a seat facing Neal Oakleigh. Between them, a wall framed halfway up with a bullet-proof, hammer-proof, explosive-proof, whatever-proof polycarbonate window separated them. Good thing, because Jake ached to get his hands on the man's throat. Or at least throw a good punch.

After a glimpse of Jake's face, Oakleigh's eyebrows lifted momentarily then beetled over his brow. He pursed his lips, picked up the telephone, and waited for Jake to do the same. "There was nothing I could do." No apology leaped from his six words, no hint that Oakleigh felt a need to defend himself.

"Which was exactly what you did. Nothing."

"Mr. Chalmers, all the legalities were in order, the facts undisputed. Worst of all was your own admission that you killed Miguel Galit."

"Killed unintentionally, and to protect Eve."

"A factor I couldn't present without Ms. Eriksson's presence to support it." Oakleigh observed him with eyes half-lidded. "My plan, Mr. Chalmers, is to subpoena her when Galit's lawsuit comes to court. Right now, no judgment has been declared, and you have not been found guilty of any crime. You have been detained to stand trial, that's all."

"*That's all?*" Jake slammed his fists against the window. "Thanks to your bumbling today, I am being *extradited* to the Philippines!"

Oakleigh glared back with equal ferocity. "For your information, I have spent the past half hour with the judge, filing an appeal against the extradition. They are seldom granted, but I am fully looking out for your interests."

Jake sat back and stared at the man. Was Oakleigh, in spite of his performance today, competent … or a bag of wind? Jake had questioned Ian MacBride's adequacy as a private investigator, and he had more than proved up to the task of finding Eve. Perhaps the same would hold true for Neal Oakleigh's skills as an attorney.

Because it mattered. Big time.

If Oakleigh didn't come through for him, within a matter of days Jake would find himself behind the bars of a Filipino jail cell.

***

Nothing like a five-bag shopping trip in downtown Chicago to lift a girl's spirits! Eve tossed her stash into the trunk of her new, crimson BMW and drove ten minutes south on Chicago's Lake Shore Drive to the Beachwood Apartments. Home sweet home, at last, where she could put her feet up and rest, safe and sound from Danny Romero's monsters.

Two long months had crawled by before she found the perfect combination of location, floor plan, and security. The Beachwood offered several options, and she had chosen one with a generous foyer, off of which all the other rooms— living room, dining area, kitchen with a large pantry, two bedrooms with bathrooms, and a half-bathroom for guests—radiated like spokes in a half-wheel. No hallway for anyone to creep down, thank you. Or creak down, as in the case of Marianne's apartment.

A doorman guarded access to the building, and another employee monitored cameras of the service entrances. Additionally, each apartment had an assigned parking spot in a well-lit lot also under camera surveillance. No more Wonder Woman trailing her every move. Danger—of abduction, at least—had been reduced to a minimum. Even her boss approved the security measures.

She braked sharply at her parking spot. A shiny, jet-black Audi was backed into it. A slender, broad-shouldered man with hair the color of the Audi, including the shine, was removing packages from the open trunk. She leaned on her horn for a good three seconds and glowered at him.

He jumped at the blare, dropping one of his bags. A head of lettuce, two green peppers, and a cucumber rolled from the bag onto the pavement. He stared at her wide-eyed and made a *what?* gesture with palms up, arms spread.

Then it hit her. An open trunk … a muscular man … a car backed in for a quick getaway. Her blood drained into a pool at her feet. Numbly, she stared back at him.

The man picked up the escaped vegetables, restored them to their bag, grabbed two more bags from the trunk, and shut the lid. His arms were full, but his face still asked *what?* as he approached her car.

No way was she going to roll down her window to speak to him. Was she even breathing? She gasped in a stinging lungful of air, and with a trembling hand shifted her car into reverse, right foot hovered over the gas pedal. Her head turned incrementally with each footstep to follow his progress around the front of her BMW to her window.

He bent at the waist to peer inside. "Is there a problem? Do you need help?"

"You're in my parking spot."

He shook his head. "Sorry, but this is mine. Apartment 3E." He pointed to the apartment number painted on the pavement in front of his car. "Oh." He lowered his arm. "3B. I'm sorry. I'll move."

She glanced at the surrounding parking spaces. Two slots on the left and three on the right were empty. It could be an honest mistake. She backed her car up so he could exit, but she didn't stay to claim her territory. Her heartbeat was shaking every moveable body part from her jaw down. Chances were good her knees wouldn't hold up if she tried to walk.

The man had said he was in apartment 3E. Was that across the hall from her, or to either side? Her security plans hadn't considered the fact that apartments near her were occupied by strangers. Any one of them could be a Romero thug.

No. She had to corral her fear. Danny Romero wouldn't go to the trouble to house someone in an apartment next to her when easier options existed. She'd just not be a friendly neighbor, that was all.

Chapter 22

Crystal Oakleigh trailed Miss Lavender, the Dean of Young Women, down the ceramic tile hallway, hoping, oh so hoping, it would take a long time to get where they were going, because the tears she was damming behind her eyes were hot and slippery and resisting her effort to blink them away. She'd been okay until the weekend ended and Aunt Betty hugged her goodbye, whispered one more time that she had to leave to go help Jake, and that Crystal needed to be brave.

She gritted her teeth and swallowed hard, over and over, until her chest didn't jerk with smothered sobs anymore. She would *not* give her new classmates reason to call her Cry Baby Crystal as her fifth-grade schoolmates had two years ago. Nobody knew her here at Arlington Academy, and she could start a new page in her life—a new book, even—and write it just as she wanted.

Really, wasn't going all the way to a boarding school in Virginia sorta like being stranded on an island again? Scary, but, maybe after a while, good? Except—she choked back a sob that jounced into her throat—here at Arlington Academy there'd be no Jake to help her.

Dean Lavender stopped, rapped twice on a door, and walked in. She beckoned Crystal to her side. A swift glance at the room revealed four walls, each situated with a loft above a desk, chair, and chest of drawers; a tall, narrow window with white Venetian blinds adjacent to one loft; and a door open to a bathroom next to a second loft. A whiff of perfume floated into Crystal's nostrils as she stepped inside.

The dean placed a dainty hand on Crystal's shoulder. "This is Room 41C, Crystal, your home for the next nine months, and these are your roommates Allie, Beulah, and Cassandra." Three girls rose from their chairs under the lofts and greeted her with smiles and a simple "Hi."

Warmth tickled Crystal's cheeks and spread to her chest. She returned their smiles with a genuine one of her own. "Hi."

Dean Lavender's hand wafted from Crystal's shoulder like a softly-blown feather. "Allie and Beulah are also newcomers to Arlington Academy. Cassandra is an old-timer, and she will help the three of you learn our ways. All of you will share the same schedule during the first semester to make things easier for you."

She pointed to the unoccupied fourth loft. "This is yours, Crystal. Your suitcases are there for you to unpack, and Cassandra will show you where to stow them when you're done. On your desk is your class schedule, as well as a folder explaining our rules. Make yourself comfortable, get to know your roommates, and I'll see all of you at supper." She favored them with a smile bookended on each side with deep, perfectly round dimples, and pulled the door shut behind her.

The three girls returned to their chairs and sat staring at Crystal.

"She seems nice," Crystal ventured.

"She's a witch," Cassandra whispered, squinting at the door as if Dean Lavender might be lingering outside. "You'll grow to hate her."

Crystal swallowed, and saw that Allie's and Beulah's throats bobbed too.

Cassandra laughed. "Jes kiddin'! Need help unpacking? C'mon, girls, let's see what of Crystal's stuff we want for ourselves."

Allie and Beulah didn't move, but before Crystal could stop Cassandra, she dumped everything in Crystal's two suitcases onto the floor. "Jes kiddin'! While you put your stuff away, I'll stow these in our closet." She half-carried, half-dragged Crystal's luggage to a third door and disappeared.

"She did it to us too," Allie said.

Crystal scurried after Cassandra, two *jes kiddins* lesson enough to not invest trust in the girl. Indeed, the door did open to a small room for storage and hanging clothes. Cassandra heaved Crystal's suitcases onto a rack above an empty rod, grinned at her, and followed Crystal back into the dorm room.

Six *jes kiddin*s later, the three newbies tailed Cassandra like ducklings to the dining hall. The room peaked in a high ceiling over three rows of three rectangular tables with benches long enough to seat four girls on either side of a table. Five three-foot-wide, floor-to-ceiling windows with white Venetian blinds overlooked the school's landscaped parking lot. Across the room, a row of kitchen workers stood behind a stainless steel counter and served food to students pushing trays along a metal rack. The aroma of fried chicken filled the room.

Cassandra led them through the dinner line, then shooed them off on their own while she joined friends at another table. Ahead of Crystal in line, Allie and Beulah found a table and sat. There was no room for Crystal. Two tables away, she squeezed onto a bench with three other students who chatted oblivious to her presence. Perfume and body odors heightened by first-day nerves mingled with the smell of deep-fat-fried chicken to churn her stomach while she pretended not to care that she was all alone in a room of seventy-two girls. She chewed and swallowed the lumps on her plate until it was time to return with her roomies to their dorm room.

When she wrote to Aunt Betty soon after, she couldn't recall what she'd eaten for supper. Instead, she told her she'd been brave.

***

By the time Betty deplaned at O'Hare, retrieved her suitcase, and hailed a taxi, she found herself arriving in heavy traffic at the Dirksen Federal Building an hour later than she'd intended. Heavens, it was almost closing time. And that dratted Chicago wind had tangled her hair into a rat's nest in the short time it took to get from the taxi to inside the building. Now she'd have to stop at a restroom to brush her hair.

Her hands shook as she wielded the hairbrush. The mirror reflected her pinched face, tight mouth, and trembling chin. And here she'd told Crystal to be brave! She whisked a prayer heavenward for both of them. Facing snakes on the island had been easier than what she planned to do now.

Wheeling her suitcase behind her with one hand, planting her cane a step forward with the other, she trudged like a broken caterpillar to the elevator. Inside the lift, her breath weighed heavier with each floor she ascended, until at last she escaped to lean gasping against the wall leading to her destination. Oh my, was jail worth doing this? She sent another prayer heavenward.

Goodness, her underarms had stained her pretty white blouse. She'd have to be sure to keep her elbows to her side. Outside the glass door of the District Attorney's office, she parked her suitcase and counted three deep breaths. Then, the picture of serenity, she opened the door.

The same pug-nosed receptionist from Jake and Betty's former visit sat at the front desk. Her mouth spread into a wide smile to greet Betty, but changed to a startled *O* as Betty approached her.

"Evedene Eriksson, please."

"I … you …" The receptionist blinked several times in quick succession, as if resetting stalled brain waves. Finally, she punched a button on her phone. "Help!" she squeaked.

Oh dear, now that man Henshaw is going to appear. Betty's heart palpitated. He would put her in jail for coming here.

Her heartbeat crescendoed in her ears. Her head spun. She clutched the edge of the front desk. She felt her eyeballs roll upward as her knees gave way.

Chapter 23

Betty opened her eyes. A man's face hovered above her, close enough to assail her nostrils with the scent of Old Spice aftershave. Franklin? She blinked several times to make sense of it. A hand with a tissue appeared and dabbed the corner of her mouth. It stung. The nasty taste of iron rose on her tongue.

"… Hit her head on the floor," a woman's voice said.

The lips of the hovering face moved. "Mrs. Parker, are you okay?"

Okay? She took a mental check. The back of her head hurt. Her bottom lip felt like a viper had bitten it.

A warm hand enveloped one of hers—left or right, she wasn't sure—and patted it. "Mrs. Parker?"

She struggled to sit up. "Yes."

"You fell and hit your head. Your mouth is bleeding. Do you feel dizzy?"

"I'm fine. I can stand."

Strong arms helped her to her feet, handed her cane to her, and stuffed the bloody tissue into her other hand. She dabbed her lip and winced.

"Mrs. Parker, what are you doing here?"

Betty looked at the man. *Henshaw.* His expression was even sterner than his voice. She swallowed. On either side of him stood the receptionist and the short, round woman with the quirky hairdo—the office manager, wasn't she? Their faces were somber, disapproving.

"I'm looking for Eve." She hoped they couldn't see her knees knocking beneath her skirt.

"Then you're lucky she's not here, or I'd have to arrest you for defying the restraining order." Henshaw paused. "You do remember it?"

"Of course I do." A corner of her mouth twitched in irritation. She wasn't daft. "I'm here because of an emergency."

Henshaw and his sidekicks looked totally unconvinced. "Doesn't matter. You'd be breaking the law. You'd be put in jail." Henshaw all but pounded a gavel. "Do you understand that, Mrs. Parker? No communication, no matter what the circumstances."

"What's the emergency?" the receptionist asked. Her boss glared at her.

"To save Jake." Betty decided not to add *Eve's fiancé.* "She needs to give testimony so he won't be extradited to the Philippines. She doesn't have to talk to me or Jake. All she has to do is go to the Correctional Center—just a short walk away—and tell the judge."

A flicker of rage twisted Henshaw's face. "Her testimony would set things straight, all right. Believe me, I want him to get his just dues. If Eve's memory returns, I'll personally see to it she bears testimony to what happened on that island."

Betty frowned. Henshaw's words sounded more like a threat than an offer of help. "Perhaps if she could see me—or Jake—from a safe distance, a legal one, it might jolt her memory. We want to help her. And now we need her to help Jake. I know she'd want to."

Henshaw took a firm grasp of her elbow and walked her faster than her legs wanted to move to the door. "We are closing the office now. I don't want to see you here again, or hear of your presence in Eve's sight. If I do, you will be arrested for stalking." He opened the office door and all but pushed her to the other side. The deadbolt clicked, and he walked away.

Betty's chest swelled, first with rage, then with choked tears, then back to rage. How dare he! She raised her cane, tempted to bring it smashing down on the glass door, through which she could see Henshaw's retreating figure. His back was stiff, his hands fisted, his stride long.

She decided against it.

Consoling herself by sucking on her injured lip, she plodded with her suitcase to the elevator and joined the employees descending to begin their journeys home. Outside, she caught a taxi on Dearborn Street and took it the short distance to Van Buren Street. The five o'clock traffic lengthened the five-minute trip into fifteen.

At the Correctional Center, she gazed up at the slotted windows and wondered which one marked Jake's cell. Was he standing at his window, staring through the five-inch-wide slit at the traffic below, hoping she would arrive soon? He would be eager to hear about Crystal's boarding school, Betty's impression of it, and how Crystal had borne the separation.

What she wouldn't tell him about was her visit to the District Attorney's office. That was her secret, and now that she'd been thrown out on her tush, she was glad she hadn't shared her plan with anyone.

How had Neal done with the extradition appeal? He had warned her that chances were against success, but she couldn't help believing the judge would grant it. Surely he'd delay such an extreme measure as extradition when Eve's testimony was all they needed to exonerate Jake. Detective Lee had accepted Jake's innocence after seeing Miguel Galit's body tied to prevent escape, and recognizing him from all the times he'd been in jail. And look at Jake's military record and the high honors awarded him! Jake was no criminal. He had served his country well, and his country would protect him.

Dodging pedestrians, wheeling her suitcase with a tight hold on the handle, she crossed the sidewalk to enter the building. A man pushed open the door from inside at the same moment she pulled it from outside.

He stepped out, and she did a double take. "Neal!"

"Betty?"

They stared at each other.

Oh dear! He wasn't on his way to the district attorney's office, was he?

She flinched as Neal pulled her and her suitcase into the Correctional Center. The door whooshed shut behind her in a loud tsk of rebuke that she'd being caught red-handed.

"What are you doing here?" Neal demanded. "I thought you were taking Crystal to Virginia."

Acid pinched Betty's stomach. It irritated her that her sister and brother-in-law had banished Crystal to a boarding school, and especially one so far away. What kind of message did that send to Crystal after already being gone for a year and thought dead? For the millionth time, Betty rued not adopting Crystal when the child's mother died in childbirth. But Franklin hadn't wanted the illegitimate child any more than Crystal's grandparents had.

"She started school today, so I flew here to see Jake."

"A waste of money." Neal huffed. "You won't be able to see him. Why don't you ask me about these things before you do them?"

"What do you mean, 'I won't be able to see him'?"

"He's gone, Betty. On his way to the Philippines. The judge denied the appeal."

"No!" A vortex of swirling darkness sucked away walls, floor, ceiling. Dimly, Betty felt arms clasp her, hands grasp her waist to hold her upright.

A floor solidified under her feet. Her legs stabilized. Air, purified by holy rage, rushed into her lungs. Swift clarity brought the truth home. "You!" she hissed at Neal. "You did this." She shoved him aside and pushed her way out the door to the sidewalk.

Neal followed, arms flailing in her peripheral vision. "What are you talking about? I did everything I could. I'm booking a flight to follow him."

Betty halted, turned to face him. "No, Neal. *I* shall follow him. *You* are fired."

Chapter 24

Crystal lowered her paper, unsure where to direct her eyes. At her teacher, or at the class? She'd forgotten her embarrassment at standing in front of the classroom and had read with enthusiasm—had even giggled at some points, and—oh, no!—read teary-voiced at others. Too late, she remembered she wasn't even supposed to *read* her essay, just use it for a prompt.

Clutching the paper in her right hand, she dropped her arms to her side and peered up at the teacher. Better her than the girls who had ignored Crystal's existence for two weeks. They were probably laughing behind hands clamped to their mouths.

"Crystal, that is amazing," Mrs. Sanders exclaimed. Eyes sparkling with sunlight captured from an open window, she clapped, stopped as if suddenly aware of her spontaneity, but resumed when the class joined her.

Crystal stared wide-eyed at the thirty applauding girls. Applauding her! It was impossible to squelch the smile that blossomed with equal spontaneity on her lips.

"Did that really happen?" a girl in the front row asked. Her voice was dreamy, not at all critical. "You were, like, *really* shipwrecked on an island?"

A forest of slender arms sprang into the air, waving eager hands like branches in an autumn wind.

"One at a time, girls," Mrs. Sanders said. "Do you mind answering questions, Crystal?"

Crystal's heart pounded all the way up to her face. She didn't know if she wanted to crow or cry. She swallowed and nodded her head.

The questions were easy to answer. Some replies earned gasps, some elicited laughter. When class ended, the girls crowded around her and walked her to her next class, asking more questions, hanging onto her answers. At dinner, they pleaded for her to sit at their tables. Homework was forgotten as they crowded into her dorm room for more stories, until finally Miss Lavender arrived to shoo them to bed.

The next morning, she was summoned to the Dean of Young Women's office. Girls she didn't know smiled at her in the hallway. For the first time since parting with Jake at the airport, a glow of happiness suffused her. She felt like the sun, radiating warmth, sowing good cheer, reaping kindness and goodwill. Did Miss Lavender want her to read her essay to the sixth- and eighth-graders? Why, she might end up popular! As Aunt Betty would say, "Goodness!"

She knocked on the frosted glass of the office door before opening it. Miss Lavender rose from her seat behind an impeccable desk and pulled forward a chair for Crystal to sit on. A tiny pucker dented the skin between Miss Lavender's eyebrows. No perfectly round dimples bookended a smile. The sunshine in Crystal's heart disappeared behind a black cloud.

"Crystal, we have a problem." Miss Lavender's mouth flatlined, and the pucker on her brow spread into furrows. "It's your grades."

Her grades? Crystal shrank into a pea-sized lump. On the two weekly math quizzes, she'd gotten every problem wrong. And the grammar definitions were like alien-talk from outer space. In French class, everyone already spoke it because they'd studied it last year.

"You missed sixth grade because you were a year on the island, is that right?"

Alarms clamored in Crystal's ears. She could see where this was going. "But … I'm almost thirteen. I can't go to sixth grade." She covered her face with her hands. Why had her grandparents made her come here?

Somehow she must escape. Find her way to Jake in Indianapolis.

**

The prison transport vehicle halted on an area of flattened vegetation. Its destination had required an hour of bumping over a rutted track that tunneled into a landscape increasingly swampy and bleak. The remote location as good as declared Salonga Prison a terminus where living cadavers were dropped off to finish their journey to the grave. "Zombie Prison," his jail mates in Manila had warned him. Dread twisted Jake's insides. Enduring the crowded conditions and filth of the Manila City Jail for two weeks had been bad enough. But here? Here the question looked to be not *if* one survived, but for how long.

The driver twisted around to face Jake. "You want, I bring." Smiley's offer finished a list of prisoner-coveted items he'd been reciting, from meds to clothing to women. Through the mesh that separated him and Jake, he smiled with perfect teeth no doubt financed by his black-market services. "This bad place."

No kidding. Jake stared out the vehicle's tiny square of window at his new residence. The prison extended farther than Jake could see, surrounded by a twelve-foot-high chain link fence topped with layers of razor wire. Inside the vegetation-chopped perimeter, the gray concrete prison walls rose one story higher than the fence. Guards, rifles in hand, gazed down from above the barred front gate at Jake and Smiley.

"If it's not legit, Smiley, I'm not participating."

"Everyone pa-tis-pate. Is good bizness."

"It's bribery," Jake snapped. He'd heard the practice had gotten worse with Marcos' regime in power. It meant Jake—and anyone else with a moral code, or too poor to *pa-tis-pate*—would have to do without basic necessities, much less luxuries.

A guard from the front gate opened the passenger door, its rusted hinge squawking, and waved Jake out of the sweltering back seat. As soon as he stepped out, mosquitos settled onto his exposed skin. There was no swatting them off until his chains were removed.

In the front seat, Smiley shrugged at Jake, bared his pearlies in a wide grin, cranked the shift into first gear, and drove off. His good cheer said he'd be back and Jake would have another chance to place an order.

Three guards in mud-colored uniforms, shirts unbuttoned over sweaty chests, surrounded Jake on both sides and his back. They were a good half-foot shorter than Jake but claimed easy authority with rifles poked into his ribs. Shouting as if he were a reluctant carabao, they herded him through the front gate into a large courtyard and released him from his chains.

His heart sank. A carabao he might well be. One of hundreds standing, squatting, lying in a feedlot reeking of human excrement. Flies—big, black, and bold—flew among the human cattle with little resistance from their victims. None wore shirts, only filthy rags—if anything— as loincloths. A large, metal trash bin in the center of the courtyard held water with debris and dead bugs floating on its brown surface. Their drinking water? In the corners of the courtyard, four fifty-five gallon drums, cut in half, spilled over with excrement.

He turned to face the front gate. Was he just being dumped here? No instructions, no bunk assignment, no basic supplies?

From behind the locked bars of the gate, the three guards stared expectantly at Jake. When their heads moved in a synchronized swivel from right to left, Jake pivoted. His stomach, already queasy with the stink, tightened.

From dozens of shadowed archways inside the prison walls, men emerged. All were adequately clothed, bony but not gaunt. Obviously not part of the carabao lot. They separated into three distinct groups, invisible lines distancing them from each other. All looked to be Filipino. Age, physique, status of health appeared evenly distributed. Jake could find nothing to distinguish one group from another. But, clearly, they were factions. Warring factions.

The men weren't merely curious. As the groups drew nearer, the carabao herd took notice, and those that could moved away from Jake. Along the tops of the walls, prison guards gathered and leaned closer from their perches.

The men encircled Jake. Breaths pulsed from open mouths. Body odor weighted with the heavy musk of adrenaline overrode the stench of feces and urine. Wary eyes knifed his.

Jake snapped to a combat readiness stance, legs apart, knees slightly bent, back straight, shoulders wide. He held his head high, chin up, and eyed the groups in a slow, rolling gaze. Either he stepped up to their unspoken challenge, or one of them would.

Three groups. Three warring factions. Challenging him to identify himself.

Who was he?

His mouth went dry … and he knew.

Chapter 25

Action was a relief. For the first time since Jake's arrest in August, he was free to make his own decision. The outcome wasn't as important as the bottom-line humanity to exert governance over his choices.

With an upward nod to signify he was taking the lead, he flared his nostrils and expanded his chest in a deep inhale that spoke of control. Of purpose. Of power. He was onstage, and drama was his communicator. What happened in the next few minutes would establish his persona in the prison. Without haste, he strolled in a direct path to the water bin. The group in his way parted like the Red Sea before Moses's rod.

There was no cup at the bin. Without looking left or right, without a glance at his enemies' proximity, Jake bent over the water and scooped a handful into his left palm, leaving his right hand free should he need it for defense. No sound came from the men, only the faint drip of water from his hand and the louder thud of his heartbeat. Pivoting, he stepped to the closest human carabao and dribbled water over the man's chapped lips into his mouth. Again, without a glimpse to left or right, he repeated the act with two more individuals. Only then did he straighten and look around him.

Two of the groups had departed, dispersing into the shadowed archways. Several members of the remaining group approached the metal bin one at a time, dipped a hand into the water, and carried it to men languishing on the ground.

When they finished, the group retreated to a third set of arches. They gestured for Jake to follow.

***

The archways reached like arthritic fingers into the prison walls. A network of crooked halls formed a maze hidden in blackness that Jake maneuvered by the soft footfalls of his companions. Dorm rooms lit by daylight through barred windows drew off members of the group—evidently *his* group now—until a bony hand, small on the middle of Jake's back, guided him into a large room squeezed full of metal bunks pushed against all four walls. A few items of clothing hanging from bedrails contributed reds, blues, yellows, and oranges to the dull gray of concrete walls and floor.

The hand parked him in the middle of the room. Except for Jake, everyone sat on a claimed bunk. He counted forty sets of almond-shaped eyes pinning him to his two-square-foot space of concrete like a new specimen in a bug collection. What was next? Some sort of test or initiation? The law laid down? Dominance established? He tensed.

As if on signal, the group turned to other business. Some curled into sleeping mode, some held up reading material to the light of the window, some chatted or crouched on the floor to play games with small rocks.

Not trusting the men's disinterest, Jake surveyed the room. Several bunks on either side of the doorway, the most vulnerable location, were vacant. Apparently he could choose among them for his small corner of the world. He lowered himself onto one of the bottom bunks and selected where he preferred to bed—across the room, farthest from the door, and under the window, where he could read assuming he got the chance. The beds were made for short men. He'd have to push two bunks end to end to accommodate his height.

Other than the clothes he wore, he had no possessions. Nothing had been permitted to leave the Manila City Jail with him, and nothing had been handed out when he arrived at the Salonga Prison. Either the basics would eventually be issued, or he was on his own to secure them. Or, like the carabao herd, do without.

He settled against the coolness of the wall backing his temporary bed. Best to wait for the opportune time to claim the other bunk location. He didn't want to bully the men. Best guess, considering these men's passivity, his group was at the bottom of the feed chain, except for the carabao. His group banded together for protection, not for dominance.

Moments later, a siren surprised him out of a doze. A blink at the window revealed the gray of dusk between its flaking bars. He scrambled to his feet, more alarmed by his falling asleep than by the siren's piercing wail. He stood, nerves taut.

His forty dorm mates assembled like automatons with depleted batteries and filed out the doorway without a single glance at him. Their lethargy spoke to conditioned habit. The siren was a signal, not an alert to danger.

He followed them. Other dorm rooms emptied shuffling men into the maze. His eyes adjusted to the gloom right before the archways unpacked the men into the courtyard. His group—perhaps two hundred in all—milled outside but didn't advance farther.

No one spoke to him, hadn't since he'd walked through the front gate. It was as if, bit by bit, the prison was already at work erasing his life. Fashioning him through isolation and loneliness into a somnolent zombie.

The faint aroma of rice wafted to his nostrils. Standard fare at the Manila City Jail, no matter what time of day—and evidently no matter what prison. Except here, the smell was mixed with the fetid odor of human waste and unwashed bodies. He clenched his fists to keep from gagging.

In the middle of the courtyard, two inmates manned a vat from which they plopped watery rice into inmates' bowls. What must be the top tier of the three prison groups filed by in two lines, each member holding two bowls and receiving two servings per bowl. Near the head of the line, one member, taller than the others and surprisingly rotund, turned back, holding out his bowls for seconds. A rifle shot spattered the packed dirt at his feet. Jake peered at the top of the prison walls. Two guards with rifles were laughing. The prisoner turned away.

The second prison group merged into the line. Their number was significantly smaller than the first group's, and each member had only one bowl into which one scoop of rice was served. Jake stiffened. The Manila City Jail had fostered a pecking order—what prison didn't?—but not at the cost of food distribution. Would Jake's group, which hadn't lined up yet, receive even one full scoop?

Two members of the first group hung around, eying the bowls of the second group as they came off the line. Jake had no bowl; these two men had two. They frowned as Jake strolled over to them and held out his hand. "I'll take those extra ones, thank you."

It didn't take a translator to interpret the words spat back at him. Jake shrugged, snatched a bowl with his left hand, and with his right hand caught the first man under the chin with the heel of his palm and powered a hard shove. The man staggered backwards and toppled like the Leaning Tower of Pisa hit by a meteor. The second man dropped his bowls and swung at Jake. Jake ducked, fisted a second meteor into his opponent's stomach. The man doubled over, gasping for breath.

Jake picked up the extra bowls. "Thanks, guys."

Keeping the deposed men in his peripheral vision, Jake sauntered to the rice vat. The two inmates dispensing the rice most likely were on the bottom tier of the first group and wouldn't resist him. He thrust the two bowls at them and pointed at the carabao herd. "Feed them."

The men stiffened, refused to move.

"Need help?" Jake grasped the closest inmate's wrist and with his other hand rammed the man's face into the vat, pulled him up by the hair, and flung him backwards off his feet. The second man brandished his ladle in a swift arc at Jake's face. Jake grabbed his opponent's fingers, twisted the ladle loose, and bopped the man on his head with it. The inmate yelped and wobbled two steps backward, hands clasped to the top of his head.

Two stories above them, the guards laughed. Jake smiled up at them, took a bow. He gulped a quick breath, grateful to have them entertained instead of interceding with rifle shots. Their ringside seats at the front gate when Jake arrived had no doubt proved a disappointment with no one fighting him. This little scrap would help make up for it.

Jake retrieved the first inmate's ladle and thrust it at him. "Feed them," he growled. "Both of you."

Scowling, the men picked up the bowls, heaped them full of rice, and began distributing clumps into the hands of men lying on the ground or propped against walls.

Jake kept the other ladle and waved the line forward. The first group had consumed half the rice in the vat. After a few minutes, he assigned an inmate from his group to dole out equitable portions of what was left.

The men whose bowls he had confiscated slunk away. Jake's nerves prickled on high alert. Pecking-order protocol called for the two men to return with reinforcements. But no one showed up. Apparently battle plans weren't on the dessert menu for tonight.

By the time he returned to his dorm room, the sun was down. The passageways glowed with electric lights, enabling Jake to study his route. No doubt there was a pattern to the maze that repeated itself throughout the ground floor of the prison. Learn this portion, and he'd have the prison's lower level memorized. The knowledge might save his neck someday.

On entering the room, he halted as the chatter inside ceased. Forty pairs of eyes fixed on him. Suddenly, the sober faces broke into smiles. The men stood and applauded.

An unexpected sob jerked Jake's chest. Nobody had acknowledged his existence since leaving the United States. There'd been no court appearance at the Manila City Jail. No sentence passed. No Neal Oakleigh or Filipino associate to represent Jake. Not even Betty or his kids had contacted him.

His throat swelled with the emotion he'd pushed back for fifteen days. He pressed his lips together and bowed in acknowledgement of the inmates' gratitude. His country had deserted him; his loved ones appeared banned from his presence. And now here were forty criminals expressing delight in his advent.

Tonight he was their hero. But tomorrow? How loyal were they if the prisoners in the first group served retaliation for breakfast?

Chapter 26

Riccardo "Ric" Romero figured his father's assignment an easy one: become friends with federal prosecutor Evedene Eriksson, push it into a romance if possible. He inhaled the scent of her perfume lingering in the Beachwood Apartments elevator, closed his eyes, and indulged in the heady tingling the fragrance teased in his senses. No question about attempting the romance part. But first he had to meet her on a basis acceptable to her.

So far, moving into an apartment on her floor had yielded no rewarding encounters. Eve was too suspicious to be neighborly. No borrowing a cup of sugar to start their acquaintance, that was for sure. He jabbed the button for the lobby and exited to follow her. He'd trailed her for weeks to pinpoint how they could meet without raising questions, and he'd found nothing.

Grocery store, dry cleaners, Ace's Gym, favorite coffee shop … he'd ruled them all out. Too much coincidence on top of living on the same floor. There must be some interest she was excited about. Something he could use on her as a blindfold to enter her life. Something pure and virtuous and lily-white.

He sniggered. Pure and virtuous and lily-white didn't exactly describe Ric's life. His father's mole at the D.A. office would have to help him.

***

Between the discomfort of his short bunk and what lay ahead come sunrise, Jake slept poorly. The siren startled him awake. Other men jumped from their bunks as well, eyes wide, blinking fast. Across the room, the barred window evidenced a dawn not quite awake itself.

An inmate in blue-checkered shorts padded over to Jake. "Siren not good."

Warmth pricked Jake's heart. So he was worthy of being spoken to now. Most Filipinos could speak a smattering of English, but until now no one had attempted a conversation. "What's wrong?"

"Too early. Trouble." More inmates gathered around, nodded, murmured.

A man with a thinning goatee grown to his midsection stepped into the room. Snow-white hair defying gravity floated about his head before coming to rest on his shoulders. The inmates hushed. "The guards have been bribed," he said. His English was accented but bore the marks of an educated man. "We are being called to a confrontation."

The group's leader. Jake's heartbeat accelerated. "I'm the one they want. For retaliation against what I did last night. Only I need to go."

"Why did you act as you did, Jake Chalmers?"

Jake wasn't surprised the old man knew his name. He was sure, too, the leader knew why he'd given water and rice to the helpless. Jake had been waiting for the question since joining the group. The old man was asking for an affirmation—for Jake to verbalize the identity he'd dramatized on entering the prison.

"Matthew 25:40," he said. A verse he had memorized twenty years ago to live by.

"*As you did it to one of the least of these my brothers, you did it to Me.*" The old man bowed. "Then we are one. We go together."

The warmth that had pricked Jake's heart earlier spread throughout his chest. This time, the men filing out of the room met him eye to eye, sometimes adding a nod, a grunt of acknowledgment, a touch on his arm. Hard to believe they were criminals. Was there another reason they'd been sent to this dead-end prison?

He followed the old man to join the crowd in the maze. The overhead lights still glowed, crushing shadows beneath the men's feet. "You know my name," Jake said. "I don't know yours."

"I am called Puno, *head*. That is good enough." Puno's white hair wafted like a cloud above his shoulders. It reminded Jake of Betty's fluff of white hair.

Sadness pierced him like a knife. She'd said she would follow him to the Philippines. He hoped he got to see her one last time before he died, if that was his fate. He wanted to tell her it was okay he'd ended up here, that God was good, that He had a purpose in everything.

He cleared the lump from his throat. "How will this play out? The guards won't stop the groups from fighting each other?"

"There will be no riot. Only champions facing off."

Champions? Jake stifled a guffaw. Was he going to fight someone half his size? "Then what happens?"

"Death follows defeat. Victor controls prison."

"I won't kill."

"You have killed once; you may kill again."

Jake stopped in his tracks. There were no secrets in prison. "That was an accident."

"That was an enemy. Killed in passion."

"I have no enemy here." No passion stirred coals in his soul. He was at peace—with God, with man, with himself.

… Until he emerged from the archway and spotted, towering above prison group one, Captain Emilio.

Chapter 27

Jake couldn't move. No blood pulsed through his heart. No oxygen dilated his lungs. No neurons jumped synapses to power his limbs. Only his eyes worked. And his brain. Telling him it couldn't be.

The man across the courtyard cannot be Captain Emilio.

The man's eyes caught his. There was no flicker of recognition. No sign of recalling Jake forced overboard at gunpoint. No flinch of culpability for nineteen passengers murdered at sea.

Yet every cell in Jake's body shrieked the man was Emilio.

Air slammed into Jake's lungs. Blood pounded hot lava to his face. Flames seared the bottoms of his feet. He took off across the courtyard.

The man yelled a challenge and charged Jake. Now there was no doubt. The hawk-like Roman nose, the square jaw and cleft chin—all were Emilio's. Jake halted and bellowed his name. "CAPTAIN EMILIO!"

His opponent stopped. Eyes wide.

"YOU MURDERED MY WIFE!"

A sharp inhale, and the man rushed Jake.

Emilio's left arm swooped at Jake's face. Instead of the uppercut Jake expected, a handful of grit stabbed his eyes. A right fist followed with a wallop to Jake's head. Too late, he tried to duck the next blow. It sent him reeling backwards. A kick to his stomach doubled him over.

Squinting through tear-flooded eyes, he saw the next punch coming. Emilio's right fist grazed Jake's ear, but this time Jake lunged inside and grabbed Emilio in a bear hug. He wasn't going to win a boxing match half-blinded, but he didn't need to see to wrestle.

In one swift movement, he hooked his right leg behind Emilio's feet and launched Emilio up and backwards. In an uncontrolled free fall, the men slammed to the ground. Emilio's back and head absorbed all the kinetic energy from both men's weight. Stunned, he gasped for breath.

Jake's arms were numb from the impact. His eyes stung. His head rang bells. His midsection had been swallowed by a shark. But what he felt was fire hot in his soul, fed by the bellows of hell.

He stumbled to his feet, shaking life back into his arms and hands, grabbed Emilio's right wrist, and flipped the man onto his stomach. Tightening his grip, he pulled his prisoner's arm up, yanked it in a half-rotation, and crushed his right foot into Emilio's neck.

"You murdered my wife!" he screamed. "I want a confession!"

Emilio moaned.

The inmates shuffled closer.

"You murdered nineteen passengers, Captain Emilio! You put them on two boats and set off explosions!" Jake twisted Emilio's arm another half-rotation. Emilio's screech reverberated off the concrete walls of the courtyard.

Blood pounded in Jake's ears. Through the red mist in his mind, he envisioned Emilio aboard the *Gateway*. Arms positioned in an *L*. Left hand pointing to the two hapless boats at sea. Right hand raised to a cloudless sky. And then the signal. Skyward arm slashing down to join the pointing arm.

Memory of the explosion ripped through Jake's soul. He screamed and wrenched Emilio's arm a full rotation. The sound of tendons tearing and bone breaking fed sweetness to his soul. Emilio's roar of agony echoed the explosion that had torn sea and bodies asunder.

"You like body parts, Emilio?" Jake shouted, chest heaving, limbs quaking. He swiveled Emilio's crippled arm back and forth in a ninety-degree arc. "What do you think? How many rotations before your arm comes off? Two? Three?" His voice rose loud, hoarse, scraping his throat. "Have you ever wrung the neck of a chicken, Captain Emilio? I have. The head always comes off by three. What do you think? Shall we start with one twist, or settle it at once with three?"

A cry went up from the inmates. Jake paused, senses perked to full alert. Barreling toward him at full speed was the tall, rotund member of group one. The man was a giant bowling ball, Jake a lone pin. Jake gulped. No bear hugs with this guy.

He dropped Emilio's arm and jumped back. His opponent extended both arms wide to sweep Jake into his embrace. For a second, Jake saw himself splatting onto the courtyard under the man's weight. He swallowed again.

The wait seemed forever. Mesmerized, he watched the rhythm of the man's heavy-footed run. A waddle. The man was a duck out of water.

At once, Jake knew what to do.

He stepped to the left and planted his feet, left foot forward. Tensed every muscle in his arms, chest and back. Hunched his shoulders. Bent his knees and leaned forward. Angled his arms out at his sides to catch the full force of the man.

His eyes he fastened on the bowling ball's right hand.

The bowling ball accepted the bait. He aimed straight at Jake's chest. Lowered his head for impact. Bellowed in anticipation of triumph.

As a batter keeps his eye on the pitched ball, Jake focused his on his opponent's right hand. His heart thumped in rhythm with the man's pace. His breath coursed in and out to the beat of the man's footsteps.

But instead of chest meeting chest, Jake snatched the man's hand in a solid catch, pivoted a hair's breadth to the side to miss him, and levered the captured arm up. The man flipped in a half circle onto his back. A standard wrestling move Jake had performed a thousand times at wrestling meets and practice. Except this time he retained hold of the man's wrist. The opponent yelped as the pressure pulled his shoulder out of socket. For good measure, Jake stomped on his opponent's sternum. The yelp segued into a whooshed shriek, and Jake grunted in satisfaction. A dislocated shoulder alone never kept an opponent down, but this oughta do.

"Anyone else?" He flung the man's limp arm aside. His whole body shook with the adrenaline of anger. He wanted more men to pummel. More release for the pain that had taken him from a cruise ship, through a second lost love, to exile.

He breathed hard until sanity leveled his blood pressure. Until the red mist disappeared from his vision. Until the daggers loosened from his nerves. He gestured at the two men groaning on the packed dirt of the courtyard. "Get them out of here."

His group surrounded him and walked him to their rooms. He expected Puno to walk alongside him, but he was nowhere to be seen. When Jake asked his whereabouts, the men looked away and shrugged.

Jake's gut knotted. Something wasn't right.

Chapter 28

"Crystal and Jonathan sitting in a tree, K-I-S-S-I-N-G," Cassandra sang. She laughed as the heat rose to Crystal's face. "Jes kiddin'!"

Crystal resisted the urge to slam the door. It would only feed Cassandra's delight. She trudged to her desk and plopped her Pre-Algebra book onto it. Stupid song. Just because she didn't talk valspeak like the other girls didn't mean she should be mocked with something fourth graders would sing. "Jonathan isn't my boyfriend, and we don't kiss." Though she wouldn't mind. Twelve years old and she'd never been kissed. Probably the only girl at the academy who hadn't been.

Allie leaned out from her loft. "Like, who's Jonathan?"

"Miss Lavender's hunk of a high school nephew," Cassandra said. "Crystal's, like, dating him."

Crystal rolled her eyes. "He's tutoring me in math, and we meet in Miss Lavender's office."

"Whatever! Can you believe it—four weeks, and she's already flunked seventh grade." Beulah shoved back from her desk and started unbraiding her hair. She brushed it one hundred strokes every night, for all the good it did. "Too bad you have to repeat sixth grade. You'll look like a giant among all those babies. Grody, fer shur."

Why did Beulah act like she hated her all the time? Crystal swallowed back the wedge in her throat and kept her voice level. "The only sixth-grade class I'm taking is French. Other seventh-graders are in the class too."

Beulah stomped to Crystal's desk and put a finger on a red textbook. "Then why do you have a sixth-grade grammar book? You're such a liar!"

"Miss Lavender loaned it to me to catch up on my own."

"Teacher's pet, teacher's pet!" Beulah waggled her head at Crystal and returned to her desk.

Crystal pinched her lips together. No use saying Miss Lavender was a dean, not a teacher.

"Here doggie, doggie, doggie," Allie called from her loft. Beulah and Cassandra laughed.

Crystal clenched her teeth. She wasn't going to let them gang up on her like this. If she slapped Beulah in the face, would the school expel her? Her breath quickened. They'd send her home, wouldn't they? And on the way she'd switch flights and go to Jake's instead.

Jake. She chewed her lower lip. What would Jake say?

"Love your enemies," that's what he'd say. And how do you do that? She sniffled. It just seemed fairer to get even.

***

"I was hoping for input on what to do now that our group is in control." Jake dumped an oversized scoop of rice into Puno's bowl. He had searched for the old man in the dorm rooms all morning with no luck. It was irritating that he'd disappeared. *A job well done* would have been nice too.

"I see our group is first in line." Puno said.

"And we're seeing to it that everyone gets the same portion. Including"— Jake nodded at the carabao herd, unsure what to call them—"those guys." He dished up his own portion and handed the scoop to another inmate to take over. He caught up with Puno. "I couldn't find you after the fight."

"I was tending to Captain Emilio. Indeed, your passion almost killed your enemy."

Flames exploded from Jake's soul and set muscles and nerves afire. "He murdered my wife!"

"Is he not in prison?"

"Not good enough! He deserves to die!" Jake slammed his bowl of rice onto the courtyard with both hands. "He killed nineteen cruise ship passengers! And who knows how many others before and since then!"

"So vengeance is yours?" Puno crouched, shooed away flies, and picked up the rice, dropping it grain by grain into Jake's bowl.

"Yes, it is!" Jake stood immobile a moment, then smashed the bowl out of Puno's hand with a hard kick. The bowl sailed like a punt to a successful field goal and crashed against the far prison wall.

Men rushed yelling to each other from the chow line and archways to surround Jake and Puno. Shouts of excitement pelted down like firecrackers from the guards manning the wall. Jake blinked at the feeding frenzy. They must think Puno was his next victim.

"Puno. I'm sorry." Ashamed, Jake crouched beside the old man to demonstrate humility. "I let my temper get the best of me. I want us to be friends."

For a long minute, Puno gazed at him. "You know how to treat one of these"—he indicated the carabao—"but not how to treat your enemy?"

Agony squeezed Jake's eyes shut. Tremors overtook his body, and he gulped hard. "I know the answer you want, Puno." His words rasped from his throat. "But if Emilio doesn't die, I will find another opportunity to see that he does."

Chapter 29

October

Eve straightened Brad Henshaw's tie. "Looks good." Thanks to him, she could relax and enjoy tonight's event. He wasn't crazy about her invitation, but he was the only man she felt safe with.

A vision of her warrior wielding the two-edged sword flashed into her mind. Well, maybe not the only man. She smiled.

"That's what I like to see." Brad tapped her chin, his finger a safe distance from her carefully applied lipstick. "Your smile is the diadem of a queen. You look beautiful."

She laughed, pleased. Compliments were rare animals in her boss's zoo. "You say that only because I didn't mess up today's court case like I did last week's."

Brad's lips twitched a smile. "Last week's was a doozy all right." He escorted her from her apartment to the elevator and out to his car. For an October in Chicago, the weather was unseasonably chilly, and she wished she'd worn a coat that was warm rather than pretty. She had to defrost in the heat of his car before she could tune back into what he was saying. "… The defense attorney wouldn't speak to me for days before I could convince him you honestly didn't know you'd accused him of perjury."

Eve sighed. Grasping the legal language of the courtroom and the correct timing of its use was proving her hardest challenge. Tonight would be a nice escape, give her motivation to keep going.

The dinner was at a modest restaurant appropriate for a fundraiser for a women's shelter. She and Brad found their assigned seats at a table for eight. Two older couples, a man her age, and a child she guessed to be twelve were already seated. Support of the shelter was a recently discovered memory, but if she was familiar with any of these guests, her recall didn't claim them.

Her seat was next to the child. "Hi, I'm Natasa Katsaros," the girl said, holding out her hand to shake Eve's. A huge smile that rivaled the grin of Alice in Wonderland's Cheshire cat animated her face. Chocolate brown eyes radiated confidence that love made the world go 'round, and that Natasa was a dispenser of its warmth.

A sudden ache pricked Eve's heart. A child, someone precious to her, hovered at the edge of Eve's memory. Another teen like Marikit, perhaps, caught in Romero's trafficking? A second pang pinched harder. No. No, this was someone close to her. Someone dear. A youngster that deep down she missed horribly.

Tears threatened Eve's eyes. She blinked them back and managed to smile. "Hi, I'm Eve Eriksson." Natasa's slender hand in hers beckoned to the girl lingering in the shadows of Eve's memory. If she could just keep hold of Natasa's sweet, little hand, maybe …

"Hi, I'm Rock Giannopoulus, Nat's uncle." The man seated on the other side of Natasa extended his hand, and Eve had no choice but to forsake Natasa's and shake his. "Mom had a crush on Rock Hudson when I was born, so my father's choice of a Greek name lost out to Hollywood."

Everyone chuckled. By the time entrees were served, the entire table was charmed by the young girl and her handsome Uncle Rock. As it turned out, Eve was correct that Natasa was twelve years old. She was not actually Rock's niece but a daughter of Rock's cousin on his mother's side. However, "niece," everyone agreed, made an easier introduction than the confusion of "second cousin" or "cousin once removed."

Rock was not married, had graduated from Stanford with a Master's, had a doctorate from Harvard, and owned a small technological consulting firm. His double-breasted, pinstriped Armani suit testified to the success of having invested in such a lengthy education.

Just the kind of man Marianne said Eve had been attracted to before her memory loss. Good looking, snazzy dresser, financially set. Ha! It was all Eve could do to listen to him yap. The man was shallow and way too full of himself. Reminded her of the jerk who'd parked in her space at the Beachwood Apartments. He'd seen her in the lobby a week later and apologized over and over for the mistake. It had taken five minutes to break free of his fawning.

At the end of the meal, two speakers shared brief testimonies to the shelter's worth: a middle-aged woman who finally dared to leave an abusive marriage, and an older teen who escaped trafficking. Both stories left Eve's heart tied in knots of compassion.

She glanced at Natasa clutching her uncle's hand, tears dripping from her eyes. Acid bit the back of Eve's throat. How dare he bring such a sweet innocent to hear these stories!

Natasa's voice quavered in a loud whisper to her uncle. "Is that where Auntie Calandra went? I'm going to tell Sissy to go too."

"Shhhhh, let's not talk about family here." Rock dabbed at Natasa's tears with his dinner napkin.

Tenderness washed the acid from Eve's throat. She could barely hold back from leaning into their huddle and slipping her hand in with theirs. Was there some way she could help this sweet child's family? It would be an intrusion into Natasa's life, but if she talked to Rock, worked her way in through him …

"—Recognize the special contribution of Rock Giannopoulus." The speaker at the microphone stumbled over the pronunciation of the Greek surname. Rock stood, and applause accompanied him and Natasa as they wound through the diners to the front of the room. "We especially want to thank Rock here for donating weeks of labor to transform our paper-and-pencil office work into something we can finally handle on a computer." The speaker rattled off technological terms that Eve could only raise her eyebrows at.

"Sounds like we could use him at our office," she whispered to Brad. He gave her a noncommittal look.

Rock stepped to the microphone, his right arm across Natasa's shoulder. "This shelter has played an important part in my life and in the family of my niece here." Natasa gave a sober nod, and a murmur of sympathy rippled through the crowd. "Never doubt for a minute that your donations make a difference. Not only does this shelter help critically needy women, but the lives of their families and loved ones outside the shelter are affected too."

Eve hung onto every word. When he closed with "God bless you," she had no doubt about asking him for his business card.

***

"There has to be more we can do than be first in line." Jake squatted by Puno and shoveled his evening meal of rice into his mouth. Without the first group taking four times their due, everyone now received one-and-a-half hefty scoops. Tonight, bits of meat and vegetables speckled the rice. Scrapings from the guards' bowls, Puno said.

"Such as?"

"Dealing with these toilets."

"The guards commandeer inmates to empty them."

"They should be dumped more often. And scoured out."

"The guards are in charge. Do they want prisoners telling them what to do and how to do it?"

Jake scowled. Certainly not an American prisoner. "What about these men in the courtyard? Why aren't they taken into dorm rooms?"

"Count them," Puno said. "They are too many."

"Not if all three groups house them."

"They are sick and dying. No one will nurse them, only dispose of them sooner. In the courtyard, at least a doctor tends them.

"A doctor? When?"

"Once a month."

Jake huffed. "No wonder this is called a prison of zombies. Zombie hearts, that's what!"

Puno stood. "Shall we start with our example of compassion then? Come."

Jake trailed him, his heart lifted. Yes, that's what was needed here—a purpose beyond mere survival, beyond waiting for death. What about all the Christians Puno said were in his group? Surely they weren't guilty of zombie hearts?

"I suggest our first example be this man." Puno stopped next to a carabao lying on his side, one arm nesting his face for protection from flies, the other arm twisted at an odd angle from his shoulder. He wore only soiled briefs barely visible under a blanket of flies.

No.

Jake's soul went dark. He used his foot to roll the man onto his back, exposing his face.

Captain Emilio.

The shuffle of feet gave evidence of silent spectators.

Jake turned and walked away.

Chapter 30

Betty stood outside the Manila City Jail and blotted sweat off her face with her fifth tissue of the morning. Had the weather been this awful on the island? Hard to believe she'd ever gotten used to the heat—though, come to think of it, there'd always been the coolness of the cave to retreat to. Goodness, going inside the Manila City Jail an hour ago had certainly provided no relief. Only one more horror in her hunt for Jake.

She bit back a weepy inhale. To think Jake had been in there with all those prisoners stuffed inside row after row of cells like chickens in wire cages. The Old Bilibid Prison consisted of twelve rusted metal buildings radiating like spokes from a central guard hub. "It's only a detention center now," a man in uniform told her. As if that excused the horrid overcrowding and disrepair. Thank goodness Jake had been transferred to a better location.

A dilapidated prison vehicle stopped next to her, and she peered inside the open passenger window. She had been directed to Smiley to take her to Jake—for a price—if she didn't mind a prisoner in the back. The driver's pearly grin easily identified him as her chauffeur. She opened the passenger door and squinted through the mesh separating her from the shadowy figure behind it. She whipped her head away as his odor hit her. Oh my, he smelled like the underarm of a bear.

"No danger." Smiley patted the passenger seat. "You sit."

What choice did she have if she wanted to see Jake? She slid onto the sticky seat and closed the door. Its hinges shrieked as if alarmed at her decision to really do this. What felt like the hot breath of the prisoner prickled the back of her neck. She leaned forward and clutched the seat on each side of her legs.

Smiley cranked through several gears and gunned the vehicle through busy streets at a speed that left her mouth spitless. "You mother of Pris'ner Jake?"

Afraid to turn her eyes away from what might be her imminent death, she nodded. *Almost his mother.* All Jake had to do was sign the documents she'd brought, and his adoption was official. That, and if she lived through this ride.

She waited until enough moisture returned to her mouth to speak. "What's the name of the prison Jake is in?"

"Som-bee Prizon." Smiley hooted a high-pitched laugh, and behind the mesh the prisoner screamed something unintelligible.

Betty swallowed. It sounded as if Smiley had said Zombie Prison. But of course that couldn't be right. The prisoner's ranting precluded repeating the question.

They drove out of the city, and Smiley pressed the accelerator. The wind from her open window lashed the sweat from her forehead and the stench of bear from her nostrils. Smiley leaned toward her. "Pris'ner Jake write letter?"

Well, drat, she hadn't thought to bring writing materials. "He won't be there long enough." Certainly not once she got Jake to agree to a new lawyer so they could get him out. The reminder of Neal Oakleigh set her stomach to boiling. She had refused to speak to him since Jake's deportation.

"Oh, no leave prizon." Smiley shook his head. "You buy penzil, paper, stamp." He grinned at her. "I have all. Guard let Pris'ner Jake write letter."

Betty frowned. "Tell me about this prison."

"Pris'ners boss."

Betty blinked. "You mean the prison is run by the prisoners?"

"Yes."

"But ... wouldn't they fight?"

"Guards shoot."

That stopped her breath. With guards not intervening, the biggest bully would reign. He'd confiscate everything, make everyone do his bidding. "But ... what about food? People could starve."

"Not worry, guards feed rice. Everything else"—he pointed to his chest—"buy from Smiley."

"What if a prisoner doesn't have money?"

Smiley shrugged. "Eat lotsa rice. Wear rags."

Jake had no money. That, at least, would soon be taken care of. And letters from Jake would be nice, especially for Crystal. Poor child. She'd been so happy to see Betty two days ago. And shocked to hear about Jake's deportation. Betty shouldn't have withheld the information. Crystal was no longer the crybaby she'd been before their year on the island.

They left the paved road for one pocked with holes and ruts. Smiley didn't slow down but drove it with twists and turns that jostled every one of her joints loose. She felt herself disintegrating into a pile of bones inside a bag of skin gurgling with stomach juices. Soon the stench of swampland overrode the underarm bear smell. Mosquitoes blew in the window.

Smiley pulled out a red and purple can of bug spray and liberally applied a mist to the front seat area. Betty barely made it to the window to thrust her head out and release every bit of fluid in her stomach. She passed the rest of the trip in a daze.

When the vehicle stopped, she breathed deeply; reassembled bones, mind and dignity; and tumbled out of the vehicle onto shaky legs. Before her, the prison rose dark and desolate like something out of *The Lord of the Rings*. She shivered. Had Smiley said this was the Sauron Prison? She approached its entrance, half-convinced it was a duplicate of the Black Gate of Mordor.

Smiley trotted up to her from the gate, where he'd delivered the prisoner. "Guard say no visitor."

She blinked as if he'd spoken a foreign language.

He lowered his voice. "You have money?"

"Only what I gave you for the ride."

"You bring money tomorrow, you visit Pris'ner Jake."

Tomorrow? Endure that ride again? For something she shouldn't have to pay for in the first place? "No! It's my right to see him *now*!" She shoved Smiley aside and hobbled to the gate.

Two guards were inside, removing chains from the prisoner Smiley had transported. A third guard stood at the gate, watching them, his back to Betty. The gate was slightly ajar.

Just wide enough for Betty to slip through.

Chapter 31

Betty crept alongside the gate until she reached the gray concrete of the prison wall. She flattened her back against it, as if, chameleon-like, in spite of her coral sundress, she would blend in. The two guards unchaining the prisoner spied her and yelled to the guard at the gate. Her heartbeat spiked, shaking her from head to toe, shutting her down. "Jake," she mewled. Her lungs had no oxygen to shout his name.

To her surprise, the guards hastened to the gate, exited, and pulled it shut. Behind them, Smiley wasn't smiling. His eyes were wide, his mouth spewing words, his hands gesticulating wildly. He must be demanding they fetch her—and the guards were refusing.

They *wanted* her inside the prison.

Her five senses returned with a wallop. Smiley's shouts, the stench of human sewage, the bile coating her tongue, the flies settling on her skin—all were eclipsed by the sight of the three guards hovering at the gate, eyes fastened on her, smiles curving their lips.

She was here for their entertainment.

A whimper crawled up her throat.

She bit her lower lip to stop its trembling and focused on the courtyard. *Jake, where are you?* The unchained prisoner stood with his back to her, immobile, his hands fisted. Beyond him, on the ground, lay dozens upon dozens of half-naked men in rags.

Movement beyond them shifted her heart into a rapid thud. Men, hundreds of them, emerged from arches in the prison walls and strode toward the lone prisoner. Surrounded him. Salivated over him.

Until they spied her.

Pretty coral dress, bare legs, bare shoulders, dainty little fingers and toes. Didn't matter she was seventy. She felt their eyes consume her. Mouths open to taste her. Hands tremble to touch her. Noses flare at the scent of her.

Her intestines knotted. She mustn't let them come closer.

Inhaling a searing lungful of air, she stepped forward, right hand high over her head, palm toward them. "I am Jake Chalmer's mother." Her words flamed hot at them.

The men halted.

"Bring him to me!"

They stared at her. A man at the back of the crowd broke away and disappeared inside an archway.

She lowered her arm to her side and gazed at them as a queen might appraise her subjects.

An eternity of seconds passed, and then Jake emerged from an archway and ran toward her. It was all she could do to maintain the sham of control before she crumpled into his arms.

***

Jake clasped Betty to his chest until his heartbeat slowed to normal. He set her on her feet, holding her arms to steady her. "Betty, what are you doing in here?" His insides twisted at the thought of what could have happened if he hadn't come.

"The guards wouldn't let me visit you." Her words shuddered out of quivering lips. "They said I had to come back tomorrow with money."

Jake clenched his jaw. Somehow, he needed to gain the upper hand with the guards.

Murmuring, the prisoners disbursed with the new inmate to the far side of the courtyard. A half-dozen men from Jake's group stayed back to form a protective arc around him and Betty. Shouts of a fight testified to the new inmate's fate.

Where have you been? Jake wanted to demand. *Why has there been no legal action?* He caught himself, ashamed at the hostility so quickly elbowing aside his concern for Betty's safety. "Catch me up," he said instead.

She did. His emotions rode a roller coaster. Eve, Crystal, Neal Oakleigh. None of her news was good. It was hard not to seethe with anger.

He told her about Emilio, but not about the fight.

"He's here?" Her face paled and she clutched his arm. "What are you going to do?"

"Finish what he started."

"You mean …" Her grip on his arm tightened. "Promise me you won't harm him."

"Harm him? I'll do worse than that."

Her face crumpled into a precursor of tears. "No, Jake, please! We'd never see you again. They'd …" She put her hands on either side of his face. "Losing your wife was awful, and I wish it had never happened. But it wasn't all loss, Jake. There was gain for Crystal and Eve and me on the island. Meeting you changed our lives. Good came out of Ginny's death. She'd like that, wouldn't she? Please, don't take that away from us." She collapsed onto his chest, weeping.

He held her, patted her back. Good things *had* happened. And he'd shared in their joy. But what Betty didn't understand was that it was over. Going forward was a futile dream.

The fight on the other side of the courtyard grew louder. Betty stepped back and dried her tears with tissues stuffed in her pocket. "I have something important to tell you." Her words came out in little jerks. "I've redone my will and taken legal precautions to protect our little family." He frowned, and she reminded him: "Our island family. You, Eve, Crystal and me."

"Oh." His cheek twitched. That reunion was pure fantasy now.

"I've adopted you as my son. Legally. All you have to do is sign this consent form." She pulled a leather wallet from her pocket and removed a document and pen.

He couldn't help a chuckle. "Adopt me? Why would you do that?"

"So you can take care of Crystal. I'm making both of you my heirs, with you as Crystal's trustee and Eve as her guardian."

"You don't need to adopt me just so I can be Crystal's trustee."

"Yes, Jake, I do. Otherwise Neal will usurp you. Somehow—maybe as her grandfather—he'll get you kicked out and take control of Crystal and her inheritance. Please, Jake, sign it."

"I don't like signing without reading it first."

The shouts across the courtyard quieted. She thrust the pen at him. "The guards are opening the gate. Trust me. I've had three lawyers go over it."

There was no time to dicker. Who knew if he'd ever see Betty again. And for sure he didn't want Neal Oakleigh controlling Crystal's life. He scribbled his signature wherever an *x* designated it. "What about having it notarized?"

"I'm sure Smiley knows someone." She tucked the document away and pulled out a small package. "I brought your pocket Bible. Will they let me give it to you?"

The prisoners were allowed reading material, but why risk the guards confiscating it? Giving it to Neal Oakleigh to pass onto Betty for safekeeping had been bad enough. He whipped the book into his waistband under his shirt and gave a big hug to Betty to hide the move. The guards ran up, a furious-faced Smiley at their back, and thrust their rifles into Jake's and Betty's ribs to separate them. Snarling, one guard marched Betty to the gate while the other held Jake at bay.

"I'll come back as soon as I find a lawyer in Manila," she called over her shoulder.

"I'll wait by the gate," he yelled. *Hurry*, he wanted to add. He didn't like postponing matters with Emilio.

Chapter 32

Eve sat back in her chair as the waiter set a monster lobster tail in front of her. She couldn't help but laugh in delight. "You're right, it's huge!" The fragrance of oregano, paprika, and cayenne pepper lightly mixed into clarified butter on the side teased her taste buds.

"You earned it—and it's cheaper than a raise." On the other side of the table, Brad Henshaw grinned at her. The invitation to dine was a last-minute reward. From somewhere in his office, her boss had pulled out a red plaid bowtie and donned it in place of his staid navy necktie. "For special occasions only," he told her. He wasn't exactly a dapper dresser, but the bright bowtie brought out a ... well, a jolly dimension to his otherwise sober personality.

She poised her fork for the first bite. "Thanks for giving me those cases." The first two she had handled well; the third stumped her twice before she could proceed.

"You did a good job—made me wonder if your memory had returned. Your law skills, anyway."

"It's more like rust removal than a point-blank return of memory. But something's working. The more I review, the sharper and cleaner my retention is."

Brad smiled. "Wonderful. How about memories connected to the Romero case? The cruise ship, what happened on the island ...?"

"No." She put her fork down, appetite gone.

His eyebrows rose at her curt answer. "Difficult to talk about?"

"Nothing to talk about. Do you think I wouldn't tell you if I remembered something?"

"I'm concerned you don't *want* to remember." He put his fork down too. The murmur of diners and the soft clatter of dishes and silverware bracketed their silence.

She forced her voice to sound reasonable. "The doctor said the bullet ricocheted enough times before it hit my head that the damage was minimal. But it still killed brain cells, Brad. Those memories are dead, not just buried. It's October, four months since my injury. The gravestones are permanent."

Brad countered by gentling his tone too. "I think trauma may still be a factor, in which case memories may yet resurface." He reached across the table and covered her hand with his. "You know I'm looking out for you." She stared at his fingers, how easily their size hid hers. His palm was smooth against her skin, his fingernails trimmed square. He gave her hand a squeeze and withdrew his to take up his fork. "Now, let's don't allow these tails to go to waste."

Her irritation dissolved. He was someone she could trust, wasn't he? She picked up her fork, the imprint of his hand on hers still warm. She wasn't sure how to take his touch—as nothing more than comfort, or as a prelude to something romantic?

If the latter, she wasn't ready. Until Danny Romero was out of her life, there was no room for affection beyond friendship. The empty spaces in her memory seemed matched with empty spaces in her heart—as if people she loved had been obliterated from each. The holes made it difficult to move on.

She sighed. "Have you given any more thought to hiring Rock Giannopoulus?" She couldn't get sweet Natasa off her mind. Or was it the mysterious girl hovering at the edge of her memory that she yearned for? "There are several things I'd like to do with my case files, and I have no idea how to set them up on my computer. I'd like at least a few tutoring sessions with him."

"I've thought about it, and he's all yours. Go ahead and schedule him for next week."

For the first time since Danny Romero's kidnapping attempt, the prospect of something good glowed like a candle inside her. Natasa wasn't a missing piece of her memory, but the young girl might fill one of the gaping holes that, more and more, haunted Eve's heart.

She flashed a grateful smile at Brad and dug into her lobster tail, careful to keep her hand from resting on the table.

***

Crystal's heart jumped as Jonathan sneaked her hand into his under Miss Lavender's study table. "I'm really proud of you, Crystal. You're getting more and more of your test questions right. You deserve a reward."

Her hand burned in his. Her throat squeezed her vocal cords so hard her question came out a squeak. "Reward?"

"A kiss." His voice caressed her ears, soft, husky, a prelude to the promise. He inched his face toward hers.

Ohhhh, she was going to faint. Her heartbeat galloped. Her breath pressed like a balloon ready to burst inside her chest.

Miss Lavender entered the office, and Jonathan sat back, dropping Crystal's hand. "Okay, kids. Time to go." She waited for Crystal to gather papers and book, and for Jonathan to scribble something on a piece of paper.

"Here's your next assignment." He folded the sheet and handed it to Crystal. "She's doing great," he said to his aunt.

"So I hear from Crystal's teacher. I'm proud of you two."

Jonathan acknowledged his aunt's praise with a smile, winked at Crystal, and walked away. It was all Crystal could do to follow him into the hallway. She was sure Miss Lavender would stop her and ask why her heart was pounding so loudly.

Jonathan's note sizzled in fingers still aflame with his touch. She dashed to her dorm room, dropped her book and papers onto her desk, and climbed into her loft. No one else was in the room. With trembling hands, she opened the folded note.

After dinner tomorrow - parking lot - blue Camaro - way at the back.

She inhaled a quick breath and held it. Tomorrow night was chapel. The auditorium would be crowded, and no one would miss her. It was perfect! She stuffed the note under her pillow.

Her breath whooshed back out. No. She was too scared.

But … maybe … for just one quick kiss.

Chapter 33

If only she had someone to share her secret with. All night, Crystal tossed and turned, read the note with her flashlight, decided yes, decided no. Her roommates grumped at her restlessness.

But she didn't dare confide in them. Miss Lavender said Cassandra was there to help her, Allie, and Beulah, so Cassandra would figure she owed it to Miss Lavender to blab on Crystal. Beulah just plain didn't like her, and Allie was jealous because Crystal, thanks to Jonathan, now made better grades in pre-algebra than she did.

So, what would Jake do? No, he was a boy. Okay then, what would Eve do? That made her giggle. For sure, Eve wasn't afraid of boys. She'd tell *them* to kiss her—or not!

Crystal folded the crumpled sheet into squares and shoved it deep into her pillowcase before getting ready with her roommates for breakfast. Too risky to carry the note around in case she dropped it or someone found it on her.

"Whatcha smilin' about?" several girls asked throughout the day. It was hard not to answer, "Cuz a guy wants to kiss me tonight."

Chapel was right after dinner. When she got into the meal line, she still didn't know what to do. But, just in case, she had stopped at the dorm room to dab a fingertip of Aunt Betty's gift of White Shoulders on her neck.

At chapel, she sat in an aisle seat at the back of the auditorium so she could leave without anyone noticing. But first, it was best to wait until everyone was wrapped up in singing. Or, well, maybe after that, during the Scripture reading. Or, okay, while the speaker had their attention.

Her stomach ached as if she'd swallowed a cement block—and suddenly she knew there was no way she was going. Relief washed over her. Kissing wasn't meant to be a game. It was meant to be special. Special enough to be done in private, but not in secret—not when you were afraid to tell anyone, or, even worse, when you were ashamed to tell them.

She felt scrubbed clean. Free.

Chapel was almost over when she felt a sharp tap on her shoulder. She turned and found Miss Lavender standing behind her. In her hand was Crystal's crumpled note from Jonathan. In back of Miss Lavender stood Jonathan, a fierce scowl on his face.

***

Betty came better prepared for a visit with Jake this time. Instead of stuffing what she could into her pockets, she carried a large handbag crammed with goodies. At the prison gate, she gave each of the three guards a soda, then handed one to Jake through the bars and opened the last one for herself.

She did the same with plastic-wrapped packages of cheese and crackers and peanut butter and crackers. One per guard and one each for her and Jake. They had a jolly good picnic together, the five of them, and polished off the meal with a candy bar apiece. It wasn't difficult to have a private conversation with Jake after that. The guards stood at a distance and smoked homemade cigarettes. The odor of cheap, reused tobacco burning was almost as bad as the human sewage stink.

"I hate that you're in this place, Jake." He looked worse than he ever had on the island. Mosquito bites covered every inch of exposed skin. His hair and beard were greasy with sweat. The amount of dirt from head to toe, not to mention the magnitude of his body odor, left no doubt that bathing was not available. "I'm going to complain about it to the authorities."

"Focus instead on getting me out of here."

Her shoulders slumped. "I'm sorry I took two weeks to come back. Everything moves so slowly here. And before that I had trouble with my passport. The last two digits of my birth year got messed up, and when I applied for a passport for Crystal, I discovered she had no birth certificate."

"Because her mother died in childbirth?"

"Because she died in a hippy commune. Evidently they didn't bother with birth certificates for their offspring, and neither did Crystal's grandfather when he got her. I tell you, I detest that man!"

Jake all but spat on the ground. "Forget Neal Oakleigh. Did you find a lawyer here?"

"Snyder gave me a name. It's a partnership of two, but competent—"

"Snyder? Isn't that Oakleigh's law partner?"

"Leroy Snyder was my husband's partner long before he was Neal's. Snyder is completely trustworthy. I told him I didn't want Neal connected in any way to me or my business matters."

Jake's left cheek twitched.

"Honestly, Jake, I think these guys here are good. I spent several days with them going over information. They said you have a defensible case but the problem is bringing it to trial. If you pay the judge—"

"I won't bribe him."

Betty bit her bottom lip. Such a simple solution and he wouldn't even consider it? "The payment is only to move the date forward, not to sway his decision—"

"No."

"Otherwise it's two to five years."

Jake's face was stony. She wanted to shake him. "There is another way. They said you could settle out of court."

Jake's eyebrows shot up. "Now that sounds like an honorable possibility. How do I do that?"

"It would take a lot of money." Not that she couldn't cover it … if Jake would let her.

"In other words, more people than the family would get compensated."

"To make it official, the lawyers and judge would have to—"

"Receive bribes?"

"Get paid, Jake. For mercy's sake, stop being so suspicious!"

"All right, Betty. Find out how much. Will the cost be a reasonable wage for the lawyers and judge? Or enough to buy a yacht—apiece?"

Betty huffed. Why did he have to be so stubborn! Why not just pay it and be done? "Okay, I will," she snapped.

"And put it in writing. A contract. With everyone's signature who gets paid—and how much they get paid."

The three guards trotted to the gate, their rifles bobbing with their pace. Was it because Jake's and her voices had gotten noticeably louder, or because a longer stay required more goodies from her handbag? She didn't want to yield to them. Nor to Jake.

"I guess our time is up." She gazed at Jake, who'd rather surrender to mosquitoes, filth, and starvation than wrong God or man. She sighed. "You're a good man, Jake. Give me a week, and I'll be back, with or without the contract."

Chapter 34

Every day, the guards dragged corpses out of the prison courtyard. Every day, the rain and mist of the monsoon multiplied mosquitoes and sent shivering men to their final destination. Every day, Jake stuffed men into the shelter of his group's maze and pulled an equal number out for the guards to cart away.

"I'm going to demand the other two groups take some of these in," he growled to Puno. "There'd be room for everyone then."

Puno flinched as if Jake had held a lit match to his cheek. "First group is criminals so bad other prisons don't want them. Compassion does not mark their souls. Second group is Muslims. They protect their customs and admit no outsiders."

So his group was the only one with pity in their souls? Jake helped Puno lay a corpse by two others at the gate. He wiped the chill of dead skin onto his shorts, his stomach bucking a spurt of vomit into his throat. "How would you identify our group?" For the most part, the men were reclusive and mild-mannered. Not your typical lawbreakers. Why were they here?

"Mostly we are political prisoners of President Marcos."

"That many of you? There must be over two hundred."

"Marcos has ruled for seventeen years. Until he dies, we die."

Jake swallowed. "You make it sound as if no one gets out of here."

"We are here to be forgotten and die."

Flames leaped from Jake's soul. Not if he could help it! Betty was here now; he was far from forgotten. And certainly his children would intervene. "Is that why the guards let inmates rule inside the prison?"

"To hasten death, yes."

"The warden allows this?"

"The warden is as forgotten as the prisoners."

In a flash, a calm as bright as sunshine on steel settled over Jake. "Then we have hope, Puno."

"Hope?" Puno snorted. "Hope was the first prisoner to die here."

"No, don't you see? If inmates are allowed to rule, then let us rule well. We can transform this place from the inside out."

Puno grimaced. "No, *you* don't see. Reading your Bible to prisoners will not change hard hearts. Few have attended your morning devotions this week. The rest scoff."

Jake smiled. "I read only to feed souls that are hungry, Puno. Hard hearts I leave to God. I'm talking about changing the prison."

At this, Puno chuckled. "Now I join the scoffers."

"You said the purpose set out for these men is to die. So that is what we change first." His mind raced. In less than a week, Betty would return. She would help initiate the first step. Smiley was next in line. And somewhere in there, the warden.

But a week went by and Betty didn't come. Two weeks passed. Three weeks.

In the meantime, Captain Emilio disappeared from the courtyard. Did his former group take him in? Or did the guards take him out? All the unrest that had settled at the anticipation of Emilio's death rose up and stalked Jake like a relentless zombie.

***

Every morning, Crystal awoke as steamed as a crab in a chef's pot. None of her roomies would tell who blabbed on her. It had to be one of them. Allie or Beulah or Cassandra—which one had heard her folding and unfolding Jonathan's note that night and dug it out of her pillowcase the next day? Ohhhh, she was *so* going to find out who and make her pay!

Even worse was how all three acted super friendly and innocent right afterward. "Tell us what happened—did you kiss him?" They gaped at her, all moony-eyed, shoulders scrunched and wiggling, giggles gushing like bubbles at the beginning of the Lawrence Welk Show.

And then what did they do with her trust? Blabbed the whole story to everyone in the school. She couldn't go anywhere without the mockery of *K-I-S-S-I-N-G in a Tree* hummed just loud enough for her ears. Just enough to make her chin quiver so she had to turn her face away.

Betrayal was a monster. She prayed to forgive and forget, but the forgetting part kept getting jabbed awake.

Jake would tell her the Bible said to love your neighbor as yourself. But what she needed to love herself was for her roomies to love her—and they weren't doing it. The whole thing was like riding a merry-go-round. Love me … so I can love myself … so I can love you … so you can love me … so I can love myself … so I can love you. Gah!

And that verse, "Love your enemies and do good to them"? Really? At night, lying sleepless in bed, all she could think about were ways to get even. Which roomie was her enemy? Did it matter? More and more, she hated all three of them equally.

So each morning, she awoke as steamed as a crab in a chef's pot. Waiting. Waiting for payback.

***

Floppy discs, MS-DOS, PC-DOS … Eve's head spun at the computer lingo and acronyms Rock spouted. Why had the Justice Department insisted on buying the new-fangled gadgets anyway? They'd just keep getting more and more complicated until only experts like Rock could use them. She heaved a sigh and poured herself a second cup from the office coffee pot. At least the computers were serving the purpose of getting her and Rock together.

Marianne joined her, wrinkling her nose at the pot's scorched dregs. "Isn't Rocky gorgeous?" she gushed. Although Marianne had more computer expertise than anyone in the office, she'd found every excuse possible to have him help her. "Has he asked you out?" The quiver in her voice betrayed her hope-against-hope that he hadn't.

"*I* asked *him* out." Eve suppressed a giggle as Marianne's eyes widened and the corners of her generous mouth plunged down. "His niece is in town next weekend, so I invited him and Natasa to the zoo. I'd like you to come too."

Another widening of Marianne's eyes, followed by a swift upward swoop of her lips. "Honest? Are you sure? Yes, I'd love to come!" Her eyelashes fluttered, then halted in a glare at Eve. "Wait. Are you inviting me to be a chaperone?"

Eve grinned. "Natasa and I will be a chaperone for you and Rock. He's all yours, girl! When you meet Natasa, you'll discover who the real charmer is."

Whew. She'd sidestepped that well enough. Natasa was the one she wanted time with, not Rock. Still, it didn't hurt to put eye candy in someone else's hands. Her two dinners with her boss, while not exactly "dates," had grabbed her by the shoulders and shook her hard. *Watch out*, the not-exactly-dates had screamed, *you're fooling yourself thinking you're not hungry for love!*

Chapter 35

"Prisoner Jacob Chalmers to the front gate." Jake's heart jolted at the blaring announcement. He'd never heard a prisoner summoned over the loudspeaker before. From the looks of the other inmates, neither had they. They stared at him as if his shirt were a black-and-white target with a red bull's eye over his heart.

Betty. Something had happened to her. Three weeks had passed and she'd never returned, never contacted him. He ran, pushing prisoners aside.

Four men stood at the gate. No Betty. The three guards huddled to one side as if cornered by a wolf. The fourth man, taller than the guards, slender, wearing a suit and tie in spite of the heat, stood with arms akimbo, staring through the bars into the courtyard. The warden?

It took a moment for Jake to recognize who he was. Disgust and anger distorted the man's face. His expression changed to surprise at Jake's approach, then returned to barely suppressed rage. Jake called out his name. "Detective Lee."

"Colonel Chalmers. This is an outrage!" Lee gestured to the guards to open the gate and let Jake out. Jake's knees wobbled as he stepped through. Was he free? His heart beat faster and faster like a staircase mounting higher and higher to the heavens.

But no, the guards, not once looking at Detective Lee, clapped chains onto Jake's wrists and ankles. Speaking in Tagalog, the detective berated them with words that had to slice their souls, leaving them cringing, hands trembling.

Even the hairs on the back of Jake's neck tingled at his fury.

"Get into my car, out of this filth," Lee snapped. He waved at a police van parked a short distance away.

"I'm afraid I'm part of the filth." Jake looked down at his ragged shirt and shorts, stained with blood from his fight with Emilio, soaked daily with copious sweat, caked with dirt not easily brushed off. His arms, face, and hair fared only slightly better from splashes of the prison's fetid drinking water. "You don't want me in your car."

Lee opened the passenger door. "Get in. I am ashamed of these officials, of this prison. I would take you away if I could."

Jake's shoulders slumped. So Lee was not here to free him.

He slid onto the front seat, and Lee joined him on the driver's side. Lee turned on the ignition, and cool air from the air conditioner enveloped them. Jake closed his eyes.

"Betty Parker called me."

Jake's moment of indulgence fled. "Where is she? Has something happened?"

"She has been deported."

"Deported!" Had he heard Lee correctly? "How can someone only weeks in the country be deported? And Betty? What could she possibly have done?"

"A difference between her passport and visa concerning her year of birth."

"Impossible. She got that straightened out before she came here. Unless the visa was incorrect …"

"All I know is what she told me. She asked if I would be your go-between until she returns." Jaws clenched, brow plowed in angry furrows, Lee glanced out the window. "You should not be in this foul place. I suspect someone has been well-paid to put you here."

Jake's stomach muscles knotted. "The judge. I was told I'd have to bribe him to move the trial date up."

"Unfortunately, that is not uncommon. What will you do?"

Jake set his jaw. "Rely upon a higher Judge who can't be bribed."

Lee raised an eyebrow. "A righteous Judge, yes, but often to be waited on as well."

"So, while I languish, is there a way to find out who bribed the earthly judge?"

Lee chewed his cheek, considering. "As a detective, I advise you to sort through your enemies."

His enemies? His only enemy was Captain Emilio.

Or was he?

Other candidates popped into his mind and stood like suspects in an eyewitness lineup: Bradley Henshaw and the Justice Department with their restraining order. The criminal that Henshaw accused Jake of being in cahoots with—Danny Romero, was it? Jake's bumbling lawyer, Neil Oakleigh, who allowed Jake to be deported. And what about that private detective Betty hired to find Eve? Ian MacBride. Hadn't Jake told him about killing the thug on the island?

Jake swallowed at the last suspect in the lineup. Eve. In one way or another, all the suspects had her in common. Like it or not, she was the starting point of his troubles. The ache he strove daily to suppress rolled over him.

"Colonel Chalmers, I must go soon. Let me tell you how I agreed to help. Mrs. Parker opened a bank account in Manila for you. With your consent, I will manage it for you and Mrs. Parker. When you need purchases, I will get them for you."

Jake nodded dully. Money wasn't what he needed.

"To ensure mail delivery, I will also take responsibility for bringing and sending letters between you and Mrs. Parker and Crystal Oakleigh."

Jake's heart perked at the prospect of hearing from his loved ones. "And my children too. If you have pen and any kind of paper handy, I'll write a quick note to all four."

Warmed by the prospect of contact with his loved ones, Jake opened up and told Detective Lee about his plans for reforming the prison.

The detective blanched. "I'm afraid my other mission today may destroy your hopes, Colonel. Even worse, it will most likely endanger you. My official assignment for coming here was the delivery of a prisoner. This is his second stay at Salonga Prison—never mind how or why. What's important is that the first time around, he ruled the inmates. Ruthlessly." Lee paused. "He will not settle for second place."

"He's inside already? Usually the inmates 'welcome' newcomers with this ritual of—"

"Scar needs no introduction. The only ones to greet him today were his fellow Muslims."

"Scar?"

"When you see him, you will understand the name. He will seek to kill you and slaughter your group. Probably tonight, out of sight of the guards. He and his men will most likely use metal from the bunk beds to fashion shivs."

"Shouldn't the warden—"

"The warden won't interfere with what he can't see."

Frowning, Jake exited the van. All those plans he had to restore hope inside the prison … he'd been so sure they were God's plans to be executed through him. He clamped his teeth, fisted his hands. Scar must not be allowed to take the leadership away from him.

Before closing the van door, he leaned back in, chains clanking, and put a hand on his quickly scribbled letters. "Make sure these get mailed, please."

If Scar prevailed, these were the last words his loved ones would hear from him.

Chapter 36

At the evening meal, Jake encountered his new enemy.

Scar was magnificent. Tall, lean of shoulder and hip, sweat burnishing well-developed muscles, skin unblemished except for a jagged scar forming two connected M's on his forehead. He wore the mark like a crown. Even the mosquitoes seemed afraid to land on him.

The man stood to the side of the meal line, not participating in the food distribution, arms folded across his chest. Eyes black as coal studied every movement, every prisoner. No one looked at him, yet each squirmed as his eyes lit on them, burning holes, leaving smoke behind. No one lingered in the courtyard.

From the dark archways behind Scar, a single voice rose and fell in a chant repeated at intervals by zealous voices. The noise filled the passageways of the maze and burst onto the courtyard like thunderclaps releasing lightning. Bolts of electricity leaped down Jake's spine. Spread to char his fingernails and toenails. Singe his hair. Melt his bones.

"Muslim prayer?"

Puno nodded. "They prepare to fight. There be no battle of champions in the open, but war in concealment."

Jake grunted. "Then we'd better prepare too." While he waited for his group to finish the food distribution and join him in prayer, he gave orders to his troop of frail soldiers.

Most of the men would be lambs easily slaughtered. He assigned leaders to each dorm room and told them to barricade their doors with bunk beds. "Make it impossible to get to you." For sure the invalids lying in the hallways would be butchered. "Move these men to the farthest point of the maze." There was no way to accommodate them in the crowded dorm rooms; distance would have to be their defense.

He shifted his own location to the dorm room closest to the archways. Men willing to fight would be stationed with him and in the dorm rooms nearby. For weapons, they disassembled bunk beds to create what arms they could.

Men who had disdained Jake's morning devotions now flocked to the prayer meeting. "You do well to come," Puno chided them. "Fear not for your bodies but for your souls. Fear Him who is the Judge, not those who send you to Him through death."

They met in the courtyard and lifted their voices to Heaven. Some with hands held high. Some with heads bowed low. Some on their knees or flat on the ground. Their supplications echoed against the concrete walls, magnifying their pleas into a thousand voices, rising like a pillared cloud into the evening sky.

Scar and his men filed out of their archways and stood at a distance, faces impassive. Jake felt Scar's eyes blaze into his, not challenging him but already triumphant. Fire ignited in Jake's soul. He lifted his head and stared back, chest expanded, power storming his lungs.

Scar raised his chin as if in acknowledgment of a dare accepted.

***

"He's playing us," Jake said. "Trying to wear us down."

Three days of waiting, and already the seventy-five men who had offered to stand with him had dropped to fifty. The volunteers' eyes were bloodshot, their limbs trembling from lack of sleep. None had experience with combat. All had vivid imaginations. Jake suspected many had laid victory alongside hope in a shallow grave.

"Scar will seek me out," Jake told the fifty. "We must use that to our advantage."

That night, the lights in the maze and dorm rooms did not come on. The darkness crimped Jake's carefully laid plan. "We'll make it work," he growled.

***

The stench of sweat exacerbated by anxiety permeated the maze and prison dorm rooms. Hours went by. Every rustle, every shift of tired feet, every grunt and cough and shuddered breath bred goose bumps and bristled hair. Mouths dried and throats wilted. Stomachs knotted and lungs shriveled. When the attack came, it would be a relief.

Dawn was the first intruder. In the dorm rooms, it cast a gray pall on every man, revealing his whereabouts, disclosing his identity. Heartbeats accelerated. Breaths came faster. Surely now their enemy would come.

A cry cut the air. Sentries or assailants? Jake's men rushed forward, stampeding the maze, jamming the archways. Flourishing weapons made from disassembled bunk beds, they shoved their opponents backwards into the guards' rifle sights. Warning shots rang out, puckering the ground.

Six assailants made it into the first dorm room. At the far side of the room, Jake jumped up from a lower bunk and brandished a four-foot-long piece of metal. *At last!*

"SCAR!" he roared.

His adversary stepped forward and charged. Behind Scar, ten of Jake's men converged on the other five assailants to cut them off. Jake tensed at the sight of the shiv Scar raised against him. He took a step back. His shoulders struck the top bunk.

One more stride, and Scar had him in striking distance.

"Now!" Jake yelled. On the top bunk, two men rose grasping a blanket between them and leaped off on either side of Jake and Scar. They slapped the blanket like a net over Scar as he lunged at Jake. The blade of the shiv ripped through the thin material and sliced Jake's forearm.

Jake grabbed his attacker's hand and spun him 180 degrees. He clamped his other arm around Scar's neck. The inside of his elbow locked under Scar's chin to imprison him gasping for air against Jake's chest. One of the jumpers grabbed Scar's shiv out of the way; the other hurried to block the breaking daylight from the window.

"Infidel," Jake's man with the confiscated shiv howled to signal the next step in Jake's plan. He backed away in tandem with Jake's men fending off the five Muslims. Eight of Jake's men fled as if yielding victory. Two slumped to the floor. In the diminished light, Jake hid behind his pinned captive. The Muslims took up the cry of "Infidel" and rushed to the bunk bed. Over and over, they plunged their shivs into the struggling prisoner beneath the blanket until movement ceased.

All at once, the overhead lights switched on. Jake's men crowded into the room and overpowered the five Muslims. "You have killed your leader," Jake bellowed. He stepped from behind his captive and flung off the blanket to reveal its victim. Eyes and mouth gaping, Scar's head flopped forward onto torn garments plastered in blood. "Take him and go!" Jake shoved the body at them.

His men let go of the prisoners, and three caught the body, two leaped at Jake. They knocked him backwards onto the bottom bunk and sprung on top of him, fists flailing his face. Jake grunted at the hatchet blow to his nose, the gouge leveled at his right eye socket. One eye functioning, he reached up and clapped hands of steel against his assailants' heads. The crack of their skulls colliding was most satisfying. He pushed the men off him and stood, legs apart to bolster rickety knees.

The two moaning opponents were pulled to their feet and thrust at their companions. Muttering guttural noises, the five men bore Scar away, and the remainder of Jake's volunteers filed into the room. Their mouths were thin lines, their faces sober. Jake grimaced at what it forebode: the battle was over, but not won.

"The guards collaborated," Puno said. "They turned the lights off for Scar's men to invade us. There will be payback."

Minutes later, Jake's name blared over the loudspeaker.

Chapter 37

Jake had wondered what the lone metal pole in the prison courtyard was for. A personal demonstration was the last thing he expected.

A rope threaded through holes at either end of the pole secured his hands and feet and suspended him fully stretched out, face to the pole. Even at this early hour, the morning sun had heated the metal to just short of scorching. He sacrificed his knees against it to keep his chest and face free of the scalding surface. The glare of sun against metal bit his one good eye.

He had been stripped of his shirt. Sweat slid in great drops over the scars on his chest and back. Scars carved by pit bull, clouded leopard, bullet holes. The cane lashes from the lone guard behind him would add a fourth species of scars to Jake's collection.

The murmur of inmates surrounding him pulsated like a three-day migraine. Close by, his group shouted protests against the injustice of his punishment. A glimpse of the Muslims showed them silently stoic, their faces equally angry but triumphant. Loudest of all were the cheers of group one. His heartbeat jumped at what looked like Captain Emilio at the back of the group.

Unable to twist far enough to confirm his suspicion about Emilio, he tilted his head and looked up. Above him, a solid line of guards filled the top of the three walls of the courtyard. Each held a rifle pointed at prisoners. On the fourth wall, the barred windows of the second-story prison offices were darkened with the heads of employees. A lone figure stood at the central window. The warden?

Black clouds had rolled in, blotting out the sky, threatening a late monsoon storm. A rare wind swept over the prison, forcing the guards to brace against it. It roared through the courtyard, trashing the air with debris, compelling the inmates to cover their faces. As if Jake were its target, the blast pommeled his body, jerking it, yanking it, jarring it until he cried out, sure the gates of Hell had been prevailed upon.

When the gale subsided, the inmates returned to their murmuring. Jake's body sagged from his bound arms down to his toes with an unholy ache. Red welts from slamming against the sun-broiled pole striped the front of his body. His vision blurred, his head swam. When he opened his mouth to gasp in air, big, black flies collided with his tongue.

And then, all at once, it was quiet. The synchronized silence of men holding their breaths.

Jake tensed. The clock of eternity ticked off seconds.

Tick.

Tick.

Tick.

And the blow landed.

Never had Jake felt such pain.

He screamed.

Again and again the supple bamboo of the cane cut into his back.

Pounding. Lashing. Pulverizing his flesh.

Until, mercifully, darkness shut him down.

***

"Jake." Puno's voice penetrated Jake's pain, brought him shuddering to the surface. "Get up."

He opened his eyes. Above him, the ropes hung empty from the metal pole. Two of his men pulled him to his knees, lifted him to his feet. He staggered, and they steadied him.

"Quick." Puno seized his arm. "We must go, before the guards shoot."

The shouts of a melee opened up Jake's ears. Clashing around him on every side were men in hand-to-hand skirmishes. "What happened?" he rasped.

"Our men jumped the guard when he refused to stop at ten blows. Then men from the other two groups attacked them." Puno tugged at him. "Quick. It's turned into a riot."

Jake waggled his head to clear his vision. "Where's the guard?"

Puno pointed to five of his men bent over a figure in a brown uniform.

"Take me to him." At the first step, pain seared every nerve in Jake's body. He doubled over and spewed stomach acid. "On second thought," he gasped, "bring him to me."

When the cluster of men holding the guard pushed its way to him, Jake pointed a shaking finger at the front gate. "We're taking him to safety."

Holding up Jake, the men, led by Puno, shoved their way through the fracas. At the gate, the guards seized their comrade, then Jake as well. With a squawk of protest, Puno slipped through with Jake. Behind them, shots spattered the ground and walls, and the echo of shouts and running footsteps swallowed the courtyard.

Without his men to support him, Jake's knees gave way and he sank to the ground. Blood seeped from his back to smear the welts on his front side and further stain his shorts. At a command from someone on the floor above him, the guards picked up Jake and ascended a set of stairs. Puno tenaciously accompanied them.

Fading in and out of consciousness, gritting his teeth at the pain, he was aware of someone cleansing and bandaging his wounds. Food and water were placed in his hands and shared with Puno. When Jake could stand, he and Puno were ushered back to the gate. Jake wore a clean shirt and shorts and carried a blanket.

"Seven days, you come to warden," the guard ordered. "You face the music." The gate clanged shut behind them.

Chapter 38

November

Did Jake know Thanksgiving week was coming up? Most likely not. Betty resisted the temptation to gather Crystal at the airport gate and immediately book a flight from Detroit to Manila. Wouldn't Jake and Crystal love that! But not, for heaven's sake, at that awful prison. She heaved a disgruntled sigh. Impossible anyway, until her passport and visa got straightened out. Crystal would have to make do with just her crusty old aunt for the Thanksgiving holidays.

"Aunty!" Crystal wove through the crowd of deplaning passengers and swooped into Betty's waiting arms, almost knocking her down.

Goodness, the child must have grown three inches since she last saw her. Betty held the sweet face between her hands and smiled so big the corners of her mouth hurt. The year on the island had bonded them beyond anything family ties could do. Jake and Eve too. Oh my, how could so many things happen to tear the four of them apart?

"Where are Grandma and Grandpa? At home?"

Betty's cheek twitched. It was all she could do not to snarl the answer. "Gone." She huffed and rearranged her attitude as if it were the hem of her skirt catching in the waist of her panty hose. "Off with friends on some kind of trip, dearie." She'd bawled Neal out for not staying home to spend time with Crystal.

"Oh good. I'm glad it's just you and me."

A catch in Crystal's voice warned Betty of the need for a serious discussion coming up. Something had happened at that boarding school Neal insisted on sending her to. The man was unjust in treating Crystal the way he did. Betty bit her lower lip. He was punishing Crystal for her mother's behavior. Probably hoping Crystal would run away from home too, when instead he should be making amends and giving his granddaughter the love he had failed to demonstrate with his daughter.

"We'll do fun things all week, sweetie, beginning tonight with that movie *E.T.* you wanted to see last summer. Can you believe it's still in theaters?"

It wasn't until Saturday, packing for Crystal's return to the academy, that Crystal finally broke down. "Please don't make me go back tomorrow, Aunty." When the child burst into tears, Betty held her until Crystal could put her misery into words. It was the first time Betty had seen Crystal cry since they left the island.

"I know how you feel, sweetheart. When I was your age, the kids at school picked on me too. Just because I was small and not growing like they were. I cried every day at how mean they were."

Crystal scrunched her shoulders. "I just want them to be nice to me, that's all."

"My mother told me we all want to be princesses. To be loved by everyone—or at least treated nicely. But you know what we don't want?"

"What?"

Betty suppressed a smile. Crystal obviously wanted to roll her eyes, just as Betty had with her mother. "We don't want *them* to be princesses."

Crystal blinked. "But I do. They just make it too hard."

"So you don't want to give them what they won't give to you."

"They're mean. Why should I? I'm not mean to them."

"And I'm proud of you for that." She kissed Crystal on the forehead and let the issue go. Just as her mother had with her. Sometimes sowing seeds was better than handing over an unwanted fruit basket.

***

After seeing Crystal off, Betty sorted through a drawer of loose keys. She felt downright sneaky, invading Neal's home office and getting into his files. Silly of her, since all she wanted was a copy of the Power of Attorney he'd drawn up for Jake and her after Jake's arrest. Oh my but it ached her back to hunch over the two-drawer cabinet, but if she kneeled on the floor she'd have trouble getting back up. She snorted at the picture of Neal returning home from his trip and finding her stretched out on the carpet inside his carefully locked office. As if she wouldn't have a spare key. The office used to be Frank's.

The document wasn't in the file folder bearing her name. She riffled through the other folders, found one labeled *Chalmers*, and limped to Neal's desk. The file was surprisingly thick. The Power of Attorney lay on top, but what was Neal doing with this—a copy of Ian MacBride's report for her on Eve?

Wait … She blinked. Not a copy, but an original bearing Neal's name as the recipient.

She gaped at the next document—pages and pages of detailed history on Jake. These also were from Ian MacBride, but this time with a bill made out to Neal. Her mouth dried to cotton. What was Neal up to?

The last document in the folder was a copy of a letter from Neal to District Attorney Bradley Henshaw in Chicago. Maybe persuading Henshaw to release her and Jake from the restraining order against Eve? Neal had promised he'd look into it.

She sat at the desk to read it.

No.

Neal wouldn't do this to her.

She flipped back to Mack's data on Jake. There it was: a personal note at the end of the report, saying Jake told Mack he'd killed a man on the island by accident. For a moment she was numb. The whole purpose of Neal's letter was to pass on this information and encourage an investigation of Jake. That the death was accidental was omitted. And nothing, absolutely nothing, was mentioned about withdrawing the restraining order on Eve.

Neal had deceived her. Worse, he had betrayed her. Outright lied to her.

She shook with fury. What else had he done? Was Jake in that filthy prison because of Neal? Was he the one who had bribed the judge to put Jake there?

She rose, her breath as wobbly as her legs, and returned the file to the cabinet. Oh, she'd been mad at how Neal treated Crystal. But now, as far as she was concerned, he was Public Enemy Number One.

As soon as he got home, she would face him—as judge, jury, and executioner.

Chapter 39

Once again, Jake's name blared over the loud speaker. By the time he trotted to the front gate, inmates packed the prison yard, curious enough to defy the furnace of the noonday sun and its militia of dive-bombing flies. The guards opened the gate wide enough to pull Jake through but refused to include Puno. Jake would have to face the warden alone.

Jake held out his hands for the guards to chain, but they shook their heads and instead motioned him forward. He braced for the prod of rifle muzzles burrowing into the tender flesh of his caned back. Instead, the muzzles stayed a respectful half-meter away. In place of an order barked to ascend the stairs, a mere nod indicated his destination. What was going on?

Behind him, the murmurs of prisoners echoed his question. With the guards busy attending Jake, the men were free to press all the way to the gate to gape and rattle the metal bars.

For a crazy second, optimism gripped him like a giant hand and squeezed the hope of freedom into a heady explosion of joy. Detective Lee … Betty … his children … Someone … had secured his release!

He climbed the cement stairs and entered the dimly familiar office where his wounds had been tended a week ago. Other than a token photograph of President Marcos, the walls were bare, as were the cheap laminate floor and four ancient desks manned by placid-faced clerks. Except for the whirr of a large ceiling fan rotating barely fast enough to displace the warm air from one corner of the room to another, the office was silent. Jake's exuberance ebbed.

One of the guards knocked on a solid wood door at the far side of the room. At a command from within, he escorted Jake inside, sat him in a chair, and stood to one side of the room, rifle ready. Behind Jake, someone closed the door. It clicked heavily into place.

In contrast to the barrenness of the outer office, this room was opulent. The rich hue of reddish-brown mahogany reflected light off floors, walls, and furniture. Photographs and paintings adorned every wall; oriental carpet in shades of purpled crimson decked the floors; black leather clothed a thickly padded couch and two armchairs—all radiating around a massive desk of deep mahogany and the man who stood behind it.

Jake sat in a spindly, high-backed, yellow cane chair. Nicked. No cushion. No carpet at his feet.

"I am Warden Mendoza." As if inviting Jake's inspection, the man behind the desk remained standing for several seconds. Jake obliged.

If the warden wished to surprise Jake, he succeeded. Judging by the careless way the prison was run, Jake had envisioned a sloven in charge. The man before him, however, was trim, his uniform a perfect fit, spotless with not even a hint of half-circles of dampness under his armpits in spite of the temperature and humidity of the room. Likewise, Mendoza's hair was tidy in both cut and cleanliness. His face was clean-shaven and his facial features comely enough.

Except for his eyes.

A black patch attached to a band around his head covered his left eye. His right eye, striated with tiny, red blood vessels, peered out of flesh almost as dark as the cloth patch over the other eye. Even a quick glance left Jake's gut feeling as if it had been walloped with a karate kick.

Was this why Puno had titled him the "forgotten warden"? Rejected because of his appearance and stowed out of sight—a zombie reigning at a zombie prison?

The warden sat down and folded his fingers together on the desk. "I thank you for saving the life of my prison guard." His words were formal. Starched like his uniform.

Jake waited. Would the warden ask for an explanation of Scar's death? Or about Jake's back healing? Perhaps even express regret at Jake's caning?

Nothing.

As if timed to the end of the warden's sentence, an office clerk rapped on the door and entered. He bore two cups of steaming tea with three small cookies on the cups' saucers. He placed one before the warden and handed the other to Jake to hold on his lap.

The warden sipped his tea, munched his cookies. Gall shot to Jake's throat. Was this some kind of token reward? He clenched his jaw against slamming the cup and saucer onto the floor. This was deemed worthy of saving a man's life?

He glared at the delicacies balanced on his lap, swallowed twice at the bile burning his tongue. No, best not to insult the warden. Defying the man would only reap retaliation. He forced a civil sip of tea and swept his gaze over the office. Ah, here was the better path. The grandeur of the room spoke clearly of what the warden valued.

Timing his consumption to the warden's, barely tasting the sugar-laden treats, Jake spoke at the warden's last gulp of tea. "I have a proposal that will benefit you and the prison."

Mendoza clacked his cup onto its saucer and cast a scornful eye at Jake.

Jake ignored the response. "Let me set the inmates up in a trade that will allow them to earn money. We will share the profits with you."

"Is this your escape plan, Mr. Chalmers?"

"Not from the prison, Warden, but, yes, escape from hopelessness and disease. At the prisoners' cost, they will improve their lot. You need only provide supervision."

The concept wasn't new. At the Manila City Jail, Jake had observed the simple trade exchange set up between prisoners and the outside world. For many, it was the only way inmates in the Philippine prison system survived. Coddling jailbirds was not considered part and parcel of punishing lawbreakers.

"The purpose of Salonga Prison is not to improve lots. Unlike your American prisons, we 'tan hides,' not pamper them." The warden twitched a contemptuous smile from one side of his mouth.

Oh yeah, he could vouch for that. Jake kept his face impassive. Better to continue offering the bait than argue. "The more the inmates can look out for themselves, the less money you spend on them. And you share in their profits."

Mendoza wasn't saying no. Jake's nerves buzzed at the encouragement. Time to bring the lure home. "Several men know how to make furniture and can teach the others. I will put up the money for wood and tools. The first profits will pay me back, then we all share."

"The first profits will include my share."

Jake pretended to chew on the idea before yielding. "Would you like to draw up the contract, or have me write one out?"

"Contract?" Mendoza spat the word at Jake. "There will be no contract."

"I am an American citizen using American money. If my government makes inquiry—or your government—we will be protected by an agreement in writing."

The warden banged his fist on the desk. The empty cup and saucer rattled. "Take him away," he shouted.

The guard snapped to and strode to Jake's side. Jabbing the rifle barrel into Jake's ribs, he prodded Jake to his feet and out the office door. The two guards standing by in the outer office joined him and escorted Jake to the front gate.

Puno awaited him. "You do not return as you left."

Jake rubbed his poked ribs. "It went better than I expected. He took the bait." He clapped Puno on the back. "Question is, will he swallow it?"

Chapter 40

Three days later, the loud speaker demanded Jake's presence at the front gate. His heart pounded as he pushed through the eruption of curious inmates spilling into the courtyard. Did the summons mean Mendoza was agreeable to a contract, or did it presage further punishment? Greed or pride—which had prevailed in the warden's heart?

This time, the guards placed him in chains and goaded him with rifles. The cement stairs to the offices presented a challenge because his feet weren't chained far enough apart to mount each step. He had to hop. The guards laughed.

Inside the clerks' office, he stood for what seemed like hours. Sweat drizzled from his forehead, cascaded over his eyes, dripped from his chin. The guards drank colas from bottles.

At last, the warden opened his office door and stood staring at Jake. Jake curved his mouth into a smile of greeting and nodded courteously. Yessir, a fan overhead, no flies licking his skin, no stench of sewage up his nose—the wait had been pleasant, thank you.

A guard prodded him to the same spindly, yellow cane chair. His sweat-sodden sandals squeaked on the polished floor, his shorts squished when he sat. Jake could almost see a hefty black cloud of body odor waft toward the warden's nostrils.

"I have a contract." The warden pulled a piece of paper from a desk drawer and nodded at the guard to hand it to Jake. The contract was brief: the prison would allow the production of furniture for trade by the prisoners at their cost, with half the profits assigned to the warden.

Jake had expected as much. "To avoid problems with my government, I need to add a few details." He kept his voice business-like, respectful. "Would you like me to use one of the clerk's desks to write them out?"

Mendoza paused, then waved a guard to escort Jake into the outer office. "Do not alter my percentage."

"Of course." Jake held up his chained hands. "May these be removed so I can write without staining the paper?" *Be submissive, maintain the warden as the one in charge.* Or as Puno had said, "Pet the beast."

Another wave of the warden's hand won Jake's freedom. A clerk yielded desk and pen to Jake, and he wrote swiftly in script tiny enough to cram everything onto the page. He and Puno had spent hours discussing what to include. "Feed the beast," Puno said, "but allow no access to the source of his food." Jake wasn't surprised to learn that Puno had chaired the business department at a prominent Filipino university until Marcos deposed him and stuffed him away at Salonga Prison.

Finished, Jake took the lolling prison guards by surprise and quick-stepped to a copy machine to print off one copy before they stopped him. "For the warden." He handed the original to a guard and pivoted to the warden's door to shield his own copy. No way he'd leave the warden with the only document of their transaction.

Seated once again in the spindly cane chair, Jake spoke before the warden's glower could harden into cement. "Please, permit me to read this out loud for your approval." Without waiting, he read the opening paragraph. For the most part, it was as close to fawning over the warden's generous permission as Jake could stomach. The next paragraph assigned the prisoners the full responsibility for the supplies, tools, production, transportation, and sale of the furniture. The prison guards would supervise them, as well as the safe storage of materials, tools, and products outside the prison walls.

The warden's scowl softened, but the gritty part of the contract was coming up. Beneath the warden's initial version, Jake had added financial terms that were more explicit. Until Jake's loan for the start-up was fully repaid, he and the warden would split the income fifty-fifty. Thereafter, the profit would be shared twenty percent to the warden as the representative of the prison, and eighty percent to split among the participating inmates. "That's twenty dollars to you, Warden, for every two dollars paid to four hundred inmates."

"That is not fifty percent."

"You're right, Warden. It's not fifty percent of what each worker makes, but ten times what each makes." Puno had emphasized presenting the payout with this configuration. Would the warden go for it? "Or we could pay them more and you receive fifty percent of their profit. But why settle for that when this amount"—Jake pointed to the contract in his hand—"would not draw my country's attention, nor, I imagine, your government's?" *Hold a sharp axe over the beast's head,* Puno had said.

Mendoza's visible eye all but disappeared beneath his beetled brow. Mouth and chin closed in tight knots, as did his fists. Jake hurried to get the worst part out into the open.

The last paragraph put the accounting into a third party's hands. Detective Lee's.

The warden crushed his sheet of paper into a ball and slammed it into a wastepaper basket. "We have no contract. No deal. Go."

Jake stood. "The Manila City Jail warden earned hundreds of thousands of pesos from the prisoners' trades when I was there."

Mendoza jumped to his feet. "Go!"

Puno awaited him at the gate. Inside, out of earshot of the guard, Jake filled his friend in. "I got to the last paragraph before he threw a fit."

"Ah, the beast has gone to lair. He will want to spit fire one more time before he concedes. Until then"—Puno pulled four fat envelopes from beneath his shirt—"Detective Lee was here and is rounding up what we need to start the furniture. He will return next week."

Jake snatched the envelopes from Puno. "Not to be rude, friend, but hold back my mail and you will have another beast on your hands." His fingers trembled. Four letters—a feast for his soul. He shuffled through the return addresses. Brett, Dana, Betty, Crystal. He headed for his bunk, the closest thing to privacy he could get, short of a pungent corner of the courtyard and piranha flies.

"Wait, Jake. There is more."

The tension in Puno's voice halted Jake's stride. He turned to face Puno.

"I learned from the guards where Captain Emilio disappeared to. After your fight, the doctor pulled him out and tended to his shoulder until his injury could sustain prison life."

Jake blinked. "The warden knew about this?"

"The warden favors him for his bribes."

All the old fury rose to Jake's throat. "I knew I'd seen him at the caning." He glared across the courtyard at group one's archways. "He's stayed out of sight since then. If he's hiding, it's not from fear. He's up to something, Puno."

Puno stroked his goatee. "Two enemies cannot rest in the same master's bosom. One of you must prevail. I suggest it be you."

Jake sighed. "Let's hope that contract didn't get me kicked out just now."

Chapter 41

None of the four letters Lee gave him bore good news. Jake raced through each one, craving the contact of his loved ones, then slowly reread them. By the end of the week, each would be memorized, yet he would still read them over and over. Touch where their hands had touched the paper. Gaze at the familiar handwriting. Hear their voices as thoughts flowed from pen to paper. And in Dana's case, inhale the perfume dabbed on her stationary. Her mother's perfume. From the bottle he had set aside for Dana when he first arrived home from the island. A lump caught in his throat.

He answered each letter prayerfully. They, too, would read and reread his letters. Memorize them. Take them to heart.

Dana's dismay was that she couldn't compete with the scores of her male peers' physical prowess. *Treasure the limits of your female body*, Jake wrote back. *God designed it perfectly as a gift to you, to your future husband, and to your children. Love being a woman. And remember, dear daughter, competition does not require domination.*

His son's distress lay at the opposite end of the spectrum. Although Brett had dated dazzling girls aplenty in high school, the charm had worn off now that he was in college. Where was the love of his life? *Patience, son. Your bride is on special order. Prepare for her by focusing on your job at hand. In two and a half years, as a graduate of West Point, you will be ready, and she will be waiting to rush into your arms.*

The letter from Betty required him to cool off first. Not only had Neal

Oakleigh betrayed them with the lie about the restraining order, but Jake suspected Betty was right about Oakleigh abetting Jake's deportation and arranging his imprisonment at the Salonga Prison. "When I confronted him with the file, he threatened to send Crystal to a different boarding school and get a restraining order against me. Jake, what do I do?"

He swallowed the rage shoving flames into his throat. *For Crystal's sake, you'll have to back off. Go ahead, though, and dig up what evidence against him you can. But whatever happens, remember what I learned (at long last) on the island—that God does not abandon His beloved. Don't look at circumstances, Betty, but instead look at God's heart.*

And then there was Crystal. Someone had framed her by putting answers to the semester pre-algebra test in her textbook. Crystal was the only one in class who got all the problems correct. Fortunately, her protest of innocence was listened to, and the whole class was given another test. Crystal aced it, but one student did significantly worse—Crystal's roommate, Allie. She admitted to setting Crystal up. At Christmas, Allie would be sent home for good. "She told me she did the other mean things to me too," Crystal wrote. "What should I do? I feel crummy about it, but I can't stop hating her. I want to be mean back to her."

Jake dreaded answering the letter. It required looking into a mirror and either turning away in denial of his own disfigurement, or rushing to the Great Surgeon for a facelift. He couldn't give Crystal answers he refused to obey himself.

He gritted his teeth and started in. *Sweetheart, we face the same problem. You with Allie, me with Captain Emilio. They've given us good reason to be angry. Yet God says payback is His job, not ours. That's because He is the great Judge, and justice from His hands is spot-on. But you and I don't qualify to be judges— not when we have our own sins to be judged for.*

The good news, Pumpkin, is that as God's beloved, you and I and all other believers are forgiven. On the cross, Jesus faced God's judgment for us and paid the penalty we owe. So our job as those who've received this sweet mercy is not to dish out punishment, but to show that God's compassion is real. He tells us we do this by "loving our enemies and doing good to them."

A wisp of a breeze touched Jake's cheek. His whole being quivered, and his soul swelled. Joy flooded him. He finished the letter, blotting moisture from his eyes onto the back of his hand. *Sounds hard, doesn't it? But loving them isn't about feeling all gooshy and happy toward them. It's about how we act toward them. When we "do good" to them, it sort of puts the spotlight on the bad things they did. I think that's what it means in Romans 12 to "heap coals of fire on their heads."*

So let's start heaping those coals, all right? We can share them in our next letter. And let's pray for each other's heart too, that God will cleanse us of hate. We need His soap for that.

It was a relief to hand over his disfigured mirror image to God. Still, his heart protested. Wasn't "doing good" to Captain Emilio the exact opposite of what would chase the rat out of the warden's bosom?

Chapter 42

December

Eve shook her gloved hand out of her pocket to grasp the stairwell's handrail. The steps inside the apartment building weren't icy, but melted snow from laden boots and coats made them slippery. Huh, so she wasn't the only one who used the Beachwood Apartment's back stairs. A month ago she'd started climbing them to add to her exercise routine at Ace's. Funny that in all that time she'd never encountered anyone.

She shifted her shopping bags of decorations to her other arm after passing the first floor. Excitement tingled the back of her neck. Her first Christmas in this apartment. She wanted the place fully decked out for Natasa. The party invitations had been hand-delivered to Brad, Marianne, and Stella this morning, but Rock and Natasa's had to be sent to his office address. She had no idea where he lived.

Two weeks until Christmas and then Natasa would be gone. Moving. Eve's elation spiraled into a noose that slipped over her heart and tightened. Why was it that no one seemed to stay long in her life? Even Chaplain Peterman had been reassigned to another state. The hospital's Sunday morning chapel service held nothing for her with him gone.

The heavy metal door to the street squealed in protest. She stepped to the banister and peered down. A man dusted in white flakes entered and stomped snow off his shoes, removed his hat, and batted more white flakes onto the floor. His black hair picked up the pinpoint of light from the surveillance camera above him.

The man with the Audi from the parking lot. The air in the stairwell swirled like a cyclone into Eve's lungs and barreled back out in one huge lunge. She grabbed the stair rail to steady herself.

The Audi-man started up the stairs, saw her, and clomped faster. "Hey, neighbor!"

Encountering him in the apartment lobby was one thing, but meeting him on steep, slippery stairs was another. The perfect place for murder if he was a Romero thug. She sprinted up the steps, her heartbeat outpacing her feet.

Above her, the third-floor door clanged open, and someone whistling a ditty took to the stairs.

Rock?

Rock!

She all but flew to him, stopping just short of throwing herself into his arms.

His eyebrows shot up, eyes and mouth wide open at the sight of her. "Eve, what are you doing here?"

She swallowed, chest heaving, grappling for some measure of dignity.

He grasped her arm. "Are you okay?" She nodded, and a frown flicked across his forehead. "Marianne said you had some kind of invitation for Natasa and me. I could have picked it up. You didn't need to make a special trip."

The Audi-man closed in and stepped around them but didn't stop. "Hey, neighbor." His glance fell squarely on Rock and avoided Eve.

"Hey," Rock said.

"You know him?" Eve shivered, not sure if it was in relief or another rise of panic.

"A neighbor on my floor."

"Your floor?" Eve stared at him. "You live at the Beachwood Apartments?"

Rock nodded. "Isn't that why you're here? To deliver the invitation?"

"I live here. Same floor."

"No kidding!" He almost sparkled with delight. "How long? I can't believe we haven't run into each other before now."

"Since September." Dread burrowed through her like a long, dark tunnel. "And you?"

"October. If Natasa had known that, she'd have bugged you all the time." His face fell. "I hate it that she's moving."

Eve's mouth ticked down. "Me too. My invitation is to a small Christmas party, which I'd like to double as a farewell party for Natasa, if you don't mind. I didn't know where you lived, so I mailed it to your office."

"How nice of you—she'll love it! Consider the invitation accepted." He glanced at his watch. "Not meaning to be rude, but I've got an appointment. See you later,"—he grinned—"neighbor."

She managed a weak smile and dashed the rest of the way to the third-floor door, shopping bags slapping her thigh. "Coincidence," Brad had warned her, "is an enemy in disguise. Don't trust it."

Rock Giannopoulus could be as much a Romero thug as the Audi-man.

With every step toward her apartment, she shook harder. It took several tries to get her key into the door. So now what? Move? Invite Wonder Woman back into her life? Learn karate?

The warrior with the two-edged sword flashed into her mind. Her fingers curled with the sensation of someone taking her hand. Warmth spread up her arm and cascaded like a waterfall to flow throughout her body. A calm of unbearable sweetness settled over her, ending in what could only be a whisper from above. *Beloved, I've got your back.*

Melted bones turned to steel. Angst transformed to mettle. She emptied her shopping bags of Christmas decorations and distributed them around the foyer, living room, and kitchen until good cheer in the apartment beamed as brightly as the exultation in her heart.

Lastly, she got out two more invitations and filled them in. One to Chaplain Peterman, who just might surprise her and come, and one to the Audi-man in 3E down the hall. It was about time she learned his name.

Chapter 43

"Dad?"

A rift the size of the Grand Canyon ripped through Jake's chest. He raced to the prison gate and plastered his son and daughter as close to him as the steel bars allowed. Their arms enveloped him, pressing his back, clasping his shoulders, gripping his neck and head with trembling fingers. First with Dana, then with Brett, he secured each dear face between his hands and smothered eyes, cheeks, and lips with kisses.

When at last they had exhausted tears and emotions, they stood back and surveyed each other with hungry eyes. Aside from copious sweat and overly friendly mosquitoes, their commonality ended there. The prison gate might as well have been the portal between two alien worlds. Jake had bathed from top to toe as best he could from the drinking water in the courtyard, but he suspected three months of ground-in grime and a bumper crop of bug bites overrode his effort to look somewhat normal. At least he wore the new shorts and shirt from the warden rather than the ragged, bloodied clothes of six weeks ago that revealed his true life in prison.

"Dad, this is awful." Dana, nose scrunched, teeth clenched, eyes squinting, grabbed his hand as if to pull him through the steel bars and make a dash for freedom.

He'd warned them about what they'd find after they wrote they were coming for Christmas. One step away from Auschwitz—how do you prepare your kids for that kind of venue? "I'll be out soon enough, sweetheart."

"When, Dad?" Brett's voice rose harshly in a battle between rage and helplessness. "We've tried everyone we can think of—the U.S. Embassy, our senator, even the commandant of the Marine Corps. They all say their hands are tied, that they can't reverse your deportation. Only the Philippine government can."

Jake's breath stilled. *The king's heart is in the hand of the Lord; like rivers of water, He turns it wherever He wishes.* If these authorities were bumping up against God's will, they wouldn't prevail. His heart squeezed, half-comforted at God's sovereignty, half-dismayed at God's choice. "It's okay, son. God may want me to walk through this, not around it."

Dana's chin and lower lip quivered. She blinked back tears. "How can we help?"

Brett nodded, hands fisted. "We'll take on Hell with you, if that's what's needed."

Joy, peace, resolution swept over Jake in a tsunami of love. He gathered Dana and Brett into his arms, mindless of the steel bars' resistance. No prison gate could separate them. He wasn't alone. It was time to stop counting zombies and start counting blessings.

***

At heart, Eve was a people-person. What a fool she'd been to cower in isolation all these months in fear of the Romeros! Happiness glowed in her chest, as bright as the crystal-clear Christmas lights suspended like icicles from the edges of her ceiling. A small Douglas fir decorated with fluffy girlie decorations in lavender—Natasa's favorite color—stood center-stage in the living room, radiating the fragrance of evergreen into every corner. Gifts, every one of them carefully selected for Eve's seven guests, tumbled from a generous pile beneath its branches. Until Natasa had to leave at ten o'clock, Eve's party was a tiny piece of eternity to be cherished.

"Natasa, could you be more beautiful?" Eve hugged her young friend, who looked at least sixteen, all dolled up in an ankle-length, velvet cranberry dress, hair snazzed into an elegant ballerina's bun adorned with holly. The gents, too, came spruced up in suits, except for the Audi-man—whose name turned out to be Robert Lopez —dressed, to Natasa's delight, as Santa. Who would have guessed he'd turn out to be such a hoot!

A week earlier, Marianne, Stella, and Eve had made a day of hitting the stores and sorting through vast possibilities of glamour. With Marianne making no secret of her wish to dazzle Rock, Eve had chosen a simple, silky red dress for herself, in contrast to Marianne's eye-catching, sparkly, silver one.

Chaplain Peterman was the last to arrive. The embrace he wrapped her in jerked a sob from deep in her soul. She clung to him for several seconds, knees suddenly weak from how starved her heart was for someone who loved her. Someone who knew her only as God's child, born as a thirty-four-year-old woman from the womb of a dark coma.

He had accepted her invitation to stay in the spare bedroom for the three days he was in Chicago. When Natasa prettily shook Eve's hand, thanked her for the party and gifts, and departed without a promise to write, disappointment wrung Eve's heart. "George,"—she plunked down on the couch, next to Peterman—"I'm trying to fill round holes with square pegs. So far, I've mistrusted two men who might be white knights, and I've trusted a princess who doesn't fit Cinderella's slipper." He took her hand, and she poured out her heart.

***

Romero's son unlocked his apartment door in time to answer the phone. Ridiculous to have to be back at midnight to receive his father's call. Even more ridiculous that Danny Romero, a prince among drug lords, would have to place the call from a stinking phone booth. He listened for the identifying raspy catches of his father's breathing, then reported in. "Party's over, Pops. Got all three mikes planted where they'll never find them." He hung up and headed back out the door.

***

Crystal's Christmas card to Jake was tucked into the same envelope as Betty's card.

Grandma and Grandpa took me to Disney World for most of Christmas vacation. Aunt Betty didn't come, she didn't say why, and I missed her horribly. We spent most of the time at the hotel because of Grandma's oxygen tank. She didn't like lugging it around, and Grandpa seemed embarrassed by it anyway. I had to go on the rides by myself, but some of the places were fun for all of us.

I bought a Mickey Mouse shirt to send to Allie as my next lump of coal. I wish she could come back to school and be my roomie again. Not to pile coals on her head, but because we're becoming friends. I think I'll ask Miss Lavender.

Betty revealed in her card that Neal had refused to let her come on the Disney trip. *Crystal told me about piling on the coals. Sorry, Jake, but it's all I can do to not hurl them at Neal's hind end.* In spite of his troubles, Jake guffawed. He faced the same challenge with Captain Emilio. Civil words through gritted teeth were the best he'd managed so far in the way of kindly coals.

Rage still scalded his gut from the destruction two days ago of the prisoners' first furniture shipment. He hoped Emilio was the rat behind it. If the warden, eager now for his fifty percent profit, could find that out, Emilio's destiny was a smoking bonfire.

Chapter 44

February 1983

The squawk of the smoke alarm jolted Betty awake. Heart pommeling, brain hurling startled thoughts, she choked in a breath and sat up. Valentines to Crystal and Jake lay nearby on the living room coffee table. A gap between the drapes revealed a coal-black sky devoid of stars. Drat that Neal, he was smoking in the house and had set off the alarm again!

She rose from the couch, halted as the acrid stench of smoke hit her nostrils. A curtain of gray gauze undulated on the ceiling. Her stomach bunched into knots. The alarm wasn't kidding. *Fire!* She sped toward the master bedroom.

"Clara! Neal!" The smoke thickened in the hallway. A vertical curtain of gray flowed from the bottom of the closed bedroom door to the ceiling. She jerked the door open.

Flames leaped halfway to the ceiling with the fresh blast of air. They had consumed the bedroom's wool carpet and sprung to the king-size bed. Bed linens writhed in blackened agony beneath a golden tongue of fire. At the side of the bed closest to Betty, Clara's oxygen tank sizzled.

"Clara!" The lump that had to be her sister under the charred bedcovers didn't move. A smaller lump lay where the pillow had burned away. "Clara!" she screamed.

She rushed toward the bed. Heat clawed at her skin. Flames bit her toes, reached higher to sink teeth into her pant legs. A wild animal, the fire forced her back from its prey. "No! Clara! Clara!"

Panting between convulsive gasps, sobbing her sister's name, she stepped back, beating the flames from her slacks. *Call 9-1-1. Get a bucket of water. Hurry!*

She stopped at the sight of Neal. He lay flat on his back on a brown leather recliner close to the bedroom door. His mouth was open, his left arm outstretched. He must have been reading a book and fallen asleep. Below his arm, the charred remains of a paperback lay on the Oriental rug setting apart Neal's chair, table and lamp from the rest of the bedroom. An ashtray lay upside down on the book. Wisps of smoke snaked a sooty path from the ashtray to the edge of the rug.

The bedroom carpet was wool; the Oriental rug was flame-retardant. Could Neal still be alive? She backed away. She didn't want to know. He didn't deserve to live.

She fled to call the fire department. "Get out of the house," they yelled. She sped toward the front door.

No.

She couldn't leave Neal to die, no matter how she felt about him.

In the narrow hallway, the smoke now hung a yard above the floor. She wet a towel, tied it around her face, and crawled on hands and knees to the bedroom. At least the carpet in the rest of the house was flame-retardant.

The heat was intense. Her clothing itched as if ready to burst into flames. Why hadn't she thought to douse all of herself with water?

A hedge of inch-high flames barred the bedroom doorway. Paint on the doorframe and plaster walls bubbled. She clamped her lower lip between her teeth and crawled faster.

With no more wool to fuel it, the carpet fire on all sides of the Oriental rug burned with low flames. She stood and stomped wobbly-legged through them to the relative safety of the Oriental rug. Groping for the recliner, she ducked back down below the roiling smoke. A glimpse across the room disclosed flames from the bed licking the ceiling.

She choked back her grief and shook Neal. Savagely. "Neal, wake up!" His skin was hot. She tried to detect a pulse in his neck, but her trembling fingers wouldn't cooperate. The towel around her head was drying. They had to get out, now.

She grabbed his legs and pulled. She weighed a hundred pounds; he was at least twice that. Impossible to put his arm over her shoulders and walk him out.

His body slid easily off the leather recliner. His head clunked with a whump onto the floor. If he was alive, it didn't wake him up. She'd have to drag him through the inch-high flames between them and the hallway, but at least his face was up.

The doorway wasn't far. She aimed her backside at it, positioned herself between Neal's knees, and tugged with all her might. At the threshold, she saw tiny sparks of red in the cuffs of her pants. Her feet were numb. She kept tugging. Smoke curled off Neal's clothes.

She was barely conscious that she was praying. The words hummed over the gray cells of her brain as if it were a beehive. When she collapsed, her ears picked up the distant shriek of sirens. Bursts of gasped air scalded her lungs. She curled into a fetal position. Her body throbbed. Smoke stung her nose, her throat, her eyes. The gauze curtain closed her eyelids.

Betty.

Jake? What was he doing here? She reached out, and a hand enveloped hers in warmth. Warmth that released her from pain. That warmed her soul. He took her other hand and lifted her to her feet.

She opened her eyes and looked up at him. But not at Jake's face … at her Lord's. His name pounded out from her throat, and she fell to her knees, bowed her head to the floor.

"Come," He said. "We go together."

She rose, knowing their destination. "*Abba!*" she whispered. Her joy crescendoed in exultation. "Our Father!"

PART 3

Chapter 45

March

Eve stiffened at Brad Henshaw's remonstrance. The words snapped like flames from his flushed face. "Don't take the girl!"

Eve's emotional thermometer skyrocketed. "You had no right to withhold this information from me!" She picked up the file folder on his desk and brandished it at him, knuckles white from her grip. He was not going to get away with this!

"I did! You were fresh out of the hospital; you'd had an encounter with your brother; and Danny Romero tried to kidnap you. The last thing you needed was more stress."

"That was nine months ago! And you've kept *on* interfering with my life. With *my* decisions!" Spittle wet the corners of her mouth. She swiped at it, lips trembling, nostrils flared. "You are *not* going to make this one. I am meeting with Crystal Oakleigh."

Brad flung his hands in the air. "Can't you see? It's a manipulation. You may as well throw your door wide open and invite Romero in."

Eve shook the file folder at him. "Here's what I see in here: Speculations. Fear. Unwarranted conclusions. A court case based on the contents of this file would get nowhere."

"Convince me."

"All right." She flipped open the folder, selected a document, and slapped it onto Brad's desk. "A report written by you about a phone call from the U.S. Embassy in the Philippines saying three people rescued by the Philippine Coast Guard claim to have been marooned on an island with me—Jacob Chalmers, Betty Parker, and Crystal Oakleigh. *No* further follow-up from the embassy or Coast Guard."

"The three said your name was Eva Gray."

She shrugged. "The name we agreed I'd use when I went undercover to Guam. Why I maintained it with those three is unknown. Any guesses are pure speculation."

Brad's clenched jaw twitched.

She slapped down the letter from Orville Marsh. "There is follow-up from the State Department: it found no confirmation of birthdates given by Jacob Chalmers for Betty Parker and Crystal Oakleigh. Unknown if they were a lie on Mr. Chalmer's part, or merely poor memory. Otherwise, all information he gave about himself was validated, including the fact that he is a veteran with high honors."

"As I recall, Mr. Marsh found his story untrustworthy."

Eve flicked her eyebrows in dismissal. "Unwarranted conclusions based on Mr. Chalmer's appearance and possible bad memory. Next,"—she tossed the letter from Neal Oakleigh onto the top of Marsh's—"a letter from an attorney encouraging you to investigate Mr. Chalmers for murder. An attorney who just happens to be the brother-in-law of Betty Parker and the grandfather of Crystal Oakleigh." She pursed her lips. "Sounds like a hidden motive in there bears checking out."

Brad opened his mouth, but before he could speak, she slammed the file's final two documents onto the pile. "Lastly, there's a sweet letter to *me* from Betty Parker, and a restraining order from *you* to keep her and Mr. Chalmers away from me—without my knowledge or consent."

"All right, stop!" Brad's face went beet red. "Sit down and listen to this." Mouth so tight his lips disappeared, he jabbed a phone number into his telephone keypad and hit the speaker button. "This is a wiretap on Danny Romero's phone."

Eve refused to sit. At Chalmers' voice on his answering machine, her heart skipped a beat —funny, since she didn't recognize it as part of her past. Then Danny Romero's voice, gruff, demanding, left a two-word message for Chalmers: *"Kill her."*

Her knees collapsed and her bottom hit the chair seat hard. She stared blankly at her boss.

***

Wringing her hands, pacing the floor of her foyer, Eve reviewed for the umpteenth time what she would say to Crystal Oakleigh. She did her best to ignore Lisa, sipping coffee in the kitchen, an irritating smile teasing her lips as the number of Eve's steps mounted. Wonder Woman's return was a concession to Brad, but, truth be told, Eve was glad for her presence. Danny Romero's mandate to Jacob Chalmers had set Eve's nerves ricocheting. *Kill her* was not the same as *kill Eve*, and the mandate could be a set-up—it was on a tape recording, for heaven's sake. But her dream at Marianne's apartment of the scarred brute on the island was incentive enough to yield to Brad's caution.

"You don't find it suspicious that all three of Crystal's legal caretakers died in one big house fire?" Brad's question cast thunder and lighting over her meeting with Crystal. Why was she even considering the responsibility of taking on Crystal as her ward in the first place? She didn't know Crystal. She didn't know Betty Parker. And she didn't know why Mrs. Parker had designated a stranger to be Crystal's guardian.

Because they might not be strangers. What if Crystal was the child hovering at the edge of Eve's memory? She had to check it out. The hunger of her heart one-upped the fear of the scarred monster in her nightmare.

The doorbell rang, and Eve halted. Couldn't breathe. Couldn't move.

Behind her, Lisa's chair scraped the floor. "Want me to answer?"

"No." The answer tiptoed from her lungs. Her fear wasn't of a gun, but of the wrong child.

She stepped to the door.

Unlocked it.

Slid her hand down to the doorknob.

Turned it clockwise.

Swallowed a cannonball of saliva.

Pulled.

Chapter 46

"Hello, I'm Hannah Lavender."

Eve blinked at the pretty face, the hand extended to grasp hers. She took it, resisted the compulsion to yank the woman out of the way.

"And this is Crystal. Crystal Oakleigh." The woman obligingly stood aside.

Crystal. Tall for a twelve-year-old. Arms and legs too long for her torso; front teeth too large for her face. She wore an acid-wash jeans miniskirt over striped, neon lime leggings that almost, but not quite, matched her shirt. Black Dance Reeboks with double tongues housed big feet. A scrunchie held a side-ponytail of long, crinkled blonde hair.

She was adorable.

***

Crystal stared at the beautiful woman in the doorway. Eve had been awesome on the island, but now, like, wow, she was totally radical. Shoulder pads huge in a stonewash denim jacket over a silk print shirt; hair big like the stars on *Dynasty*. Jake would fall over backwards.

She swallowed. Aunt Betty had said Eve didn't remember them. Didn't remember the island. Didn't remember they were family. Miss Lavender said Eve wanted to meet Crystal. Meet. Not live with her. Not be her guardian.

Not be her mom.

Only one way to deal with this. She raised her hand and fluttered her fingers. "Hi, Mom."

Eve's eyes went huge, her hands flew to her mouth. She stepped forward and pulled Crystal into her arms. "Crystal." Eve's voice choked. "I don't remember you, but my heart knows you."

A sob stirred to life in Crystal's lungs. "Oh Eve, I missed you so much, and now Aunty's dead." She threw her arms around Eve and hugged back.

***

The noise of hammering and men's murmurs faded as Jake read through his mail. Slim pickings today—only two letters, one from the twins, one from Crystal. Nothing from Betty. He used Crystal's envelope to fan his face and scatter mosquitos while he read the twins' letter. With Detective Lee's weekly visit to oversee the transportation and sale of the prisoners' furniture, the number of letters didn't bunch up anymore.

He stuffed Brett and Dana's letter into his pocket and opened Crystal's letter. It was surprisingly short. Usually she wrote every day and sent it as one long letter. This one was not only short but hastily scribbled in large script.

Jake!

Aunt Betty is dead. And Grandma and Grandpa. I can't stop crying. Miss Lavender came and told me. It's awful! The house caught on fire and they were in it. I can't write, it's too hard. I wish so much you were here. What am I going to do? I love you, Crystal

Betty, dead? For a moment, Jake couldn't grasp it. He read the letter again. Slowly, the reality poured over him like wet cement, weighing him down, blocking his brain. He sank to his knees. A groan scraped up his throat. Moans choked his breath.

Several men dropped their tools and ran to his side. "What's wrong?" Puno asked. He glanced at the letter crumpled in Jake's fist. "Bad news?"

"Betty ..."

"Your mother?"

"Dead."

The men dropped to their knees, placed warm hands on Jake, bowed their heads. Prayers surrounded his grief, reached out to lift their brother's leaden soul to heaven.

But there was no comfort.

He inhaled a jagged breath. A behemoth with coals for feet tromped from his lungs, through his windpipe, and out his throat, shoving his heart before it with broken wails.

Chapter 47

"It's only for three months." Eve patted Crystal's hand. "Your Aunt Betty put her will on the fast track, so we'll be good to go by the time school ends. Our trial period will be done, you'll officially be my ward, and we'll have all summer together."

Crystal turned her face to the airplane window, the corners of her mouth down, lower lip imprisoned between her teeth. Her lip quivered nonetheless. "Can I call you *Mom* then?" The words were barely a whisper above the muted roar of the plane's engines.

"You can call me Mom now." Eve smiled. The kid was like a flame on a candle, constantly melting Eve's heart. She had not a smidgeon of doubt this was the child from her memory. No matter what Brad said, Crystal was not a ploy of the Romeros. She was staying.

"Can we talk about the island when I come live with you?" Crystal rotated her head enough to see Eve out of the corner of her eye.

Eve's throat tightened. "Not until I'm ready." A shiver ran from her spine and down her arm, transplanting itself onto Crystal's palm. "We've talked about the island enough for now. It's giving me nightmares." Nightmares of the scarred man seizing her screaming from the jungle floor.

Crystal squeezed Eve's fingers and turned to fully face her. "I heard you yelling in your sleep. I'm sorry. There were some scary things that happened."

All it had taken to shut Eve down was Crystal's admission that Jake had scars on his face. *Kill her*, Romero had ordered him. Had he already tried it once?

"I bet,"—Crystal's face brightened—"like, maybe it was that python—"

"Stop." Eve withdrew her hand and raised it flattened at Crystal. "No more. Our lives from now on have to be based on this day forward, and not on what happened on the island. Can you do that?"

"But what about—?"

"Those are my terms, Crystal. Can you do that?" Her demand came out harsher than she intended, but taking Crystal on as her ward was already loaded with more challenges than she knew how to handle. "What will you do when the charm wears off," Brad asked. "Throw her back into the water like an unwanted fish?"

She wouldn't do that. Would she?

Crystal's mouth quirked down. Her shoulders slumped. "All right. I won't talk about it until you want to."

"We'll make new memories, okay?"

Crystal nodded, but there was no sparkle in her eyes.

"Now, tell me what Arlington Academy is like, what you're studying, and who your friends are."

Crystal screwed her mouth into a do-I-have-to expression. "Okay, but first, who's Marikit? You yelled her name in your nightmares."

Marikit? Eve hadn't thought about her since moving out of Marianne's apartment. She'd as good as thrown the young girl back into the water, hadn't she? The guilt stung. "Someone who died. I'm looking for her friends."

And she would. As soon as she returned home.

***

What would the warden think of Jake's new idea? For sure Mendoza liked the money he had pocketed the last several months from the furniture sales. Constructing a fenced-in area at the back of the prison had done the trick. The area was easier for the guards to monitor, and it protected the furniture from destructive inmates. Jake huffed. They still had no proof Emilio was behind the sabotage.

Tarp placed over the furniture at night was used during the day to provide shade by attaching the pieces to the tops of ten-foot-high poles. Heat rose to the underside of the tarp and rolled off to a hungry sky, creating a nature-made, if somewhat warm and humid, fan. Unfortunately, it had no deterring effect on the swarms of mosquitos attending the laborers.

Jake peered through the new fence to the land enclosed by the outer, twelve-foot-high chain link fence surrounding the prison. There had to be a swamp back there to generate so many mosquitos. He'd need binoculars to see where the fence ended, the land was that extensive. He grinned. Perfect for his plan.

A plan he ached to share with Betty. Grief stumbled from his gut to his bruised heart, past lungs shoving broken sobs into hiding, up and over his tongue to swipe the grin from his lips. He blinked back tears, pretended they were sweat to rub from his face. Hard, so hard to believe there'd be no more visits from her. No more hugs of encouragement. No more interceding for justice.

Crystal is with Eve. Betty is in heaven. Jake's heart leaped. Yes, Lord. Yes! Yours is the perfect plan! He slid his hand into his pocket, touched Crystal's letter conveying the good news about her and Eve, and smiled.

The men's chatter stopped, signaling the warden's daily visit to the furniture yard. Jake joined the others in dropping tools to the ground and standing with arms bent at the elbow, hands flattened to show they held nothing. Six guards trailed the warden, rifles at the ready, pushing men aside for the warden to inspect their work. He stopped at Jake's station last for a report on their progress.

"More men want to join us." Jake avoided the term *prisoner* or *inmate* in order to emphasize the men's humanity—a concept Mendoza sneered at. "To accommodate them we would have to expand the fence and buy more tools."

"Do it." Clearly it was no skin off the warden's back. The cost would come out of the prisoners' pockets, and the increased profit would line the warden's.

"I have a suggestion for using their labor in an even more profitable way." Jake waited for Mendoza to respond. "Keep him in charge," Puno warned. "Never be a rung above him on the ladder."

The warden ran his fingers over a finished table, stooped to examine its underside. "This work is inferior. Too many of these pieces are."

"I'm bothered too. As you've pointed out, unskilled workers hurt our products and waste our time. What do you think of putting those workers to better use—to bring in money from another trade?"

Mendoza eyed him warily.

"Horticulture." Jake swept his hand across the vista outside the furniture yard. "All that fertile soil is going to waste. In May the rains will start. Enclose the land to grow food, and the unskilled laborers can plant and harvest it to sell to the prison at a sizable discount. Salonga will have money left over from its food allowance for other purposes."

Most likely the savings would go into Mendoza's pockets. But Jake couldn't be responsible for what the man did with the government's money. And at least it would place food in the prisoners' bowls.

Mouth puckered in skepticism, Mendoza gazed at the weed-choked terrain. "I will think about it." His eye patch slipped downward on the sweat beading his face. He pushed it into place and exited the yard, his rifle-bristling retinue marching in his shadow.

Jake winked at Puno. They had the contract thought out and ready to go. It included a survey of the land, ostensibly to find the best agricultural site.

Only Jake and Puno knew its additional purpose.

Chapter 48

May

Eve accepted Rock's dinner invitation only because she wanted to help a broken-hearted Marianne. And, well, after all, it was Eve's birthday. A fact she kept secret as a defense against critics who would voice concern that, at thirty-five years of age, Eve was not married. The fact was certainly not a point of dismay for her. Although she couldn't recall the line of suitors Marianne said Eve had swept through, Eve had no doubt that Mr. Right wasn't among them. Unthinkable that such a man could have fallen through holes in her memory.

Remarkably, Rock happened to choose one of her favorite restaurants. Classy, with china, crystal goblets, sterling silver, and a centerpiece of fragrant, freshly-cut roses on white linen tablecloths. Soft music just loud enough to shelter conversations from nearby tables drifted from a pianist on a low, centrally located stage. Marianne had never mentioned a date with Rock as elegant as this.

She waited until the entrées were ordered before bringing up the romance. "Is it too forward to ask what happened to you and Marianne?"

Rock's mouth twisted into a grimace. "I figured I'd end up the bad guy." He shook his head, glanced at the ceiling, heaved a sigh of exasperation. "Your question presumes something happened between Marianne and me in the first place. Nothing happened. Ever."

Eve's mouth dropped open. "You mean ... but Marianne said ..." She corrected herself: "implicated ... that you two were a couple."

"Never."

"You didn't date?"

"She hired me to set up her new personal computer and tutor her. Treated me a few times to dinner because of the late hour. Or to a drink before we went to her apartment."

"Oh." Eve suppressed a groan. Poor Marianne.

"Stupid of me not to see what she was up to. I like her—she's pleasant, smart, a quick learner. The perfect client to work with." He puffed out another sigh. "When she asked why I didn't ask her out, I saw the light and, well, set her straight."

"Kindly, I hope."

"Of course."

"And you invited me to dinner because ..."

"Because my job at your office is done and I don't see you anymore. I thought you'd like an update on Natasa."

"I do." Heat rose to her cheeks. She'd forgotten all about the child now that Crystal was in her life. "And I'll update you about my ward, Crystal."

Rock's eyebrows rose, but his face didn't express surprise. Perhaps he knew about Crystal from Marianne. Her stomach gave a sharp pinch, whether from hunger at the aroma of her steak as it was set before her, or from ill-ease that Rock knew what was going on in her life, she wasn't sure which. Would she ever stop being suspicious about a Romero thug behind every bush?

***

Jake all but licked his empty rice bowl at lunch. He was ravenous from the hard labor of tilling the soil, and dehydrated from working under a hot sun with no water. He wanted to shake the warden for refusing the request for a five-gallon drum of drinking water in the field, and for a double portion of food to the horticulture laborers for at least one of their meals.

Puno informed Jake of the reason: Emilio. "A bribe in the hand sours benevolence in the heart."

Jake huffed. "Why would Emilio care about water and extra food?"

"You defeated him only in physical battle. The war is not ended."

And it wouldn't end as long as the two of them occupied the same turf. Fights between prisoners broke out daily, but no one had challenged Jake since Scar's death. Jake and Emilio's conflict was a Cold War, with the warden as the battlefield.

"Tarp," Jake growled. "We'll stake out pieces in the field to collect water when it rains." He should have thought of it earlier.

At least the grueling work of putting up new fence and removing vegetation from the field was finished—tasks that had to be done by hand because construction and farm machinery were too expensive to transport to the prison. Over two hundred men, more familiar with cultivation than carpentry, had signed up for the horticulture trade. Puno divided them into morning and afternoon teams to minimize the effect of inadequate food and dehydration.

At the end of the month, the field was striped with row after row of beds. "We're ready for delivery of the seedlings," Puno announced to Smiley. Two days later, the young plants arrived. Dried up. Dead.

"Smiley, come here." Jake beckoned him at the front gate. "What happened?"

Smiley shrugged, eyes wide with innocence. "Plants good last night. Too much heat today."

"Quick." Jake held out a check. "Buy new ones and bring them back as fast as you can."

"I hurry, but cost more." Smiley stepped forward for the check. Smack into Jake's trap. Before Smiley could escape, Jake reached through the bars, grabbed the front of Smiley's shirt with his left hand, and landed a powerful blow on Smiley's cheek with his fisted right hand. Man and check fell to the ground.

The guards laughed. Jake smiled and bowed. Nice to be able to count on them for entertainment humor.

Before Jake could grab him again, Smiley scrabbled backwards like a crab. Jake scooped up the check and pocketed it. "No more bribes, Smiley. Either deal with me or deal with Emilio, but no more doubling up. If you aren't back in four hours with new plants, I will tell Detective Lee to find us a new transportation partner."

Rubbing his jaw, Smiley trotted to his truck, skirted the trailer of wilted seedlings, and jumped into the cab. A cloud of dirt erupted from the back tires as he tore out of the parking area.

Puno joined Jake. "Vigilante justice?"

"Compassion, my friend, compared to what I'm going to dole out to Emilio. I'm sick of his bribes." He pivoted on his heels and strode toward the archways of group one. His fist tingled in anticipation of contact with Emilio's jaw. Or a hard punch to the solar plexus would prove equally satisfying.

"To heap coals on your enemy, I take it."

Jake halted. The rebuke landed a penetrating blow to his heart. Punishment was the prerogative of God, whether straight from His hand or through His approved means of man's legal system. He hung his head. "I told Detective Lee I'd rely on a higher Judge who can't be bribed. But retribution"—he shook his head—"trouble is, swift retribution brings such sweet satisfaction." He grunted in reluctance. "Guess I need to wait on God's timing for that too."

Puno chuckled. "Ah, heavenly retribution—now that makes me feel sorry for Emilio."

Heavenly retribution? Huh. All it made Jake feel was impatience to see how soon God executed it.

Chapter 49

June

"How's it going as an instant mom?" Marianne poured two cups of coffee from the office coffee pot for her and Eve. Marianne's cheeriness was forced, but better than the tears she'd been choking on since her "break-up" with Rock.

In contrast, Eve had to tone down her buoyancy. *I love being a mom!* she wanted to shout. Instead, she said, "So far, so good. I like it." She flinched at the acrid taste of the coffee. Definitely motivation to keep the conversation short and get back to work.

"What'd you and Crystal do on your week off?"

"Shopped. Decorated Crystal's bedroom. Saw *Return of the Jedi*. Oh, and found a private school we both like for next fall." No way was she going to send Crystal far away to Virginia. "The summer day camp didn't go over very well though—you know how it is making new friends at her age. But I didn't want her sitting home alone all day. We settled on one run by a church we might start attending."

"You, attend church? That's quite a concession."

Now, that surprised her. "Why not, I'm a Christian."

"Uh, you were quite the atheist, Eve. With fangs. Part of your memory loss?"

Eve did a quick assessment of brain, spirit, and heart. No question about it, she believed in God and loved Jesus as her Savior. "Whatever I was before, I'm solidly a Christian now."

Amazement swept across Marianne's face, followed by a fat-cat look of glee. Eve knew what that meant: h-e-l-l-o from the top of Marianne's office gossip list.

"Did you two talk about the island?"

"A bit." Eve couldn't help but snort. "Crystal said I was in love with Jake." Teenagers and their romantic fantasies …

"I can believe it. I saw him. Definitely handsome—although not the glitzy type you usually go for."

Glitzy? Eve sniffed in annoyance. "Was his face scarred?" A spasm pinched her throat at the thought of the brute from her nightmares.

Marianne's eyes widened, evidently remembering Eve's description of him as well. She eked out the briefest of nods.

"Wait. You saw him?"

"When he and Mrs. Parker came to the office and asked for you." Marianne described the visit and Jake's resistance to showing his ID to Brad. "But don't worry. He's in the Philippines awaiting trial now."

"He was deported?"

"Last September. Brad represented the U.S. at the hearing."

"He did what?" Eve slammed her coffee cup onto the breakroom table and stormed down the hall to Brad's office. Her high heels clicked on the marble floor like the timer on a bomb set to explode. "Are you deliberately hiding information from me?" Her voice boomed against the four walls of his office.

Brad's hair all but stood up. "What are you talking about?"

"Jake Chalmers' deportation." The three words sizzled.

"What about it?"

"You didn't tell me about it, that's what, much less your part in it."

"What's to tell?" His eyebrows punched downward in bewilderment. "It was a standard hearing, with the expected outcome."

"So … you played a recording for me of Danny Romero ordering Jake Chalmers to kill someone—someone you said was me—but you didn't think it was important for me to know that earlier there was evidence he murdered someone in the Philippines? Enough evidence, in fact, to substantiate his deportation."

Brad's face said *Oh*. "Honestly, Eve, once the man was no longer a threat to you, I moved on. I simply forgot about it."

"That man was reportedly on an island for a year with my ward, Crystal Oakleigh, and you forgot to inform me he might have killed someone there?"

"I told you not to take her on."

"Yes, without telling me Jake Chalmers was awaiting trial for murder." Her eyes flung daggers at Brad.

"Both of us were hot under the collar with that conversation, Eve."

"So why wasn't a transcription of the deportation hearing in the file?"

"Because the file was personal, one I kept for you. You just happened to find it before I was ready to give it to you. The transcription of the hearing is filed under official business."

So, Brad was looking out for her. Eve's anger deflated like a balloon. He wasn't trying to hide anything. Maybe she should have listened to him after all about Crystal.

She sank into one of his office chairs. "I have nightmares," she whispered. "I'm in a jungle, hiding. He finds me." She gulped. She could never get beyond that point. Terror always woke her up, erased what happened next.

"Have you and Crystal talked about the island?"

"A little."

"Has she brought up Chalmers' deportation?"

Eve shook her head. Did Crystal know about it?

"So she hasn't asked for your help in exonerating him?"

Eve startled. "No."

"Mrs. Parker, her great-aunt, came to our office, asking for you,"—a muscle in Brad's jaw twitched—"in spite of the restraining order against her. She wanted you to go to the Correctional Center to testify on Chalmers' behalf against deporting him."

A shudder vibrated ice-cold waves over Eve's shoulders and down her spine. That brute had been within walking distance of her office? And he'd wanted *her* to testify in *his* defense? What kind of power did he have over her to expect that?

She blinked. Was this why Betty Parker had made her Crystal's guardian—their connection with Jake Chalmers? What had happened on that island that put him in control of their lives?

She stood, agitation fueling her like rocket propellant. "I'm sorry I doubted you, Brad. Maybe taking on Crystal was the wrong thing to do after all." Her body quivered. "I'm picking her up in an hour, and we're going to have a long talk."

Chapter 50

It didn't help that Crystal was bubbling with excitement over her day at summer camp. In the car and on into dinner, she shared minute-by-minute details of every event, and word-by-word conversations with every friend. Eve ate it up. Again it came home to her how much this girl filled an empty spot in her heart. A spot she never should have filled with so little thought and way too much emotion.

After dinner, instead of turning on the news, Eve started her unhappy inquisition. Crystal stretched out on the couch, unaware her life with Eve was at stake, while Eve camped stiffly in an overstuffed chair to the side. She got straight to the point. "You've told me a little about Jacob … Jake … Chalmers. Do you know where he is?"

The immediate change in Crystal was unsettling. She sat straight up, darted a glance at Eve, then stared down at the floor. Eve could all but hear Crystal's heart pounding. It was a full minute before she answered. By then, Eve's heartbeat was burning fuel in its own race.

"He's in the Philippines." Crystal's throat bobbed in a hard swallow. "In prison."

Well, that was straightforward. Eve's shoulder muscles relaxed. "Why?"

"Because you didn't testify at his hearing. Aunt Betty tried to get you to go."

Eve inhaled sharply. Everything Marianne and Brad had told her, in a nutshell. "I meant, what is he accused of?"

"Killing a man."

No cover-up from this kid. "Did he? Do you know?"

Crystal nodded her head.

"Can you tell me about it?"

Another nod. "He told me and Aunt Betty. And Detective Lee."

"He told you. So you and your aunt didn't see it happen?"

"No. You didn't either."

Eve's eyebrows did a quick jump. "Then why did he want me to testify at his hearing?"

"Because you were with him when it all happened."

The interview was like pulling teeth one at a time. "I'd like to hear everything, from beginning to end, okay?"

"Okay." Crystal heaved a sigh and pulled herself into a crossed-leg position. "I was the first to see the yacht. It sailed into our cove, and I yelled for Aunt Betty because you and Jake were gone. Aunty and I hid in the trench and then in the cave cuz Jake wanted to check people out first in case they were bad guys—and they were. Like, big time. Pirates. Only we didn't know it till later."

Already Eve had ten questions to ask. She shifted into a more comfortable position and hoped the floating story pieces would eventually come together.

"We hid for a long time until Jake and you finally came. That's when we heard what happened." Crystal paused to stare at Eve. When Eve said nothing, Crystal continued. "It was bad. Two guys from the boat found you and tried to take you with them. Jake accidently killed one of them, and so did you. Then the two guys still on the boat came and caught you and sailed away."

"I killed one of them?" Eve could hardly get the words out. No one had mentioned a word about that.

"Uh huh. You made him fall and break his neck."

"I ... on purpose?"

Crystal sucked in her bottom lip and chewed on it. "I don't think you meant to break his neck. Just to make him fall so you could get away."

The fist-like grip on Eve's throat relaxed, and she gulped in a breath. "How did the other man die—the one Jake killed?"

"I don't know, except it was an accident, and to protect you."

"How did it protect me?"

"You were running away from the first guy, and Jake stopped the second guy from helping him. Then Jake found you and the first guy, dead, and then you and Jake went back to the second guy and found him dead."

The explanation left Eve cross-eyed. "What happened with the other two pirates?"

"They caught you and beat up Jake and tied him to a tree, so you said you'd go with them if they didn't kill Jake."

"You witnessed all that?"

"Jake told us. But we came out of the cave in time to see the yacht leave. Jake was mad at you for going with them."

Or mad because she had escaped him? Everything Jake said had no witness to corroborate his story—except, evidently, *her*. She shivered. Had he counted on her to be scared enough at the deposition to support him, no matter what the truth was?

"Mom, can you testify for him now?"

Eve quelled a nasty laugh. "I can't testify to what I can't remember, Crystal. I'd be of no help." Nor did she want to help. If anything, quite the opposite.

She gazed affectionately at her ward. She'd detected no guile in Crystal. Only confirmation that the warmth she felt in her heart toward her ... and the bond her blocked memory screamed was real ... tugged her in the direction of maintaining their relationship.

She had enough information now to adequately handle the tension between her memory loss and what had happened on the island. As long as Danny Romero and Jake Chalmers didn't touch her and Crystal's lives, there was no reason for her and Crystal to part.

***

A week later, a letter came in the mail for Crystal. From Jake Chalmers. Eve all but pushed Crystal into the living room for another couch conference.

"Jacob Chalmers is writing to you?" Eve's tongue sharpened the words into hurled spears. This must stop!

The spears appeared to not even part Crystal's hair as they flew over her head. Again without guile, Crystal said, "We write, like, every week. I'm almost done with my letter. It needs a special airmail stamp for overseas. Can we get one today, Mom?"

Eve stomped on her reaction to immediately forbid the correspondence. She took two big breaths to downsize her voice from shriek to normal. "I don't like the idea of you writing to a man in prison."

"But he's only there because …" Crystal let her voice fall.

So she was the bad guy. Eve gritted her teeth. "It would be best to wait until he's had his trial."

For a long moment, Crystal said nothing. Then, "He's fixing up Aunty's house—my house now. He needs to write me about it."

"How did he—" Eve's shoulders stiffened as understanding dawned. "Your aunt made him your trustee."

Crystal nodded. "Until I'm twenty-one, he's in charge of my money."

This was worse than Eve expected. The man had been given every advantage to manipulate Crystal and her money. Eve was remiss in limiting herself to only overseeing Crystal as her ward. To protect the child, Eve needed to know everything about Betty Parker, about her will, and about Jacob Chalmers.

And about the island.

Nightmares or not, she had to discover what had happened there. Somehow, Chalmers had bamboozled Betty Parker into putting him in charge of her estate. How big was it, and how could Eve kick the man out of power?

Crystal watched her from the couch, mouth drawn downward, body curved into a slump. Pity swelled Eve's heart. She'd never let go of Crystal now. "It's okay, honey. We'll get it all straightened out. I'm going to contact your lawyer to find out how to coordinate Jake's responsibilities and mine. In the meantime, how about if I read your and Jake's letters? That will help me understand what's going on."

"I'll get them." With the fire of a zealot, Crystal sped to her bedroom and returned with a large bundle of rubber-banded envelopes. "These are all his since we came back from the island, and I'll let you read the one I'm writing before we mail it."

Eve set the bundle aside to read later without Crystal's appraising gaze. So many letters! Surely they contained a gold mine of evidence to bring Chalmers down.

Chapter 51

October

Why did it seem as if God had put her in a long-distance hurdles race all summer long, and now into autumn? Eve's footfalls beat a steady rhythm against the track at Ace's Gym. Her breath labored from her lungs as she counted the frustrations she'd barreled into instead of leaping over.

The highest hurdle was her complete lack of success in finding the Sampaguitas. How could Danny Romero keep this "club" of trafficked Asian children so well hidden? In one way or another, she'd searched every inch of Chicago's 234 square miles. Romero must be moving the girls around. She clenched her fists. Was he getting the lowdown from someone—a mole in the office perhaps? Something to talk over with Brad …

Jake's letters to Crystal were another hurdle she'd bungled. No gold mine there after all. Thirty-five letters, and each glowed with good cheer and sage advice. Not one smidgeon of evidence for his manipulation of Crystal. The man was clever. She hated the helplessness of having to wait for him to blow his cover.

But the hurdle that sent her sprawling on her face was the one set up by Betty Parker's will. Crystal's lawyer had sent the dismaying information that not only was Jacob Chalmers the trustee for Crystal's inheritance, but he was also an heir along with Crystal. Of all the crazy things Mrs. Parker could do, she had adopted Jake as her son! She'd created a moat around her castle that made it impossible to unseat Chalmers from his role as trustee, or to forbid Crystal from corresponding with him.

To her surprise, Eve learned Mrs. Parker had left money to Eve too. A smoking-hot million dollars. Was it a bribe? But for what? She ground her teeth. Her memory loss was its own long-distance hurdles race. The doctors were now saying she had retrograde amnesia—with no hope of recovery. The race would never end; she'd never cross the finish line.

She stopped, bent over to catch her breath, grabbed her towel to blot the sweat beading her brow. Wait. Was that Rock at the weights? Her heart perked at the sight of him. She had recommended Ace's to him, and often they ended up at the gym at the same time. Lately it had become an occasion for them to catch a cup of coffee in the down time before Eve picked up Crystal from summer camp.

She sauntered over to him, liking the way his lips twitched into a smile when he spied her. His expression changed to a grimace as he set the weights down. Four hundred pounds for a bench press, not bad. "I'm glad you're a friend and not a foe," she teased. "You up for coffee?"

Rock rose to a sitting position, dismissed the man spotting him, and mopped his face with a towel. "Coffee it is."

The way he said it suggested he'd go for a better offer. A bit of a hint from her, she suspected, and they'd start dating. Ha! That was the last thing she needed in her life right now. Still, it was tantalizing to contemplate the relationship as a future possibility. More than a possibility, thanks to her neighbor Robert Lopez replacing Rock in Marianne's affections. The two were dating and often stopped by Eve's apartment to hang out.

Should Rock's niece Natasa be invited to Crystal's birthday party? It would be interesting to see if the two girls hit it off. Perhaps she'd bring it up to Rock while they had coffee. It was a long shot with Natasa living so far away, but maybe she could come for a weekend visit with Uncle Rock.

***

Eve frowned at Crystal across the kitchen table. Putting on a birthday party for Crystal's fourteenth was becoming an ordeal. "I don't want Natasa to come to my party, only my church friends." That was Eve's first disappointment. The number grew until it exploded in her face.

"A party at ChuckECheese? Mom, I'm turning fourteen. That place is for little kids. I want the party here."

Eve squirmed. That meant some moms would wait, sitting in the kitchen to chat. Which meant Eve being the odd woman out. No husband, no family growing up with other families in the church, and no idea of whose children were whose in the first place.

The explosion didn't hit until after Crystal and the girls gravitated from the living room to Crystal's bedroom, out of sight, out of hearing, freeing the mommy murmurs to focus on the girls. "Crystal is such a blessing to our youth group," a mother said, leaning toward Eve. "She's brought a genuine excitement and fervency to their prayer time for missionaries."

"Oh?" Crystal hadn't mentioned any prayer time, much less any missionaries.

"Our missionaries visit our church, of course, and talk to the youth group, but it's not the same as being intimately involved in their lives like Crystal is," another mother chimed in.

Eve pasted on a smile. Irritating that these women knew more about Crystal than she did. What missionaries did Crystal know, and what was her involvement? A carry-over from her Aunt Betty, perhaps?

"Crystal's stories about the men grab the kids' hearts, and my daughter prays for her assigned prisoner every day." The mother laughed. "I've started doing it too."

"Prisoner?" A sense of foreboding hit Eve's gut, and her stomach crunched into accordion folds. "Crystal hasn't told me about that."

"From Chaplain Jake's prison ministry in the Philippines." The mother frowned. "Crystal tells about each prisoner's response to the gospel, and assigns him to someone interested in praying for him."

Eve felt the blood drain from her face. "Are the girls writing to them?"

"No, just praying—"

"Because that's the last thing you want—any kind of personal contact between the girls and the prisoners." She could see the intensity of her words hit the moms like a slap to the face. But the message was too important to soften. Too dangerous to underplay. "I'm a federal prosecutor, and I can't warn you enough of how prisoners will manipulate the emotions of young girls and young women. It's a step down the road to sure disaster."

She stopped as the mothers' faces paled and alarm rounded their eyes. Alarm at her passion, or at Crystal's endangering their daughters? Her rage dropped like mercury in a thermometer at the end of a hot day. She forced a weak laugh. "Prayer, of course, is a wonderful involvement."

Should she tell them Jake wasn't a chaplain but a prisoner no different from the others? Tell them that Crystal—the girl without guile—had lied? That Eve's heart was broken, and it was all she could do not to bawl her eyes out in front of them?

No. She bit her tongue. It was better to talk to Crystal first.

She hadn't felt this fragile since waking up in the Cook County Hospital sixteen months ago. From that time on, she'd done her best to put her life together, to assemble the scattered puzzle pieces of her memory, to move forward. But all that effort involved her mental faculties, not her heart. Her heart's joy, next to God, was Crystal. Only the betrayal of Eve's father and brother hurt worse than Crystal's duplicity.

The awkwardness of Eve's explosion shortened the party. Less than fifteen minutes later, the mothers herded the young birthday guests out the door. Crystal, giddy with success, plopped down onto the couch. "Oh, Mom, thank you! Everything was like, so perfect! I love this church, love my friends in youth group, love that they love me!" She giggled.

"Crystal." Eve's voice was sober.

Crystal's elation vanished. She sat up. "Mom? Has something happened?" Panic sharpened her words.

"Yes. The mothers told me you said Jake is a missionary. A prison chaplain."

"Uh-huh. We're praying for the prisoners Jake tells me about."

Eve blinked at Crystal's bravado. "Crystal, you told them a lie."

Bewilderment spread across Crystal's face. "What lie?"

"That Jake is a missionary and a chaplain." She let her vexation color her words.

"But he is! That's not a lie."

"He's a prisoner, Crystal, just like the other men."

"That doesn't mean he can't share the gospel with them. He's in a foreign country, telling people about Jesus—that's what missionaries do."

Eve's fingernails cut into the flesh of her palms. She wasn't going to play semantics with a fourteen-year-old. "Does the church know he's a prisoner? That he's there for killing a man?"

Crystal's mouth screwed into a pout. "He's awaiting trial. He hasn't been convicted of anything."

"Do they know Jake is a prisoner?"

"No." The word punctuated a huff.

"I want you to inform anyone you've told about Jake that he is a prisoner. By the end of next youth group."

Crystal shrugged. "Okay, but it won't make any difference." She rose, snatched up her birthday gifts from the girls, and stalked stiff-legged like an indignant Pinocchio to her bedroom.

But it does make a difference, Crystal. Now I know I can't trust you—especially anything you tell me about Jake.

She slumped into a chair, head aching, heaviness settling into her chest. Foolish woman! Deep down in her heart, she'd half-believed she might have been in love with Jake after all—the heroic, head-and-shoulders-above-other-men-Jake that Crystal described from the island. Stupid romantic notions, all of them based on Crystal's integrity. She pressed her hands against her face.

Well, she was done with them. She got up, disposed of the trash from the party, collected the decorations and found a place to store them. The busyness helped clear her mind. Perhaps it was time she found reality in the man across the hall, who had given every indication he was ready to move ahead in their relationship.

Chapter 52

December

Jake stared at the number deposited in the bank account Betty had set up for him. "This can't be right."

"My thoughts too." Detective Lee grinned at him through the prison's front gate. "Perhaps the letter from Mrs. Parker's lawyers will explain it." He retrieved the bank statement he kept for Jake in running his account, and replaced it with a bundle of letters.

Jake selected the envelope from *Parker, Snyder & Oakleigh, Attorneys at Law*, opened it, and pulled out a sheaf of closely printed pages. He grunted. "This is going to take a while." He read the first page and flipped through the rest. "Apparently the amount is not a mistake."

Lee whistled a loud whoop. "You poor man, you're a multi-millionaire!"

"I had no idea Betty was rich, much less this rich." Jake shook his head. "I'd never have agreed to be her heir if I'd known it included an inheritance—especially one of this size. I'll write and tell them to give the money to Crystal."

"I'm going to do you a favor, brother." Lee reached through the bars and clapped a hand on Jake's sweaty left shoulder. "I'm going to let you read the rest of that document before I mail any letter to them. That may be Mrs. Parker's will you're holding in your hand, and she may have special instructions for you."

"Makes sense. But Lee, not a word of this to anyone."

"No problem." The detective headed for his car, then turned to hold up the letters Jake had given him to mail. "Here's an idea for you: set up a private post office as a trade."

Jake harrumphed. Another service the prison should offer but refused to prisoners. He sought refuge in his dorm room from the sewage stench and flies and read the letters from his children and from Crystal. Dana and Brett didn't have the funds to fly to Manila for Christmas, so they were spending the holiday with a friend. Jake felt sorry for himself; even more so now that, with Betty's money, he could have paid for their trip.

Crystal had already received news of her inheritance and was beyond excited. He unfolded the document from Betty's lawyers and confirmed it included her will. He and Crystal inherited the same amount of money, except that Crystal's was under his care as her trustee until she turned twenty-one.

In addition, there were gifts—among them, a million dollars to Eve, and ten thousand to Detective Lee. Jake chuckled. No wonder Lee had grinned. He must have already received his good news.

And what did Eve think of her gift? Now that Eve read his letters, he didn't dare ask Crystal. She probably wouldn't know anyway. Eve most likely would tell no one, perhaps even stuff the money away and not touch it, suspicious of Betty's motive.

After reading the will, he changed his mind about refusing the money. Lee had been right about special instructions. *Jake, at Salonga Prison we talked about your dream. If it hasn't already happened, I'd love to be part of it through your inheritance. You're a good man, Jake. However you spend the money, I know I can trust you to benefit others.*

Excitement sprouted like newly sown grain and grew exponentially. His dream—so that's why Betty had asked so many questions about it. Had even requested he draw a sketch for her. He found it and placed it inside the large envelope containing the land survey taken last spring. Hours later, he added a long letter, sealed the envelope, and addressed it for Detective Lee to mail. Hopefully, he'd have to wait only a few days to see the warden to present the dream—his and Betty's dream.

DON & STEPHANIE PRICHARD

He jumped from his bunk and trotted, head ensconced in silver-lined clouds, to the front gate to make the appointment with Mendoza.

***

"I have a dream, Warden, that can make you and Salonga Prison renown in all the Philippines."

December was usually the coolest month of the year, and Mendoza was about as cheery today as Jake had ever seen him. That pumped up Jake's hopes all the more. There were no Christmas decorations in the warden's office, but the desk of every office worker sported something of the season. Jake made it a point in his now-frequent visits to always greet every clerk and guard, and this afternoon they reciprocated his "Merry Christmas" with warm smiles.

"Fame at your hands is a frightening prospect, Prisoner Chalmers." Mendoza's snicker was as close to a laugh as Jake had seen the warden come. "What is this dream?"

"To design a new Salonga Prison. World-class. State of the art. There'd be nothing like it in the Philippines—perhaps in all of Asia—and you'd become the premiere warden of your country's penal system."

A flicker of surprise crossed Mendoza's face. He stared wordlessly at Jake.

So, their dreams meshed! Jake's heartbeat leaped like a racehorse out the gate. "I've sent a request to my former architectural firm for drawings to show you. I will cover the initial costs with a no-interest loan if it's agreeable with you that the prisoners build it with free labor." Actually, with incentives in the way of food and other amenities, but that was best addressed later. "The new prison will house more prisoners, with greater security—a model others will look to. It will be self-sustaining with food industries and prisoner trades to cover the cost of running the facility."

"My prison works well as it is."

"For zombies." The words were out of Jake's mouth before he could stop them.

Mendoza's head jerked. His nostrils flared in a long inhale. "So you are the savior who will raise the dead?"

"Or at least offer dignity until death."

Mendoza swiveled his chair to gaze out the window. "I will look at your plans when they come." Without looking at Jake, he dismissed him with a wave of his hand.

There had been no resistance, but Jake's footsteps weren't light. Instead, he felt the warden's pain. The pain of a forgotten man who yearned for recognition.

***

Christmas in Detroit. Eve snugged her heavy coat closer and puffed away a snowflake on her half-frozen nose. Of all the places in the world they could have gone on holiday, Crystal had voted for Detroit.

"It's a lovely house, honey. You sure you don't want to go inside?"

"No. I don't want to see where they burned to death. I just want to see it one last time now that's it's sold."

Ten frozen toes later, Eve walked with Crystal back to the taxi. The ride to the cemetery was long enough to thaw out nose and toes, but was no defense against the next bite of sub-zero temperatures.

In spite of the snow obscuring gravestones more than an arm's length away, Crystal had no trouble finding the two she sought. "Grandma and Grandpa." She pointed to a gray marble headstone, stood briefly in front of it, then stepped to one beside it marked Betty Lamar Parker. "Aunt Betty," she said. She removed her glove from her right hand and ran her fingers over the stone and the etched name. "Pink Rosato marble was her favorite. It's pretty, huh?"

"Very pretty." Sadness seeped in with the cold's icy teeth sinking into Eve's skin in spite of her heavy clothing. Betty Parker had written a sweet note trying to make contact with her. Things might have turned out differently if only they'd gotten together.

"The firemen said Aunty was trying to pull Grandpa out of the fire. I'm sad he's dead, but I'm glad it's you and not him I get to live with, Mom."

Mom. It had been two months since Crystal had used that name. Eve put her arm around Crystal's shoulders and snuggled the child against her side. "I'm glad too."

More than anything, she wanted her memory back. Wanted all the puzzle pieces of her life in place. Wanted to control her present and her future through knowledge of her past.

Who was she? Deep down and wide across, where the treasures and monsters of her life lay hidden and her secret self dwelt, what had made her who she was? And how were they influencing her, even now, on the pathway her feet unwittingly took?

At least she had Crystal. Someone to love and be loved by. Someone who bridged the gap between past and present. She mustn't let anything—or anyone—come between them.

Including Jake Chalmers.

Chapter 53

With every day a carbon copy of the one before it, and promising equally monotonous ditto marks for the next day, Jake sought to make good use of the eight weeks before the architectural documents arrived. In January, a letter from the firm updated him on advances in prison design, and he shared the information in increments to entice the warden.

Hot tea and three small cookies always accompanied their meetings in the warden's office. Jake timed how much data he shared by how slowly or quickly Mendoza consumed his treat. In January, Jake barely got to dispense crumbs. "'Direct supervision' marks state-of-the-art prisons now, Warden. As you know, prisoner surveillance has typically been linear—jail cells lined up one after another, guards patrolling the walkway alongside them. They can only see what's happening with the prisoners when they walk by."

"Salonga is not linear."

"No, but the men can't be observed except in the courtyard." Entombed zombies, out of sight, out of mind. "Almost fifteen men a month die in your prison, half of them because of prisoner violence where you can't see it to control it." The fact wouldn't tug at the warden's heart, but the loss of men affecting trade income might tug at his wallet.

Jake's crumbs fared no better at the next meeting. "State-of-the-art prisons use circular pods now. Jail cells are placed around the perimeter so guards stationed in the middle can see into all the cells all the time. Prisoners are safer, and remotely controlled doors keep the guards safe. More prisoners can be managed by fewer guards. A money-saver."

The warden's face with its one eye on Jake was a disinterested mask, and the tea, three cookies, and Jake's crumbs were swallowed in silence.

Jake proceeded at their next meeting as if there had been no interruption. "Disease takes the other half of your prisoners who die. Each jail cell in the new prison has its own toilet and sink, with plumbing handled by the prison's own sewage disposal plant. No more drums to drag out and empty, no more flies to spread disease, no more stench to flavor the air." Jake figured that alone was a winner, but the warden's face remained stony, his tea-sipping and cookie-crunching unaffected.

"No resistance says your fish has swallowed the bait but not pulled on the line," Puno said. "When the documents arrive, his belly will be ready."

The first week in February, Jake didn't bring up the prison. The next week, the warden surprised Jake by agreeing to tromp through vegetation to the new prison's most likely site. "When the topographical map arrives, it will show how many pods you can have." Jake waved his hand at the farthest distance of the prison lot. "I think there's even enough land here for trades like farming, livestock, and fish ponds. That would save on your food budget."

Still no response from the warden. Not one word. Not one question. So once again, Jake ate the next meeting's treat with no mention of the prison.

Finally, the week arrived when Detective Lee brought the documents. Jake could hardly breathe as he waited for Lee to open the doc-tube and unroll the plans. In spite of Jake's growing friendship with the guards, they weren't about to let him touch the suspicious-looking tube. It took sharp words in Tagalog from the detective before they allowed even Lee to shake out its contents.

"Good, the topographical map and schematic design." Jake longed to grab them and run. He allowed himself a glimpse of each page before asking Lee to deliver them to the warden. "Better you than the guards," he grumbled.

He contented himself with letters from Crystal, the twins, and his sisters while he waited for Lee to descend the stairs from the prison offices. "Let me guess," he said when he saw Lee's irritation. "He didn't say anything."

"Just set them to the side of his desk."

Jake couldn't help grinning. "I suspect the tube set the hook, and I'm going to feel tugging on the line soon." He handed Lee a list of materials. "Now that we have the map and schematic design, we can start a fast track on the foundation and canopy—assuming the warden agrees." Jake shook his head. "Man, I've been dying to order these and get going."

Dying. He laughed. He was the zombie architect, wasn't he? Giddy with a dream he hoped was about to come true.

***

With the floor plan spread out on the warden's desk, Jake explained *fast track*. "Once you okay the schematic design, we don't wait for the next stage of documents to arrive. Instead, we go ahead and put in the foundation wherever load-bearing walls and columns are called for. Pouring concrete and smoothing it—easy for the inmates to do. Along with that, we set the poles for the canopy roof and attach it."

Mendoza nodded. "No waiting." After days of studying the documents by himself, he had found his voice. "March and April is weather still dry and cool. Perfect." The gleam in his eye and the cock of his head witnessed to his confidence that he was back on the rung above Jake. "Construction can proceed under canopy when rains come in May and after."

Jake was pleased the warden particularly liked the idea of the canopy roof. True, it provided shelter from the rain and shade from the sun. But best of all, it allowed air movement from the floor up through the vented ceiling to an attic pocket under the canopy and on out to the atmosphere. Instead of the ceiling receiving the brunt of the sun's heat, the canopy took it. Simple and cost-effective, the physics of the layering made a difference of twenty to thirty degrees inside the prison.

Convincing Mendoza to offer incentives to the construction workers was not easy. "Why should they leave the income of their trades to work for nothing on the prison, Warden? There are morning and afternoon prison teams that work in the fields. How about more food for those who are willing to use the other half of their day to do construction work—maybe throw in a can of pop and a candy bar too?"

The warden's jaw muscles jumped, and his lips tightened downward. "They can have more food, no free pop or candy."

Jake grunted an unhappy consent to hide his smile.

"We can get prison workers besides the field teams," Mendoza said.

Exactly what Jake didn't want, but it wasn't wise to put down the warden's suggestion. "Theft of rebar—the steel reinforcing rods we put in the concrete—could be a problem among the more militant prisoners. Are there enough guards to oversee them?"

Mendoza frowned and switched topics. "Order the next level of documents from your firm, and what we need to start the foundation and roof."

"I'll get Detective Lee right on it. I'll also set up a 'critical path schedule' to define what's most important to work on at any given point in time. With the schedule, you'll always know what's going on, and what happens next."

Trouble was, so would Emilio if he got access to the plans through the warden. Even worse would be Mendoza allowing Emilio's group or the vengeful Muslims to work on the construction. Stolen rebar would make a formidable weapon against Jake and his men.

Chapter 54

April - May

"I knew it was too good to be true. We almost made it through April without problems, and now this." Jake, accompanied by the warden and his rifle-bristling retinue, surveyed the cables sprawled like dead snakes over the five prison-pod foundations. "One man with bolt cutters could do this in twenty minutes." He wanted to say a *guard*—bribed—but left the warden to accuse his own men.

They examined the five cranks that fed cables to a system of pulleys controlling canopy extension and retraction over each pod. The canopies, which yesterday had lain fully extended, now lay folded like accordions on their frames. No shade from the sun. No shelter from rain.

"How long before more cable can arrive?" The warden's question was unusually gruff, probably not because he cared so much about shade for the workers as he did about delay in the construction because of rain. Everything was set to go. The design development drawings had arrived yesterday, and last week all the materials necessary for laying the concrete block walls and inserting electric power conduits and plumbing lines had been delivered.

"Weeks, probably three," Jake grumped. "I suspect Smiley may know something about those bolt cutters. They aren't part of our tools." C'mon, Warden, take the hint, he wanted to yell. Let's see some justice here for once.

As if hearing Jake, the warden lifted his chin. "I will question him. Order the cable and tell the prisoners to keep on schedule. Rain in May is not frequent."

It was a week before Smiley's next delivery and consequent confession, another week before intermittent rain interfered with construction for three days. The warden gave Jake no details on solving the cable-cutting, but Puno, with his back-door connections, found out what had happened. "Smiley caved in when the warden threatened no more prison deliveries."

"Was the culprit Emilio?"

"Smiley knew only the guard, who conveniently vanished before Mendoza got to him."

"Convenient," Jake snarled. "Do you think Mendoza is covering up for Emilio?"

Puno shrugged. "A bribe in one hand, versus a few days' labor lost in the other … what do you think?"

"I think another dislocated shoulder will help."

Puno held out his hands, palms up. He raised his left hand. "Jake's retribution, or"—he raised his right hand—"God's retribution?"

Jake huffed. "You're right, Puno. I don't want my impatience to let Emilio off God's hook."

"Setbacks do not mean God is failing us."

Jake ducked his head. Is that what, deep down, he believed? That God was failing him, falling short as the Just Judge? Jake's eyes were focused on circumstances, weren't they, and not on the One sovereign over those circumstances. Guilt smote him like a sword to the heart.

Father, I know You are Master in all things, not man, and yet I keep flunking when tested. Center my eyes on You and my confidence in Your goodness, so that circumstances neither rule nor rattle me.

A sweet peace settled over him. He would be tested again. And again. Life was like that. Prison was like that. Emilio was like that. He snorted. God was like that.

And it was good.

***

Eve smoothed down her dress and checked out its fit in her full-length bedroom mirror. Rock had promised to make her birthday tonight unforgettable. It would have to be amazing, as already the past three months of dating had been like clinging to a raft shooting down canyon rapids. Once she had given the nod to begin a romantic relationship, Rock had pursued her with zeal.

Every day was touched in some way by his attention. At first with simple gestures like her favorite candy bar in her mailbox, or a single Easter lily tucked under a windshield wiper, eventually moving to gifts of Swiss-imported petit fours wrapped in gold foil, and perfume-exhaling bouquets of long-stemmed roses delivered to her door. He didn't bug her with daily phone calls or surprise visits. They saw each other only on weekly dates. He salted her, made her feel special, coaxed sweet awareness of him.

And he was going to top that tonight?

The evening was to begin with dining and dancing. She had shopped long and hard before she found what she wanted to wear: a deep-violet Victor Costa cocktail dress with huge cabbage-rose sleeves and a tightly fitting, ruched torso that hugged her curves. Four-inch spike heels she might need to shed for dancing, big hair, and big earrings to complete the drama, and she was powered for the night.

Crystal's response was gratifying. "Like, rad, Mom!" Then it must have dawned on her that Eve was decked out for Rock. Her shoulders slumped, and her mouth followed suit. Between Crystal and Eve stood the Unmentionable One. Jake Chalmers. Eve continued to monitor their correspondence, but beyond that, he didn't exist.

Eve sighed, wishing once again Natasa hadn't moved so far away. Surely the two girls would like each other and become fast friends. Rock would have a chance in Crystal's heart then.

Rock surprised her with dinner and dancing, not at any old expensive restaurant, but aboard an exclusive skyline cruise along the Chicago lakefront. She had worried she might be overdressed, but her fellow diners wore fashions from every top designer Eve knew. Women exchanged compliments and showed off their dresses for each other, boosting egos and everyone's delight in the evening. Another ego-boost was Eve's discovery that she was a skillful dancer. So, some of those suitors from her past must have been proficient dancers as well. She and Rock rarely sat out a dance.

"I didn't know how you could possibly do it, but you truly gave me an unforgettable evening." She cuddled up to Rock on the taxi ride home, and he put his arm around her shoulders. "I don't know when I've had so much fun."

"Oh, but there's more."

"More? Impossible!"

"I know you don't like coming to my apartment, but your birthday demands one last addition."

Eve quirked her mouth to the side. "I can't stay. Church tomorrow morning, and Crystal won't sleep until I'm home."

"Fifteen minutes max."

Eve laughed. "All right." He had piqued her curiosity. It must be a gift of some kind.

Chapter 55

Eve had been in Rock's apartment before, but an addition to its décor was immediately apparent. Before she even stepped inside the door, the scent of roses drifted into the hallway. Multiple roses. Their perfume was just short of inducing a migraine. A trail of crimson petals led from the front door into the living room and straight to the couch. Attending the petals on every side were vases of different sizes, all containing crimson roses. A lone long-stemmed rose sat on the coffee table in front of the couch. Next to it lay a gift exquisitely wrapped and ribboned in, yes, red.

"Oh my!" She blinked as Rock turned overhead lights onto the dim setting. She slipped off her heels, put her purse next to them, and walked to the couch. The rose petals, cool from the air conditioning, placed silky kisses on the bottom of her feet.

He sat next to her and placed the gift onto her lap. "Happy birthday."

The wish was spoken so soberly that she decided to follow suit and not make light of the situation. No giddy *for me?* No shaking the gift and making a silly guess. She simply unwrapped it.

Inside was an elegant gold box. Clearly one designed for jewelry. She swallowed. If it was pricey, she couldn't accept it. She didn't know where the moral came from, except that it was part of who she was.

"Go ahead, open it." Rock gazed at the box as if curious himself.

She removed the lid. An indigo pouch with a pale sliver of ribbon for a drawstring lay inside. The velvet of the pouch caressed her fingertips as she picked it up and emptied its contents onto the palm of her left hand.

Her heart lurched into her throat. It was a ring. A diamond ring. The diamond was at least three carats. She stared at it.

"Eve." Rock took the ring, turned her hand over, and slipped the glittering rock onto her ring finger. "I love you. I've never met a woman as amazing as you. Will you"—twice, he cleared the hoarseness from his throat—"will you marry me?"

She didn't know what to say. *I don't love you.* But her heart was headed that direction, wasn't it?

Rock slipped his arms around her and nuzzled her neck.

"We"—she gasped in a breath as warmth spread across her chest and down her arms—"we've only dated three months."

"We're not children. We don't need more time." Rock turned her face to him. "I love you, Eve." His lips settled on hers, gently prodding. He slipped his fingers into her hair at the nape of her neck, pushed her into a more demanding kiss. His other hand slid to her chest, caressed the skin above her dress.

Eve's warrior jolted into her mind. Scowling. Sword gripped in both hands. Her eyes flew open. "Rock, stop!" She put her hands on his, pulled them away, rose to her feet. "I have to go."

He stood up with her. Pulled her tight against him. "Eve …"

"Don't!" Panic scorched her throat. She shoved fists into his chest. "Let me go."

Rock dropped his arms and stepped back. "I'm sorry, I didn't…"

She strode to the front door, swept heels and purse into her hands, and left.

At her own door, fumbling for keys, she dropped her purse twice. Rock didn't follow her, but he was probably watching through his door's peephole. The back of her neck prickled, driving a hail of goose bumps down her spine. It took three tries to insert her key and unlock the door. By the time she stepped inside, she felt like a fool.

In the foyer light, she saw Crystal standing in her bedroom doorway, eyes wide, mouth gaping. Eve's cheeks heated in sudden awareness of her disheveled hair, crushed cabbage-roll sleeves, and a rose petal peeking from the bottom of her right heel. How explain this?

It wasn't until Crystal's eyes settled on Eve's left hand that she remembered the ring. She was still wearing it. She grabbed hold of it, blurted out, "He asked me to marry him."

Crystal's face froze into a mask. She sucked in both lips, blinked several times.

"I didn't say yes."

Crystal's chin corkscrewed into a clutch that pulled the corners of her mouth down. She backed into her bedroom, a sniffle barely above a whisper accompanying a jerk of her chest.

Eve exhaled a weak sigh as Crystal disappeared. The ring on her finger didn't exactly say no either, did it?

For sure, she wasn't trekking across the hall to return it right now. She needed to regain her composure, think of what to say. What a fool she'd made of herself! Of Rock too. He'd been presumptuous in his expectations, but aside from that, the evening—even the proposal—had been perfect. He didn't deserve the bad ending she'd given him.

Would he be willing to wait on an answer? She didn't want to say no, but she wasn't ready to say yes.

Ready had to wait not only on her heart, but on Crystal's heart too

Chapter 56

June

Forget Ace's Gym. Today was one of those days for dumping caution and yielding to the great outdoors. Eve exited her car, spent several minutes stretching leg muscles, checked the security of her water bottle's attachment at her waist, and took off down Lake Shore Drive. At six o'clock in the morning, the jogging path was relatively free of pedestrians and runners. Good. Her emotions were in a jumble and needed soothing. Running leveled her out: pinched what was low into a jump skyward, squashed what was high into a slope downward.

Her emotional high was a week old. High? She snorted. More like a rocket blast to Mars. In a matter of weeks, she would become a magistrate, an appointment that could jump-start a career as a federal judge. Given her memory loss and absence of over a year from the courtroom, her chances for nomination to circuit and appellate judgeships were doomed. Experience as a magistrate, however, opened a back door to the positions. The opportunity gave wings to her heart, and she stepped up her pace from a jog to fly down Lake Shore Drive's footpath.

On the downside was Rock. His response to waiting for her answer had, understandably, been cool. Their next three dates were increasingly tepid. Then, on the very day she'd received the news of her appointment, he said goodbye. "I got a job offer in California I can't turn down." No regrets for the end of their relationship colored his words. Within two days, he was gone, his apartment vacant, no forwarding address. She felt as if their relationship had stepped off the roof of the Sears Tower.

She stopped on the footpath and lowered her head, heaving breaths of air in and out of her lungs. Wiped tears and sweat from her face. Straightened and trotted back to her car.

Elation and depression. Where was the middle ground? She'd been praying for relief.

"No answer doesn't mean no listening." Chaplain Peterman had done his best to comfort her in last night's phone call. "Don't let misery be your interpreter of God's providence."

She smoothed a towel over the driver's seat to catch her sweat and plopped onto it. In other words, if she could see behind the scenes into God's mind, she'd probably slap herself upside the head at how perfectly everything—good and bad—was working together.

Crystal had suggested they move too. A house this time. A place the two of them chose.

The distraction appealed to her. They'd start looking on Saturday.

***

Jake leaned into the cool gust of the car's air conditioner. Detective Lee's weekly visits were the one time he could fully escape the torments of heat, stench, and insects. "Any news from the lawyers?" Occasionally he had Lee check with the two men to bug them if nothing else. How could they keep saying the judge had Jake on his docket after a year and a half of inaction?

"Same story. No progress," Lee grumbled.

Jake's spine curved into a limp C. The slump always surprised him. Every time, he was sure he had his hopes in a tight grip. Every time, they slipped through his fingers to his feet.

God had him here for a purpose. The reminder straightened his shoulders. "At least we're making progress here. The working drawings arrived, and we're ready to go for the long haul." If rain, typhoons, and delays in deliveries, not to mention sabotage, didn't interfere, that would be eight months. February.

Brett and Dana would graduate from West Point next year. With the new Salonga Prison completed in February or March, Jake hoped it was on God's critical path schedule to free him to attend the twins' graduation ceremony in June. He glanced at his hands. Calloused. Fingernails jagged. Dirt so ingrained it looked like a tattoo. He'd be gripping that hope mighty tightly.

He handed Lee a paper. "Here's what we need to hire in the way of skilled workers and technicians. Nothing more here the prisoners can do."

Lee folded it and slid it into his shirt pocket. "We'll have to start digging into your inheritance now."

"Money is only a means of exchange"—Jake grinned at the ease of a philosophy afforded by a deep pocket—"and I appreciate your honesty in being my exchanger." He didn't doubt Lee's integrity, but that didn't mean Jake declined balancing his checkbook with the bank statement and receipts either.

They swapped Jake's letters to Crystal and his family for their letters to him. Savoring them in private gave him the incentive to leave the car and trudge back into the prison.

Crystal's envelope was thick with several folded sheets of paper. Jake chuckled. There must be news items beyond the who-said-whats of school and youth group that comprised most of her letters. And indeed he was right. His heart jumped at the changes she reported in Eve's life. Not that Eve had been appointed a magistrate, but that Rock had moved away.

Crystal had never called the man Eve's "boyfriend," but the letter Crystal wrote after glimpsing the engagement ring on Eve's finger had spilled every bean in the pot. Up until that point, Jake, for the most part, had been successful in corralling his thoughts and longings for Eve. Had done his best to channel them into antiseptic prayers for her welfare. Had abandoned all intent of pursuing her should he get out of prison.

But now, with that … that … interloper gone, he found himself kicking down the corral rails and setting its captives free.

Fool!

All he was doing was making himself all the more a captive. To Eve, he was nothing but a convict. A murderer. An intruder in Crystal's life. Even if he got out of here, he was forever branded with the prison bars of Salonga.

No magistrate would align herself with someone on the wrong side of the law.

Chapter 57

September

Eve and Crystal stood on the sidewalk and gazed at the house. "I think we found it." Impulsively, Eve grabbed Crystal's hand and squeezed it. Crystal let out a hoot and threw her arms around Eve. They had visited the house on South Hyde Park Boulevard four times. Each time they'd crossed off other possibilities for faults the Hyde Park house surmounted. It was time to take the big step and buy it.

The plum-red brick house, draped with a shawl of ivy over its north side, dormer windows crowning its third floor, a three-car detached garage in the rear, and a six-foot, black, wrought-iron fence marking its boundaries, was a matriarch of the neighborhood. Most of the other residences on the street were apartment buildings converted into condos with six to eight units.

The boulevard, lined with stately maple trees at least eighty years old, was a noisy conduit of urban traffic, with city buses that hurled down the street at breathtaking speeds every twenty minutes. At the southern end of the boulevard lay the Museum of Science and Industry, a majestic limestone structure converted from its original 1893 construction as the Palace of Fine Arts. Shops and restaurants of every ethnicity began a block away in every direction, along with parks and more condos.

"You should have a reception," Marianne exclaimed the day Eve closed on the purchase. "Celebrate your new home and your promotion to magistrate at the same time."

Once the idea took root, Eve moved swiftly to execute it. The busyness helped push Rock to the back of her mind. Rooms were painted, drapes selected, and plush carpet installed in the living room and her and Crystal's bedrooms. Crystal's furniture and antiques undamaged by the fire at Aunt Betty's were moved out of storage and delivered, and a moving date set to vacate Eve's apartment.

"Install security devices," Brad insisted. "Alarms, cameras, monitors, the whole deal."

"A bit of overkill, don't you think?" Eve flipped through a catalog listing hundreds of security gadgets. For almost two years, there had been no threats from Danny Romero. And now that she was a magistrate, she wouldn't be able to prosecute him anyway. He was free of her.

Then the newly installed security system revealed three mikes hidden in the furniture moved from her apartment. Her stomach pinched for a week. She felt violated. Her apartment, her privacy, her life—all had been exposed to somebody's scrutiny. Who had been spying on her? And why? She upgraded her security to top-of-the-line.

A possible answer came a week and a half later. On the third Saturday in September, she stopped by a Hyde Park florist to determine whether she wanted to use its services for her reception next Saturday. Her order filled a sheet of paper. Grand bouquets for the foyer and for the dining room table, flashy but smaller arrangements for every room in the house, and simple vases of multiple flowers to supplement the flower power in her living room. Any flowers but roses.

Chin, the owner, an elderly man of Asian descent with brown, almond-shaped eyes and as many wrinkles on his face as silver hairs on his head, showed not only patience but delight in waiting on her. For two hours they pored over books of flowers and bouquet arrangements and toured his refrigerated storage room. He knew his flowers, and it was obvious he loved them.

How could she not place her order with him? The bill made her swallow twice as she paid it, but for the first time since learning about the microphones planted in her apartment, she felt as if she could breathe without her stomach stinging with pinpricks.

The jangle of bells on the door of the shop drew her attention to an African American man of slight build wearing gray slacks and a white lab coat. *Chin's Florist Shop* embroidered the left breast of the lab coat. Outside the door, a white van sported the same logo.

"I'm double-parked," he said. He sauntered past Eve, and the pungent odor of cigarette smoke machine-gunned the fragrance of the shop's flowers.

"Excuse me." Chin flashed a smile at Eve, handed her a receipt, and hastened to the back of the shop. He opened a door to a room with a central counter surrounded by metal bookcases. Every horizontal surface was stuffed with vases of flower arrangements. "Eight bins." Chin pointed to the right and stepped aside for the deliveryman to enter. "The blooms are fragile, so be careful."

"All these to the same address?" The man emerged hugging a large bin with tiny white flowers peeking over the top. "What are they anyway?"

"Sampaguitas. All eight bins to the same address, yes. A nightclub."

Eve dropped her purse. Fingers trembling, she picked it up and shuffled backward out of the way. At the sixth bin she came to her senses.

She had to follow that van.

Trouble was, her car was parked too far away to get back before he drove away.

She dashed out to the street. Squeezed between parked cars. Stopped to look both ways. Where was a taxi when you needed one? *Please, God!*

The man brought out the seventh bin, placed it into the back of the van.

Was there room for her to squeeze in and hide? She waited for the man to reenter the shop before sticking her head inside the raised hatch. The perfume of the Sampaguitas filled her nostrils.

No. There was barely room for the last bin.

Please, please, please, God! She moved away, looked up and down the street again. She should have run to her car, risked she'd get back in time to follow the van.

252

Behind her, the van door slammed shut. She pivoted and saw the left turn signal flutter red. The vehicle pulled out into the left lane and stopped at a traffic light, its signal still blinking.

Eve sprinted across the street to the corner. The light turned green, and the delivery van made a left. Eve chased it, high heels clattering on the sidewalk, slamming her knees. If only she had her tennies on, she could keep up with it. The van wouldn't outdistance her in this stop-and-go traffic.

And then God answered her prayer. "Hey, lady!" A brown face poked out of the driver's window of a yellow vehicle and flashed a smile. "You wanna taxi?"

"Yes!" *God bless you, friend—you are going to get a tip that will feed your family well tonight!* She jumped into the taxi, gasping heaves of air, and stretched her arm into the front seat, finger pointing at the windshield. "Follow that white van, but don't let him know."

The driver laughed. "Jus' like in the movies."

"Exactly." She echoed his laugh in a panting chortle of relief, then louder in gratitude to God for the answered prayer. Not just the answer of a ride, but of what might be the answer to a decade-long chase.

When the van pulled behind a building to make its delivery, Eve noted its address and had the taxi driver return her to her parked car. She had read about the Brits' portable Vodafone featuring thirty minutes of wireless talk time. She wished she had one to call Brad Henshaw.

He'd probably be at the office. Should she drive there, or go home to call him? Her house was only minutes away. What if the office was bugged, or maybe the mole was there to overhear? Risks she didn't want to take.

She called from her house. "Brad, can you meet for coffee in fifteen at the Corner Café?" Did he detect the tremor in her voice? Her hands shook when she got behind the wheel again. By the time she arrived and found a parking spot, she had to walk five blocks to her destination. The thump of her heart pulsated against her eardrums with every step. Her breath wrenched out from lungs tight with excitement. The top of her head felt as if any second it might lift off from her skull and rocket to the heavens.

By the time she collapsed into the booth across from her boss, exhilaration had her torn between tears and hysteria.

Brad signaled for a waitress. "Catch your breath and order your coffee. I can tell you're about to burst."

When she finally settled down into a cheek-stretching grin, she let the news bust out. "We've got him, Brad. We've got Danny Romero! I think those were his mikes in my apartment. Maybe that's how he knew where I was sending the detectives all the time to check for trafficking in his nightclubs. Or maybe it was a mole in our office. Doesn't matter. My mikes are gone, and there's no mole here to hear us. We can get him."

She told him about the large delivery of Sampaguita flowers. "That's what Marikit said she and the other children were called—Sampaguitas, because the girls were Asian, like the flower. Brad!"—she grabbed his hand—"I think Romero is featuring them tonight, putting them up for show. Please, you've got to check it out!"

Dignified, Lincolnesque Bradley Henshaw actually cackled. Actually rubbed his hands together in delight! "I'll send an undercover cop tonight and have a raid ready to go—without going through our office." His grin radiated to the corners of his eyes and lit his face brighter than the Christmas tree lights at Millennium Park. "Let's hope the big honcho himself is there."

"Let me go with you, Brad. It's the culmination of everything I've strived for against Danny Romero."

Brad frowned, tapped the fingers of his right hand on the table. "You know I can't let you participate. I'm sorry."

Eve huffed. Okay, then she'd find her own way to be there.

Chapter 58

Brad would kill her if he knew she was here. Eve leveled her binoculars at the nightclub nestled in darkness down the street. She was parked too far away to see anything. Anyway, she should have brought binoculars with night vision.

"Here they come! See 'em? No lights flashin' to give warnin'." Beside her, her new cabbie friend from earlier in the day pointed at half a dozen police cars and vans screeching to a halt at the front and rear of the nightclub. "Want me to pull up so we can see better?"

We. Eve laughed. 'Lijah's excitement almost exceeded hers. After her generous tip this morning, he'd given her his name and said he'd come running whenever she called, day or night. "Not yet, 'Lijah. Not till they come out with everyone cuffed."

It was hard to sit. To wait. To inhale the stale scent of passengers-past that radiated from the cab's back seat. She cracked her window open. "Have you ever been in a raid, 'Lijah? I want to know what it's like."

'Lijah inhaled a noisy snuff. "Once maybe." He peeked at her, took in her grin. "Maybe more 'n once. Cops, they come bustin' in, send your heart through the roof with their yellin' and pistol-wavin'. 'Don't nobody move,' they yell. 'Hands behind your heads.' And all you wanna do is run."

"Did you?" Her stomach lurched to her throat. Would Danny Romero have an escape route handy?

"They got ya cuffed before your feet can move. Got ya inside the police van and hauled off to jail, and all ya can think about is you hope your mama don't find out."

They both laughed.

"Here ya go—they got 'em outside, stuffin' 'em in the vans."

"Go!"

'Lijah stomped on the accelerator, cab tires squealed, and Eve's head hurtled toward the windshield. She barely caught herself in time. "Whoa, 'Lijah! Slow and steady or we'll end up cuffed in the paddy wagon too."

Too late. Every face was turned toward them. Two policemen approached the cab at a run, pistols in hand, arms locked in a straight aim at her and 'Lijah.

"Oh Lawrd help us!" 'Lijah moaned.

"Get out of the cab, hands up," the policemen roared.

Eve slowly opened her door. "Don't run, 'Lijah. I've got your back. We'll be fine." She stepped onto the roadway and up onto the sidewalk. Before she could open her mouth, a policeman had her hands cuffed behind her back and was marching her toward the arc of police vehicles now barring the street.

"I'm Judge Eriksson," she barked at her captor. "Take me to Attorney Bradley Henshaw, right now."

A tall figure broke away from the crowd of blue uniforms and strode toward her. "What the—" He halted and glared at Eve. "I told you to stay away!"

"I did. The raid is over." She gave him a sweet look instead of the defiant one she wanted to fling at him. "C'mon, Brad, don't cut me out now."

"Let her loose"—Brad snagged Eve's arm in a steel-tight grip—"and hold the cabbie."

'Lijah moaned.

Eve eyed the group of young girls being escorted to a police van. Sixteen of them. All Asian. A half-cry, half-whimper escaped her throat. "Sampaguitas!"

"Not all of them are. I'm sorry, Eve." Brad's hold on her arm softened.

She looked closer. The tallest girl, clad more provocatively than the others—probably the "hostess" of the girls—turned her face toward Eve.

Raised her eyebrows in apparent recognition. Smiled. No … sniggered.

Eve's breath stopped, caught in a bear trap.

Natasa.

"I … that's not …" *No.* It must be Sissy, Natasa's cousin … or whatever she was. This girl looked like Natasa, but older, much older. Wicked … not sweet and innocent.

Her knees went weak, and Brad's grip tightened to support her. "Natasa. I'm afraid so. And not twelve years old, by any means." His voice went gruff, the way it did when he had something to say he didn't like. "It gets worse, Eve."

"You didn't get Romero?" Shock burst like a spark inches from a pool of gasoline in her chest. She inhaled heavily to extinguish it.

"We got Danny Romero. Red-handed."

"Then what—?" Her gaze traveled in sluggish confusion along Brad's raised arm to his pointed finger to its target.

Rock.

A policeman was pushing Rock's head low enough to miss hitting it in his climb into a police car's back seat.

The car door slammed. Her heart echoed it in a jump-start to her brain.

Rock?

He had been in the nightclub? He visited prostitutes? She blinked at the fog creeping into her gray cells.

Her eyes leaped back to Natasa, Or selling their services?

She gasped, grabbed at Brad's arms. Horror churned her stomach. Sucked the marrow from her bones.

"Another deception," Brad growled. "He's not Rock Giannopoulus. He's Ric Romero, Danny Romero's youngest son."

Everything inside Eve went cold. Shut down. Hardened to stone.

From far, far away, she heard a voice of steel say, "Get me to the cab. I'm going home."

***

The next morning, Eve rose from a sleepless night and telephoned Brad. "I want those flowers that were delivered to the nightclub." When they arrived at her house, she stuffed an armload into the back seat of her car and mashed the rest into the trashcan. She told Crystal she'd be back in an hour and drove to the cemetery where sixteen-year-old Marikit Santos Torres was buried.

She hauled the flowers to Marikit's grave and dumped them in front of the gravestone. "I made you a promise …" The words struggled from her mouth.

She sank to her knees. The ground was cold on her legs. Hard as stone. One by one, she broke the stem of each flower and piled the debris like a funeral pyre onto the grave. The harsh treatment of hauling and dumping the Sampaguitas had loosed their blossoms. Her throat caught as the oval petals, white as snow in sunlight, settled like a satin blanket across the gravesite.

The memory of young Marikit came to her, as fresh as if she'd visited her in the hospital last night. A white sheet had covered the slender teen up to her chest, revealing a spectrum of black and blue bruises across her arms, bare shoulders, and face. Her left eye was swollen shut. Blood caked her lips, both ears, and a swath of cuts across her cheeks.

Marikit. Danny Romero had gotten to the girl and ended her life before Eve could get her to a safe house. But now he'd pay for it. Pay for all the young lives he'd ruined. Tears blurred Eve's eyes, washing away the memory. The tightness gripping her throat loosened.

"These flowers are laid to rest with you, Mari. I'll bring different flowers next time. The Sampaguitas are done. It's over. The girls have been rescued, and Danny Romero arrested."

She stood, fighting the tears that made her voice crack. "You were brave, Mari. You risked your life to save little Tala, to get her back home." She clenched her eyes shut and inhaled deeply, as she had four years ago, fighting the horror of Tala, only eight years old, trapped in trafficking by Danny Romero. Mari's rescue failed, and Mari had paid the price of her life.

"Tala was there with the girls, twelve years old now. She doesn't talk." Eve stopped, her lungs clamped shut. The tears she'd been damming flooded her face until finally she could breathe again. "But maybe," she whispered, "maybe it's not too late and she can be helped."

"I'll tell her about you, Marikit. And I'll tell her … I'll tell her justice has been done."

Chapter 59

January 1985

Jake slammed his fist onto Mendoza's desk. "This has got to stop! I tell you, Emilio is behind this sabotage."

Seated behind his desk, the warden glared at the spot of mahogany Jake had dared to violate.

Jake took a step back. "I'm sorry. I shouldn't have done that." He inhaled twice to lower the flames fanning his anger. Offending the warden was not going to win the man away from Emilio and his bribes. "There must be something we can do to stop this destruction." *We*—as if he and the warden were on the same page.

"Soon, Emilio will be gone."

"Gone?" Jake lowered himself into the spindly cane chair facing the warden's desk. Gone where? To trial? To death row?

"He has served his time. Papers have come through."

"Served his—" Rage blasted Jake out of his chair. It fell backwards onto the floor with a loud clatter. The prison guard in the corner jerked his rifle to his shoulder. "Served his time?" Jake slapped his palms onto the edge of the desk and leaned in. "You mean paid a bribe!"

The warden shot to his feet. "Sit down! How dare you talk to me so." Lips and eye tightened as he watched Jake place the cane chair back onto its legs and plop down. "Guard, remove him."

Jake snarled at the rifle barrel poked into his ribs. He wasn't chained. It took every bit of grit he could muster to not smack the rifle away and slam the guard to the floor. This time he didn't apologize. Didn't kowtow. He hated all this groveling before the warden to win his cooperation for something the warden should be doing in the first place.

And releasing Emilio from prison? Jake strode through the prison offices, banging the doors behind him so hard they sounded like rifle shots. The guard ran to keep up with him. At the prison gate, Jake flung the gate wide after the guard unlocked it, making the little man chase after it, cussing.

He stopped in the middle of the courtyard, every muscle taut, fingers flexing in and out of fist mode. As for Emilio … he'd rather kill him than see him go free.

***

Jake let Puno persuade him to wait the two days until Detective Lee made his weekly visit. "No bribe is big enough to set free a murderer," Puno insisted. "Lee has access to records. Get facts, then act."

Lee arrived a day early with a contingent of technicians to work on the new prison. The warden, as usual, toured the construction site with Jake and Lee. Not once did the unmasked eye look Jake's way, nor did the tight lips address him.

"A bit of tension between you and Mendoza?" Lee asked, once he and Jake were alone in Lee's car.

Jake cranked his neck to release the tension that had ridden his shoulders like a cowboy with spurs during the inspection. "Emilio," he grunted.

"Now what?"

"Mendoza said he's served his time and is getting out soon."

"And you aren't saying good riddance?"

Jake stared at him for a minute. "You don't know, do you?" How could that knowledge have slipped by the detective? "Emilio is the captain of the *Gateway,* the cruise ship that disappeared after he murdered all the passengers except Eve, Betty, Crystal, and me."

Lee's head jerked backward. "I didn't know." His eyes darted from side to side, as if scanning his memory. "I remember about the hunt, but there was nothing in the newspapers and nothing said in the police department about the captain being caught." His eyes latched onto Jake's. "I would have heard."

"Then he's in prison for some other reason." The tightness in Jake's stomach flipped into a chest-radiating glow. It soared to his throat, the tips of his ears, the top of his head. "Emilio has never been arrested for the *Gateway* murders. We can get him!" He grabbed the detective's shoulders as if to hug him. Lee leaned away, and Jake laughed and slapped him on the back. "How soon can you find out what he's here for?"

Lee shoved a bundle of letters at Jake. "Get out of my car, and I'm on my way."

"Get right back to me. I can't wait a week."

"You bet. A soon as I find out what crime he's here for—and I've stopped his release."

Jake didn't hug the guard who escorted him back to the gate, nor the two guards holding open the iron bars. But when he got to Puno, he locked the little man into a bear hug, lifted him off the floor, and danced around his dorm room, laughing and laughing.

***

Dear Jake, Crystal wrote. She went on for pages about returning to school after Christmas vacation, and the usual who-said-what among her classmates and youth group friends. Jake jumped ahead to the end of her letter, where she always talked about Eve.

Eve's still grumpy about Danny Romero getting out on bail. She says last year a good law was passed that wouldn't let him get bail if he was a danger to the community, but the judge said he wasn't and let him go until trial. Oh, I said judge, but it was a magistrate. I'm learning all about the differences now that Eve's one. She said Romero is going to postpone the trial for as long as he can. But she's also happy because, whenever it happens, the evidence against him will put him away for good.

Jake smiled all the way through his letter back to Crystal, telling her about Captain Emilio. He left room to add onto it when Detective Lee returned with further news. He also dared to ask a question Eve probably wouldn't want brought up: *Have you ever told Eve about Captain Emilio and what happened with all the passengers?* He knew Eve read his letters. Maybe his question would prompt her to ask Crystal about the event. Even better would be if it prompted Eve's own memory of what had happened.

Dana's envelope contained two letters. He opened both before reading them. One was from a young man whose name had been mentioned more and more often in Dana's letters. Bentley Hampton. Jake read it first.

Colonel Chalmers, Sir:

We met four years ago at West Point soon after you returned from being shipwrecked. I am in love with your daughter and want to ask you for her hand in marriage. We would like to marry soon after we graduate in June.

I will leave it to Dana to present my character to you to avoid presumption on my part.

Respectfully, Cadet Bentley Hampton

Jake bowed his head. He'd missed out on Dana's years at the Point. He had left her there as an eighteen-year-old girl, and now she was a woman of twenty-two. Soon to be a second lieutenant in the United States Army. Soon to be a wife. In those four years, he'd gotten to see her three times. Once after he returned from a year of shipwreck on a Philippine island, and twice at Christmas break while he was in a Philippine prison.

Not sadness, not regret, but a sweet joy permeated his soul. How good of God to have placed her in the safekeeping of West Point, of her brother in the same place and time-frame, and now of Bentley. Jake's journey over those four years had been a turbulent one. He was grateful it was he who had borne a burden, and not her.

He turned to her letter and chuckled through her lengthy lionization of Bentley Hampton. If the man was half the knight in shining white armor she said he was, why, he was certainly worthy of his daughter's hand in marriage. But Jake already knew that. Had read his character four years ago when they first met. Had heard of his Christian testimony through Brett's letters.

The big surprise in the letter came at the end.

Dad, I know you've been sad to miss out on so much of Brett's and my life these past four years. I don't want you to miss out on my wedding. I'm coming there to the Philippines. I'm proud of you for building the new prison. I want to see it. I want to be married in it.

Jake almost dropped the letter. Every molecule of oxygen in his lungs leaped out his mouth and nose, maybe his ears too. *What?* His brain numbed over.

He blinked until a reverse inhale finally ballooned body and mind into sensibility.

Almost into sensibility.

Because, deep down, he wanted to do it. He wanted the new prison to host his daughter's wedding.

Chapter 60

February

"Papa?"

Danny Romero stiffened. Clutched the phone to his ear.

Only one of his sons ever called him that name. His office disappeared in a shroud of silence. His body functions ceased. Nothing there but ear-crushing numbness. Then his heart began to beat. Louder and louder, as if hammering on the underside of a coffin lid. His breath chuffed through nostrils strained to capture oxygen. A tremor stirred in his chest. Shot to his brain. Spattered into shudders that shook his whole body.

"'Milio?"

It couldn't be.

"Yes, Papa, it's me."

A wail sprang from his lungs. Wild. Primeval. A beast awakened from a long sleep. Sobs choked his throat in guttural rasps. "Emilio"—his lips shaped the words in awkward spurts—"is it ... really you?"

"Yes, Papa. I'm sorry. I've been in hiding from my brothers. They killed my wife and son, and—"

"No, 'Milio, not your son. He is here, safe with me. Come home. I thought you were dead." His lungs threatened more sobs.

"I can't, Papa. I'm in prison. I need help. I don't have much time to talk."

Romero gripped the phone, grateful the line was no longer bugged, and listened to Emilio's hurried account of serving time in the Philippines for a bar fight and resisting arrest.

"Last month, my sentence was up. I was coming home to see you, Papa, but now they've arrested me for"—his son hesitated—"for murdering the *Gateway* passengers."

The *Gateway*? Romero's heart lurched. He had dismissed the disappearance of the cruise ship back when he thought it and Emilio had been lost at sea. "What murders?" he growled.

"I gotta go, Papa. I staged the shipwreck so my brothers would think I drowned. Please, I need money to hire a lawyer for the trial." Another hesitation, as if to give Romero a few seconds to process the information. Or the lack of it.

"And I need you to hire an assassin for me, send him to the prison. Salonga Prison, north of Manila. The swine broke my shoulder so I can't fight. It's a matter of vengeance. But I don't want him killed; I want him maimed for life."

"Who?"

"Jake Chalmers."

"I know that name." A click on the other end, followed by a dial tone, gave Romero plenty of time to remember. Yes, Jake Chalmers—the man whose answering machine Romero had used to retaliate against District Attorney Bradley Henshaw for his wiretap.

Chalmers had hurt his boy. Romero breathed in fire. His bones shook in the inferno of his wrath. Oh yeah, he knew just who to hire. If it cost every penny he had, it would be worth it.

***

Jake stood by Lee's side, observing the new prisoner as the guards unchained the man. Short, dark, of indeterminate ethnicity. Which of the three prison groups would claim him? "I may need to intervene for this one," he muttered to Lee. "Doesn't look Muslim, and Emilio's group will pare him to nothing in minutes."

"Hate to tell you this, Jake, but you're his target."

Jake groaned. "I figured I'd be in for it after Emilio's arrest."

Sure enough, the groups were barely out of their arches before Emilio strolled up to the new prisoner. They exchanged what looked like two words before Emilio marched away with the little guy trailing him.

Jake grunted. "Doesn't look like much of a challenge."

"He's known as Pamukpok. Translated from Tagalog, it means Mallet, if that gives you any idea of what you're facing."

"Can't be anywhere as bad as Scar."

"Worse. Far worse. I'll tell you about him after our inspection with the warden."

There had been no more sabotage on the furniture and construction sites since Emilio's arrest in January. Every morning, skilled workers transported from Manila arrived at the prison and worked until dusk. Still, as Lee said, progress seemed as slow as the Palawan Forest Turtle. They were a month behind schedule. "But then," Lee asked, "what's the hurry anyway?"

Plenty. Jake had told Lee nothing about Dana's request. Nor Puno. Certainly not the warden. But more and more, the idea was elbowing its way into Jake's heart. He'd give it a month, let it simmer on the back burner of his mind.

Since Emilio's arrest, the warden no longer frowned on Jake. "Looks like you won the competition for Mendoza's favor," Puno said. "Or perhaps Emilio simply lost it with his arrest."

Jake smiled. "Or maybe it's simply the Just Judge prevailing." The turn of events gave him renewed hope that eventually God would extend that justice to him.

When he and Lee were free after the site inspections to sit in the detective's car, Lee updated Jake on his new opponent. "Are you familiar with Eskrima?"

Jake shrugged. "Only that it's a Filipino martial art that uses weapons instead of bare hands and feet."

"Correct. Mallet is best known for using bastons, sticks made from rattan. Two of them."

"Sounds defensible enough."

Lee's eyebrows lifted. "He uses them ambidextrously at different angles at the same time. One to strike your head, for example, while at the same moment smashing your arm with the other stick. Defend yourself against one move, and you still get hurt by the other. Not just hurt. Damaged. Pulverized. Thus the name Mallet."

Weariness sucked the juice out of Jake. "Why did you let him in here?"

"I'm sorry, Jake. I have no choice. The best I can do is forewarn you."

"I know." Jake shortened his sigh to a huff. "I appreciate it. You're a good and faithful friend, Lee. I thank God for the day our paths crossed."

"You aren't going to try to hug me again, are you?"

Jake grinned. "Not until I get out of this place and have had a long, hot shower, I promise."

Scar had worked on Jake's nerves by delaying his attack. Every day for Jake had meant looking over his shoulder for stalkers, peering around corners for ambush, questioning his defense tactics for weak points. This time he didn't want to wait. Instead, he'd make himself available for Mallet's assault. The sooner, the better.

"He couldn't bring his bastons inside the prison with him, so probably someone hid them where Mallet could best get at me. That has to be the construction site," Jake mused.

Puno agreed. "Your morning inspection, before the construction crew arrives. There is a new guard. If he accompanies you, he is most likely Mallet's accomplice."

The next morning, a cloudless sky already shimmering with heat greeted Jake at the front gate. Standing on the other side, rifle hefted, was the new guard.

Chapter 61

At the construction site, the new guard trailed Jake at a distance. How would the guard admit Mallet to the site, and at what point would Jake be confronted? Shadows clung to the concrete walls on the west but bounced back the bright light of the morning sun on the east. Doors and windows hadn't been installed yet, and although each of the four prison pods consisted of a simple circular space, the large, central office pod offered a maze of rooms. Plenty of options for an ambush.

Jake carried no weapons. Only a clipboard and pen on which to jot notes. Nor did he spy anything he could use to defend himself. All tools were carefully stored away and accounted for before the working crew left in the evening.

February was the driest month of the year, yet Jake found himself sweating profusely. In contrast, his tongue was a cotton ball in an oven set to broil. His stomach was all teeth, gnawing on tangled guts. Never in his life had he felt so vulnerable.

Last night, Puno had further enlightened him on the sport of stick fighting. Eskrima was a long-standing martial art of the Philippines. Bastons, in addition to being wielded ambidextrously, could also be used to pommel an opponent with multiple blows per second like a jackhammer. Repeated blows to the same area of the body resulted in either broken bones or muscle tissue damaged beyond repair.

Even if Jake disarmed Mallet of one of the bastons, he could still be harmed by Mallet's empty hand. The *live hand*, Puno told him, was a distinctive feature of eskrima. There'd be no fencing, baston against baston with the off-hand safely tucked behind the fighter's back. Instead, the live hand would be used as a weapon for trapping, blocking, and striking the opponent.

Odds were that if Jake tried to deflect blows with his arms, they'd be broken. Then, defenseless, he'd simply be beaten to death.

Fight or flight. If he couldn't fight, was that his only recourse, to flee?

He kept to the perimeter outside the office pod. Once Mallet showed himself, Jake could use the labyrinth of the interior to his advantage. He was familiar with the rooms and the passageways between them. Even if Mallet had scouted the layout beforehand, he wouldn't have them memorized as Jake did.

Where was the man? Jake all but tiptoed, subduing the slap of his sandals on concrete. Silence stormed his ears. No bird calls. No buzz of insects. No distant murmur of guards at the front gate. Only his heart, pumping.

Pumping ice. Frosting corpuscles in arteries. Chilling oxygen molecules in his lungs.

A footstep rang out like a gong, and Jake's nerves zapped to life. Flames consumed the ice, flared muscles to full alert.

Mallet stepped from the shadowed entryway of the office pod. He halted, sticks raised, face grim.

Adrenalin shot through Jake's body. He snapped to his combat readiness stance, legs apart, knees slightly bent, arms wide. Nostrils flared, he breathed deeply, steeping brain and muscles in oxygen.

Slowly, Mallet stooped and laid one of the bastons on the ground. He retreated several feet. Nodded at Jake in apparent invitation to pick it up.

Jake's heart skipped a beat. Was Mallet evening the odds by giving Jake a weapon? Or luring Jake into false hope?

Fight or flight? Hairs on the back of his neck prickling, Jake advanced, grabbed the stick, stepped away. The baston was lightweight, about two feet in length. Made of rattan, colored a candy-cane stripe of light and dark browns, highly polished. He tested it with a smack to his open palm and winced. Unlike the bamboo cane that had lashed his back at his prison beating, the baston was inflexible. Solid. Meant to break, not be broken.

Fight or flight? He had a weapon, muscles strengthened by hard labor to wield it, and towered over his opponent. Surely that gave him the advantage.

So thought Goliath with David.

Jake blinked. Okay, flight it was.

He pivoted to his right and dashed through the entryway. Behind him, Mallet screeched a howl that followed him in his pursuit of Jake. Outrunning the little demon wasn't a problem, but neither was it a solution. At some point there had to be a confrontation. And what if the new guard stepped in to help, blocking Jake's path? Then he'd have two opponents to contend with instead of one.

To keep track of Mallet, Jake made sure his pursuer observed his path of flight—every corner he turned, every passageway he ducked into. Twice he stopped as if to confront Mallet, but fled before his adversary closed in on him. Little by little, he led him pounding the concrete floors to the only destination that held out any hope for him.

The large dining area offered several doorways. Jake sped across the empty room to the kitchen. The stainless steel serving counter stretched to his right, with access to the kitchen straight ahead. A backward glance made sure he was in Mallet's line of sight. Mallet had to see him enter the kitchen. That was important.

Huffing to slow his breathing, he turned to a food service door set at a right angle to the serving counter. From the dining room, the exit was invisible. He dropped to his knees and crawled alongside the serving counter to its end where he had entered the kitchen. Where Mallet also would enter the kitchen.

Heavy panting punctuated the slaps of Mallet's running footsteps like the dots and dashes of a Morse code message. Good. The labyrinth chase was sapping the Minotaur. Hopefully his aim and the power of his strikes would be thrown off.

Positioning himself in a tight crouch, Jake gripped the end of his baston. Tensed his muscles. Prayed to God for perfect timing.

Mallet strode into range, and Jake slammed the stick with all his might into Mallet's shins. The chunk of man fell screaming onto his face, and Jake pounced on him. Mallet twisted and landed a blow with his baston onto Jake's arm. The angle was awkward, though, and the blow lacked Mallet's full strength. Jake grabbed Mallet's hand and bent it back until he felt the wrist snap. Mallet's baston clunked to the floor, and Jake swept it out of reach.

Jake tossed aside his own baston to better deal with his writhing opponent. With his one good hand, Mallet tore at Jake's clothing, clubbed his face, and jabbed his ribs. Trying to pin the little man was like riding a bucking bull. Mallet's teeth sank into Jake's forearm, and Jake slugged the swarthy face as hard as he could. Mallet's eyes rolled into the back of his head, and his mouth went slack. A low, guttural sound wheezed from his throat. His body went limp.

Jake staggered to his feet. When he leaned over to make sure Mallet had a pulse, his head reeled. He sat down at a safe distance until the faintness dissipated. With each breath that heaved from his lungs, he rasped a humble thanks heavenward. Then he gathered the two bastons and left the defeated Minotaur for someone else to help.

When Jake emerged, victor of the labyrinth, the new guard dropped his cigarette and clutched his rifle. "Get Mallet"—Jake jabbed the bastons at the office pod—"but first open the gate. I'm taking these to the warden."

The voices of construction workers arriving from Manila wafted from the parking lot. The guard opened the gate for them to file through, followed Jake outside, and locked the gate. Pointing his rifle at Jake at a distance safe from the bastons' reach, he escorted Jake to the steps of the prison offices, then turned and sped, not in the direction of the construction site, but away from the prison complex. As far away as possible, Jake figured, from the warden.

The guard hopped into the passenger side of a pickup truck parked at the far end of the lot. The door barely closed before the truck took off, back tires spurting dirt and dried vegetation into the air. A well-executed getaway. Was Mallet expected to be with them?

Jake gazed after the disappearing vehicle. How could he even think of letting Dana get married at the prison? Safety was too big a factor. Perhaps, with Detective Lee escorting Jake, the warden would permit Jake to attend the wedding in Manila.

Yes, that was the way to go. He'd ask the warden on that basis.

Still, the idea tugged at him to stick with having the wedding at the prison. More than tugged. Yanked. Practically hog-tied him.

Almost as if he were being commanded to do it.

Chapter 62

April

Eve's hands shook. She didn't know which envelope to open first, the one from the U.S. District Court for the Northern District of Illinois, or the one addressed to her—not Crystal—from Jake Chalmers. With Crystal tucked next to her on their living room couch, reading her own letter from Jake in the fading evening light, Eve opted for her letter from him. He had never written to her before.

A bitter taste settled onto her tongue as she used a letter opener to slice through the envelope. It was bad enough he manipulated Crystal. Was he going to try his wiles on her now?

Dear Ms. Eriksson, he wrote. What, he wasn't going to address his "fiancé" by her given name? Eve snorted. *I would wish to call you Eve, but I suspect the familiarity would not be respectful between a prisoner and a magistrate.* Eve sniffed in disdain that he'd anticipated her response.

My hope with this letter is to invite Crystal and you as her guardian to attend a special occasion. My daughter, Dana, will be graduating from the United States Military Academy in May, along with her twin brother, Brett. In June, she will marry Cadet Bentley Hampton here in the Philippines so that I can walk her down the aisle. My request is that you and Crystal join us as my guests, at my cost for your transportation and lodgings.

I won't say anything to Crystal about this invitation but will wait on you for

273

an answer. Before you make a decision against coming, however, please, will you meet Dana and Brett, who will be in Chicago in two weeks? Through getting to know my children, you may feel more comfortable about their father. Dana will call to set a time and place if you agree.

He signed the letter, *In humility, Jacob Chalmers.*

"Is that from Jake?" Crystal, voice peaking in excitement, leaned across Eve's arm.

What could she say except yes?

"Can I read it while you read mine?" Crystal thrust her letter from Jake at Eve.

There was no avoiding an exchange; she might as well tell Crystal what he'd said. "He wants us to go to the Philippines for his daughter's wedding."

Crystal shrieked. "Tubular, dude! My dream come true, and I get to meet his kids too!"

"No, Crystal."

Silence. Then the sound of air sweeping into Crystal's lungs and stopping, caught in her throat. Her eyes bulged wide open in a stare of disbelief at Eve.

Eve squirmed at the magnitude of Crystal's reaction. She hated denying Crystal. Hated hurting her. Hated Jake for setting up the conflict.

"I'm sorry, honey. He's a—" She broke off before the words *murderer* and *manipulator* left her tongue. "—a prisoner. He's off-limits."

Crystal exhaled slowly through her mouth, then nodded and rose to her feet. Dropping her letter onto Eve's lap, she executed a numb exit up the stairs to her bedroom.

Eve sat, arms wrapped over her chest, and rocked back and forth, releasing herself to a hug from God. *Help me, help me, please, God. I just want to be a good mother.*

She closed her eyes and sank into the despair of her prayer. When she opened them again, she was curled up against the couch cushions. Her wristwatch showed an hour had passed. Guilt for neglecting Crystal's sorrow knifed her stomach. She didn't know what to say to Crystal, but she knew she needed to put her arms around the child and hold her tight. For both their sakes.

Her heart thumped in accompaniment to her heavy footsteps on the two flights of stairs to Crystal's bedroom. The dormer room, which included a bathroom, took up the entire third floor, a teenager's dream of privacy, with the additional wow-factor of space for entertaining friends.

Crystal lay asleep across her bed where she must have flung herself in tears onto her pillow. Her hair was in disarray across her face. Dried tear-tracks ran from her eyes, alongside her nose, and down to a jumping-off point at her chin. A thicker track of drool from her open mouth joined the tear-track.

Should she wake her up? Betty's old-fashioned alarm clock on the bedside table pointed its hands to 9:20. No, they'd both be better off with a good night's sleep. She draped the bedspread as best she could over Crystal. The movement disturbed a photo inches from Crystal's right hand, and it fluttered to the floor.

Eve picked it up.

And gasped.

It was her warrior.

A headshot, close up and personal. Grinning at her. Same shaggy hair, same shambled beard. Same steel blue eyes crinkled at the corners by the grin. The only thing missing was his sword.

She stumbled to a chair, turned on a lamp, and sat, mesmerized by the picture. How could this be? A deep joy welled in her heart and flowed to every part of her body. She felt her face brighten with a sweet radiance, felt the touch of strong fingers caress her cheeks.

She closed her eyes and basked in the love.

***

"Mom?"

A hand clasped Eve's shoulder and shook it. Startled, she opened her eyes to find herself still in the chair, with Crystal leaning over her.

"Are you okay?"

Eve blinked, sat up straight. "I must have fallen asleep. I …" Her drowsiness whisked away as she remembered her warrior, the love, the lightness of her heart. She looked for the photo. She could ask Crystal now who he was.

"What are you doing here?" Worry edged Crystal's question.

"I came to give you a hug. I figured we both needed it." The corners of Crystal's mouth curved downward, pulling a sad face with it. Eve stood and embraced her, held her a long time.

She spied the photo to the side of the chair and broke the hug to retrieve it. "Crystal, who is this?"

Crystal's face flushed. "It's, uh, Jake, before he shaved his beard when we came home from the island."

Eve sat down hard on the chair. "Jake? Jacob Chalmers?"

Crystal sucked in her bottom lip and nodded.

Betrayal grabbed Eve's neck in iron fists. Choking, she shot her hand to her throat to break the hold. Her face bloated with pressure. Her scalp prickled in flames.

"Mom?" The blur of Crystal's panicked face came into focus. "What's wrong?"

"I thought he—" The words released the grip on Eve's throat. *I thought he was from God. That he was my protector.* Renewed rage burned like coals. He'd fooled her! Or God had.

The assessment stunned her.

No.

Thoughts like that said she was on the wrong track. No one had betrayed her, least of all, God. She sagged back into the chair.

"You thought what?" Crystal worried the edge of the photograph with her fingers.

"I recognized him, but not who he was."

"Maybe from your memory? From way down deep?"

From the mouths of babes. "Maybe."

Crystal plopped her bottom onto the carpet and looked up with pleading eyes at Eve. "Why won't you believe me, Mom? Why won't you let me even talk about Jake, about you and him? Why won't you trust that I'm telling the truth?" Her voice cracked, and she looked down at the floor. "It hurts so bad."

Crystal's pain burrowed into Eve's heart. *Because I have a stockpile of reasons to revile the man, topped by his own admission that he murdered someone.*

Set all those on the scales against a fifteen-year-old's emotions, and of course the scales wouldn't tip in her favor.

"Do you even *want* to believe me?"

Believe that she loved Jacob Chalmers? No. "It's not about you, Crystal. It's about him."

"You won't even give him a chance."

"We need to get cleaned up now, eat breakfast." Eve stood and walked to the stairs.

"Mom."

Eve turned. "What?"

Crystal held up Jake's photograph. "Your memory gave him a chance. You recognized him."

Eve drew in a sharp breath. Yes. Her memory had as good as said she loved him.

"I'll think about what you said, Crystal. That's all I can promise."

She sighed, half grumpy, half resigned to a new direction. She wanted to erase Jacob Chalmers from her and Crystal's lives, not start a new chapter.

All right, if she was going to do this, she'd better accept a meeting with Jake's children. She had prayed to be a good parent. Maybe it was time to help Crystal attempt a stockpile on her side of the scales.

Chapter 63

Eve discovered the letter from the U.S. District Court crumpled on the couch where she'd dozed off last evening. All this time waiting for its arrival, and then she'd forgotten about it! She sliced open the envelope and smoothed out the rumpled page before sitting to read it. The temptation to scan the contents teased her, but she remained resolute to read every delicious word one by one.

At the title *Drug Czar*, she smiled. It should be *Anti-Drug Czar*, but since it wasn't a public label, it didn't matter. Only a small number of people within the judicial system would know about Eve's new designation in order to protect her from becoming a target. Excitement jittered a silly tap dance across her nerves. So it was official now: from this moment on, her focus was to combat illegal drugs in the Chicago area by coordinating law enforcement assets.

Thank you, Danny Romero! The success of her decade-long quest to nail him had put this judicial hammer in her hand.

The only disappointment was that she had to keep the assignment a secret. If she told one person, that person would, like her, feel compelled to tell one other person. And that person, one other person. And so it would go, multiplying like rabbits, until a public announcement might as well have been made in the first place. So Crystal was out. And Marianne. And Stella. And Chaplain Peterman. None of them could be told.

At least her former boss was part of the "inner circle." Brad Henshaw would have been her first choice as an ally, anyway, so she was grateful for his inclusion.

She poured a cup of coffee and climbed the stairs to her home office. The room was simple in its furnishings but rich in decorations. With her identity lost in a miasma of soggy brain cells, she found it rewarding to define the "new her" by impulsive choices in art, literature, and music. Were the selections true to who she'd always been, or were they indicative of a totally "different her" who had moved on with her life?

Her first task was to answer Jake's letter. She made it fast and simple: yes, she and Crystal would accept a visit with his children, and no, she and Crystal would not attend the wedding. She folded the single sheet in thirds, inserted it in an envelope, addressed it, and added one of the air-mail stamps she had bought for Crystal's overseas letters to Jake.

Done. Would he even get it in time to write back to his children? Maybe she'd luck out and miss their visit to Chicago.

***

When the telephone rang two weeks later, Eve knew the call was from Dana or Brett Chalmers by Crystal's squeal of delight. Rats! She put down her morning coffee and listened.

"I can't wait to meet you, I'm, like, so excited, I can't believe it's really going to happen!" The words pelted from Crystal's mouth like kernels of corn in a hot popper. "Sure! I'll get her for you." She swiveled and thrust the phone at Eve with lips spread to the max in a wide grin. "It's Dana!"

Eve winced. So she was going to have to go through with this. It was Saturday, with no excuse of school for Crystal or a workday for her. Best to get it done and over with as soon as possible. No telling what the Chalmers kids were like, but she would at least approach them with dignity. Mentally assembling herself in a judge's robes, she squared her shoulders and took the phone. "Hello, Dana."

Dana's greeting was as stiff as hers. Eve startled. She hadn't thought about how the rendezvous might be as difficult for Dana and Brett as it was for her. To them, their father was the victim and Eve the culprit. Why had she ever said yes to this meeting?

A glance at Crystal's face gave the answer. As if she had heard both sides of the icy exchange, Crystal's glee had transformed into uncertainty and was rapidly converting into dread.

Eve cranked out a pitiful rendering of a smile for the child's sake and attempted a friendlier voice. "Crystal and I are"—she managed not to choke on the next words—"looking forward to meeting you and Brett. Is there a time that's good for you?"

"We're staying at the Hilton. Is it too late to meet for breakfast, or brunch?"

Good. There was no way Eve was inviting them to her house. Not that safety was an issue, but getting together with anyone even remotely connected to Danny Romero was reason enough to meet in a public place. "That would be perfect. Does forty-five minutes from now work?" Hopefully, the Chalmers didn't expect her and Crystal to spend the day sight-seeing with them.

When they hung up, Crystal gave her a hug worthy of a grizzly bear and dashed for the stairs. "Gonna brush my teeth and change into somethin' totally choice and be right down."

Eve followed her up the stairs to her own room to get ready. It was hard not to want to make a good impression on someone who found her the guilty party.

***

When Eve and Crystal entered the restaurant, the hostess, told to expect their arrival, escorted them to a table where a young man and woman sat. A striking pair. Chestnut hair with sun-streaked red highlights, copper freckles sprinkled lightly across nose and cheeks, mahogany eyes that observed every step of Eve and Crystal's approach. Assessing them. Just as Eve and Crystal were assessing them. Were their hearts beating as fast as hers? Their mouths as cottony?

Differences became apparent as Eve and Crystal reached the table. Brett stood to hold out Eve's chair—really?—exhibiting a height of about six-two. Dana, Eve guessed, since the girl was sitting, was probably a half-foot shorter. Brett was straight and lean; Dana was curvy with pleasing proportions. The boy had high cheekbones; the girl's face was round. Both were attired in jeans, tees and Members Only jackets.

"You look just like your mom and dad," Crystal said. From there, Brett and Crystal carried the conversation until the cardboard finally leached from Eve's and Dana's britches. It helped that the talk centered around the twins' four years at West Point instead of events on the island. By the end of the meal, Eve, doggone it all, liked them.

"What are you doing the rest of the day?" Hello? Had she really asked them that? Eve smiled at herself and made the question into an invitation. "The Museum of Science and Industry is right down the street from our house. If you're available, we could make a day of it and finish up with dinner at our place."

Brett and Crystal immediately claimed they were in. Dana was slower to respond. "I need to make up my mind between two wedding gowns before we leave tomorrow. Could I talk you into coming along, Eve? I'd love to have your input."

Dana's request was like walking into a rose garden on a sunny day. Gowns over trekking around a museum? Not a brain buster. "I can't think of anything I'd rather do! Are you okay with taking Brett to the museum, Crystal?"

Fifteen-year-old Crystal glanced at twenty-two-year-old Brett and grinned. "I can't think of anything I'd rather do!"

Chapter 64

Crystal and Brett took a city bus to the museum while Eve and Dana marched into their quest for treasure, two princesses armed with credit cards. They expanded their search to include dainty items Dana hadn't bought yet, as well as gowns at boutiques Eve knew of within walking distance.

The Saturday pedestrian traffic wasn't crowded, but steady enough that Eve wanted to make sure she didn't lose Dana when the girl stopped to gaze in store windows. Rather than hang over Dana's shoulder like a pesky mosquito, Eve often stepped ahead to window-shop nearby. The April weather was brisk but sunny. Perfect for sauntering along the downtown streets and indulging in the sights, sounds, smells, and occasional shoulder bumps of Chicagoan humanity.

A boutique with jewelry Eve favored was two stores ahead. When Dana lingered at a department store window, Eve made a beeline for the boutique. A tired-looking woman with a coat draped over her arm stood in the middle of the sidewalk, slowing down the foot traffic, peering up and down the street as if lost. Before Eve could dodge her, a man elbowed past Eve in the narrow gap between the two women, knocking Eve off balance. He hesitated, muttered "Sorry," but didn't stop to help her regain her footing.

At once, Eve knew what had happened. "Stop him," she yelled. "He stole my purse!"

The man broke into a run, threw something into a trash container at the edge of the street, and fled around the corner. Eve sped after him. A glimpse over her shoulder showed Dana frozen, mouth gaping along with other pedestrians staring at the disturbance.

A fat lot of good she was! Eve clenched her jaw and pushed through the gawkers ahead of her. At the corner, she halted, torn between chasing the thief and turning back to examine the trash container for her purse before someone else did.

Dana was nowhere in sight. Eve strode to the container and peered into the yawning opening. Most of the trash was food cartons and cups. She could almost hear the sighs of contented flies that had found their corner of detritus heaven.

Her purse was nowhere in sight. Gritting her teeth, she stuck her hand in and pushed aside the top layer of debris. The smell of fermented garbage assailed her nose, as did a landing force of angry flies on the defense. She swatted them with one hand and finished her nasty invasion of their homeland with the other hand. No purse, no wallet, nothing she could claim as hers.

She stepped away from the war zone, only to face the raised eyebrows and tittering of passersby, who gave her a wide berth. Her face flushed hot. Come on, people, bag ladies don't dress in Gloria Vanderbilts.

Gah. Her right hand was filthy with the contamination of trash. Perhaps the boutique would let her use its employees' bathroom, or at least grant her paper towels to clean off her hand. Spying a policeman entering the store, she ran to intercept him and report the crime.

Inside, her heart jumped at finding Dana in an arm-wrestle with an older woman at the check-out counter. The policeman was trying to pry them apart.

"Here she is," Dana cried out, breaking away to point at Eve. "She's the real Judge Eriksson."

"What's going on?" Eve stormed up to them. Had Dana been caught shoplifting and was claiming guilelessness because of Eve? Chagrin that she'd been fooled by Dana and Brett knifed her heart.

"Compare their signatures, officer." Dana squirmed as the policeman clamped onto both her and the other woman. "You'll see this woman is lying.

She and a colleague stole Judge Eriksson's purse minutes ago, and are using the judge's credit card."

Eve gasped and wrenched the older woman around. It was the same woman who had been standing near her on the sidewalk when the thief bumped into Eve. And the same coat still draped over her arm. Eve grabbed the coat and pulled it away, revealing her purse. "That's my purse, officer. If my wallet is still in there, the picture on my driver's license will identify me."

The policeman released Dana and pulled the purse off the woman's arm. He handed Eve the purse and resumed his hold on Dana. "Show me," he said to Eve.

Eve did. Relief swamped her at finding everything intact inside. The vexation of having to get a new driver's license and make phone calls to stop her credit cards evaporated. She made arrangements to press charges against the woman, and after the policeman left with his handcuffed prisoner, she all but leaped on Dana in a huge hug. "How'd you know?"

Dana hugged her back. Her face glowed as they broke apart and Eve continued to hold Dana's shoulders in affection. "I thought I saw the man pass your purse to her. It happened so fast, I wasn't sure. I felt bad not joining you in the chase, but I wanted to see what she'd do. When she turned and walked straight into the boutique, I followed her. Using a stolen credit card right away allows the thief to make pricey purchases before the credit is stopped. The woman wasted no time selecting expensive jewelry. When the clerk took her credit card and called her Ms. Eriksson, I grabbed the woman and told the clerk to call the police."

Eve shook her head in admiration. "I'd never have thought to suspect her." She looked at her right hand, saw it was as good as clean, and hoped she'd wiped it off on the woman's coat and not on Dana's back with her bear hug. She dropped her hands from Dana's shoulders and removed a tissue from her purse to finish the task. "How can I ever thank you?"

"Oh goodness, you don't owe me a thing." Dana laughed, then lifted her eyebrows. "You know, there is something. I'd love it if you and Crystal would attend my wedding. Even better, if Crystal could be my bridesmaid."

Eve drew in a sharp breath. Dana's lips were pressed flat, holding her breath as well. Funny how easy it was to release the air and say, with a genuine beam, "You know, I think we will."

***

Jake didn't have much to take with him into the prison cell. A few items of clothing, a blanket, and letters from back home were about it. His pocket Bible was lost. Or stolen. He suspected it fell out of his pocket in the tussle with Mallet, but it was nowhere to be found when he went back to look. He mourned its disappearance. Not only because he couldn't read it, but because important dates were written next to Scripture passages. Like when he became a Christian. Same with Crystal's and Eve's dates. And Ginny's, Brett's, Dana's, his dad's and mom's.

Making matters worse, he now had no bunkmate. He and Puno decided to locate in two different pods to oversee group three since it was large enough to have to split up. Group one, Emilio's men, including Mallet, was in a third pod. The Muslims, unhappy to be on round-the-clock display to their pod guards, were in the fourth pod.

He set his meager possessions on the lower bunk. It was too short for him, but at least it had a mattress. The biggest plus of moving into the new prison was that each cell had a toilet and sink. Jake's design had included showers, but the warden had cut them out. There was clean water to drink and bathe in, but it was restricted to two hours in the morning and two hours in the evening. That meant sewage sat until it could be flushed, but the stink was nowhere as bad as when they'd had to use the fifty-five gallon drums cut in half.

His dream was pretty well accomplished. The nasty drums and their hordes of flies were gone. The old Salonga Prison now housed the furniture and other trade industries that had sprung up. There was purpose—hope even—for those who wanted it. No human carabao languished in the courtyard but were bunked in the new prison. All the prisoners were free to move about within the confines of Salonga, but at night they were secured in their cells with electronic locks controlled by the pod guard on duty.

The four prisoner pods radiated equidistant from the central administrative pod, where Mendoza could survey his kingdom in both the old and new prisons with surveillance cameras. The offices and barracks for the guards and other employees were upstairs; the kitchen, cafeteria, dispensary, and other rooms were downstairs. Gravel defined a new parking lot, and trees and plantings around the entrance gave a pleasant appearance to the whole structure.

"You are rewarding prisoners with a five-star hotel," Mendoza grumbled at his weekly meeting with Jake.

"They are getting decent facilities, Warden, that's all. Take away a man's freedom, and you take away his choices. What you give him is slavery." Jake scowled. "Believe me, the loss of liberty bears no comforts.

"What you do have, however, is a five-star prison. Word will get out, and it will become a model for new prisons throughout the Philippines." Jake smiled. "You best prepare yourself for visitors."

Beginning, perhaps, with a wedding. If security at the prison proved reliable, he would ask the warden next month if Dana could be married on Salonga Prison's premises.

It was a big *if*. He had to be one hundred percent sure. Ninety-nine percent wasn't good enough.

Chapter 65

June

Eve declined a meeting with Jacob Chalmers at the prison. "I don't want to intrude on your time together and all the planning you need to do for the wedding," she told Dana. Truth to tell, she wanted to skip the whole event. But for Crystal's and Dana's sakes, she'd have to at least put in an appearance. Remain way at the back of those attending the ceremony. Unfortunately, there wouldn't be many guests to hide behind.

It had been a long time since she'd had the nightmare about the man wrenching her screaming and flailing off the jungle floor. It had returned last night after setting foot on Philippine soil. The thought of seeing that monster at the wedding in two days shriveled her insides. Turned her stomach inside out so that she couldn't eat. "Jet lag," she told Crystal. She tried to hang onto the image of Jake Chalmers as the man in Crystal's photo, but the grip of the brute's fingers squeezing her arm in the nightmare was far more real than the flat two dimensions of Crystal's photograph.

She didn't know how to reconcile the two.

Thank goodness for the appointment with Detective Lee this afternoon. His request to interview her about what had happened three years ago was unnerving since she had no memory of the events, but at least the meeting was another handy excuse for bowing out of the trip with the twins and Crystal to Salonga Prison.

The detective was sober of face and quick of mind. A bit younger than she, a bit shorter, neither by much. Dressed in a sports jacket and tie in spite of the sun hammering the tops of heads like nails. She was grateful for the air conditioning of the cafe they walked to.

Lee placed a manila folder on the table and they ordered tea. "Thank you for meeting with me, Judge Eriksson. I'm hoping you can help with some open cases I have from 1982."

"I'm glad to help." Surely he knew about her memory loss, but she was curious to hear what he would reveal about its circumstances.

"We found you with two dead men aboard a stolen yacht, the *Cameron's Castle*. Can you tell me about that?"

"I have no memory of it. Neither of the yacht nor of the two dead men."

Lee withdrew a photograph from the manila folder and slid it toward her. "Does this help?"

The photo was of a beautiful yacht at a distance. *Cameron's Castle* identified it across its stern. When she shook her head, Lee showed her pictures of the interior. "I'm sorry, detective, I don't recognize any of it." She handed the photos back.

"May I show you the two dead men?"

"Certainly." Photographs of corpses were common enough in the criminal cases she handled. She moved aside her tea as the waitress set it down, and Lee slid a photo to her. A Filipino man of small stature, glasses askew, hands plastered over a bloody shirt at his stomach. She shook her head, slid it back to Lee.

The next photo showed a large man, eyes open, mouth in a grimace, at least a dozen scars carved on his face. A pool of shiny red blood beneath his neck and head reflected the flash of the camera. Eve leaped to her feet, air knotting her windpipe in a loud gasp. She shoved back from the table. Her chair toppled with a rattling crash behind her. Tea flooded the tabletop and slopped onto Detective Lee.

He stood, swiping at his lap area with a paper napkin. "Are you okay?" He picked up the photo and flapped tea off it. "You recognize him?"

Eve couldn't control the sobs that tangled her throat. Her chest heaved like a blacksmith's bellows. When at last she quelled the shuddering breaths, she righted her chair and flopped into it. The waitress sopped up the spill with a cotton towel and replaced their teas. "I'm sorry." Eve lowered her eyes. "About your clothes." When they left, he'd probably look like he'd wet his pants.

Lee pshawed and sat down gingerly. "I take it you recognized him." He held up the photo, now wrinkled from its baptism.

Eve turned her head away. "He's …" She swallowed, forced herself to look at the photo. "Only from my nightmares."

"Not from the yacht? Or the island?"

"No." Was the man Jacob Chalmers? He couldn't be. Jake Chalmers was the man in Crystal's photo.

"What happens in your nightmares?"

She suppressed a whimper. "I'm hiding in the jungle, and he finds me. Grabs my arm. I scream and … wake up."

"So you remember being in a jungle?"

"Only in my dream."

"Tell me about the island."

She shook her head. "No memories."

He pulled more photos out of the manila folder, slid one across to her. "Recognize him?"

This one was a police photo. Another Filipino man. "No." Nor did she remember the second Filipino man in a similar kind of photo.

At the third photo, she drew in a quick breath. It was the same bearded man as in Crystal's photograph. The man in her fantasy with the two-edged sword. The Protector. "Crystal showed me a photo of him, said he was Jacob Chalmers."

Lee didn't confirm it. "Do you remember him?"

"No. Is that who he is?" *Please say yes.*

Lee stared at her. She didn't flinch.

Finally he nodded.

She'd been holding her breath. She released it with a hearty sigh through her nostrils. "Who is the other man? The scarred one?"

"He goes by Jojo. Does that ring a bell?"

"No." She wet her lips. "What happened on the yacht with him and the other man?"

"We think they got into an argument and managed to kill each other." Lee flicked a glance at the scar on her forehead. "And almost you. Probably killed the first mate and owners of the yacht too."

He pushed the police photos of the other two Filipino men back into her view. "Let's talk about these. Witnesses say they were part of the crew on the yacht."

Her heartbeat doubled. "Witnesses?"

He pulled out two more photos and held them up. An old lady and a younger Crystal. Both were horribly bedraggled. Hair disheveled, clothing ragged, skeleton-thin with haggard faces. Her breath punched out of her lungs.

"Recognize them?"

Her voice wobbled. "Crystal, my ward. And … I'm guessing, Betty Parker?" She took the photo of the old lady and examined it. This was the multi-millionaire who left her all that money?

"They say you witnessed this man's death." Lee tapped the police photo on her right.

"No." Alarm buzzed over her face like an electric razor. "Or if I did, I don't remember it." When Lee said nothing, she squared her shoulders. "How did he die?"

"He fell. From a long ways up. From the top of a tree. Landed in a crunch that folded him like an accordion."

Her lower lip jerked in a spasm. "Did I … did I push him?"

"You're the only witness."

"I don't remember." Horror pushed her stomach into her throat. "I don't remember," she whispered.

Lee stabbed the other photo with the same finger. "Jacob Chalmers killed this man."

She felt her eyes widen, her sight jump from the second photo to Lee's eyes. "Any witnesses?"

"He confessed to it."

Confessed. Her shoulders slumped.

Crystal had told her why Jake killed the man. "He was protecting me," Eve said to Lee. She believed it now. It was no longer a question, but a declaration solid in her heart. Jake Chalmers was her Protector.

She sat up straight. "Jake … and Crystal. They're in my memory—even though I don't remember them." Lee frowned, and she tried again to explain the conundrum. "I recognized them in my memory. When they popped into my mind, I knew I knew them. I just didn't know how. Or who they were." She faltered.

"Like you remembered Jojo from your nightmare."

"Yes!"

Lee slipped all the photos back into his folder. "Anything or anyone else from your memory you can't explain?"

"No. Only those two. But Jake … someone's defending him, right? Is his case ready for court?"

"He has competent lawyers, yes. A judge, no."

"His trial is being delayed?"

"For three years so far. He is waiting on the Just Judge." Lee pointed heavenward. "The earthly judge demands a ransom Jake refuses to pay."

Eve's brow furrowed, smoothed as comprehension dawned. "The judge wants a bribe. What's his name? I will gladly confront him, judge to judge."

"An American making such an accusation, judge-to-judge or not, will only make things worse for Jake."

"And you, a police officer, can't do anything about the judge?"

"I would if I could, but there is no proof. Only tradition, and a government that practices it as well."

"It's not right!" she spat out. Lee made no reply, and they sat quietly, staring at the table, sipping their teas. At last, she asked, "Do you think he's guilty?"

"No more than you are guilty." He corrected himself. "Than you may be guilty."

She ducked her head. All these years she'd pointed her finger at Jake, labeled him a murderer, when the same accusation could be leveled at her. She could be in prison. No attorney career recovered. No promotion to judgeship. No Crystal. Everything a loss.

But she wasn't in prison. Because there was no witness.

Jake was in prison. Because there was no witness.

Her.

She couldn't testify to say it was self-defense and that Jake had been protecting her.

Because she couldn't remember.

She didn't look up when Lee thanked her and said he had to be on his way. Didn't raise her head because tears would have spilled down her cheeks.

Chapter 66

Eve peered out the window of the limousine Jake had sent for the wedding party and guests. In spite of her reluctance to attend the ceremony, she'd gotten caught up in the excitement of the moment. Dainty Filipina hairdressers had styled her, Crystal's, and Dana's hair into elaborate arrangements and insisted on applying their makeup as well. She feared they'd turn out looking like plastic dolls, so was pleased when the unique beauty of each was brought out instead. Dana was the radiant bride, Crystal the buoyant maiden, and Eve the elegant … well, judge.

Brett, Bentley, and his parents were in a separate limousine ahead of them so the groom could make his exit without seeing the bride. Both the groom and his best man, Brett, wore their Army formal blue mess uniforms. In contrast, Dana had selected attire that would be comfortable in the blazing heat and humidity. Foregoing fashionably massive shoulder pads and sleeves, she chose a gown with spaghetti straps that topped a deeply scalloped V-neck. From her waist to her toes, lace graced the sheath with tiny rhinestones that shone in the late morning light as if she had stepped from a sun-drawn chariot. Crystal, also dressed for comfort, wore a bright yellow, spaghetti-strapped gown that flowed to her ankles and swirled like a golden mist around her slender body when she walked.

Eve opted to forego spaghetti straps since every dress she tried on with them insisted on showing off the opulence of her bosom. Not exactly what she wanted to feature to the hungry eyes of prisoners, and especially not to the man who reportedly was in love with her and had last seen her three years ago in as disheveled a state as Crystal and Betty had been in Lee's photos. Instead, she wore a soft emerald, full-length dress with a high, wide-scooped neck that ended in fashionable puffy sleeves halfway to her elbows. She was pleased to see the groom's mother was similarly dressed, with a touch more glamour. As she should be.

Eve still balked at the idea of holding the wedding at the prison, but the warden refused to allow Jake to leave. If he was to walk Dana down the aisle, it had to be at Salonga. Jake, the warden, Detective Lee—all three insisted it was safe with all the new security hardware. The prisoners would be locked in their cells, with only a few handpicked men from Jake's group permitted to help at the reception.

The road to the prison was newly paved. From a distance, the prison appeared a strangely shifting gray blur against a greening landscape that Jake had told Crystal was once a swamp but now agricultural fields. Closer up, Eve discovered the moving parts of the prison were canopy gently flapping above five circular concrete pods. On the wide arc of the concrete apron at the front gate, pots of tropical trees, ferns and flowers surrounded a small arrangement of rattan chairs for guests. The gate's black iron bars were hidden behind an arch draped with white cloth and made festive with colorful flowers. On each side of it, at full attention, stood three National Policemen in dress uniform. Everyone in the car, even the driver, murmured in admiration. Dana beamed.

The first limousine deposited its passengers at the apron, and Bentley escorted his mother and father to chairs on the front right side of an aisle already dressed in red carpet. He and Brett then took their places under the arch, where a Filipino man, presumably the preacher, joined them.

The bride's car pulled up next. "Your turn, Mom," Crystal whispered. A prison guard opened the car door, and Eve stepped out into the heat-borne fragrance of tropical flowers. The warden awaited her, and she greeted him, glad she had been forewarned he was her escort. He too was in full uniform, but between his eye patch and grim visage, he looked more the part of an usher to hell than the host of a wedding facility. She took his arm and matched her step to his down the red carpet to the set of two chairs on the left second row. Jake would be sitting in front of her. Her throat felt as if it were stuffed with a 500-pound bale of cotton muffling her heartbeat. She sat, and then the warden next to her on the aisle.

Detective Lee was one of the three National Police standing to the left of the draped arch. His almond-shaped eyes were round, staring at her with frank admiration. The bale of cotton in her throat poofed away, and the tension in her shoulders with it. She smiled at him, and the stern line of a soldier's mouth at attention swept into a reciprocal smile.

Emboldened, she tipped her head and spoke to Mendoza. "I'm sorry I missed the tour of your new prison yesterday." She had been wallowing in self-pity and excused herself from joining the twins and Crystal. "I heard many compliments on it."

Mendoza turned his head to give her a stiff stare. "I admit I was surprised since your fiancé designed it and supervised its construction."

The ice on his words shoved the cotton bale back into her throat. She rankled at the designation of Jake as her fiancé, but the fixation of Mendoza's flesh-sunken visible eye on her eyes quelled any thought of correcting him.

The revelation that Jake truly was responsible for the new prison astonished her. She'd figured his letters to Crystal about it were just one more way to dazzle a foolish child. After all, who had ever heard of a prisoner having that kind of freedom, much less cooperation, from the warden of his prison?

A choir began singing Wagner's *Bridal Chorus*, and she turned her head from side-to-side seeking its source. The voices were all male with no instrumentation, sung in English with a Filipino accent. The song's power caught at her heart.

"Prisoners," the warden muttered, "behind the gate."

The nuptial arch and line of three National Police on each side all but hid the front gate, but once she knew the choir's location, she spied the men standing in back of the iron bars. Bentley stepped forward and his parents rose, as did the warden. Apparently everyone but her knew the cue. She joined them in standing and turning to gaze down the carpeted aisle.

Crystal, flowers artfully gracing her hair, hands clasping a simple bouquet of the same blossoms, floated like a moonbeam down the aisle. Her gown swirled in gentle folds about her legs, revealing dainty, sandaled feet with each step. A smile devoid of self-consciousness but dispensing joy like petals tossed upon the audience completed the picture of utter ebullience.

Eve inhaled a muffled sniffle. *Thank you, Lord, for giving me the heart to bring Crystal to the wedding.* She followed Crystal's journey all the way to the arch, where she entered and stopped in place opposite Brett. When Crystal's eyes landed on the young man, she grinned and shot him a wicked little wink.

Why, that little flirt! It was all Eve could do not to laugh out loud.

Standing between Brett and Crystal, Bentley suddenly stiffened, his eyes widening, his gaze fixed on the back of the aisle. Eve pivoted, smiling in anticipation of the loveliness that would grace Dana's appearance. The bride, like her bridesmaid, was also adorned with flowers, but all of her blossoms were white. They shone in her ginger-red hair like a halo, and cascaded from her hands in a bouquet that feathered like froth in a waterfall against the glittering rhinestones of her gown.

A whimper of awe escaped Eve's mouth at the picture of purity Dana presented. Next to Eve, the warden emitted a guttural huff of admiration.

Before Dana started down the aisle, her escort stepped into view, and she slipped her arm into his, tipped her head back, and smiled up at him. Eve frowned. Instead of Jake, an officer in a Marine Corps mess dress uniform was accompanying Dana. Where was the father of the bride?

Disappointment clamped Eve's mouth shut, and she glared at the big shot standing next to her. Mendoza must have forced Jake to watch from inside the prison. She shifted to one foot, sorely tempted to kick the warden in the shins.

Chapter 67

Whoever the man escorting Dana was, he had Eve's heart thumping into a rapid pitter-patter. She'd always been a sucker for a man in uniform, and this dude, as Crystal would say, was definitely rad.

He was in his mid-forties, tall, with a clean-shaven face bronzed by the sun, and a smile as broad as his shoulders. Definitely handsome in the formal military attire, with its black jacket, brass buttons, and gold braid at the ends of the sleeves. The jacket cut away to reveal a wide, red cummerbund over a white shirt, with more color added by a line of miniature medals across the jacket's left breast. The trousers, also black, featured a red and gold stripe on the outside of each leg. The same stripe encircled the white barracks cap he wore, and gold braid decorated its black bill. Above the bill, a silver and gold emblem of an eagle atop a globe and anchor identified the man as a member of the U.S. Marine Corps. Honestly, it was hard to keep her eyes off him.

"First time in three years I see him without a beard." Mendoza peered up at her, evidently aware of the focus of her gaze.

She felt her cheeks go hot. Had she been gawking? "Who is he?" was on the tip of her tongue when the answer hit her.

Jake!

Her chest expanded in a gasp, and her eyes zipped to his at the same moment he looked at her. His eyes flew wide open, and his lips tightened into a quick inhale. He faltered a step, recovered both pace and smile, and turned away his gaze.

Her breath tore out of her with claws. She felt a hand on her arm steadying her, saw it was the warden's. Was that a grin quirking one side of Mendoza's mouth? She stifled a glare and turned her attention to Jake and Dana, now standing at the nuptial arch.

She stared at Jake's back, vaguely aware of the wedding ceremony. Emotions, raw, undefined, shifted and pooled and contracted like the colors of a kaleidoscope. When Jake's voice rose strong and clear, affirming he gave his daughter with every blessing into Bentley's care, she barely averted her eyes before he turned and took his seat in the row in front of her.

The chair creaked under his weight, moved slightly back as he adjusted his posture. For a crazy moment she wished it were she who sat behind him instead of Mendoza so that she could lean forward and inhale the smell of him. It would be clean, slightly musky with the sweat of the morning sun on his skin. A thin line of perspiration would gleam on his hair where the rim of his cap rested on his head.

Good grief, woman! She pulled her eyes off him and focused on Bentley and Dana, holding hands side-by-side as they faced the man preaching a sermon on God's good purpose in marriage. Out of the corner of her eye, she caught the glint of sunlight on Jake's shoulder. She peeked at it without moving her head. It was a silver eagle with outspread wings, pinned on a shoulder board the same color and material as his jacket, only trimmed in red. The insignia of his rank—Colonel?

His hair must have been cut at the same time as his beard. The color was a dark chestnut, almost brown. A sprinkling of gray touched the hair at his temples. She had a quarter-view of his face. High cheekbones, no scar on his skin. Crystal said he had a scar, so it must be on his right cheek. Deep wrinkles creased the skin at the corner of his eye. She couldn't tell the color of his iris. His eyelashes were short and straight.

Could he see—out of the corner of his eye—that she was examining him? She sat back against her chair and again focused on the bride and groom. The two were now facing each other, holding both hands, saying their vows. Bentley's forehead was beaded with sweat, and Dana's elaborate hairdo was beginning to sag. Eve touched her own "do." It'd be just her luck to have hair and makeup drizzling onto her neck when the ceremony ended and she had to face Jake.

Seconds later, the preacher pronounced Bentley and Dana husband and wife, and they brushed lips in a chaste kiss. Eve snickered. Dana was a practical gal and was no doubt looking out that her makeup didn't smear because of the heat. The bride was wearing more cosmetics than Eve, and Eve was glad she'd held back the hairdressers from applying more to her own face.

The wedding party and guests clapped at the introduction of the new Mr. and Mrs. Bentley Hampton. The couple, instead of marching back down the aisle, turned and walked to the back of the arch, through the now-open prison gate, and into the foyer of the central pod. Crystal and Brett, arm-in-arm, paraded after them, then Bentley's parents, followed by the preacher and Jake, and finally Eve arm-in-arm once again with Warden Mendoza. The clang of the front gate shutting reverberated down the hall, with the thud of boots on tile testifying to the accompaniment of the six National Policemen behind them.

Flowers festooned the hallway leading to the main dining room, where two of the tables bolted to the floor were lavishly decorated. In spite of the fact that Eve and Warden Mendoza were the only guests, a reception line had been set up. The bride and groom greeted them first, then the bridesmaid and best man with wide grins, followed by Bentley's parents and the preacher, and, last of all, Jake.

Even the warden smiled at the jollity of the lineup of merry-makers. Congratulations, compliments, and jokes were shared back and forth until, with a gulp, Eve reached the end of the line … and Jake. Her smile felt plastered, her handshake cold and clammy. Her tongue cleaved to the roof of her mouth, while her voice crumpled into her larynx. How could she even look him in the eye when she was the reason he was here. A prisoner.

"Judge Eriksson." Jake held her hand with both of his. His fingers were strong, clasping hers with tenderness, warm like a toaster. He didn't smile. His eyes, she saw, were blue. They swallowed hers, hungry like a starved man. His lips parted, and her heart jumped. "Eve," he said, "may I call you that?"

Air shivered through her nostrils to her lungs, but her voice remained locked. She nodded. When he loosed her hand and tucked it into his arm, she let him lead her to one of the tables. Everyone else was already seated. She scooted into place on the bolted bench where Warden Mendoza sat. Every cell in her body tingled when Jake slid in next to her.

***

Jake's heart hadn't stopped pounding since he caught sight of Eve seated in front of the nuptial arch. Had the same lightning that struck him struck her also? Her eyes had said so. For a fragment of a second, everything in him had shattered into splinters. His breath had disintegrated, his feet stumbled. If Dana hadn't been on his arm, he'd have bolted down the aisle and swept Eve into an embrace that surely would have spiraled them to heaven's door.

Every second of sitting on the seat in front of her during the ceremony had been a tug-of-war between torture and ecstasy. He was sure Dana and Bentley got married, but he didn't hear a word of it. Instead, his ears caught every rustle of Eve's dress, every creak of her chair, every whisper of breath in and out of her lungs. Was she as conscious of him as he was of her?

Or was he the big, bad prisoner who had dragged her and Crystal to Manila? Declining the prison tour with his children and Crystal yesterday had as good as declared her lack of interest in him.

Still, the heart was resilient. Today he had tromped the steps to heaven in anticipation of seeing her. In the reception line, he'd watched her every movement, the shifts in her facial expressions, the grace of her body as she advanced toward him. Had hung onto the laughter exchanged with his kids. Had relished her quivering hand and speechlessness when she finally stood in front of him.

A meek Eve had been a rarity on the island. He held back a delighted guffaw.

And now he sat next to her. Oh how he wanted to slide that one little inch closer so their shoulders touched! Her gaze was clearly averted from his, so he took up his fork to capture her attention. "This salad is from our fields. The men grow its components and sell it to the prison. Helps us eat healthier and puts money in the men's pockets."

She turned her head so that he had a three-quarter view of her face. Her cheeks were pink, her lips lightly lacquered with lipstick. He wanted to reach over and caress her skin with the back of his fingers. Kiss the curve of her neck. Move his lips on around to her throat and up to her mouth.

"What do they do with the money?" she asked.

He watched her bring a scant fork of salad to her mouth. Watched her lips close on the lettuce. He blinked and cleared his throat. "Some send it to family. Some buy clothes, books, candy, soda."

Her eyes settled on his right cheek. It took a moment to realize their focus was his scar. Lee had told him she'd mistaken Jojo for Jake. No wonder she'd wanted nothing to do with him.

"How's Crystal getting along?" His question eased their conversation into a comfortable exchange that even evoked laughter twice. At the next table, Crystal beamed at their mirth. It was still hard to believe the beautiful, confident fifteen-year-old seated next to his son was the same scrawny scaredy-cat he'd taken under his wing four years ago on the island.

The delivery of the main meal interrupted them, and the warden took advantage of it to engage Eve. Before Jake could regain her attention, the prison choir put in a second appearance to sing a medley of wedding songs. Puno conducted them with energetic gestures, white hair floating like an animated cloud about his head. Tenderness stirred a lump in Jake's throat at his friend's gift of love. It had been a major undertaking for Puno to find men willing and able to sing parts, teach many of them how to speak the words in English, and then come together in such striking harmony.

After much applause, the choir exited, and a prisoner entered the dining area from the kitchen, pushing a wheeled metal cart draped in white. Atop it sat a cake glistening in white icing, a miniature bride and groom on top, and delicate fresh flowers pressed into each of the three layers. A stack of dessert plates lay next to it.

The man halted the cart within a few steps of the wedding party's table, smiled in acknowledgement of the exclamations of praise for the cake, and left.

Jake frowned, brain and body on sudden alert. Wasn't that a member of group one, Emilio's men? Only men from Jake's group were allowed to help with the wedding.

Dana and Bentley slipped with some awkwardness off their bolted bench to approach the cart. Bentley carried a dull table knife for slicing the cake since a sharp knife wasn't permissible in the prison.

"Stop!" Jake slid off his bench. "Let me check that cake out."

Everyone laughed, evidently thinking he was teasing the bride and groom.

Bentley grabbed Dana's arm and backed away.

The cake looked fine. It just—

A man burst from the kitchen and hurled himself at full speed against Jake. *Mallet!*

Jake fell backward. Scrambled to his feet.

Mallet grabbed the cart. Sped in the opposite direction. Two steps, and a flash from the cart lit up the room. A loud boom followed.

Chapter 68

Eve screamed as the explosion spit gray plumes into the middle of the dining room. The man with the cart stiffened, then collapsed to the floor. Three of the National Police ran toward him while the other three herded the wedding party to the hallway. "You must leave," Mendoza roared at the wedding party. He led the way to the front gate at a spanking march.

"Eve," Jake shouted. "Please! Come see me tomorrow. Detective Lee will bring you."

Eve looked over her shoulder at him. The tabletops were in disarray. Ashes fluttered to the floor like paper feathers. The odor of acrid smoke crawled into her nasal passages. Across the room, men in uniform barked orders at the man on the floor and hauled him to his feet.

She didn't know why, but she nodded.

***

Jake rose early, paced his cell until the electronic lock opened the cell doors, and hastened to the infirmary. Mallet lay on a bed in a locked cell. His whole head was in bandages with openings for his eyes, nose, mouth and ears. More bandages wrapped his chest and no doubt continued under the thin, white blanket to swathe his stomach and groin. An IV connected his right arm to a bag of dripping fluid on a pole. A plastic oxygen mask cupped his mouth and nose. Bruises and cuts, many of them stitched, dotted his arms, probably his legs under the blanket too. Behind him, a monitor blipped the pattern of his heartbeat.

There'd be no information wrung from his throat today.

Jake raced to Emilio's pod, every hair on his body bristling. The room was full of men. Few of them worked in the prison trades, Puno said, because most of what they earned ended up in Emilio's pocket. In the area between the cells and the wire cage protecting the guard on duty, men collected in small groups or sat at bolted tables and benches. Emilio stepped away from a man to confront Jake.

Jake grabbed him by the front of his shirt. "You planted that bomb!"

Several men encircled them, forming a barricade to the guard's sight. Emilio snickered. "I heard there were unexpected fireworks at your little tea party."

"You almost killed my daughter!" Jake let the spittle at the corners of his mouth sit. He pushed his face closer to Emilio's. "The only reason I let you live is so I can attend your trial and execution. But if you *ever* try to touch my family again, I'll wrench off your other three limbs and let you stew in your putrid impotence. In fact,"—he released the shirt and secured Emilio's uninjured arm—"I should start right now. What d'ya think, an arm or a leg?"

Two men grappled with Jake and pulled him off Emilio. Emilio jacked back his good arm and rammed a flying fist into Jake's cheek. Spittle and blood flew from Jake's mouth. "I think your head will do as a good substitute, Chalmers." Emilio's men laughed, and his group crowded closer.

A gunshot jerked everyone's face toward the prison guard. Above their heads, the bullet pinged off a wall and splattered into the concrete of another wall. "Next shot at your bellies," the guard yelled. "Back off!" He pointed the gun at Jake. "You, go! Don't come back!"

Jake spat on the floor and left. He didn't dare risk defiance. If he got thrown into solitaire, he'd miss his appointment with Eve.

***

Jake cleaned up, and in midafternoon, joined Eve in a visitor's room in the central administrative pod. Detective Lee provided them some privacy by replacing the prison guard who oversaw the room. He winked at Jake and stepped into the hallway.

Eve wore green cotton slacks, a sleeveless white blouse with an oriental collar, and flat leather sandals. The extravagant hairdo of yesterday was replaced with hair loose on her shoulders. Flashy jade earrings peeked from her curtain of hair, and an equally flashy jade necklace and bracelet belied any impression she might be a woman of simple tastes.

Gone, of course, was Jake's impressive wedding attire. He wore khaki shorts and a plain navy tee, sandals on his feet and a day's growth of beard on his face. After the wedding and its attendant fiasco, he had changed clothes and sent the uniform back to Brett's safekeeping via Detective Lee.

"Thank you for coming." He wished he could take Eve's hand into his, but a table separated their chairs, and her hands were in her lap. Tightness framed her shoulders, and her face was sober. *She doesn't want to be here.* His throat constricted, and he cleared it with a cough. His thoughts tumbled uselessly from his brain.

They sat in silence. Finally he said, "It meant a lot to me to see Crystal. To see you."

Eve cast her eyes down.

This was going nowhere. What did he have to lose? May as well straight-out ask her the question burning in his soul. "Do you remember me now that we've met again?"

She peered up at him, opened her mouth in a small inhale. "Yes, and no."

His heart jumped. He raised his eyebrows, waited for her to explain.

"An image ..."—she shrugged her shoulders—"a fantasy ... came to mind one day. A bearded man with auburn hair to his shoulders and a sword sheathed across his back. In times of pressure, I thought of him. He became my warrior, my protector, who helped me out." A blush pinked her face. "Two months ago, I was surprised to find a photograph of him in Crystal's bedroom. She said it was a picture of you, from when you returned home from the Philippines."

Jake's heart went into orbit.

She drew in another breath, this time a big one, and released it in a soft huff. "So you see, you were in my memory, but I didn't know it. I had no idea what you looked like. All I knew of Jake Chalmers was that he was a prisoner, in jail for a murder he confessed to."

Jake crash-landed.

"When I first got out of the hospital in Chicago, I had a nightmare. I was hiding, and a horrid man, a brute with scars all over his face, found me—"

"Jojo."

She looked at him with wide eyes. "You knew him?"

"I fought him on the island so you could get away."

"But ... I was on the yacht with him."

"You went with him so he wouldn't kill me. I begged you not to." Jake's muscles knotted. If she had listened to him, none of this—the yacht, her memory loss, his imprisonment—none of it would have happened. It was hard to swallow back the words and not shake her by the shoulders with them.

"I ... I thought the man in my nightmare was you. Someone in the DA's office told me a man with a scarred face kept me captive on an island. Then I met Crystal, and she said you had scars on your face." The corners of her mouth drooped. "I didn't know you weren't that man—Jojo—until I met with Detective Lee three days ago and he showed me pictures."

"So there's hope?" Jake's head spun with the prospect of leaving this wretched place. Of winning back Eve's love. Of making Crystal his daughter and Eve his wife. He blinked at the sharp pain that Betty couldn't be included. The island family would limp a bit because of her absence.

"Hope for what, Jake?"

"That I can get out of here."

She shook her head. Tiny little movements side-to-side. Over and over, as if she couldn't stop. As if there were no hope.

His breath stilled.

Tears flooded Eve's eyes. "Don't you see? I don't remember you ... what happened on the island ... none of it." Her tears escaped and splashed onto her cheeks. "I can't testify to what I don't remember. I can't free you, Jake. I'm sorry." She didn't try to stop more tears. Didn't hide the quaking of her chest or the muted sobs that tripped from her throat.

"I love you, Eve. Do you remember that?"

She inhaled sharply. "I believe you. But, no, I don't remember."

His throat tightened. Did she remember loving him? Any part of it at all?

He couldn't ask. A denial would be the equivalent of a firing squad. But he did dare to express it for her. "You loved me, Eve. I want you to know that."

She gazed at him with sad eyes. Wiped her tears with the back of her hand. Stood. The legs of her chair scraped in protest against the concrete floor as she pushed back the chair. "I'm sorry, Jake. My memory is empty. And my heart." Her voice faltered. "All of it ... it's been forgotten."

The crack of rifle fire stung his heart as she walked out the door.

Chapter 69

The next morning, the strutted jangle of the hotel telephone awoke Eve. She stumbled across the room in hopes of catching it before it woke Crystal too. Once that girl opened her eyes, any hope of snuggling back down for more zzzz's was lost. Especially when the day held their last visit with Jake before flying home.

"Judge Eh-reek-son!" The hotel concierge's voice popped with excitement. "President Marcos—his secretary call for you!"

Every nerve snapped to attention. "President Marcos?"

"She give message you come for visit this afternoon, two o'clock."

"Did she say why?"

"Customs Office always tell President when U.S. officials come to Philippines. Warden at Salonga Prison also report you come two days to see new prison. President Marcos make few minutes today to welcome you. He extends great privilege."

"Yes. Yes, it is. Thank you." She hung up, her mind spinning like a dog chasing its tail.

"Who was that?" Crystal sat up and tossed aside her bed covers.

"Can you believe President Marcos's secretary called? I've been invited for a visit at 2:00."

"But that's when we'll be with Jake."

Oh. "I said goodbye to him yesterday, sweetie. A second goodbye would be awkward." Understatement of the year. Relief washed over her that she had an excuse to not see him again.

Yesterday, leaving Jake had been a reality check. Face it: She had permanent retrograde amnesia, and she wasn't getting her memory back. As much as she hated her inability to help Jake, his future was out of her hands. For three years she had struggled with her identity because of her lost past. It was time now to settle down and proceed with her new identity—mom and magistrate.

She'd been a good mom, hadn't she? Had opened the door and stepped through it to fulfill Crystal's wish to see Jake. And now, President Marcos's invitation to her as Judge Eriksson was as good a sign from heaven as any that the judgeship was her destiny.

Not Jake.

Pushing aside the sadness that swamped her, she rang the concierge. "I have a suit that needs pressing. Can you see to that? And a taxi for the visit with President Marcos."

***

She sat for half an hour in the President's office waiting room. A good reminder that she was a humble servant of the law, not a big shot. Did Marcos know the difference between a mere magistrate and a full federal judge? Surely he didn't know she was the newly conferred Drug Czar of Chicago? Her throat tightened. If that had gotten out, then the Romeros knew too.

Finally she was escorted into the office. Marcos greeted her with a handshake. And a perceptible jump of the eyebrows. "What good fortune to have a beautiful and charming visitor to share tea with."

She bet that wasn't a scripted part of his welcome. "The honor is mine, Mr. President."

They sat in comfortable chairs across from each other, a highly polished mahogany coffee table with a magnificent bouquet of flowers between them. Before a word could be spoken, the secretary appeared with tea and poured it into china cups with saucers. Eve accepted cream and a lump of sugar. She was a coffee person herself, but tea could be made palatable enough, especially when shared with the President of the Republic of the Philippines.

"You have visited our new federal prison, Salonga?"

"I have, Mr. President, and I am impressed. It rivals anything we have in the United States." She could kick herself for skipping the prison tour. Hopefully Marcos wouldn't ask too many questions about it, and Jake's letters and the kids' comments would supply her with enough information to get by.

"Warden Mendoza will receive an award for its design. Salonga is a model for new prisons on my agenda. He will be promoted to oversee their construction."

"He is an excellent man, very appropriate for the job." She managed not to wince at her recall of his eye patch and blackened visible eye. Marcos made no mention of Jake, whom the warden had acknowledged to her as the actual designer and builder.

All too soon, fifteen minutes by her calculation, the visit was over and President Marcos was walking her to the door of his office. The door shut behind her, and she collapsed against the wall to capture her wobbly breath and strengthen her shaking knees. She had been bold with President Marcos. She was a lowly magistrate, not a federal judge, and she may have presumed upon Marcos's ignorance with her last-minute request. Hopefully, there would be no backlash against Jake.

***

She returned to her hotel room and found everyone still gone. The room felt hollow, barren—like her heart felt about Jake. She sat on the edge of her bed, chin suddenly crumpling, lower lip quivering. Snuffs of air vibrated in bumps to her lungs, set off tremors in her chest. Regret, soot-black, thorny, scratched up her throat. Rasped against her vocal cords. Shuffled out her nose in keening moans. She opened her mouth and gave in to cavernous sobs.

At length, face hot and puffy, eyes swollen half-shut, she rose and splashed cold water over her face, toweled it dry. Okay. She crunched her lips between her teeth until her breath calmed, raised her chin and addressed her splotchy reflection in the bathroom mirror. Time to close this chapter of her life. A chapter whose pages were years of misguided emotions and erroneous conclusions about Jake. A chapter not well-ended. Nevertheless, one that needed to end—*had* ended in the visitor's room at Salonga Prison.

It was too late to change things for Jake, but there was someone whose life she could affect for the better. She'd told Brad she needed to find a way to be who she was *now*, instead of chasing ghosts of the past for her identity. The new her—the *now* her—could be different. Whatever she remembered … or didn't remember … didn't need to define her. God's mercies were new every morning. She'd let Him be the one to create her anew.

Confidence perked every cell in her body as she picked up the hotel phone and arranged a long-distance call. Still, her hands trembled, and desert heat wilted her tongue into rawhide.

"Hello?" The voice was edged with sleep, colored with thinly-veiled irritation. She hadn't thought about what time it was in New York. Early morning—very early. She almost hung up.

"Dad?" she croaked.

His lungs wheezed a sharp inhale. "Eve?" Her name was a half-gasp, half-cry. "Are … are you all right?"

"I am, Dad. I didn't mean to wake you. I can call back." Would she? Her nerve endings were frayed rope. She wrapped the coils of telephone cord around and around her pointer finger.

"No, no. Now is perfect." An awkward pause, then, "How are you?"

She had to jump in feet-first or end up turning tail. "I forgive you, Dad. You and Dax."

"Eve—" Her father's voice jerked.

"I'm not going to just say the words, Dad. To help me truly get past this, I'm going to share the venom of my hurt. For your sake as well as for mine." Her heart pattered against her chest as if a Loving Hand was patting her back. A deep calm infused her words, removed the bile from her tongue.

"What Dax did wasn't just a matter of being drunk and a stupid teenager. And what you did wasn't just misplaced ambition. What you did, what you both did, was betrayal. Betrayal of my love, of my faith in you, of Mom's faith in you as family who would take care of me.

A sob hobbled from her father's chest. "I'm sorry, so sorry …" Grief, raw with pain, crusted with remorse, scraped from his throat. "God forgive me, I'm so, so sorry."

Tears coursed from Eve's eyes as the poison of twenty-five years oozed from her heart, misted into a fog, evaporated into the heavens. Hugging the phone to her ear, she wept with her father.

When their emotions lay spent, he thanked her. "I love you, Evie."

But she couldn't reciprocate. That would take time. She'd get together with him—him and Dax. Brick by brick, they'd remove the wall between them. Perhaps slowly, perhaps quickly. The foundation of forgiveness would help them.

***

Jake milked the five hours with his kids, Crystal, and Bentley for all they were worth. The visitor's room was theirs for the day. Two actually decent meals were served for lunch and dinner, and the warden stopped in for a brief visit. The rest of the time was spent sharing stories from the graduates' four years at West Point, and from Jake and Crystal's year on the island.

Eve's absence was not referred to.

When, with hugs and tears goodbye, they parted, Jake jogged to the exercise yard. He walked the perimeter, over and over, waving away Puno and other prison mates. He held up his heart to God. Placed its broken pieces at the feet of Jesus.

Piece by piece by piece. So many pieces.

Hear me, O Lord God of mercy and compassion. I give you my thanks, but also my complaints.

My children have departed. Second Lieutenants now. Who knows when they'll be free to visit again?

Crystal is gone. Next-to-last year in high school coming up. Fat chance Eve will ever bring her back to the Philippines.

Lee's job of managing prison construction is over. No more weekly visits with him.

The prison is completed. Functioning well. My job is done.

Same with the prison trades, prospering under Puno.

Emilio's trial is coming up. Water-tight case against him, Lee says.

It took several hard swallows to bring up the next broken piece: *Eve's memory loss is permanent. So is her departure.*

And then he had to work on breathing. Breathing so his lungs would expand and contract. So they'd empty out carbon dioxide and draw in oxygen. So his legs could walk and his brain could talk and his soul could continue praying.

Still waiting on you, Lord. Still holding out for you as the Just Judge. Still trusting.

Gotta tell you, though. I'm giving up on the earthly judge.

And then he gathered the pieces and placed them one-by-one at the feet of Jesus again.

And again.

And again.

Chapter 70

Two weeks later, the warden summoned Jake. Jake huffed. Even Mendoza had set him aside after Jake's family left. Hadn't even toured the furniture workshop, where Jake was burying his sorrows in work. Not that Jake cared about the warden's lack of attention. Anymore, Jake didn't care much about anything.

At least he was worth tea and cookies in the warden's office. Mendoza said nothing as they munched their apportioned cookies and sipped tea, and Jake sure had nothing to say. He felt the warden's eye on him, though. Yep, something was on Mendoza's mind.

"I have been promoted," Mendoza finally said. "Departmental head over new prison construction in the Philippines. I will leave Salonga tomorrow."

"Congratulations!" Jake's smile was genuine. Someone was no longer forgotten anyway.

"You will leave too."

Jake stared at him. What—as Mendoza's employee? Some kind of exchange deal—ten years of Jake's labor for his eventual freedom?

"You do not wonder how or why?"

"I do." Jake flashed a grin. May as well give the man some satisfaction. "I'm afraid to ask what you have in mind."

"Your freedom."

Jake's cheek twitched. At what price?

"Tomorrow you walk out. Detective Lee will drive you to airport."

Jake's mouth fell open. If Mendoza laughed, said it was a joke, Jake would land a fist in that one good eye.

But Mendoza only nodded his head toward the door. "You may go." Face as sober as ever.

"You aren't kidding? You mean it?" Jake stood up on wobbly knees.

"Yes. You are free to return to your country."

"How—?" Jake swallowed back an onslaught of tears. "What—?" He inhaled what had to be all the oxygen in the room. "Good grief, Warden, tell me about it!"

This time Mendoza smiled. The rat had been waiting for the satisfaction of Jake's reaction. "When I was told of my promotion, I was also told your case has been dismissed. No more accusation of murder. No more court trial to wait for."

"*Who* told you?" The words came out gruff. "How do I know it's official, that it won't come chasing after me?"

Mendoza held up a piece of paper. "Special delivery this morning." He handed it to Jake. "From the office of the President of the Republic of the Philippines."

"Marcos?" Jake dropped back onto the chair. His eyes could hardly focus, but, yes, the letterhead was there. The signature. Everything in between he needed. "I'd say that's mighty official." He wanted to hug the one-eyed ogre, but settled for a handshake across the expanse of mahogany between them. "Thank you."

"Thank your Judge Eriksson. My source tells me she initiated the request to bring you home immediately."

"Judge Eriksson?"

"The day before President Marcos left on a trip two weeks ago."

"Two weeks ago?"

Mendoza outright laughed. "You sound like lovesick parrot. Go. You leave tomorrow."

***

What did he have to pack? Nothing here he wanted. Except his lost pocket Bible. And letters from home. Home! The Just Judge was sending him home!

His kids, sisters, Crystal—he could imagine their screams over the telephone. He chuckled in anticipation. He'd call them at the airport. Using Mendoza's phone required a bribe.

And Eve? What had happened after she left him? Judge or not, she couldn't just show up at Marcos's door, pleading for Jake's freedom. And she wouldn't have held back the possibility of Jake's release from him if she'd been working on it all along. He knew her too well for that. No way she'd snatch away that hope and leave him as she had, with his heart facing a firing squad.

Would it make a difference in how she received him now? Her heart was empty, she'd said. She didn't love him. Would she turn away if he tried to win her back?

He sighed and selected tomorrow's outfit: parachute pants—at least a bit more dignified than shorts for the long trip home—and a reasonably clean shirt. Everything else he'd give away. Didn't have a suitcase anyway. Lee would have his plane ticket, and, no doubt, cash. That's all he needed. All he wanted. Almost …

His group had a party for him. Snacks, treats, candy, and soda pop came from hoarded stores. In the fine American tradition, they "roasted" him with funny stories—safe to tell now that he was leaving—but at the end they thanked him, man after man, for the kindness and compassion he had bestowed on them with the new prison.

When the men trailed away to their bunks for the night, Puno hung back until last. "I am glad for you, sad for me." Unashamedly, they clung in a long hug.

***

He skipped breakfast the next morning. Didn't want to face goodbyes again. These men were seeds sown into his heart, much as his buddies in Nam had been. Parting was like ripping them out by their roots to make room for new plants.

The pod emptied quickly after breakfast. Echoes of the prisoners' footsteps and voices faded to silence as they left to work in their various trades. The odor of multiple males confined in a small area dissipated to the canopy.

Inside his wire cage, the guard nodded off. Jake felt as if he'd been sealed inside a coffin with a somnolent mouse.

He was dressed and ready to go. Nerves jumpy, restless to move on. To get out of here. He stared out his cell window at the empty road. Lee's normal routine was to come late in the morning, well before the sun reached its peak, but he might come early today. If only Eve and Crystal, or the twins and Bentley, had known of his release, they could have journeyed home together.

His vacant house in Indy was the last place he wanted to go. But what choice did he have? Chicago wasn't an option. He couldn't—and didn't want to—take Crystal away from Eve. And Eve had made it clear there was no future for the two of them: "My memory is empty … and my heart," she'd said.

His memory was full. His heart brimming.

Did the two have to be irreconcilable?

"Chalmers."

At Emilio's voice, Jake whipped around. His archenemy stood in the doorway to Jake's cell, two of his thugs on either side of him.

Chapter 71

"Get out of my cell," Jake growled. It had taken less than a day in the new Salonga Prison for the inmates to establish the rule that every man's cell was his domain, and no man could enter without permission. A lot of good that did Jake now, with the pod empty and the guard asleep. Or bribed.

His last day in prison, and he might exit it with three shivs in his gut. Jake's sightline to the guard was blocked. While a shout would alert the sentry to Jake's danger, the show of helplessness would acknowledge Emilio's ascendancy. No way Jake was going to give him that.

"I want to talk," Emilio said.

"I don't. Get out."

"At that table." Emilio sauntered to the nearest table and sat. His two men settled into a table farther away.

So, this was to be a private conversation …

Behind them, the guard had his eyes on the intruders, his hand on his rifle. Remaining in the cell would label Jake a coward. He strode to Emilio's table but didn't sit. "So talk."

"You're outta here." Emilio's voice expressed no emotion. "I'm not."

Jake flashed a wicked smile. "It's called justice."

"It's called you win, I lose. Simple as that."

"This is what you wanted to talk about?"

Emilio took a photograph out of his shirt pocket and laid it on the table. Jake gave it a cursory glance. A toddler with curly dark hair and nut-brown eyes, smiling. "My son, three years ago," Emilio said.

Jake's nostrils flared. "You met my kids three weeks ago. With a bomb."

Emilio slapped a second photograph onto the first. "Same boy, a week ago." Flames lashed from the anger in his voice.

In spite of his reluctance, Jake cast a quick eye over the photo. The same curly-haired boy, about five, crouched in a corner, naked except for briefs, covered in bruises from his chest down. Terror, not smiles, defined his face. Jake quashed the sick feeling seeking entry to his heart.

"My three half-brothers did this."

Jake refused to ask why.

"He's been in my father's care ever since my brothers killed my wife. This photo is their promise of what awaits little Dan once my father lands in prison and can no longer protect him."

"You try to maim my daughter and son-in-law with explosives, and you want me to feel sorry for you?"

"For him. I want you to go get him and raise him as your own."

Jake stared at Emilio in disbelief. "You kill my wife, send assassins after me, attempt to injure my daughter … and you have the gall to ask me to save your son and raise him?"

"You're the only one I trust."

Jake sputtered. "What about the eighteen passengers you killed from the *Gateway,* besides my wife? And how many countless others I don't know about? Tell me, do you feel any remorse at all? Any guilt for what you've done?"

Emilio set steely eyes on Jake. "I will face a firing squad for what I've done. My son has done nothing."

"Your son is not my responsibility." Jake turned on his heel, grabbed his bag from his cell, and stormed out to wait for Lee at the front gate.

***

Every step fanned the coals of Jake's fury. Emilio had no soul. No conscience. He had pre-meditated the deaths of the *Gateway* passengers. Had made sure Jake saw him give the signal for the explosions. Had relished Jake's horror as the blasts sent living humans into sudden oblivion. No remorse. None at all.

Did Emilio care about his son? Or did he only want to deny his half-brothers the glee of control over anything belonging to Emilio? Or was the appeal for Jake's intercession a manipulation to set him up for yet another assassination attempt?

He strode past the infirmary, then stopped and retraced his steps. Yes, Mallet was still there. An IV remained in his right arm, but the oxygen mask and bandages were gone. His cell door was unlocked, an aide at his bedside. Jake stepped inside.

The aide startled at Jake's appearance. "No. Go!" Anger furrowed the smooth skin of his brow.

"I want to say goodbye to your patient. I leave Salonga today." Actually, he had a question he wanted Mallet to answer. It had been gnawing at him like a hungry cannibal ever since the bomb went off at Dana's wedding. Until today, Mallet had been inaccessible.

"No. Go!"

Mallet tapped the aide's arm. "I talk." The words gurgled from a lipless mouth.

The aide clenched his jaw but stood back, hands tightened into fists at his side.

Jake moved closer and got his first close-up of Mallet. Skin and tissue had been ripped from Mallet's face, head, and torso. He looked like burnt bacon. Jake was familiar with bomb injuries from Viet Nam, but the horror was always fresh.

This could have been Dana and Bentley lying here. Jake fought back the rage tearing at his heart. A rage of righteous wrath. Of indignation at the cruelty of man. A rage that demanded just judgment but that he was helpless to render.

"Mallet." His question crept out of his mouth in perplexed humility: "Why?"

He could swear a smile shone from Mallet's face, even though the bacon had no flexibility to crinkle at the edges of his eyes or mouth. "Gift," Mallet croaked.

"Saving Dana and Bentley was a gift?" The answer only baffled him further. "I … I can never thank you enough." He stared at the mutilated flesh. "You paid an awful price—the sacrifice of your own body—for the precious lives of my children. I am forever grateful." His question prodded him to dig deeper. "But I don't understand why you did it. Why, when only five months ago you tried to kill me?"

"God. You gift me." Mallet struggled to pull something from under his pillow. His fingers scrabbled like a burrowing crab until finally he withdrew a small book and plopped it onto the blanket covering his stomach. Gilt letters spelled out *The New Testament & Psalms.*

"My Bible!" Jake barely stopped himself from snatching it away.

"I read all." Mallet held up two mottled fingers.

"You read it two times?"

"Yes." Mallet fumbled with the book until it opened to a page folded in half. The opposite page identified it as the first chapter of the gospel of John. Mallet smoothed out the folded page, and, with a hand almost too weak to lift the book, raised it for Jake's eyes. Names and dates written in small script crowded the margin next to verses twelve and thirteen. "I add."

Jake took the book, sure of what he'd find. The three dates recorded his, Crystal's, and Eve's acknowledgement of Jesus as the Son of God. A fourth name and date increased the tally: Pamukpok, 4-85. Jake's throat tightened. "You believe?"

"Yes, Christian." Mallet brought his hands together in a gesture of prayer. "Love God … neighbor … Jake."

Jake's heart squeezed tremors up his throat to his chin. He gulped a snatch of air.

Shallow coughs dribbled spittle from Mallet's mouth. The aide blotted it and gave him a sip of water. "'Milio want hurt Jake. How?" Mallet's chest rose and fell with long pauses in between. "Find out: wedding. Bomb." Ragged breaths pulled his eyelids down.

The rest of the story, Jake knew first-hand. Mallet had rammed Jake aside, commandeered the cake, and fled to face the bomb alone. To pay the price of sacrificial love. Every muscle in Jake's face quivered.

The aide pointed at the cell door. "No more. Go."

Jake laid the pocket Bible back onto Mallet's middle and gently placed Mallet's skin-peeled hand on it. "Thank you, brother." The words came out in chokes. Blinking back tears, he stumbled toward the front gate.

Mallet's gift of saving Dana and Bentley was God's gift. A gift joyfully delivered by Mallet with no thought to cost. With no reluctance to demonstrate the compassion of God that had saved him. Mallet was a spiritual babe of two months; Jake a God-loving man of twenty-three years. Yet, tested, he had failed. He had chosen to live based on his past rather than on his future—his history with Emilio rather than his destiny of Heaven, won for him by Christ. No wonder his heart was hard.

He changed the course of his footsteps. It wasn't too late.

In group one's pod, Emilio immediately spotted him. Taking his time, a sneer on his lips, he joined Jake at the pod's entryway. "Come to gloat?"

"I've come to forgive. I'm letting you go, Emilio. You said I'd won and you'd lost. But you were mistaken. Every time you hurt me or wronged me scored a win for you. It was one more link chaining me to you, putting you in control of my emotions and behavior."

Emilio's eyebrows twitched upward.

"I'm not excusing what you've done—no way. But I don't have to." Jake shrugged, surprising himself with the smile that accompanied it. "Fact is, it's a judicial power I simply don't have. What I do have is a Savior who loves me and gives me the freedom to put the past behind me. So, do what you may, Emilio, my focus is no longer bound to you. I'm breaking the chain."

Emilio snorted. "And leaving your wife and all those passengers in my keeping, huh?"

"Your guilt chains *you* to *them*, Emilio, not the other way around."

"Oh? Does refusing to save my son chain you to him?"

The memory of Mallet racing away with the wedding cake rose to Jake's mind. "No, but God's compassion motivates me. I will do my best to help him."

"Good. Here's the info." Emilio whipped the photo of the toddler out of his pocket. "Everything you need to know is on the back. Name, birth data,

Social Security number, address, phone number. My father is his legal guardian; he'll need to transfer it to you."

Jake slipped the photo into a pocket of his parachute pants. "God's compassion extends to you too, Emilio."

"Yeah, well, I can take care of myself. Just don't forget my kid." Emilio turned his back and ambled into his venue of vultures.

For a minute, Jake watched him, until the reality hit home. *Hello, Jacob Chalmers—you are free!* Free of the enemy he'd let enslave him for three years with bitterness. He had wanted Emilio put in prison for the murder of the *Gateway* passengers, but Jake had put himself into prison too—had built his own cell, even—by hanging onto Emilio's offenses.

He trotted through the admin pod to the front gate. Lee stood outside, his van at the curb. Jake laughed, and like a kid on his last day of school, ran whooping down the hallway. He'd bathed at the sink this morning, and, good to his promise, he was going to give Lee that big hug!

Chapter 72

Eve peered through the van window, her heartbeat ticking faster as Jake emerged from Salonga Prison's front gate. So, Marcos had truly come through, and she'd been able to help Jake after all! Doubt had stalked her for two weeks while she and Crystal killed time with a sightseeing spree in the Philippines. Every day, she woke with misgivings hissing in her ear that Marcos's promise was nothing but political posturing.

Her unsolicited request to the President had been nervy. "I wish to bring prisoner Jacob Chalmers back to the U.S. with me, with his case dismissed. Can you help me expedite that?" Her heart pinging off every rib belied the calm of her voice. Marcos had all but snapped his fingers at his secretary to get on the phone and start the process. Showing off his power? Didn't matter. She'd kiss his feet now!

Crystal scooted in tight against her to share the view out Eve's window. They giggled when Jake grabbed Detective Lee in a big bear hug. Would he do that to them after they stepped out of the van to surprise him? To Crystal, no doubt. But not her. Last thing she'd told him was that whatever had been between them was over. Forgotten. As good as never happened.

The hurt on his face as she left was a knife in her heart. The man had just told her he loved her, and that she had loved him. She fled the visitors room because the guilt was more than she could bear. Maybe she wasn't accountable for her memory loss, but she was responsible for how she'd mismanaged it.

And now, here she sat, with Jake and Detective Lee ambling across the prison apron toward the van, laughing at their horseplay. Jake had no idea she and Crystal were in the back seat. No doubt Lee was chomping at the bit in anticipation of Jake's shock.

Jake wore parachute pants, a tee, and ragged sandals. A good two weeks' growth of stubble marked the start of a beard. Impressive was not exactly descriptive of his appearance. In his Marine Corps uniform at the wedding, he'd been dazzling. With his beard and longer hair, he'd been the valiant warrior and protector. Yet, the man striding toward her with a bounce in his step, animation in his face, and exuberance in his voice had her heart sprouting wings.

He'd said her memory loss was not an obstacle to his love. So why should she let it stand in their way? Why look to her past to define herself? To cross a river, she didn't need a road behind her; she needed a bridge in front of her. A bridge like the one she'd built to her father and brother. A bridge made of new experiences and new relationships and new memories.

Crystal reached over, opened the van door, and scrambled out. "J-a-a-a-k-e!" she squealed. He stopped short, eyes wide, and barely got his arms open before Crystal pounced on him with her own bear hug.

Her turn. Eve stepped out, aware her greeting would send signals to Jake. Aloof—no expectations, please. Or friendly—just don't step over the line. Or warm—open to possibilities. Her mind fogged at which she wanted.

Before she could act, Jake took the lead. Astonishment, then delight, lit his face at the sight of her. "Eve!" Crystal released Jake and turned to watch them with the biggest smile Eve had ever seen.

Jake didn't exactly race to her, but his strides were long enough that he may as well have. She took a step backward, leery of a collision, but at the same time conscious of a wave of excitement crashing over every nerve in her body. Two steps away, his arms opened. One step away, and they reached out for her.

The air whooshed from her lungs as he seized her arms at the outside of her shoulders. Gave a little squeeze. Slid his hands down her arms to clasp her fingers. "Thank you for my freedom." His voice was deep. Steeped with emotion. Intimate.

She inhaled. Swallowed. Nodded acknowledgment. Tried to synchronize tongue and lips to form words. Could think of nothing but the track of his hands down her bare arms, the tenderness of his fingers curled around hers. Inanely she whispered, "My pleasure," then caught herself and said, "It was long overdue. I'm sorry."

"You can stand here and stare at each other all moony-eyed, or you can get in the car and catch a plane to the United States," Lee said. "Which is it?"

"I vote for the moony eyes," Crystal said.

Eve withdrew her hands from Jake's. "Catch the plane and don't look back."

"We're flying out together?" Jake opened the van door for Eve to climb inside. "Where to?"

"Chicago, if you don't mind. We need to do a little legal debris clean-up." Eve winked at Crystal. "Maybe throw in some sight-seeing and"—she looked pointedly at Jake's attire—"some clothes shopping."

Jake's chuckle trailed him to the opposite side of the van, where he opened the door for Crystal to slide in next to Eve.

Crystal shook her head. "Nope. You hafta sit between us, dude."

Jake ducked his head, eyebrows raised, to peer in at Eve.

"Only if you promise no moony eyes." Eve grinned and patted the seat. They'd save that for later. Include it as part of her new bridge to the future.

Jake slid in, then Crystal. His arm rested lightly against Eve's as the three of them squished together. Warmth radiated from his skin to hers. Warmth from his heart too. She breathed a quiet sigh of contentment. The struggle that had separated them was over. It could be put away.

Forgotten.

The End

Dear Reader,

Your comment posted on Amazon is a pat on our back for your reading experience of *Forgotten*. Positive or negative, long or short, your input is helpful to us and other readers. Simply go to http://www.amzn.com/B01N639LXP, scroll down to "Write a Review," and post your comment. Thank you!

CURIOUS ABOUT WHAT HAPPENED TO
JAKE, EVE, BETTY, AND CRYSTAL ON THE ISLAND?
Go to http://www.amzn.com/B00OQGJBUY for *Stranded*,
their adventure as survivors.

You can CONTACT us at our website at
http://www.donandstephanieprichard.com

Sign up for our NEWSLETTER there to keep updated
on our next book about Jake, Eve, and Crystal.

Our author FACEBOOK page is
www.facebook.com/4u2read

17053829R00190

Printed in Poland
by Amazon Fulfillment
Poland Sp. z o.o., Wrocław